THE BELIAL CHILDREN

BOOK FIVE IN THE BELIAL SERIES

R.D. BRADY

D1572126

SCOTTISH SEOUL PUBLISHING, LLC

BOOKS BY R.D. BRADY

Hominid

The Belial Series (in order)
The Belial Stone
The Belial Library
The Belial Ring
Recruit: A Belial Series Novella
The Belial Children
The Belial Origins
The Belial Search
The Belial Guard
The Belial Warrior
The Belial Plan
The Belial Witches
The Belial War
The Belial Fall
The Belial Sacrifice

The A.L.I.V.E. Series
B.E.G.I.N.

A.L.I.V.E.
D.E.A.D.
R.I.S.E.
S.A.V.E.

The Steve Kane Series
Runs Deep
Runs Deeper

The Unwelcome Series
Protect
Seek
Proxy

The Nola James Series
Surrender the Fear
Escape the Fear

Published as Riley D. Brady
The Key of Apollo
The Curse of Hecate

Be sure to sign up for R.D.'s mailing list to be the first to hear when she has a new release!

'But Jesus said, Suffer little children,
and forbid them not, to come unto me:
for of such is the kingdom of heaven.'
Matthew 19:14

CHAPTER 1

BALTIMORE, MARYLAND

Delaney McPhearson knew she should focus. It was important. It was life-changing.

She sighed and pushed away from the desk. Who was she kidding? It was paperwork.

She ran her hands through her auburn hair, wishing she had brought a ponytail holder with her. With green eyes she stared at the desk, imagining what relief one good swipe could bring. But then she imagined herself picking all the papers back up and reorganizing them, and she wanted to scream.

She'd been struggling for the last two hours to reduce the pile on her desk and somehow it seemed to only be getting bigger.

Her eyes roamed over the rich wood paneling that covered the walls, the heavy drapes that contrasted with the more contemporary office furnishings added by the Chandler Group. She was sitting in the administrative offices of the Chandler Home for Children, which had taken over what used to be the Breckenrich School, a well-to-do boarding school that apparently hadn't had enough students to stay afloat.

Laney sighed. *From dodging bullets one minute to filling out forms for Child and Family Services the next. The good times never end.*

The phone rang and Laney grabbed it, looking for a reprieve. "Chandler Home."

"Hi, Ms. McPhearson. This is Leslie from The Bed Place? I'm calling about the order mishap?"

"Hi, Leslie. When will the other beds be delivered?" The last truck had been two beds short.

"Um, well, you see, we have a problem? The beds, they're still at the warehouse?"

Laney rolled her eyes toward the ceiling and prayed for patience. Pulling on her inner calm, she said. "Okay, Leslie, I need those beds here by tomorrow morning."

"I understand. But you see—"

"No, Leslie, you don't understand. I have a dozen kids arriving tomorrow; kids who have literally been through hell. And I mean *hell*. And the least they can expect is to have a bed to sleep in. So do whatever you have to do, but get the beds here tomorrow, understood?"

"Um, yes, Ms. McPhearson. I'll have them there."

"Thank you."

Laney disconnected the call and blew out a breath, feeling a little bad about how she'd bowled over the poor woman. But honestly? She had way too much on her plate right now to be dealing with delivery problems.

Laney stared at the piles of work on her desk. Was it her imagination, or had it actually increased in size while she was on the phone? She ran her hands over her face. *Come on. You need to get this done before the kids arrive tomorrow. They need this.*

And that was true. The Chandler Home for Children had been a haven for Fallen and nephilim teens ever since the Chandler Group took down Amar Patel and learned of a training camp he had set up in Indiana. They'd raided it and liberated the twenty teens that had been held there.

But then the problem had been: what to do with the kids? A few were over eighteen and had decided to strike out on their own—not that Laney could blame them after what they'd been through—but the others were still minors who either didn't have family or didn't have family they wanted to go back to. And no one could see how dropping the kids in foster care would benefit anyone.

So Henry Chandler, Laney's brother, had purchased this old boarding school about a twenty-minute drive from the Chandler Estate, and dubbed it the Chandler Home for Children. The kids, however, called the home "Broken Halo." Personally, Laney preferred the kids' name.

That first camp in Indiana had led them to another one in Texas, and all told the facility now housed twenty-eight kids ranging in age from twelve to nineteen, more than half of whom had abilities.

Even more kids were expected to arrive soon: a third training camp had been identified just outside Boston, and Laney's love, Jake Rogan, along with Henry and Jennifer Witt, one of Laney's best friends, were off liberating it. That left Laney basically in charge of the school.

She glanced out the window. It was a gorgeous day: bright blue skies, a few white clouds, and a light wind. *Oh, I so want to be anywhere else but here.*

Cleo, the giant black Javan leopard that Laney had rescued from Amar's home, was stretched out in a spot of sunlight behind Laney. When on all fours, Cleo was on eye level with Laney—a result of some growth hormone experiments done on the cat while still in the womb.

In spite of her massive size and intimidating presence, though, Cleo had become part of the school, almost a mascot of sorts. And while the kids had been a little startled by the cat's presence at first, they'd quickly gotten used to her. She was just another facet of Broken Halo.

Laney watched with envy as Cleo let out a yawn and repositioned herself with a lazy stretch. "Oh sure, rub it in," she muttered.

A brunette with a cute pixie cut appeared in the doorway. "Having fun?" Kati Simmons asked.

Laney glanced up with a grimace. "Compared to a root canal? Yes."

Kati walked in and sat in the seat in front of the desk. "Oh, who are you kidding? You love it."

"Don't get me wrong, I love helping the kids out." Laney gestured to all the paperwork. "It's *this* stuff I could do without."

"But someone needs to do it."

"I know, I know." She glanced up at Kati with a grin. "I just heard from the gang. They're ahead of schedule and should return with the kids early tomorrow morning. And Maddox will be back tonight."

Maddox Datson had been an integral part of the last raid, but ever since Amar, he had been staying with Kati and her son Max, as an extra protective bodyguard. When he'd gone off on this latest raid to Boston, Kati and Max had come down from New York to stay with Laney instead—and Laney loved it. She had missed the both of them incredibly over the last year. And these last few weeks reminded her why.

"I just finished setting up the beds for the new kids," Kati said. "Clean linens, towels, a little basket of toiletries for each of them. It should get them started at least."

"You are a godsend." Laney rifled through the pile on the desk. "Jen sent me sizes. I have it here somewhere. I was going to see if Sasha could go to the store and pick them up some clothes and pajamas." Laney looked up just as Kati looked down.

And Laney felt the guilt crash over her again. Ever since the attacks two months ago, Kati had been incredibly nervous about going out in public—hence the need for Maddox's protection.

4

And Kati's concerns for Max's safety were even greater than her concerns for herself. Laney had really hoped that Kati would begin to feel safe, but so far they'd only made baby steps in that direction.

"You know, we really could use someone like you around here permanently," Laney said.

It was true: Kati had a knack for seeing what needed to be done in the school and taking care of it. And although Laney was more than capable of handling fallen angels, ancient treasures, and hand-to-hand combat, when she was faced with a leaky faucet, she was clueless.

Kati gave Laney a small smile. "I know. I'm thinking about it. And I'm leaning toward moving. It would make things easier. And Maddox can't stay with us forever."

"I don't know. He seems to be enjoying himself."

A small blush colored Kati's cheeks. "Yeah. Somehow he fits right in."

A little boy, five years old and the mini-me of Kati, ran in and threw his arms around Kati's legs. "Hi, Mom!"

Kati's smile was huge. "What have you been up to?"

"Yoni was showing me how to subdue someone with a Chapstick."

Laney stared at Yoni Benjamin, who had appeared in the door-way. Yoni had been part of the Boston raid as well, but he'd come back as soon as the kids were safe. He hated being away from Sasha and their eight-month-old, Dov.

Yoni looked at his feet. "Actually, I was showing Danny. But Max wanted to try, too, and it's important to encourage kids to learn."

Laney shook her head and looked over at Kati, who was looking slightly green. *Great.*

A tall statuesque blonde walked in, tsking at Yoni. "Yoni, I told you not to teach him that. He's too young."

Yoni nodded. "Sorry, sweetie."

Sasha Benjamin leaned down and kissed his bald head. "I love you anyway."

Laney marveled once again at the difference between the two. Sasha had been an Olympic volleyball player a few years back for the Ukraine. She was almost six feet tall and stunningly gorgeous. Yoni, by contrast, was barely five foot two, with large eyes that dominated his face and biceps the size of willowy Sasha's waist.

On paper, they made no sense. Yet when you saw the two of them together, they just seemed right.

Sasha turned her blue-green eyes to Laney. "Laney, do you have the list?"

Laney rummaged through the papers on her desk and found it under the receipt for the plumber and an order for pizza. *Who ordered pizza?* She shook her head as she handed it over. "There are ten kids. I broke the list down by gender and Jen's guesses on sizes."

Sasha looked over the list and nodded. "No problem. Should take me about an hour or two. Dov will be up from his nap in a few minutes and then we'll head out."

"Can I come?" Max asked.

Sasha opened her mouth, then closed it, looking at Kati. "Well, that's up to your mom."

"Um, I don't know..." Kati said.

"You should go too, Kati," Laney said. "Maybe you guys could get some dinner."

Yoni rubbed his stomach. "Well if dinner is involved, I'm going, too."

"And I'll send along a couple of guards. They've been wanting to get away from the grounds," Laney added, trying to sound casual.

Kati looked at Laney, and Laney could read the indecision on her friend's face.

"It'll be okay," Laney urged. "And it'll good for Max."

Kati kept her eyes on Laney for a long minute before nodding. "Okay. Sounds good."

Laney smiled. "Bring me back something, would you?"

"Hamburger and fries?" Sasha asked.

Laney smiled. "Perfect."

The group trooped out of the office and Laney let out a sigh, wishing she could go with them and just relax for a few hours. Instead she pulled over a stack of resumes for the psychologists they were considering interviewing. Her uncle, Patrick Delaney, had been pinch-hitting as a counselor, and had been doing a fine job, but they all knew that with the problems some of these kids would be dealing with, they would require professional help.

"Okay, Dr. Shields, what do you bring to the table?"

She spent the next hour going through the files. Finally she stood up and stretched. Cleo raised her head expectantly.

Laney smiled as she shrugged on her jacket. "Okay. A quick walk. And then back to work."

Cleo got to her feet, kneading her claws on the carpet as she stretched.

Laney shook her head and added a carpet to the list of things she'd need to have replaced.

But then she smiled. In the grand scheme of things, if her biggest worries involved carpeting and beds, she was doing all right. In fact, she could most definitely get used to this.

CHAPTER 2

D anny Wartowski sat at the wall of monitors in his office at the Chandler School. Henry was off helping bring back the new kids, but Danny had chosen to spend his time at the school. He liked being around kids his age, even if he wasn't exactly hanging out with them.

A yell from the hallway seized his attention and his head jerked up. Three kids went running by, tossing a football between them.

Danny had been at the school a couple of days a week since it opened, but he still didn't know many of the kids well enough to do more than say "hi" in passing. Some of them seemed nice enough; Danny just didn't know how to talk to them. They had nothing in common. Almost all of these kids had abilities, but Danny didn't. And Danny had an off-the-charts IQ, which none of the kids had. So there wasn't a lot of middle ground there.

Danny turned back to the screen. He might not have many— okay, any—friends among the kids at Chandler Home, but it didn't matter. Because right now, he had much more pressing concerns.

He bit his lip as he examined the latest data output. "This can't be right," he murmured.

He flipped through the screens of code he'd written. There must a problem in the syntax. Maybe he reverse coded the variable. He stared at the one he thought might be causing the problem. No, it was coded correctly.

He hit a button and the monitors filled with pictures of children. Danny looked carefully at each child's face in turn, his worry growing. Finally, he hit another button to remove the pictures from the screen. But the faces stayed lodged in his mind.

He printed out the computer code he'd used to generate the results: all one-hundred-plus pages of it. He walked over to retrieve it from the output tray, then headed back to his desk. Pushing his other papers out of the way, he sat down and started going through the code, line by line. It would take hours, but he needed to make sure.

And for the first time Danny could remember, he hoped that he was wrong.

CHAPTER 3

L aney pulled up in front of one of the cottages on the Chandler Estate. The five-hundred-acre estate boasted over two dozen cottages along what was known as Sharecroppers Lane —all of them, unsurprisingly, former sharecropper homes. Henry had renovated them when he'd decided to turn the estate into the headquarters of his business. Henry's own home was located just behind the main building.

Laney and Jake had a cottage here too, and Kati, Maddox, and Max were in the cottage right next door. Her uncle Patrick took the one on the other side of her when he was in town.

She smiled as she looked at the row of rock-faced homes. It was like something out of a fairy tale, with old-fashioned lampposts and flowers overflowing from window boxes.

Laney had spent the last few hours arranging all the final details for the kids arriving tomorrow. Once they arrived, she'd be staying out at the school while they got settled, so tonight would be her last chance to sleep in her own bed for a while.

Cleo put her head over the back of Laney's seat. Laney reached up and rubbed the side of the big cat's face. "And you are going to have to spend a little time in the cage while the kids get settled."

Cleo let out a grunt.

"I know you don't like it. But tonight you can sleep with me. Come on, let's go say goodnight to Max."

Laney got out of the car and Cleo followed. A very tall man opened the door of the cottage and stepped out. With his long dark hair and muscular build, he looked like he was part of an extremely tough biker gang.

Laney put up her hands. "Just me."

Maddox Datson smiled. "You're just in time—Kati's tucking him in."

She returned the smile as she walked up to him. "We thought we'd say goodnight."

Maddox reached down and ran a hand through Cleo's fur. "Hey, girl. Danny was hoping you'd stop by."

"Both of us, or just Cleo?"

Maddox grinned. "Let's pretend it's both of you."

Laney shook her head as she headed for the stairs. Cleo had won over Max, hook, line, and sinker. And Laney wasn't ashamed to admit that she was a little jealous. She used to be Max's number one friend. But now Max had Maddox, Cleo, Dom, Danny, Jake, Jen... the list went on and on. She was happy for him, but still selfish enough to want him to like her just a little bit more than the rest of them. After all, she *had* helped raise him.

Laney headed up the stairs with Cleo right behind her. She could hear Kati and Max talking, and put up a hand to stop Cleo.

Laney peeked in Max's room. Kati was tucking the blue blanket around him. "Who were you talking to before, honey?"

Max looked up at her, then his eyes drifted away. "Um, Dad?"

Laney had been just about to say hello, but now she stopped. Dad? Max's dad had passed away in a car accident before Max was even born.

"You mean you imagined him here?" Kati asked.

Max shook his head, his voice a little nervous. "No. He, uh, visits me sometimes."

"How do you know it's your dad?" Kati asked.

Max shrugged. "It looks like him."

"Is he here now?" Kati asked.

"He's over by the window," Max said.

Kati looked over at the window, and so did Laney. A chill stole over Laney even though there was no one there. What was she expecting? Max was imagining things.

She looked back at the boy with concern. Ever since the attack in Hershey, Max seemed to be making up more and more imaginary friends. His dad was just one more. That was all.

Laney's concerned gaze shifted from Max to Kati. Her friend's hands shook as she reached out to push a piece of hair from her son's forehead. "Well, it's nice your dad comes by to say hi."

Max smiled. "He wants you to know he loves you. He said he should have taken the other road that night."

Kati went still, but then she continued straightening his blankets. "What do you mean, honey?"

"Dad says he's sorry. He should have listened to you and taken the other road."

Kati just stared at Max, her eyes wide, her mouth open.

What's going on? Laney thought.

Just then Max looked past Kati and caught sight of Laney. "Laney! Cleo!"

Laney tried to smooth her face as she stepped into the room. *At least I got top billing.* "Hey, little man."

Kati let out a breath and smiled. "Hey, Laney."

Laney went and sat on the other side of the bed. "Thought I'd come say goodnight to my favorite little guy."

"Me?" Max asked. He drew out the word, his eyes big.

Laney laughed. "Yes, you."

Cleo came over and put her head right next to Max's. He leaned over and rubbed her ears. "Good night, Cleo."

Cleo stayed still for a moment before stepping back and slinking out of the room. Laney shook her head. When she'd first met Cleo she'd been terrified, and now she trusted her implicitly. It was strange the turns her life had taken.

"Where's Lamby?" Kati asked, drawing Laney's attention back to the bed.

"I left him downstairs." Max started to climb out of the bed.

Kati gently pushed him back down. "Oh, no you don't. I'll get it." She looked over at Laney. "You want to tuck our little guy in?"

"Absolutely," Laney said.

Laney pulled Max's blankets up to just below his chin. "So what did you do today?"

"I went to the park and played with Sally. We played trucks."

"Is Sally a new friend?"

Max nodded.

"That's nice." Laney tucked the blankets tight around him. "Snug as a bug in a rug."

Max giggled. "I'm not a bug."

"You're my little love bug."

Max giggled again, but then his face went serious. "Your friends play with me sometimes, too."

"Oh? And who's that?"

"Rocky and Drew."

Laney went still. Rocky and Drew had been two of her best friends. Drew had died at the beginning of all of this craziness, and Rocky had died saving Laney's life just a few months ago. Laney swallowed. "Um, what did they say?"

"That it wasn't your fault. And that you need to keep fighting because something's coming. Something bad."

Laney couldn't think of anything to say to that. *Something bad?*

Kati bustled back into the room, holding up the stuffed lamb that Laney had brought to Max in the hospital when he was only a day old. It had been well loved: once white, it was now a light grey, and both of its eyes were missing.

"Lamby!" Max yelled with a smile.

Kati handed him the lamb. "Now to sleep for you."

"Okay." Max leaned on his side, pulling Lamby to his chest. He closed his eyes and immediately started to snore.

Kati playfully whacked his blankets. "*Real* sleep."

Max stopped snoring with a grin, but kept his eyes closed.

Kati kissed him on the forehead. "I love you forever and always."

"No matter what," Max replied.

Laney shook herself from her surprise and kissed him on the cheek. "Goodnight, buddy. I love you too."

He snuggled deeper into the blankets. "I love you too, Laney."

Laney followed Kati out of the room, pausing in the doorway to glance back at Max. He looked so tiny, swallowed up in the big bed.

She looked over to where Max had said his dad was sitting. A chill crept over her again. What had all that been about Drew and Rocky?

Shaking her head, she caught up with Kati at the top of the stairs. "Kati?"

Kati turned, and Laney could tell that the smile on her face was forced. "Hey. Wasn't sure you'd make it."

"Everything okay?"

Kati nodded. "Sure. Good."

Laney glanced back over her shoulder at Max's room before turning back to Kati. "Max just told me that he talks to Drew and Rocky."

Kati's mouth fell open. "Uh, well, he's imagining things."

"I heard what he said about David."

Kati shook her head. "It's nothing. Just his way of coping. I was about to make myself something to eat, would you like to join me?"

"Um, sure."

Kati headed down the stairs.

Laney watched her friend go. What was going on? Kati was hiding something. Laney was sure of that.

She sank down onto the top step, her chin resting on her hands. Was it possible that Max really talked to Rocky and Drew? She ran her hands over her face. *Okay. Now you're looking for the supernatural in everything. He knew Drew and Rocky, and of course he heard about his dad. Kati was right. It's just his way of coping.*

Laney stood up. No point in looking for problems that didn't exist when she had plenty of problems that did.

CHAPTER 4

Early the next morning, Henry Chandler drove the large van down the rough, potholed side road. Last winter had been murder on all the roads in the area, and apparently this particular one, rarely used, didn't yet warrant attention by the state.

"How can they sleep through this?" Jen asked from the passenger seat.

Henry smiled over at her. Her Korean-American features were striking in the morning light, even with her dark hair pulled back and no makeup. "I believe that's a special power attributed to only teenagers."

He glanced in the back: three of the teens were sleeping, and the two right behind them were talking quietly. Jake was a few minutes behind them with Jen's brother Jordan and another five kids.

Jen glanced out the rear window and then faced forward again, biting her lower lip.

"They'll be okay, Jen."

She nodded. "I know."

Henry reached over and took her hand. "They will. You did good."

Jen met his eyes and Henry once again was taken aback by her beauty. She had an almond shape to her pale brown eyes. At six feet, she was still fourteen inches shorter than him, but a lot closer than most females.

Jen had found one of the teens before the girl had even been recruited. But the girl had volunteered to allow herself to be recruited anyway, so that she could lead them to the camp and save the others. Jen hadn't much liked the idea, but the girl convinced her, and in the end they did successfully liberate the camp.

Still, Jen's feelings about the whole thing were mixed. On the one hand, the kids from the camp were safe, which was wonderful. But knowing that this camp existed at all... it meant that someone else besides Amar was *still* recruiting potentials. And they had no idea who it was.

Jen smiled sadly. "I just wish none of them had to go through that."

"I know," Henry said softly. "But we can't control that. We can only help them from this point on."

Jen dropped Henry's hand, and he felt the loss. But they were taking baby steps with one another. And that was okay. He could wait.

As he drove, Henry became aware of the debate going on behind him between the two teenagers.

"Yeah, but he would totally be able to escape. I mean, why stay there?" Dark hair framed Lou Thomas's serious face.

"Maybe he didn't have enough strength to escape," said Roland —a.k.a. "Rolly"—Escabi, the sixteen-year-old African-American boy.

"But then he wasn't one of us," Lou countered.

"What are you two talking about?" Jen interrupted.

Lou looked over at Rolly, one eyebrow arched. Rolly grinned before turning to face Jen and Henry. "I think Prometheus was a nephilim or a Fallen. One of the good ones like us."

Henry glanced back in surprise. Prometheus was the Greek god who allegedly gave fire to humans against the wishes of Zeus. As punishment, Zeus condemned Prometheus to have his liver eaten by an eagle.

Each night, though, the liver regenerated, only to be eaten the next day by the same eagle. And the punishment was said to be eternal.

Lou shook her head. "But *I* say that if he was like us, there's no way he would just stand still and let his liver be eaten every day. There would be nothing that could hold him."

This was one of the problems with teenagers learning about their abilities. Non-super-powered teenagers tended to think they were invulnerable. Super-powered ones were a step above even that dangerously uninformed belief.

Jen looked over at Henry, and he knew she was thinking about his torture at the direction of Sebastian Flourent. He clenched his fists on the steering wheel as a vision of Hugo slashing his torso with a knife flashed through his mind.

"Henry," Jen said softly, grabbing his attention. And although telepathy wasn't part of their nephilim bag of tricks, he could hear the words in her mind clearly. *It's over—it's in the past. It can't hurt you any more.*

"It's okay." He glanced back at the kids. "We're not omnipotent. We can be restrained, held against our will—hurt. You guys need to remember that."

The teenagers seemed to realize that Henry wasn't speaking idly, and they both went quiet. Then Lou spoke. "Do you think the story's true?"

"I don't know," Jen said. "Personally, I look at all of the myths a little differently now."

"But does that mean—" Rolly looked over at Lou.

Lou looked back. "What?"

"It was an eternal punishment, right?" Rolly asked.

Lou nodded.

"Do you think there's any chance Prometheus is still locked up somewhere? Being pecked away?" Rolly asked.

Henry jolted at the image. *No. It wasn't possible. Was it?*

"I'm sure it's..." Jen stopped speaking. "I don't know what it is. But whoever he was, he must have died a long time ago. We're not immortal, either."

"Yeah, but that's really not the way I want to go," Rolly muttered.

Henry rounded a bend and all the trees disappeared. A field of grass stretched for a mile straight ahead and a massive three-story building sat at the end of it, nestled against a tall rock outcropping. A ten-foot-high wrought iron and stone fence surrounded the school. And today, the gates were open, waiting for the new arrivals.

"Wow." Lou moved up so her head was in between Henry and Jen. "That's the school? Fancy."

Rolly poked his head up right next to Lou, then let out a low whistle. "Nice."

Jen rolled her eyes. "All right, you two. Try to tamp down the excitement. You're not lord and lady of the manor. You get a room. And you'll probably have to share it."

"No problem," Lou said, her eyes wide. "I bet mine has some serious velvet drapes and a window seat. I've always wanted a window seat."

Henry smiled over their heads at Jen, who smiled back. A fresh start: something they all could use.

"Hey, is that Laney?" Lou asked.

Laney stood by the front door, waving. Henry nodded.

"She looks kind of small for an all-powerful nephilim," Rolly said.

Jen laughed. "Just don't let her hear you say that."

"Where's her pet?" Lou asked, craning her neck.

"Probably in her cage," Henry said. "Cleo is... well, she requires a special introduction." A few seconds later, he pulled to a stop next to the main entrance. "All right. Everybody out."

The kids scrambled out of the van, stretching and gawking as they huddled together.

Laney walked over to them. "Hi, everybody. Welcome to the Chandler House."

Some of the kids smiled back at her. Most just looked around nervously.

Laney gestured behind her. "If you head inside, Yoni and Sasha will show you to your rooms. We'll meet in the dining room in about forty minutes and tell you all about the place."

The kids filed passed her, but Henry and Jen grabbed Lou and Rolly before they could go inside. They led them over to Laney.

"Laney, this is Lou and Rolly," Jen said.

"The heroes," Laney said.

Lou blushed and looked at her feet.

Rolly grinned broadly. "Yup. That's us."

Laney laughed. "We're really glad you guys are here. You saved a lot of lives."

"Does that mean we get better rooms?" Rolly asked.

Jen swatted him on the shoulder. "Get inside before your ego makes it impossible for your head to fit through the door."

"Bye, guys," Laney said as they disappeared through the entrance. Then she greeted Jen with a hug. "I'm glad you're back."

"Me too." Jen pulled back and tilted her head toward the door. "I'll go help Yoni and Sasha. See you in a few?"

Laney nodded.

Henry smiled down at Laney. "Hey there, sis."

Laney hugged him. "I'm glad you're safe."

Henry returned the hug, amazed at how a little hug could make him feel like he was home. He looked around. "Where's Danny?"

Laney looked around, her eyes ranging over the teenagers through the open doorway. "I don't know. I thought he'd be here."

Her phone beeped and she pulled it out. Her face went pale.

"What is it?"

She turned the phone around so Henry could read the text. "It's from Danny."

A pit formed at the base of Henry's stomach as he read the text:

I've found more kids.

CHAPTER 5

Laney clasped Jake's hand as they made their way down the hall. He had arrived a few minutes ago with another group of students. But even as Laney had greeted the new students, Danny's text had stayed in the forefront of her mind. More kids in danger.

As they walked, Laney had to keep herself from sprinting down the hallways to Danny's office. When they'd set up the school they'd all agreed that it was important to provide the kids here with a calm and soothing environment. Laney and Jake charging down the hall wouldn't exactly inspire feelings of tranquility.

To distract herself, she told Jake about her last few days. "I swear, Jake, the paperwork is multiplying. Someone is sneaking into my office while I'm not looking and adding piles of the stuff."

Jake was fighting a losing battle to keep a smile off his face. "I'm sure that's exactly what's happening."

"You are *not* being sympathetic."

He pulled her to a stop and kissed her. "Better?"

"Better."

Whistles and claps from down the hall made her pull away.

She could feel her cheeks flame. But Jake held her hand and performed a deep bow.

But despite her embarrassment, Laney knew the kids' reaction was a good sign: it meant they were beginning to feel comfortable here.

Laney knew all twenty-eight kids at the school by name. And they all knew her. Somehow, though, the fact that she was the ring bearer had also become common knowledge among the kids. At first, it had resulted in the kids being a little frightened of her. She could understand that; after what she'd observed in Amar's camp, she could see why they'd worry about someone with the ability to control them.

It didn't take long, though, for Laney to show them that she wasn't interested in controlling anyone. Besides, she very rarely wore the ring, at least on her finger, which she thought probably helped allay their concerns. And the fact that they thought they could whistle when Jake kissed her meant they were feeling at home. So she'd take the embarrassment.

She reached up and grabbed the ring on the chain around her neck as she and Jake continued down the hall. Making sure the kids felt safe was one of the reasons she kept the ring on a chain. But it wasn't the only one.

The power of the ring was seductive. It gave her control over nephilim, Fallen, weather, animals, and probably gave her a few other abilities she hadn't figured out yet. That much power was not something anyone should wield on a daily basis. So she kept it close if she needed it, but tried to avoid using it.

On the way to Danny's office, she reminded herself how important it was for these kids to feel at home here. So she forced herself to say hello to each one as they passed, even though all she really wanted was to sprint past them and hear what Danny had found out.

Three teenagers, two boys and a girl, headed down the hall toward her. "Hey, Laney. Hi, Jake," they called as they approached.

"Hi, guys," Jake called out.

The girl stopped and said something to the boys before jogging over to Laney. "Um, Laney?"

Laney smiled at the young girl. Theresa was tall for her age, making her appear older than her sixteen years, and had been with them since the school had opened. She hadn't had any abilities prior to being in the camp, but they had been turned on by that brutal experience.

Laney was happy to see a little color in Theresa's cheeks and to see her spending time with some of the other kids. Theresa was one of the few teenagers here who knew about the abilities of one of her parents. She and her sister had been separated and moved into foster care after her parents' deaths.

Laney smiled. "Hi, Theresa. What's going on?"

"Um, hi, um. Yoni… he said that they found my sister."

"I know. I heard. That's great."

Theresa smiled. "Yeah. Yoni said she'll be here tomorrow afternoon. I was wondering, though: is there anyway we could share rooms?"

Laney nodded. "I'll take care of it."

Theresa's shoulders sagged with relief and she gave Laney a quick hug. "Thank you."

Laney hugged her back. "You're very welcome."

Laney watched with a feeling of contentment as Theresa dashed back down the hall in the direction her friends had gone. They were really making a difference here.

Jake raised an eyebrow at her.

"Okay," Laney said. "Maybe all the paperwork is worth it. Come on." She tugged Jake down the hall, the smile dropping from her face as the worries about Danny's text started to crowd her mind once again.

"We'll find them," Jake murmured next to her.

She didn't ask how he knew what she was thinking. He just always seemed to. And his voice held no doubt—only confidence.

It made her own confidence increase a little. She, Jake, and Henry had taken on incredible odds before. This situation would just be one more opportunity to succeed. She leaned into him. "Yes, we will."

They turned the corner together and could hear Danny and Henry talking. "Lou's here. You should go say hi," Henry said.

Danny groaned. "Henry..."

"What? She's nice."

Laney smiled and shook her head.

Before they reached the door, Jake stopped her and tipped her face up toward his. "Just remember, whatever it is, we face it together. Okay?"

Laney nodded as she reached up to kiss him. "Together."

CHAPTER 6

MEDFORD, OREGON

Reverend Nathaniel Grayston stepped to the pulpit. The squirming in the seats stopped automatically, as did the whispers and quiet murmurs. All eyes turned to him. The only sound was the hum of the tall fans blowing the hot air around the big tent.

Nathaniel nodded, pleased with the response. For a man who had been largely overlooked his entire life, these last few years of his ministry had been ego enhancing.

Nathaniel had no illusions about his appearance. He was not a tall man, nor an imposing one. But he knew his words would ignite his followers. His congregation was small but it grew every week.

He glanced around the "church." The tent traveled with them from venue to venue. It took hours for his followers to set up, but it was worth it. The beams of the tent were draped in a deep red fabric that contrasted with the white of the tent itself.

An eight-foot-tall crucifix hung behind Nathaniel on the

portable stage. Jesus, bloodied and scarred, looked down on him, as if to give Nathaniel his blessing.

His congregants sat on metal folding chairs. More than half of the attendees were male. The majority of them wore some sign of their military background. The wars in Afghanistan and Iraq were a boon to his ministry. All those lost souls in need of guidance.

And it is my honor to provide them with it, Nathaniel thought as he placed his worn Bible on the podium. The Old Testament was dog-eared, marked with words or insights. The New Testament was practically pristine. Jesus was a divine force, but the true message of God could be found in the Old, not the New Testament.

"My friends," Nathaniel began, casting his eyes over the group. Although the tent was filled to capacity, none of the one hundred twenty people said a word, their attention rapt, except for a few in the back who looked around uneasily. There were always doubting Thomases in the crowd—at least at the beginning.

All of those in attendance had been invited to attend due to their support of Nathaniel's weekly online sermons, with, of course, a few of his already devout followers sprinkled throughout the crowd. Now was the time to solidify these supporters to the cause.

"My friends," he said again, mentally discarding the sermon he had prepared. These people needed to know their duty. They needed to know what they risked through their inaction.

"We have been much blessed. We have been born into a country the likes of which the world has never known. Many of you have helped defend the freedoms and ideals of that country and have lost friends along the way. We are forever in your debt."

He paused, allowing his words to wash over the crowd.

"But now, another, even more insidious, danger has appeared. And we have been chosen to fulfill God's word—to protect the innocent, to protect the faithful. God is not pleased with our sinful ways."

Nathaniel picked up the Bible, holding it above his head, his voice louder. "'I will execute judgment on him with plague and bloodshed; I will pour down torrents of rain, hailstones and burning sulfur on him and on his troops and on the many nations with him.

"These are our God's words. He has been unhappy in the past and mankind has paid the price. He is unhappy again. The time of the judgment has begun. Are you ready?"

He peered at a man in the second row, waiting for the man to nod back. Then Nathaniel scanned the crowd, making eye contact with others. "Are you? And you?"

"I'm ready." A muscular man with a shaved head in the third row stood, his back straight. Tyrell Nichols, Nathaniel's right-hand man. Tyrell kept his eyes locked on Nathaniel, his commitment apparent to everyone there.

And the tidal wave of proclamations began.

"Me too."

"I'm ready."

"I'm with you, Father."

The noise increased, and soon almost all in the tent were standing, declaring their unity. Nathaniel let the outpouring continue for a few seconds more before he put up a hand, waving everyone back into their seats.

He nodded, coming to the front of the stage. "I never doubted it, my friends. You have all been called to God's mission, just as I have. And what a glorious duty it is: the ushering in of a new age, a better age. We will save the human race from this danger. We will show them the way."

His voice took on a hushed, urgent whisper. "But to do this, we must become God's weapon. We must strike down evil where we see it, no matter what face it hides behind.

"We have known we are the chosen people. Now God has instilled within us a glorious duty. It is not an easy task, but we must stay the path. The consequences of failure are too steep for us to pay, but the rewards for success are great."

His congregation nodded back at him, their faces serious.

Nathaniel opened up his Bible to the passage he had highlighted. "For the Lord God said, 'Upon the wicked He will rain snares; Fire and brimstone and burning wind will be the portion of their cup.' We, my friends, have been chosen by God for this duty. You who hear His call, you who are lost: fear not, for God has a plan for you. All that you have been through, all that you have seen has been designed by God Himself to bring you to this moment—to bring you to Him. We will be God's righteous weapon. We are the chosen ones of God. How many of you will answer His call?"

A few people called out.

"I will!"

"Yes!"

Nathaniel eyed the crowd, pulling his voice from deep in his soul. "I said, How many of you will answer God's call?"

The tent thundered with the voices calling back at him. Nathaniel smiled as his flock shouted their affirmations of their duty. He finally waved his hands to quiet them down. It took a few minutes for them to return from their blissful states.

Nathaniel's eyes lingered on the blond teenager in the front row. The boy met his gaze unblinking, his devotion apparent. He had none of Nathaniel's features, only his mother's.

Nathaniel peered into the eyes of his son, holding up the Bible. "This is our God. These are His words. This is our duty."

CHAPTER 7

L aney stepped into Danny's office, Jake right behind her. While Jake said hello to Danny and Moxy, Laney's eyes traveled across the monitors.

As usual, Danny had six monitors running, each presenting different data. Laney knew they weren't all regarding the "potentials," as they'd come to call the kids they were looking for. Danny's brilliant mind made it difficult for him to focus on only one project at a time. He needed to be constantly challenged.

Fifteen years old, Danny had reminded Laney of Elliot from the movie *E.T.* when she'd first met him. Big freckles dotted his cheeks, dark brown hair fell over his eyes, and he always looked like he could use a few hamburgers. But Laney knew eating wasn't a problem: he put away more than his body weight in fries.

Danny concluded his conversation with Jake and gestured to the monitors in front of him. "I found more."

"*We* found more," came a voice from the desk.

Jake reached over and grabbed the iPad, propping it up. "Hi, Dom. Sorry—didn't see you there."

"Dom" was Dr. Dominic Radcliffe, a brilliant agoraphobic who also worked for the Chandler Group. His hair was a little longer than usual, making the halo of salt and pepper curls springing from his head that much bigger. His glasses were patched with tape and kept slipping down his nose.

Dom grinned and gave them all a wave.

"How'd you find them?" Laney asked.

"We used my database," Dom said.

Back when this all began, they'd learned that Dom had created a database with the present and past incarnations of the Fallen. He'd been aware of their existence for decades longer than anyone else, and they had been playing catch-up ever since.

Jake was about to cut in, but Laney shook her head at him. She knew from experience that it would be faster to let Danny and Dom explain their methodology rather than ask them for the results. Dom had sometimes sent her result printouts with not-so-descriptive variable names like "X23." She'd learned the hard way that having them explain everything in their own way usually saved time in the long run.

"The problem has been trying to tease out the kids we're looking for from all the kids that go missing every year," Danny said.

Dom cut in. "Do you have any idea how many kids go missing annually?"

"Eight hundred thousand," Laney replied.

Dom's expression was one of comic shock.

Laney tried not to feel exasperated. Geniuses always seemed surprised when other people were brighter than they expected. "I do actually have a Ph.D. in criminology, Dom."

"Oh, right. I'd forgotten about that," Dom said.

Most people do, Laney thought. Her academic career felt like it had happened a lifetime ago. "And the problem," Laney said, "is that the majority of those missing kids are either familial abductions or runaways."

Danny nodded. "Right. So we had to figure out a way to pull out the stranger abductions. Occasionally there's a witness and a police report that helped, so we tapped into those files first. But even then, we couldn't tell anything about the nature of the child grabbed."

"That's where my database came into play," Dom said.

"I cross referenced Dom's data with birth records going back twenty years to see if anything popped," Danny said.

"And it did," Dom added.

Danny nodded. "Then for those names, I cross-referenced against missing kid reports as well as just general information, like school records about current whereabouts, in case for some reason the kids weren't reported as missing. I added in the information about the kids we already know about and the ones we found in Amar's files. Then I added in some variables for what I called 'specialness'—extreme physical capabilities—"

"Or psychic capabilities," Dom chimed in.

Psychic abilities? Laney thought. *How the heck did they do that?* But she kept her thoughts to herself. She'd ask later.

"Right. And we finally got our results," Danny said.

"And you found some kids?" Jake asked.

Danny nodded as he handed Laney a sheet with an output table. He handed the same sheet to Jake and Henry. Laney's eyes scrolled over the report, thankful that Danny had at least created variable names with some actual meaning this time.

She stopped when she got to the age variable. She ran her hand across the sheet to make sure she had linked the right coefficients with the right variable. Then she looked up, knowing the disbelief was on her face.

Danny nodded at her, his face serious. "You found it."

Laney shook her head. "This can't be right."

"What?" Henry asked, staring at his own sheet. Laney glanced at Jake and he nodded back at her. He'd seen it too.

Dom was more sober than Laney had ever seen him. "It is. We've run it again and again, adjusting variables, reworking the coding. The results are always the same."

Danny's voice was quiet. "They're not grabbing teenagers this time. This time they're grabbing children."

CHAPTER 8

BALTIMORE, MARYLAND

Henry sat down heavily in a chair, dread filling him.

Laney was making Danny go over the methodology again. Dom had gone off to work on some other project; he didn't take well to having his work questioned.

Henry knew Laney was looking for something Danny and Dom had missed. But he also knew she didn't expect to find anything. After all, the chances of two super-geniuses messing up was pretty slim.

Henry only half listened to their conversation. Mostly he studied Danny. The boy's face was drawn and there were bags under his eyes. Henry knew those signs: Danny hadn't slept last night. No doubt he'd been hunched over his computer, trying to find more info on the missing kids. Henry closed his eyes. *It's not supposed to be like this.* He opened them again. This was not the life he wanted for Danny.

Laney sat back in her chair. "So there's no doubt about it: they're going after children."

Danny nodded.

Laney grabbed the output sheet and glanced at the variables. "And if I'm reading this correctly, the oldest is ten and the youngest—" She swallowed. "One."

"Yeah," Danny said. "We found them in the files. Twin boys, age thirteen months."

Henry felt like he was going to be sick. He looked over and saw Laney swallow hard. Laney had raised Max since he was a baby. This had to be hitting her pretty hard. Even Jake looked shaky as he spoke. "Okay, we're looking at, what, a dozen cases?"

Danny nodded. "Probably a little more than that."

Henry looked at Danny for a moment before he understood what he meant. "You've only been able to track the nephilim. If Fallen are being tracked too, the numbers will be higher."

Danny nodded. "And the strangest part of this is that all the abductions have occurred within the last month."

Henry felt nauseated again. He knew that the chances of finding a kid alive were reduced dramatically the longer a case went unsolved.

"But why grab them at all?" Danny asked. "Having one parent with powers doesn't guarantee the child will have abilities, right?"

"Actually in most cases, the children don't," Henry said.

"Have any of these kids demonstrated any abilities?" Laney asked.

Danny shook his head. "Not that we could find. I mean, they're too young to come into their abilities, aren't they?"

Henry thought of Jen, who'd come into her powers early. He spoke slowly. "Usually, people are older, yes."

"So, why even take them?" Danny asked, his eyes big, the confusion and fear plain on his face. "They're too young to come into their powers anytime soon. They're not a threat."

Henry was once again reminded of how young and innocent Danny really was. He had been isolated from the world in many ways, and his intelligence put yet another barrier between him and the rest of the world. Henry hated that Danny had become involved in this.

Jake spoke, his voice gentle. "They're not a threat right now. But one day they will be. Maybe someone wants to take care of them before then."

"Because in a few years, humans won't be able to hurt them," Laney said.

Jake turned to her. "You think it's humans?"

She shrugged. "I don't know."

"Has there been any sign of the kids since they disappeared?" Jake asked.

Danny shook his head. "We're still cross-referencing with hospitals and… morgues. But so far, none of the kids we've identified have shown up anywhere. They're just gone."

Laney leaned back. "Well, maybe that's good news. Maybe they're just being held somewhere."

Or maybe someone buried them where no one will find them. Henry wanted to chase the voice away, but he knew it was all too reasonable a thought. *After all, these graves would be awfully small.*

He knew how easy it was to hide a body—or twelve. Look at Jimmy Hoffa or many of the victims of suspected serial killers. Even today, no one was sure just how many people Ted Bundy had killed. And the Green River Killer managed to kill for years before anyone even realized who he was.

Were these disappearances the work of a serial killer as well—one targeting nephilim? Or was it something else? A picture of John Jamelske popped into his mind. He'd abducted four different girls between 1998 and 2003 in upstate New York. He kept them for an extended period of time and then let them go. And no one was the wiser.

"How did whoever took them find them?" Jake asked, pulling Henry from his dark thoughts.

Danny shrugged. "I guess they could have done what we did."

Laney nodded. "I suppose, but that feels kind of piecemeal.

And there are probably more kids we haven't identified using your methodology. So how did whoever grabbed them find them? Or even know, for that matter, that they were potentials?"

"I don't know." Danny hit a button on his keyboard. "These are the kids that Dom and I uncovered."

Henry stared at a little boy who couldn't be any older than three. "They're all so young."

"Is there anything from the investigations?" Jake asked.

"I only just started going through them, but there's not much so far. No video. No trace evidence. The kids are just gone." Danny bit his lip, his hair falling into his eyes, but Henry read the sadness there.

And Henry couldn't stand it. He spoke before he even knew what he was going to say. "Well this is good work. Why don't you send us everything and then you can go take Moxy for a walk or something? We can finish this up."

Danny looked over at him. "What?"

Henry ignored Laney's and Jake's dual expressions of shock. "I just don't think it's necessary for you to be part of this."

"*Part* of this?" Danny asked. "The only reason you even *know* about this is because of me."

Henry nodded. "I realize that, but you've done your part, so I think you should—"

"What?" Danny demanded. "Run along and play? I'm not a child."

"Yes, you are," Henry lashed out. "You're *my* child. And I don't want you to be involved in this."

Danny stood up. "I'm not your child. Legally, I'm not anybody's child."

Henry felt like he'd been slapped. He took a breath. "Fine. Then as your boss, I'm telling you, you are off this project."

Danny's mouth fell open and a look of hurt appeared on his face. Then his mouth slammed shut and the hurt was quickly replaced by anger. He punched at a few buttons on the keyboard.

"I just sent you all the files, *boss*. Come on, Moxy." He stomped out of the room, Moxy at his heels.

Henry watched Danny go, wishing he could take back the last five minutes. *'As your boss'?* He'd never pulled that with Danny before.

Henry turned. Jake and Laney watched him silently, yet that silence seemed to be filled with words. "What?" Henry demanded.

Jake raised an eyebrow. "Well, out of the three of us, I'd usually say you were the most diplomatic. And yet Yoni could have handled that better."

Henry gave a heavy sigh, feeling wearier than he had in a long time. "You don't understand. Danny's just a kid. He shouldn't be dealing with life and death issues. Especially not life and death issues involving other kids."

"He's not a kid," Laney said softly. "He hasn't been for a long time."

Henry sighed, knowing she was right but knowing he was too. "I don't know what to do. I know he's not technically a kid. He's a teenager, and legally he's already an adult. But how can I want him to be a part of... *this?*" He waved his hand toward the monitors.

The room went silent, and Henry's eyes roamed over the kids on the screen. Each additional face just made his resolve that much stronger. Danny was not going to be a part of this.

"Look," Jake said finally. "We can keep Danny out of it from here on out. I'm okay with that."

"Me too," Laney said.

"Thanks." Henry felt the weight on him lift a little.

"Okay, so now the problem is, who's grabbing these kids?" Jake turned to Laney. "You're sure it's not the Fallen?"

She shook her head. "Of course I can't be sure, but I just can't see why they would. Not this young. They'd require too much care for too long."

"Maybe someone thinks they're rescuing them," Henry said.

"Rescuing them from what?" Laney asked.

Henry shrugged.

"Or maybe someone's just killing them," Jake said softly.

Laney nodded. "Yeah. That's what I'm afraid of."

"Okay, so where do we start?" Henry asked.

Laney pointed to the picture of the little girl with brown pigtails and big brown eyes. "With Sophia Watson. She was grabbed three days ago. I'm thinking Jake and I should head down to Atlanta and see if we can find out anything."

"I can go," Henry said.

Laney shook her head and looked down the hall in the direction Danny had disappeared. "I think you're needed here."

"There is one other option," Jake said thoughtfully.

Laney and Henry looked over at him.

"There are two triangles, right?" Jake asked.

Last year, they'd learned that Laney, Henry, and Jake made up an ancient triad that only comes about when the world has reached a dangerous point. They worked on the side of the good, protecting mankind. Unfortunately there was also another triad, one that was far less concerned about the welfare of mankind.

Henry and Laney nodded.

"But there's also three groups," Jake said. "The Fallen, us, and—"

"The Council," Laney finished. The Council was a shadowy group of humans with extensive resources who, for financial reasons, helped the Fallen. They'd been around for centuries, operating behind the scenes, using whatever they uncovered from Atlantis and the Fallen to their financial benefit.

Jake nodded.

"But what reason could they have for being involved in this?" Laney asked.

Jake shrugged. "Who knows? But they're always around, always at the periphery, and we haven't paid them much attention because the Fallen have always been the greater threat. I think, though, we might need to start paying them some attention."

"Why?" Henry asked.

Jake gestured to the monitors. "Whoever grabbed these kids did it before the kids' powers manifested. Which means the kidnappers are most likely human. And whenever humans are involved..." He left his sentence unfinished.

Henry nodded with a sigh. "Whenever humans are involved, it's in the form of the Council."

"Uncle Patrick may know something," Laney said. "He's been going through the Council books."

"The ones from Flourent's house?" Henry asked.

After they had rescued Henry from Sebastian Flourent's home, they'd uncovered a set of books in Sebastian's office. The books had survived the destruction by pure luck: the bookcase had been bolted into a rock alcove, giving it some protection from the destruction of the home. Not all the books survived, but more than half had, and Patrick had slowly been going through them, one by one. Together they formed a history of the Council's activities that went back centuries.

Laney nodded. "Once he's gotten the kids set up, let's pull him aside. See what he knows."

Jake stood up, his eyes straying to the monitors. "Actually, I think we can let Patrick focus on helping the new kids, for right now anyway. Henry and I can get the rest of the investigation reports."

"Okay. What about me?"

"I think there might be someone else you could call who may know a thing or two about the Council."

Laney looked from Jake to Henry and back again, then paused before nodding. "I'll make the call."

CHAPTER 9

D anny headed toward the back of the school with Moxy at his side. All the new kids were getting settled in and Danny wasn't in the mood to meet a bunch of new people.

Of course, Lou will be getting settled in too, he thought. Danny could feel the blush crawling up his neck at the mere thought of her. He'd only met her a few times, back when he'd helped Jen set her up with a tracker. But there was something calming about Lou. *Maybe I should go say hi.*

His subconscious laughed at him. *Then you'd have to meet all the other kids. And you're never in the mood to meet new people.*

Danny was honest enough with himself to admit that that was true. In fact, he couldn't remember there ever being a time when he was anything but terrified of meeting new people. New people were only another chance to get hurt.

Freak. The word slashed through his brain. His brothers' voices, still loud all these years later.

A memory of his father, angry at Danny for using up all the pages in his notebook, popped into his mind. "Are you going to pay for more books?" his father had yelled, slapping Danny across the face.

Danny stopped in his tracks, a tremor in his hand. He tried to pull up a memory of his mother. He remembered sitting and reading to her when she was sick. And when he was done, she would always whisper, "I love you, my brilliant, sweet boy."

She'd said the same words to him every single day, up until the day she died. He sighed. Why did the memory of his father's and brothers' angry words still hit him more powerfully than her words of love?

Moxy nudged his hand, and Danny leaned down to rub her head. "I'm okay, girl. Let's go see Cleo. I bet she could use some company."

Danny turned the corner and spied the door leading outside. As he pushed it open he heard Cleo's screech. *Oh no.* His heart pounding, he ran to the end of the building and turned a corner.

Cleo prowled the edge of her cage as two teenagers, a boy and a girl, tried to swipe at her with a garden rake.

Summoning his courage, Danny marched toward them. "Get away from her."

The teenagers turned, and Danny realized it was Michelle and Collin. He groaned. *Why did it have to be them?*

"Oh, look, super brain has arrived," Michelle taunted.

"What are you going to do, super brain? Think bad thoughts at us?" Collin mocked.

Danny crossed his arms over his chest, feigning a confidence he didn't feel. "Maybe I'll just let Cleo out to defend herself."

"Yeah, well, how are you going to get to the door?" Collin took a step toward Danny. "You're not faster than us."

"I'm betting we are," called out a female voice from behind Danny.

Danny turned his head and saw Lou heading toward him, followed by a tall African-American boy.

Lou stopped next to Danny and gave him a smile. "Hey, Danny."

He nodded back. "Hey, Lou."

"Stay out of this," Michelle warned.

Lou snorted. "Why? Cause a Barbie told me to?"

Collin took a step forward. "You really should listen to her."

The boy next to Lou sighed dramatically. "See? That's the problem with youth today: no understanding of when they're about to get their asses kicked."

Michelle rolled her eyes and turned to Collin. "Whatever. Come on."

Collin feigned like he was going to throw the rake at Danny.

Danny flinched.

Collin laughed before dropping the rake to the ground. He followed Michelle back to the building, stopping at the door just long enough to give them the finger.

Danny let out a breath. "Jerks."

Lou laughed. "Hey—watch the language. My pristine ears."

Danny could feel the blush creeping up his neck again. "Sorry."

"No problem," she said with a smile, and Danny realized she was even prettier than he'd remembered. Much prettier.

The boy next to Lou coughed and raised his eyebrows. Lou smiled again. "Oh, sorry. Danny, this is Rolly. Rolly, this is Danny, the super-genius who put that tracker on me, traced our call, and saved our butts."

Rolly held out his hand. "Heard a lot about you. Thanks for what you did. We all owe you."

Danny shook Rolly's hand. "It's no big deal."

"Well, it is to me. I like my butt," Rolly said.

Lou whacked Rolly in the arm. "Ignore him," she said. Her eyes moved past Danny to the cage, and she let out a low whistle. "Wow. That is one giant cat."

She approached the cage but stopped a few feet short of it when Cleo let out a hiss.

"Uh, Lou, maybe you should come back here with me," Rolly said, a tremor in his voice.

Lou took a step back. "I thought Jen said she was friendly."

"She is." Danny stepped up next to the cage and Cleo walked over to him. He reached in and petted her through the bars. "You just need to get Laney to introduce you."

Rolly shifted from foot to foot. "Um, Danny?"

"Yeah?"

"Um, I was wondering. I know you don't know me or anything, but I was hoping you could help me out."

"If I can," Danny said.

Rolly looked at Lou, who nodded back at him. Then he took a breath. "My sister Alicia... I think she might have been in one of the other training camps. I was hoping maybe you could find a record of her?"

Danny swallowed, knowing that whatever he found might not make Rolly happy.

"He needs to know, Danny—one way or the other," Lou said quietly.

Danny looked at her for a moment before turning back to Rolly. "I'll see what I can do. Do you have a picture?"

Hope flashed across Rolly's face as he dug a picture out of his wallet and handed it over. "It's my only one."

"I'll get it back to you." The girl in the picture looked a lot like Rolly, except with higher cheekbones. "She's very pretty."

Rolly gave a half smile. "Yeah—we're a good-looking family."

Lou shook her head. "Although not a humble one."

Danny smiled.

"Listen, we're going to go to that carnival thing," Rolly said. "You want to come?"

Danny looked between Lou and Rolly. For the first time, the idea of just hanging out with kids his age sounded like fun. "Yeah. That sounds good."

CHAPTER 10

L aney's mind churned as she walked down the hall and outside. She needed a little fresh air after everything Danny had showed them. She pictured Sophia Watson with her blond hair and bright blue eyes. A shiver ran through her as she imagined all sorts of dark possibilities.

But she forced herself to close down that line of thought. *They're alive until you know otherwise,* she ordered herself, even as her stomach rolled.

Henry and Jake were pulling together everything they could on the investigations into the disappearances. But Laney couldn't help but wonder how the abductor had identified the children. The only person who could identify a potential, as far as she knew, was herself.

Over the last few weeks, Laney had come to realize that she could feel a slight electrical charge from any potential nephilim or Fallen. Even so, the sense was minimal, barely there.

And that was for kids who were close to coming into their powers. She couldn't imagine she would get a reading from a kid who wasn't even close. Plus, as far as she knew, no one but her had this ability.

She sank onto a bench at the side of the school with a view of the front gate. The fight between Danny and Henry slipped into her mind. She wished she could help there, too, but she couldn't figure out a way to ease the tension between the two of them.

She knew Henry was feeling out of his depth. Being Danny's surrogate father had been pretty smooth sailing until the last year. *Until the Fallen started making their presence known,* she thought, with more than a little resentment. How many aspects of life could they possibly disrupt?

Laney shook her head, her eyes straying over the outline of the large school. A few of the kids wandered by now and then; others sat and talked beneath the magnolia to the right of the main drive. More were inside unseen, starting a new life here.

All these kids—their lives uprooted because the Fallen had plans for them. Were there still more of them being rounded up into a camp right now?

As she pictured the little kids that were missing, her gut clenched. They were all so young. So unfairly young.

She pulled out her phone and dialed Victoria, unsurprised when she got her voicemail. "Hi, Victoria—um, Mom. It's me. Can you call when you get a chance? I need some help with something."

She disconnected, frustration rolling through her. She was never able to directly reach Victoria. And she knew Victoria would have information. She always did.

Her eyes narrowed. There might be someone else who would know something else about the Council. She hit speed dial number eight. *I can't believe I have this guy on speed dial.*

Agent Matthew Clark of the Special Investigative Agency, or SIA, spoke cheerfully through the line. "Laney. How are you?"

The SIA was a highly secretive branch of the Department of Defense. Clark had said their goal was to monitor the Fallen, but Laney couldn't shake the feeling that there was more underneath the shadowy group.

"I'm good, Matt. How are you?" She paused. "How are the interrogations going?"

"Slowly. Our guests are not being overly cooperative."

Laney frowned, feeling uneasy. After they'd taken down Amar, Clark had collected all the Fallen who hadn't been killed. Six were now residing at one of the SIA's facilities. Laney had never really been comfortable with that decision. Still, it's not like there had been a better option. The people captured were too powerful to be housed in a regular prison, and the only other option would be to kill them—which was not an option, as far as Laney was concerned.

"So, have you reconsidered my request to come down and speak with them?" Clark asked.

Laney paused again. Clark had been asking her with increasing frequency to come down to the facility. After all, as the ring bearer, she could compel the Fallen to speak.

She had visited once and questioned one of the inmates. But the place felt too much like a prison—a very *bright* prison—and the questioning had felt... wrong. It was one thing to use the ring to defend herself or others in the heat of battle. It was another thing altogether to force someone—someone who was no threat, someone who was completely in her control—to do something against their will.

"Matt, I told you I'm not comfortable with that."

"But the stakes, Laney—"

"Are not dire enough at this moment to warrant me overriding their will, Matt. I said no."

Clark sighed. "Okay. I'll let it go for now."

"Thank you."

"Did the kids arrive all right?"

"Yes. They're getting settled in. A few more will arrive in the next few days when they're released from the hospital."

"Glad to hear it." He paused. "So, what's the reason for your call?"

The picture of the pigtailed girl ran through Laney's mind. "Well, we have a problem with some children. Just not the ones here." She quickly explained about the missing children.

Clark was silent when she finished. An uncomfortable feeling swept over her. "Matt, you didn't already know the kids were missing, did you?"

Clark hesitated. "I knew."

Laney stared at her phone, stunned. She literally could not think of a thing to say to that.

"It's not what you think, Laney."

"It's not what I think? What I think is you knew kids were missing and didn't try to find them."

Clark's angry words burst through the phone. "We did try! In fact I lost men trying."

Laney paused. "Lost men? How?"

Clark's sigh was audible. "I thought there might be a link between the abductions and the Council. I had two of my agents investigating. They got close. One's disappeared, and the other one..." He paused. "We recovered his body a few days ago."

Laney closed her eyes. Damn it. More deaths. "Why do you think it's related to the Council?"

"Probably for the same reasons you do. A Fallen wouldn't need to grab kids before their powers manifested. And there's a good chance some of these kids won't even have powers. That makes humans the most likely candidates. And when it comes to this stuff, 'humans' means the Council."

She couldn't fault his logic. "Okay. So have you found out anything?"

"There's been a lot of turmoil in the High Council in the last two years. New members have been added to the High Council."

Surprise filtered through her. *New members?* They'd learned that within the Council was a higher council composed of six members, one each from six ruling families. They were the power behind all of the Council's activities.

"And how does one become a new member of the High Council?" Laney asked.

"You have to demonstrate that you're a descendant of Atlantis."

It took Laney a moment to find her voice. "How on earth do they accomplish that?"

"They used to require a well-documented family tree. But now there's a much easier and more foolproof method."

"What's that?"

"A DNA test."

CHAPTER 11

L aney stared at the phone. *A DNA test that proves Atlantean lineage?* Then it hit her. "Haplogroup X."

"Yep."

Haplogroups, Laney knew, were a sort of genetic marker that could be used to identify groups of people with a shared ancestry. People from northern Europe would might tend toward one haplogroup, and people from southern Asia another. By measuring the types and distribution of haplogroups in a population, it's possible to determine where that population's ancestors came from.

Haplogroups proved to be particularly useful in understanding the global ancestry of Native Americans. Original testing indicated that Native Americans shared four distinct lineages: Haplogroups A, B, C, and D. Haplogroups A, C, and D migrated from Siberia, entering the Americas around 35,000 BCE. Haplogroup B was associated with populations in Southeast Asia, China, Polynesia, and even Japan, and migrated to the Americas much later, around 11,000 BCE.

Laney knew there was controversy about these dates. Some scientists argued that all the Native Americans migrated at the same time. Others suggested four separate journeys. The most popular theory, based upon linguistics, was the Greenberg theory, which argued that there were three distinct migration periods.

But then, in 1997, a different haplogroup was discovered: group X. Haplogroup X was found in about seven percent of Europeans and Middle Easterners as well as three percent of Native Americans (although in some tests it comprised a whopping twenty-five percent of certain tribes).

The problem was that haplogroup X indicated a much earlier habitation of America than most scholars were comfortable with. According to genetic testing, haplogroup X first appeared on American shores around 34,000 BCE—and then it showed up again, in even greater numbers, in 10,000 BCE. Both dates coincide with the alleged destructions of Atlantis.

A flicker of memory stirred in the back of Laney's mind. She remembered that Edgar Cayce had made some predictions about early America. He argued that parts of the Southwest had been inhabited ten million years ago. And Cayce also argued that the Atlanteans became the Iroquois, although he did allow that some of the Iroquois were not actually from Atlantis but were indigenous to North America. And the more recent research linked Haplogroup X to the Iroquois.

Laney also remembered something about the X group being tied to the Mound Builders.

"So the Council believes that people with haplogroup X are descendants of Atlanteans?" Laney asked.

"Yes. And this new DNA testing requirement caused a schism in the Council. Families that had formerly been held in high regard were unceremoniously dumped. In fact, you know one of them."

Laney thought for a moment. "Flourent."

"Yes. He was denied membership, although I doubt even he knows why."

Laney nodded. Sebastian Flourent had been incensed when his

membership to the Council had been denied. In fact, it was that denial that had spun him off on his own mission to recover the Atlantis library from Ecuador—a mission that had resulted in dozens of deaths, mostly from among the Shuar tribe.

The anger at the senseless destruction in Ecuador flared inside Laney yet again. She tamped it down. She needed to stay on track. "Okay. So the High Council is having some membership issues. How does that related to the abductions?"

Clark's voice was heavy. "In our records, it mentions that there are only six members of the High Council. One of whom is its head."

Laney nodded. She knew the current head of the Council was Phillip Northgram, the well-known CEO of Banchfield Trust, a hedge fund based in Chicago but with offices in Los Angeles, New York, and Atlanta. Billions of dollars ran through Banchfield annually. He had taken over as CEO when his father had retired. And reportedly, he was grooming his young daughter to take over after him one day.

"Well, it turns out that those records are wrong. There are not six members—there are seven."

"Seven? Who's the seventh?"

"The *real* head of the Council. And I have no idea who he is. In fact, I didn't even know he existed until a week ago."

"What happened?"

"One of my men managed to intercept a piece of correspondence between two members of the High Council. In it, they spoke of this seventh member. My agent tried to track him down. We found his body a few days later. His partner is the one who's gone missing."

Laney closed her eyes. "I'm sorry."

"We pulled in one of the High Council members. The man was terrified. But not of us. He was terrified of this seventh member. He wouldn't say anything about him. In fact, he claimed he didn't even know who the head really was. He said the man's identity was never revealed. He sends emissaries on his behalf to all meetings and is never seen."

"Has anyone else ever gone looking for him?"

"No. And the emissaries always show up dead a few days later as well."

"And there's nothing in the SIA records on this seventh member?"

"I've combed the SIA archives looking for a hint, but no luck. And to be honest, I think the man we interviewed was telling the truth: not even the other members of the Council know the identity of their leader. So whoever the seventh member is, they're covering their tracks exceptionally well."

Clark was quiet for a moment.

A seventh member? Laney thought. *Was it possible? And did it matter? Were the inner workings of the High Council related to the missing kids?*

"There's more," Clark said. "Like I said, the Council dates back centuries. And this seventh member's identity, whoever he or she is, has been anonymous since the Council began."

"How do you know that?"

"The Council member we grabbed? We grabbed all his journals as well."

"But you can't mean to say it's been the same person for centuries?"

"No, I can't see how that's possible. But if you'd let us see those Council books you got from Flourent, we could put them together with this other set and probably figure out what family the seventh member represents."

Now it was Laney's turn to pause. "Actually, I think we'll hold on to them. But we'll go through them ourselves. And if we find something, we'll let you know."

"Okay. But Laney, I think you should make that a priority."

"Well, the missing kids are the priority right now."

"I understand that. But if they're linked..."

Laney nodded, knowing he was right.

Clark's voice was serious as he spoke. "Laney, it's getting dangerous out there. And if you've been called, we know it's only going to get more so. Having a player on the board but unknown, well… that makes me nervous."

Laney nodded and dropped her head back against the couch. "Me too, Matt. Me too."

CHAPTER 12

BALTIMORE, MARYLAND

Laney sat back from the desk in her office and glanced over at the window. Darkness was just beginning to creep across the sky.

She stretched her back, trying to work out the kinks. Her head was pounding. She had just spoken with Henry and Jake. They hadn't found any new information about the kids' abductions. Jake still had a few more leads to try and run down, and Henry was arranging for them all to go speak with Phillip Northgram of the High Council tomorrow.

The building was quiet, which was unusual. With over two dozen teenagers under the roof and another dozen staff members, it was usually bustling. But most were out back where Henry had set up a carnival to welcome the kids.

Laney crossed the room to the coffee machine, poured herself a large mug, and took a sip. Her mind yet again sifted through all the information she'd read on the abductions, trying to find a string she could tug to unravel the knot. But there were no clues and no witnesses. The kids were simply there one minute and gone the next.

The closest they'd come to a suspect was a cable guy. Sheila Macintosh, the mom of the twins, had let him in for the scheduled visit, showed him where the TVs were, and then stayed with him while he worked. After about thirty minutes, he finished up and left, and she went to check on the boys. They were gone.

Originally the police thought the cable man was in on it—distracting the mother while his accomplices made off with the twins—but the man had no criminal record and further investigation cleared him. Once again, it was a dead end.

In her heart, Laney knew the kids were probably already dead. They'd been gone for too long. There was no reason for someone to hold on to them. But even if it was too late to save those kids, they still needed to find out who was behind this, and quickly, so they could stop them before some other child was grabbed.

No. You can't think that way, she warned herself. She needed to believe those kids were alive until she had hard proof that they weren't. And she'd find whatever asshole was behind their abductions and make sure they paid.

But right now, there were some different kids she needed to focus on. She glanced at the clock. She had maybe an hour before the welcome dinner began.

Laney crossed back to the desk and dropped back into her chair. She glanced over the list of things that still needed to be done with a sigh. Then she opened the drawer on her right, pulling out a bottle of aspirin. She dropped two aspirin in her mouth and washed them down with a swig from her water bottle.

Her eyes strayed to the stack of papers held together with a binder clip in the open desk drawer.

"Hey, Lanes." Yoni Benjamin stuck his head in the door with a grin.

Laney pulled her eyes from the drawer. "Hey, Yoni, what's going on?"

"Just wanted to let you know the toilet's backed up in the boys' wing. I called the plumber. He'll be here in an hour."

Laney stared at the piles of paper on her desk: plumbing issues, kitchen re-stock, new supplies needed for the kids coming later today, and a hundred other things. What was one more?

She ran her hands through her hair, sighing. "Yoni, how did we go from saving the world one day to plumbing issues the next?"

"Just lucky, I guess." He shrugged. "Sasha said the kids are all situated."

"You have one hell of a wife, Yoni."

"Don't I know it," Yoni replied before disappearing.

Laney's eyes strayed back to the open desk drawer. She knew she should get back to trying to find some clue about the missing kids. She could review the files again; maybe something would pop this time.

Yet she found herself reaching into the drawer and pulling the printout onto her lap.

On the front page, in a twelve-point Times New Roman font, were printed the words "The Army of the Belial." Nothing more. All very normal-looking. But underneath that front cover was the translation of a book that dated back to before 10,000 BCE. And if they were right, that book foretold the end of the world.

Or at least the attempt *to end the world. Apparently I keep that from happening somehow.*

Laney shook her head, thinking of everything that had happened in the attempt to get this book. An incredible number of lives had been lost between the time they first found it in an ancient collection down in Ecuador to the time they defeated Amar and his minions in Tennessee and recovered this book from amid the ruins.

An image of Rocky drifted through her mind. One of her best friends had given her life to save Laney—the ring bearer destined to save the world.

Her heart clutched at the thought. "God help us all," she mumbled.

Cleo unwound herself from her spot and glanced at Laney.

I'm okay, girl. Cleo looked at her for a long moment before placing her head back down.

Laney had taken Cleo out of the cage before heading back to the office. She knew she'd have to put Cleo back in her cage before dinner; even though Cleo wouldn't hurt any of the new kids, her size was enough to make even a grown man blink. But Laney wanted to keep her out as long as possible. Cleo wasn't a big fan of being locked up.

Laney flipped through the first few pages of the printout. By now, she had the entire manuscript practically memorized. She passed the description of how the angels fell. She barely scanned the section on the angel's reincarnations—how they didn't know who they were early on, how that awareness only came later.

She moved on to the section that they didn't have a name for. The one labeled with only a symbol: two entangled triangles. This was the section she had been obsessed with ever since Henry had given her the translation. It described the rise of the triads—both of them.

In a time when all members of the triad exist, the world shall be in great peril.

The words still struck fear in her. But they weren't the words that replayed time and again in her mind. That honor belonged to the last two lines on the page:

When the triads intersect, the time of judgment is at hand. The choice of sacrifice or death will be made.

Laney stared at the words, willing herself to understand. Who was judging? Who chose the sacrifice?

She clutched at the ring on the chain around her neck. Was choosing the sacrifice her job as the ring bearer? Because she wasn't sure she could sacrifice one more person she cared about.

Maybe you *are the sacrifice,* a voice whispered in the back of her mind.

That was the thought that kept her up late at night. Because isn't that what always happened to the hero in the ancient tales? They sacrificed themselves to save the many? And whether she liked it or not, she seemed to be cast in that role.

Another thought struck her. *What if the missing kids are part of this sacrifice?*

"You know, I don't think those words are going to change if you stare at them for the three hundredth time."

She looked up in surprise. Her uncle, Father Patrick Delaney, leaned against the doorframe. She quietly placed the printout back in the drawer and shut it with her foot.

She placed what she hoped was an innocent expression on her face as she looked up into his knowing eyes. "Oh, I don't know. Haven't you heard the old saying, 'The three hundredth time's the charm'?"

Patrick chuckled as he took a seat in one of the two chairs in front of the desk. Cleo padded over to say hello, placing her head in Patrick's lap. Patrick gave her a good rub behind the ears. "Hello, sweetheart." Satisfied with her greeting, Cleo retreated back to her corner.

Patrick turned his attention to Laney. "The burden of what's to come isn't on only your shoulders."

She sighed. *So much for my poker face.* "You know that's probably not true."

"Only if you let it be. Henry and Jake are here for you. And even though I'm not part of the triangle, I'm here for you too. Jen and Victoria as well."

Laney felt herself stiffen at Victoria's name. "Oh, Victoria's here for me, is she?"

Patrick sighed. "Laney." He drew out her name.

Laney felt a small ball of resentment curl up in her chest. Somehow, whenever the topic of Victoria came up, Laney and

Patrick seemed to be on opposite sides. And it hurt. If anything, the news that Laney was the biological daughter of Victoria Chandler should have driven a wedge between Patrick and Victoria. But instead, that knowledge had turned Patrick into Victoria's strongest defender.

Laney supposed the relationship between her and Victoria had been improving over the last few months. They'd seen each other a few times and talked on the phone every few days.

But no matter how much effort Laney put into the relationship, there was always one huge sticking point that kept her from getting any closer: Victoria refused to talk about how she saved Jake's life in Saqqara, Egypt.

The image of Jake, his deep brown eyes staring up at nothing, his dark hair contrasting sharply with the sandy ground… It was an image that would always be with Laney. And so whenever she was with Victoria, she had a really difficult time talking around the elephant in the room.

Laney put up her hand. "Look, let's not go there. I know you think she has a good reason—"

"Laney, she's helping all of us. She trying to figure out who the members of the other triad—"

"I know, I know. I just wish she wasn't quite so wrapped in mysteries."

Patrick looked at her for a long moment before pulling his chair around the desk and turning her chair so she was facing him.

"You know, I never talk about Vietnam," he said.

Laney squeezed his hand. He had been a Marine before joining the priesthood. In fact, Laney was pretty sure that it was the things he'd done and seen in Vietnam that had pushed him toward the priesthood. "I know. It was a difficult time. You don't have to—"

He squeezed her hand back. "Yes. It was a difficult time. Just as the time with your uncle was difficult for you, which is why you don't talk about it."

Laney looked away as an image of her other uncle's fist appeared in her mind. Even all these years later, it was impossible to forget how powerless she had felt.

"We don't know Victoria's story," Patrick continued. "But I have a feeling it's not an easy one to tell. And as much as you and Henry and Jake and everyone wants to know, we need to respect that it's her story to tell when she's ready."

Laney looked into the crystal blue eyes that she knew so well and blew out a breath. "I know you're right. I hate that you're right, but I know it."

"Good. Now tell me what else is bothering you."

Laney strove for innocence. "What? Nothing's bothering me."

"Delaney McPhearson, I know every look on your face. You are currently wearing your 'I'm lying but I hope he believes me' look. So I ask again, what is going on?"

Laney didn't know why she was trying to keep it from him. Scratch that—she *did* know. The idea of small children being missing was eating her up inside. She didn't want her uncle to go through the same turmoil. But he had his arms crossed over his chest and his face resolute, and she knew he wouldn't budge until she told him the truth. Taking a breath, she did.

Patrick's face grew progressively paler as Laney spoke. Finally, she stopped and waited.

"Dear God, those poor children."

Laney felt his pain, and more of her own.

"But who could it be?" he said. "Samyaza's dead."

Laney watched her uncle for a minute and knew she had one more thing to share. "Actually, I don't think Samyaza *is* dead."

CHAPTER 13

L aney and Patrick decided to take their conversation outside. Kids had begun to wander by the office and Laney didn't want anyone overhearing their conversation.

They made their way to the gardens at the back of the school. Or more accurately, to what had once been the gardens. They had become overgrown, so the realtor had simply had them mowed over.

But you could see what the garden would once again become one day, with a little TLC. Laney planned on hiring a landscaping staff as soon as she took care of all the things ahead of that task on her to-do list—which, at her current rate, should be about two years from Tuesday.

Laney and Patrick took a seat on the bench in the old gazebo, which sat in the middle of the roughly one-acre space, with six separate paths leading toward it.

"How young are we talking?" Patrick asked as soon as they sat.

Laney sighed. "Too young. The youngest abductees are actually twins. They just turned one last month."

Patrick gasped.

Laney nodded, then explained about the data search Danny

and Dom had conducted. When she was done, Patrick bowed his head and said a little prayer. Laney closed her eyes, saying her own informal prayer. *Please, God, keep them safe.*

"What did you mean when you said Samyaza wasn't dead? Is Amar alive?" Patrick asked.

Laney looked at him and then away. She had never explained to her uncle her doubts about Amar being Samyaza. It's not that he wasn't evil enough, because he was. It was just that, from everything she'd read, Samyaza was supposed to be this incredible strategist—and Amar wasn't.

"No. Amar isn't alive." She paused. "I just don't think he was Samyaza."

Patrick sat back and then shook his head. "Taking down Amar was too easy."

"Yes. Samyaza was supposed to be this gifted orator, a leader of men. Amar was egotistical and didn't care about his followers. But to be a good leader, you need to at least make people *think* you care about them. And we found his estate awfully easily."

"But Rocky..."

The stab of grief was fresh and familiar. "I know. We lost good people. But for a great strategist, it should have been harder than that."

"It's still possible that it's the Fallen behind these abductions," Patrick pressed. "Maybe some other Fallen wants to gather the kids before they get their powers. Keep them under his control."

"That would take years." Laney paused, looking at her uncle, speaking slowly. "Some of these kids have already been missing for weeks."

She let her words hang in the air.

He looked at her, his face paling. "You think they're already dead."

Laney blew out a breath and looked across the destroyed garden, trying to imagine it blooming with life. "The criminologist in me says yes. In stranger abductions, the likelihood of a victim surviving for this long... it's slim."

She felt Patrick's eyes on her. When he spoke, his voice was quiet. "You don't really believe that, though, do you?"

Laney shook her head, thinking about what Maddox had told her about the camps. "I don't know. The children are of no use to the Fallen until they come into their powers. And even when they do come into their powers, the Fallen will only use them if they have that killer instinct. I can't imagine them taking care of children for potentially years until they figure all that out. I mean, a few of them are under the age of five."

"But that's not entirely true."

Laney glanced at him, confused. "What do you mean?"

"About them having to wait years to come into their powers," Patrick clarified. "Jen turned early."

Laney felt lightheaded. "You don't think—" She paused, the horror of her thought making it difficult to get the words past her throat. "You don't think someone is trying to turn their abilities on early, do you?"

Patrick stared at her silently, but with his hand he made the sign of the cross.

Laney knew Jen had come into her abilities early because she was being relentlessly tormented by some foster brothers. The day her abilities kicked in was the day they threw her out of a tree —a really tall one.

Laney looked at Patrick as realization and horror washed over her. "Do you realize what they'd have to do to make that happen?"

Patrick nodded; he looked a little shaky himself. "Yes." He swallowed. "What do you need from me?"

"The new kids need a calm, peaceful introduction to the school. I had planned on staying here to help, but Henry, Jake, and I need to look into this. Can you take the lead? We're heading out of town first thing in the morning."

Patrick nodded. "Of course."

Laney stood up, but Patrick grasped her hand. "Do you really think someone's trying to turn the kids' powers on early? That's just evil."

Laney stared back and spoke slowly. "When dealing with the Fallen, do you really think there's any limit on evil?"

CHAPTER 14

SACRAMENTO, CALIFORNIA

Nathaniel sat behind the desk, his ear to the phone but his eyes focused on his son sitting across from him.

Nathaniel's wife's blue eyes and blond hair graced the boy's angular features. He was a beautiful boy. He and Beatrice had taken great joy in the similarities between his wife and Zachariah when he had been born. Now, Nathaniel struggled not to cringe at the sight of him.

"Your son has a lot of talent," Coach Ferguson said. "I told him he needs to be on the soccer team, but he said he wasn't allowed. I thought I'd press home just how much skill he has. I could easily see him getting a full scholarship to college. Is there—"

"I'm afraid Zachariah is needed at home. Thank you for calling." Nathaniel hung up the phone. He let out a breath as he tried to calm the rage building inside of him.

Zachariah stared at the floor, his hands clasped.

"What did you do?" Nathaniel asked.

His son continued to stare at the floor.

"*What did you do?*" Nathaniel yelled.

Zachariah jumped like he'd been hit. "Nothing, nothing. It was just gym class. I played soccer in gym class."

Nathaniel narrowed his eyes. Disdain dripped from his words. "And you felt the need to show off. You had to be *better* than—"

"No!" Zachariah yelled, and then immediately looked stricken. His tone shifted to a more humble one. "I mean, one of the boys was making fun of me, so I just played without holding back as much."

Nathaniel narrowed his eyes. "'Everyone who is arrogant in heart is an abomination to the Lord; be assured, he will not go unpunished.'"

Zachariah paled at the words.

Nathaniel's eyes pinned his son in place. "You are sinful by your very nature. You must be more humble, more obedient than any others." He stood up, undoing his belt and pulling it off. "Come, submit to God's will."

Zachariah hesitated for only a moment before he stood and pulled off his shirt. He leaned his two arms against the desk.

Nathaniel walked behind him, curling the end of the belt around his fist. With a practiced move he lashed out at his son's back, the buckle digging deep into his son's skin.

"What are you?" Nathaniel growled as he let go with two more hits. His anger only grew as the wounds on the boy's back began to heal.

"An abomination," Zachariah said softly.

CHAPTER 15

A few hours later, Laney slipped away from the welcome dinner. She'd tried to focus on the kids and not on her earlier conversation with Matt, but it was difficult.

An unknown player. As if they didn't have enough to worry about already.

She'd stayed at the dinner for two hours, making sure she spoke with each new kid. Most of them seemed like typical teenagers, if maybe a little nervous. A few had attitudes that might cause problems down the road.

Laney rubbed her temple as she walked down the hall. She, Jake, Henry, Clark, and Patrick had all spoken before about what they were going to do if one of the teenagers went rogue, but so far they had come to no resolution. Clark made it clear his facility could hold more; Laney prayed there was a way to avoid that possibility. But at the same time, she knew that any one of those teenagers could hurt a lot of people if they wanted to.

Laney just hoped they could find a way to ensure they never wanted to.

At the dinner, she'd been surprised to see Danny walk in with Lou and Rolly—surprised and happy. She'd been worried about him after the fight with Henry. Danny had stayed for quite a while and had left only a little before she did. As he left, he caught her eye, and she nodded back at him—silently confirming that their training session was still on.

After Amar, Danny had wanted to learn self-defense. Laney had been a little unsure at first, thinking that maybe Henry should be the one to teach him. When she'd mentioned that idea to Danny though, he'd had a very reasonable response: "Henry doesn't fight the way you and I have to."

So they'd started training that night. And they now trained five days a week, although Laney suspected Danny was practicing a little more on his own. Every once in a while, Yoni or Jake would also step up to teach Danny something as well. At first, Laney had been worried about Danny's ability to pick up the moves; he'd never really been an athletic kid. But he had made incredible improvements in the last few months.

She had thought about cancelling tonight's session, but she needed the workout as much as he did. Sometimes after a nice strenuous workout, she thought a little more clearly. And right now, she needed a little of that.

Laney jogged down the hall, making a mental note to take Cleo out later for a walk, when she heard the sounds of a bag being hit in the gym. Laney smiled. *He's already at it.* She hurried to the locker room and changed quickly.

Pushing through the gym's double doors, she tucked her chain with the ring on it into her shirt. Danny was on the far side of the gym, hitting one of the heavy bags. Laney watched as he bounced around the bag, staying on the balls of his feet. He darted in every few seconds to hit or kick, then quickly danced away.

Laney smiled. *Yup. He's definitely getting it.*

She jogged over to him. "Good job, but you're dropping your guard when you kick. Try to keep your hands up by your face at all times, okay?"

Danny nodded, wiping at the sweat on his brow. "Okay."

Laney glanced over at the clock. "Let's start thirty-second rounds, ten seconds in between. Pick one series of punches and kicks for each round. Okay?"

Danny grinned. "Okay."

Laney lined herself up at one of the other bags. With a glance at the clock, she yelled, "Go!"

They worked in the gym for an hour. After the bag work, they moved on to some hand-to-hand work and then some situational scenarios. By the time they were done, both were dripping with sweat. They both grabbed showers before meeting back in the gym.

Laney slid down the wall to the floor. Danny took a seat next to her.

Laney took a drink from her water bottle. "You're really coming along."

Danny ducked his head. "Thanks."

She glanced at him out of the corner of her eye and realized he was really growing up. His face was starting to lose that boyish quality and he'd easily grown five inches since she'd met him. She pictured how his face had looked when Henry told him to stay away from the missing children project. She debated whether or not to say anything about it, then figured she might as well.

"Danny, you know Henry loves you."

Danny groaned. "Not you too, Laney."

"What do you mean?"

"Jen already laid into me about it. Telling me Henry's trying to protect me."

"Well, he is."

"Yeah, but maybe I don't need his protection. And those kids could use my help. I'm not a little kid anymore."

"We all know that, but when you care about someone, you try to protect them. Heck, I tried to keep Uncle Patrick from learning about the missing kids."

Danny's mouth was just shy of a smirk. "How'd that go?"

Laney rolled her eyes. "About as well as you'd think. But I had to try. And Henry worries that you've seen too much violence. He doesn't want to expose you to more."

"I was exposed to plenty before I even knew him."

Laney sighed. Danny never talked about his family. Just like she never spoke about her time with her other uncle and aunt, Patrick never spoke about Vietnam, and Henry never spoke about his torture. They were all walking around with these open wounds and pretending they didn't exist.

"I know you were," Laney said softly. "And that's the point. Henry doesn't want you to go through any more."

"Yeah, well, you know what they say: life happens."

"Ain't that the truth." Laney took a drink just as the doors to the gym pushed open. Standing silhouetted by the hallway light was a tall woman with pure white hair cut in a no-nonsense bob.

Laney nearly choked on her water. "Victoria?"

CHAPTER 16

Victoria Chandler crossed the room toward Laney and Danny. "Hello, dear."

Laney scrambled to her feet. "Um, hi."

"Hi, Victoria," Danny said shyly, getting to his feet next to Laney.

Victoria smiled at him and held out her arms. He walked into them and they hugged for a moment.

Finally breaking away, Danny looked up at her. "What are you doing here?"

"Well, Laney called and said she needed to speak with me. I wasn't too far away, so we headed here."

At the mention of "we," Laney glanced back toward the doorway and saw Ralph, Victoria's bodyguard. She waved and he waved back, but he didn't leave his position at the door.

She turned back to Victoria. "I didn't mean to make you change your plans. We could have spoken on the phone."

Victoria gave a small shrug. "It was a good excuse to visit. It's been over a week since I've seen you."

Danny took a step back. "Well, I'll let you two speak."

"Oh, Danny," Victoria said as he started to walk away. "I picked up a copy of *Chaos Rules* and left it in your office."

Danny went still. "Seriously? That's not supposed to be out for months."

Victoria shrugged. "I have a friend."

Danny ran back to her and threw his arms around her. "Thank you, thank you thank you!" he said, before dashing across the room and disappearing through the doorway.

Laney smiled. "Well, that made his night."

"It's a grandmother's prerogative to spoil her grandson. And I have a lot of lost time to make up for."

Laney nodded, and suddenly the distance between them seemed filled with all the words they never seemed to be able to say. "Uh, I was going to let Cleo out. She's been locked up all day. Do you mind if we walk and talk?"

"That would be lovely," Victoria said.

Laney led Victoria through the series of hallways that led to the back of the school. As they walked, she explained to Victoria about the missing children.

"That's horrible. What can I do?" Victoria asked as they stepped out into the night air.

Cleo screeched at them.

"Hold that thought for a minute." Laney headed toward Cleo's cage.

Cleo's thoughts got louder the closer Laney got. Laney stopped at the cage door and looked through the bars at Cleo, whose black coat was beginning to fade into the darkening sky. "No," Laney said to the big cat. "I didn't know some kids had done that. Yes, I'll speak with them. No, you can not disembowel them."

Victoria chuckled from behind her. "She sounds like she's had quite a day."

Laney unlocked the gate. "Apparently."

Cleo sprang out of the cage. She held her head up in the air as she walked past Laney.

"Fine. Be that way," Laney muttered.

The cat walked over to Victoria and lowered her front paws, her head down. Laney stared at the two of them, dumbfounded.

Victoria ran her hand over the giant's cat's head. "Hello, Cleo."

Cleo got to her feet and ran off into the courtyard.

Stay in the courtyard, Laney warned. *There are new kids at the school and I don't want them getting scared.*

Cleo gave only the slightest of responses but it was enough for Laney to hear.

She turned to Victoria. "What was that?"

"What?" Victoria asked.

Laney gestured in the direction the panther had disappeared. "Cleo. She just bowed to you."

"She was just being polite."

Laney stared at her mother, all the questions she had about her piling up in her mind. She thought back to the first time she had seen Victoria and Cleo interact. Victoria had stopped by Henry's unannounced. Cleo had been outside and had sprinted for Victoria before anyone had realized what was happening.

But then Cleo had just stopped. Victoria had walked up to her and patted her head. And then Cleo went on her way and Victoria kept walking as if nothing had happened.

"You're the only person I didn't have to introduce Cleo to. She automatically behaved as if you were a friend. Why is that?"

"Is that what you wanted to discuss?" Victoria asked, amusement in her voice.

And with those words, Laney knew she wasn't getting an answer to that question either. "You *are* going to tell me one day though, right?"

Victoria nodded. "Yes. When the time is right, I will tell you."

Laney thought about pressing the point now, but she remembered her conversation with Patrick. She let out a breath and pushed her questions about Victoria from her mind. She had other priorities.

She steered Victoria toward the bench outside Cleo's cage. "Okay then. So the reason I called is sort of about the missing kids. I don't think it's the Fallen, but I'm not sure."

"Okay. What do you need?"

"We know there's someone else collecting potentials—the teenagers—like Amar was. This last camp is proof of that." She let out a breath. "I think it's Samyaza. I don't think Amar was Samyaza. I don't think Samyaza is dead."

Victoria looked back at Laney, her expression unchanged.

"You're not surprised," Laney said.

"No."

"You don't think Amar was Samyaza either."

Victoria shook her head. "No. I don't."

"*Is* Samyaza dead?"

"No. Amar wasn't Samyaza."

Laney had been expecting the response, but it still stung. "Is Samyaza behind the latest abductions?"

Victoria shook her head. "I would doubt it."

"Why?"

"Probably for many of the same reasons you don't think he's behind it. But most of all, it's just not Samyaza's style. When he kills, he kills. There is no grey. Grabbing children... it's cowardly. If Samyaza wanted them dead, he would wait until they came into their powers, see if they were of use to him, and if not, kill them."

Laney tried not to dwell on the fact that Victoria spoke about Samyaza as if she knew him personally. Instead she focused on Victoria's interpretation. And her mother was right: everything about these abductions smacked of cowardice.

"Do you know who Samyaza is?" Laney asked.

Victoria paused. "No. But I'll keep digging. I'll find him."

"I know you will," Laney said.

Laney thought about asking Victoria about the High Council, but she wanted to speak with Northgram first. Besides, after what Clark had said about his men going missing, she wanted to learn a little more to make sure they were even related to the missing kids.

As Laney watched Cleo creep along the grass after some poor unsuspecting bird, she couldn't help but be aware that Victoria wasn't telling her the whole truth. After all, if there was one thing Laney could count on with Victoria, it was that she was holding back. Still, there was another, darker part of her mind that wondered if this time she was holding back more than the normal amount. Victoria knew so much and shared so little.

Laney glanced at Victoria out of the corner of her eye. "But it's safe to assume Samyaza is part of the other triangle, right?"

Victoria nodded before her gaze turned to follow Cleo's antics. "Yes. That's a safe assumption."

Laney watched Victoria in profile. Who was this woman she had learned was her biological mother only a few months ago? And why did she know so much? Laney clutched her ring. She knew Victoria wasn't a Fallen. But she was *something*. Of that she had no doubt.

Laney turned to watch Cleo as well, but her mind wasn't done with its thoughts about Victoria. And a question that always lurked in the back of her mind came to the forefront:

But is she a good something or a bad something?

CHAPTER 17

CHICAGO, ILLINOIS

Laney glanced out the window as the Escalade pulled up in front of the Hanover Building the next morning. It wasn't the tallest skyscraper she'd ever seen, but it was definitely up there. Northgram's company, Banchfield Trust, had floors five through ten.

The doorman hurried over, first opening Jake's door in the front and then Henry's in the back. Once on the sidewalk, Henry extended his hand back to help Laney out.

"Thanks," she said.

He grinned down at her. "Any time."

But then all their smiles faded as they headed into the lobby. Laney rubbed the ring on her finger.

Jake leaned down, whispering. "Sense anything?"

"No. Nothing. The only nephilim or Fallen nearby is Henry. Henry?"

He shook his head. "I don't sense anyone, either."

"Well, great," Laney grouched. "So much for my superpowers."

Jake put his arm around her. "Guess if there's a fight you'll just have to fight like us mere mortals."

"Hey, I can still affect the weather. And if Northgram has a pet cat, they're toast."

Jake laughed. "Well, let's hope Fluffy is hanging around."

They headed through the revolving glass doors, and a brunette in a tight-fitting grey suit and "how do you walk in those" heels strode over with a smile. "Mr. Chandler, Dr. McPhearson, Mr. Rogan. I'm Olivia Reid, Mr. Northgram's assistant. I hope you didn't have any trouble finding us."

"No, no problems," Henry replied.

Olivia smiled. "Wonderful. Mr. Northgram is waiting for you upstairs. If you'll follow me."

She headed away from the main elevator bank and over to a private elevator. She inserted a key and the doors slid open. "This way, please."

As they stepped into the elevator, Laney noted Jake eyeing the ceiling at each corner, pausing at the left hand corner over the door. Laney looked at it for a moment and finally noticed the small camera lens.

Jake looked back at Laney and she shook her head, answering the silent question: still no Fallen or nephilim.

The elevator whisked them up ten floors smoothly. The doors opened with a small burst of air. Olivia stepped through, holding the door open with one arm. "Here we are."

The hallway was lush, with dark wood floors, a navy runner, and stark white walls. Olivia led them to a door at the end of the hall and knocked.

"Come in," came a male voice from the other side of the door.

Olivia held open the door for them and called out each person's name as they stepped through. "Mr. Northgram, Mr. Henry Chandler, Dr. Delaney McPhearson, and Mr. Jake Rogan."

Laney couldn't help but think of old movies she'd seen when the butler would announce the lord and lady's arrival at the ball.

Northgram came around from behind his large desk, his hand extended. "Mr. Chandler, wonderful to meet you. Dr. McPhearson and Mr. Rogan. It's a pleasure."

He was pushing sixty but he kept in good shape. And judging by his tan, he obviously spent a lot of time outdoors, or at least a tanning booth. His eyes, though, were distractingly small for his face, and his chin was tiny.

He gestured toward three chairs placed in front of his desk. Laney hesitated. The chairs were slightly lower to the ground than normal chairs, which would make anyone sitting in them at least a head lower than Northgram.

She smiled at him and gestured to the conference table in the corner. "I think the table would be preferable."

Northgram's smile faltered for only a moment. "Of course. Whatever you prefer."

Laney smiled sweetly. *Nice try, buddy.*

She led the way over to the table and took a seat on the side nearest the wall. Henry took a seat on the other side. Jake eschewed a seat altogether and stood behind Laney, leaning against the wall.

Northgram sat down at the end of the table, between Laney and Henry. He looked back and forth between them. "Now, what can Banchfield Trust do for the Chandler Group today?"

Henry sat back, the picture of a confident CEO. "We had some questions regarding the Council."

Northgram tilted his head to the side. He reminded Laney of Moxy when you mentioned biscuits. "The Council? What Council?"

Laney pictured Sophia Watson, the missing little girl with the braids. "The Council. The one you head."

Laney could almost see Northgram's gears moving as he debated what to say. "I'm sorry. I'm afraid—"

Laney arched an eyebrow. "Why don't we cut through the bull-shit? You know who we are, and we know who you are."

Northgram's eyes narrowed, and for just a second Laney could see the man behind the smooth veneer. But just as quickly, the facade returned. "Of course. Delaney McPhearson, the ring bearer. And Henry Chandler and Jake Rogan, the other two members of the triad."

"And you're Phillip Northgram, the head of the Council." Laney paused. "Well, sort of."

Northgram raised an eyebrow. "Sort of?"

Laney kept her gaze on Northgram. "We hear you're more of a figurehead. And we're more interested in the real head of the Council."

Northgram tried to act nonchalant, but the tremor in his hand gave him away. "I don't know what you're talking about."

Henry leaned in closer. "There are children missing. And we think the Council is involved. Now, who is the head?"

Northgram pushed back from his chair. "I don't know what you're talking about. Now I'm afraid I'm going to have to ask you—"

He tried to stand, but Jake pushed his chair back in, forcing him back in the seat. "How dare—"

"Enough," Laney said. "Who's taking the children?"

"Children? What children?"

Laney studied him and realized she believed his look of ignorance. He really didn't know anything about the children. Damn it.

"Does your organization keep track of the offspring of the Fallen?" Jake asked.

Surprise flashed across Northgram's face. Laney wasn't sure if it was because of the topic or their knowledge. "I don't know what you're talking about," he said.

"Mr. Northgram." Henry's voice was smooth. "I took the liberty of reviewing your portfolio on the plane ride over. Over the past several months, your firm has lost quite a few clients."

Northgram bristled. "We have not lost any critical clients. And it was a mutual agreement to end our business relationships."

Henry glanced at his tie and flicked off an imaginary speck of dirt. "Be that as it may, I was quite happy to see that a number of my business contacts *remain* your clients." He looked up. "I've found them to be very happy clients—and always *very* appreciative of my business advice."

Northgram paled. "I didn't realize that."

"Yes. I was just speaking with Frank Catalino over at the Grevigor Group this morning. We have plans for golf soon."

Northgram stiffened.

"I do hope nothing happens to any of your other clients. It does look like your firm would have difficulty coming back from losing the Grevigor, Access, or Trident accounts."

Laney knew those were Banchfield's top three clients. She looked at Henry with a new respect. Every time she thought she understood him, she saw one more facet of his personality.

Northgram's voice was stiff. "There's no reason they would choose to leave."

"Hmm," Henry mumbled. "Now, I believe Mr. Rogan just asked you a very reasonable question about the Council's record-keeping habits regarding the Fallen. What was your answer again?"

Northgram paused. He licked his lips. "Um, I um... I may have some information on that. But I'll have to check to see for sure."

Henry smiled and stood. "Of course. But we'll hear something by the end of tomorrow, I'm sure."

Northgram stumbled to his feet. "Of course."

Laney bit back her own smile as she stood and exchanged an amused glance with Jake. Laney and Jake often thought of themselves as badasses. Today, that title belonged to Henry.

Northgram walked stiffly to the door and opened it.

Henry stopped at the door, using all his height to his advantage. "We will hear from you by tomorrow. Correct?"

Northgram nodded. "Yes." He paused, his voice quiet, his tone ugly. "You three, you think you're so powerful. But you're not. You're not even unique. There's another triad."

He smiled with no warmth in his eyes. "As for the head of the Council, you should go looking for him. Let me know how that turns out."

CHAPTER 18

Laney stepped out onto the busy sidewalk, Jake and Henry right behind her. "Well, *that* earned us nothing."

"Not true. We confirmed that the head of the Council is a complete asshole," Jake said.

Laney laughed. "Totally worth the trip then." She glanced over at the Escalade. The driver had already gotten out to open the door.

She looked back at Henry and then Jake. "I don't know about you guys, but I am not ready to get back on the plane. Anyone hungry?"

"There's a place a few blocks over," Jake offered. "Supposed to have great egg sandwiches."

"I'm in," Henry said.

An hour later, Laney pushed her plate away. "That's it. I'm stuffed."

Henry leaned over and plucked a piece of toast off her plate. "I'll take this, then."

Laney glanced out the window. She could see the top of the Hanover building a few blocks away. "So what do we think?" she asked. They hadn't discussed the meeting with Northgram yet.

"He'll call," Jake said with a grin at Henry. "He's terrified of losing those contracts."

"He knows about the other triad," Laney said.

Jake nodded. "Has Victoria had any luck tracking down the members of it?"

Laney shook her head. "No. Not yet."

Of course, if she's a member of it, she wouldn't share any of that information with you, would she? Laney shooed the voice away, but the thought was always there in the back of her mind.

"Northgram also mentioned the other triad. He knows more than he's saying," Henry said.

Laney put up her hand. "How about one crisis at a time? We'll deal with the second triad after we find the kids."

Henry nodded. "Okay. So what's our next step?"

Laney and Jake exchanged a look. "Clark arranged for us to visit two of the families of the missing kids. We're going to head down to Atlanta, meet with the Watson family. See if maybe there's something we can learn. Then tomorrow we'll stop over in North Carolina, meet with the Seeleys. See if there's anything they can share."

Henry nodded. "Well, why don't I take the—"

Laney took Henry's hand. "Jake and I can handle it. Why don't you head home? Spend some time with Danny?"

Henry blew out a breath. "Not sure he *wants* to spend some time with me."

"Maybe not. But you have responsibilities there. We can handle this," Jake said.

Henry nodded agreement. "Well, let's get back to it."

They stepped out onto the sidewalk, blending in with the flow of pedestrians, and headed back for the Hanover Building, where the driver and Escalade awaited. Jake slipped his hand around Laney's. She smiled and took a deep breath. Okay, the air quality might not be the best, but there was something about the bustle of a city that just energized her.

They made it back the two blocks quickly—too quickly in Laney's opinion. For that short time, she could pretend that life and death were not in the palm of her hand. That she was just a normal person out for a walk with the love of her life and the brother she loved more than life.

They had just turned the corner onto Northgram's street when a familiar electric tingle slid over Laney's skin. Her head jolted up and she stopped short as her gaze swept the street. Her eyes came to rest on a man exiting the building across from the Hanover Building.

He stopped suddenly too, but his eyes rested on Henry.

Laney's heart raced and she took off at a run. "Fallen!" she yelled back at Henry and Jake.

Henry and Jake leapt into motion behind her. Henry quickly outpaced them, although for appearances' sake he kept his pace at a human one. A really fast human.

The Fallen paused for a moment, his eyes darting back down the street before he ran back into the building.

What the hell's he doing? Laney thought.

Henry disappeared into the doorway after him. Laney looked up at the building. It was easily twenty stories high. *Oh, please let him be going out the back door and not to the roof*, she thought as she sprinted inside.

The lobby was empty but the door to the stairs was wide open.

"Stairs!" Jake yelled, pulling his gun and pulling ahead of Laney.

"Of course it's the stairs," Laney grumbled, but she picked up the pace. She sprinted behind Jake, taking the stairs two at a time and thanking God for her grueling workouts. Nonetheless by the ninth floor, her thighs were screaming from the exertion.

Still, Laney didn't dare slow. Not with Henry up there, facing the Fallen alone. *Please don't let there be any more.*

Grunting sounds and a yell came from the next floor, the tenth. Jake threw open the door; Laney burst out next to him. Her skin tingled, telling her that a Fallen and nephilim were down the hall.

"Second door on the right," she said.

Jake nodded and again took the lead. The door was open.

Or, more accurately, demolished. Inside, Henry wrestled with the Fallen they'd seen on the street.

The Fallen threw his head back, catching Henry under the chin. Henry looked dazed, just for a moment, but that small distraction was all the Fallen needed to wrench himself from Henry's grasp. But then he caught sight of Laney, and his eyes went wide.

Laney opened her mouth to command the Fallen to stop, but he was already on his feet, sprinting away from her. Before she could make a sound, he flung himself through the window.

"Shit." Jake ran to the edge of the window and looked down. Laney peered out with him. The Fallen lay in a heap on the sidewalk, not moving. It was a miracle he hadn't hit anyone.

"I need to get down there," Laney said.

Henry grabbed her without a word and sprinted from the room. Laney held on as Henry vaulted down the steps. She closed her eyes, willing the egg sandwich she had enjoyed at breakfast to not return.

When they reached the sidewalk, Henry placed Laney on the ground, keeping a grip on her to steady her. The Fallen was just getting to his feet.

"Stop!" Laney ordered, feeling the power from the ring flow through her.

The man went still, although from the grimace on his face, Laney knew he didn't want to.

Laney walked toward him, conscious of the onlookers. She pulled her badge from her pocket. "We'll take it from here, folks."

"Walk over to me," she ordered the Fallen.

He took two steps—and then a boom rang out though the

street. It sounded like a jet, but somewhere low in the city. Henry pushed Laney to the ground, covering her with his body. Pedestrians scattered with screams.

Laney looked over at the Fallen. He lay on his side, his eyes locked on hers—a giant hole where his heart should be.

CHAPTER 19

SACRAMENTO, CALIFORNIA

Energized, Nathaniel strode down the hallway. He'd just taped his latest sermon and that always gave him a high. Not that he would know exactly what a high was. After all, he would never disrespect his body with such toxins.

He smiled at his wife, Beatrice, as he approached his office.

She nodded toward the closed office door. "Tyrell is waiting for you."

Nathaniel rubbed his hands together. "Good, good. Hold my calls, please."

"Of course," she replied.

Nathaniel paused, wanting to share a bit of his good mood. But Beatrice had already returned to her paperwork.

When his marriage to Beatrice had been arranged, Nathaniel had thought he'd won the lottery. Tall, slim, with dark blonde hair and blue eyes, Beatrice was everything that he had hoped for.

Her warm looks had hid a cool demeanor, but that was all right. She performed her wifely duties when requested—if not with passion, at least without complaint. Most important, though, they were joined by their faith—their shared belief that the next age was coming. That humanity was going down the wrong road. And that it was their duty to save it.

Or at least some of it, he thought.

He watched Beatrice as she finished her note and pulled a file from the stack on her left. She didn't glance at him. She never did. *It would be nice if she looked at me every once in a while,* he thought.

Shaking his head at his own foolishness, Nathaniel turned toward his office. He steeled himself, then opened the door.

Tyrell stood by the window, the afternoon sun glinting off his shaved head. His hands were clasped behind his back, his posture perfect.

Nathaniel straightened his own back, sucking in his stomach just a little. "Tyrell," he said.

Tyrell turned around and bowed his head. "Reverend."

Nathaniel nodded toward the chairs in front of his desk. "Please, take a seat."

With a nod, Tyrell crossed the room to sit, just as the Reverend took his own seat behind the desk.

Nathaniel took stock of his right-hand man, his lieutenant. The man was tough. He'd been through five tours overseas and had been honorably discharged. And he maintained a rigorous physical standard—one Nathaniel admired but never tried to emulate.

Nathaniel had never been very good at sports. He'd always wanted to be, though; there was something so manly about being muscular and athletic. But his natural pear shape made that impossible—or at least, that's what he told himself. So when he'd started his ministry, he aimed it at the people he admired most: the soldiers. And they came running.

Tyrell looked over at the reverend, uncertainty creeping onto his face. "Um, Reverend... is something wrong?"

"No," Nathaniel said, realizing he had gotten lost in his thoughts. "No, not at all. In fact, you've done very well."

Tyrell relaxed, sitting back in his seat. "Thank you, sir. That means a lot."

And Nathaniel knew it did. Tyrell might look like a tough, indestructible man, but the reality was, he craved acceptance and approval. He was a large puppy.

"Not at all. I am pleased. God is pleased. But now I have another mission for you."

Tyrell nodded, back in his comfort zone. "Who is the target?"

Nathaniel smiled. "Another child. But this one is different. Special. And he will have security surrounding him."

The soldier frowned. "In all the other cases, we've been sure to grab them without being seen. Those were your orders."

"This case is different," Nathaniel repeated. He slid a folder over his desk to Tyrell. "For this child, that won't be possible. The gloves are off. Get him through any means necessary." Nathaniel felt a little thrill at the words. Why, he could be in a movie right now.

He smiled as Tyrell leafed through the folder. Tyrell was an important weapon in his arsenal. An arsenal he assembled under his Shepherd's guidance—an arsenal that allowed Nathaniel to hold life and death in his hands.

Tyrell glanced up at him. "I'll need to take more men."

The reverend waved his hand. "Take what you need."

Tyrell stood. "Yes, sir. I'll begin preparations immediately."

"Good. You're dismissed."

Tyrell nodded, turned on his heel, and left.

Nathaniel smiled as his lieutenant closed the door behind him. He laced his fingers behind his head and twirled his chair to look out the window.

Yes. Tyrell was a weapon. One Nathaniel intended to wield ruthlessly.

CHAPTER 20

CHICAGO, ILLINOIS

L aney watched the body get loaded into the ambulance. The white sheet was stained red as it disappeared behind the ambulance doors.

She shuddered. Jake said it had to be at least a fifty-caliber bullet to have done that much damage. There was literally a hole through the man's chest. You could actually see through the body, the hole was that big.

Whoever had shot him had wanted to make sure he wouldn't heal. But who the hell was that?

Laney looked up again at the buildings that surrounded them. They hadn't seen a hint of the shooter. Jake said he could have been as far away as almost three thousand feet, which meant the shot could have come from over a dozen buildings.

Laney had caught sight of Northgram being ushered into his car by security just after the shooting, but she didn't think he was involved. It was too straightforward a kill.

She blew out a breath. *Like Samyaza.* But was this related to the missing kids, the Council, or Laney, Jake and Henry? Or was it all of the above?

A burly police officer walked over to Laney, his words coated in hostility. "We've got the body loaded. It'll be at the airport in about ten minutes. Anything *else* the Chicago PD can do for the federal government?"

Laney plastered a smile on her face. "No, thank you, officer. You've been most helpful."

He grunted and strode back toward his car without a word.

Laney sighed. *Oh, I'm just making friends everywhere.*

The police had at first been suspicious of Laney's and Henry's badges. Not that she could blame them. She herself had only learned about the existence of SIA a few months ago. Clark had deputized Laney, Henry, Jake, Maddox, and Jen just after the Amar incident—*Just in case*, as Clark had explained.

This was the first time Laney had had to use the badge, and even so, it took a call to Clark and a call from Clark to the chief of police to get them to cooperate. *What's the point of having a badge for an agency no one's heard of?*

The body was now being taken to the airfield where SIA would pick it up, but the high-handedness was not going over well with the police, who had been relegated to crowd control after a shooting in the middle of downtown Chicago. Laney couldn't remember the last time she had been on the receiving end of so many nasty looks.

She turned to Henry. "I'm going to head upstairs. See what Jake's found."

"Okay." He gestured to the street. "I'll keep an eye out for the SIA agents Clark's sending."

Laney nodded and headed inside. She pressed the button for the elevator, her thighs still protesting her earlier unexpected leg workout as she stepped inside. When the doors slid open on the tenth floor, she badged the two officers by the demolished door. They nodded at her with less hostility than the guys downstairs.

Must be new to the force, she thought.

She climbed over the door Henry had taken off its hinges an hour earlier. Jake stood over by the desk, looking at some papers on a clipboard. After making sure that Henry and Laney were all right, he had headed back up here—said he wanted to go through the room and see what he could find about their John Doe.

"Hey there," Laney said as she stepped through the doorway.

Jake looked up. "Hey yourself."

She walked over and hugged him.

"You okay?" Jake asked.

"Well, if looks could kill, some of those officers would have done me in."

"They just don't like people stepping on their turf."

"Yeah I get that, but—" She sighed. "Can't we just tell everyone we're doing this for their benefit and have them say thank you? Would that be too much to ask?"

"Yup. It would."

"Gee, don't soften it."

Jake chuckled, stepping away from her, and pointed to the computer. "So—would you like to know what I found?"

"All right. Tell me what you've got."

"First, I don't think they were here for us."

"Really?" Surprise flashed through her. Every time Fallen appeared, she assumed it had to do with her. *Ego, ego.*

"No." Jake picked up a plastic dome with wires attached at the apex. "This is a parabolic mike."

Laney glanced out the broken window. "Can it reach across the street?"

Jake nodded. "They enhanced it."

"So they were listening to us meet with Northgram."

"Maybe. I think this was more likely for street surveillance. I'm willing to bet they have bugs stashed somewhere in Northgram's office. But we weren't the original surveillance targets. They've been here for a while." He gestured toward a garbage can in the corner; it was overflowing with takeout containers and coffee cups.

Laney narrowed her eyes. "How long?"

"Hard to tell, but weeks at least. I found a receipt in the trash—Chinese food from two months ago."

"So they were watching Northgram. But who is *they*?"

"I think if we figure that out, we'll know who killed him," Henry said as he stepped in, two men in dark suits following. Henry introduced Laney and Jake to the two SIA agents. Then he pulled Jake and Laney into the hall while the agents documented the scene.

"You're saying the person who hired this guy is the same person who killed him? Why?" Laney asked.

"To keep him from revealing what he's found," Henry said.

"That's cold," Laney replied.

Jake shrugged. "Cold, but probably accurate. If this guy had any intelligence, he would have sprinted down the street when we caught sight of him—gotten lost in the crowd. Instead he ran back here."

Henry nodded. "When I came in, he was entering something into the computer. I think it was a kill command to wipe it. I tackled him before he was able to initiate it." He glanced at Jake. "You didn't touch the computer, did you?"

"No. I stayed with the paper."

"And the trash." Laney winked, and Jake smiled.

"Find anything useful?" Henry asked.

"Other than that he was here for two months? Afraid not. There's no indication of who he was hired by."

Laney glanced back into the room, but in her mind she could still see the Fallen on the street below, the hole gaping in his chest. "Yeah. And somebody made sure he wouldn't tell us either."

CHAPTER 21

VENICE, ITALY

Gerard Thompson disconnected the call, resting the phone against his lips. *Just what* was *the ring bearer up to?*

He stood in the central archway of the Rialto Bridge, leaning against the railing. The bridge spanned the Great Canal, providing a view of the shops that lined both sides of the waterway.

Below him he watched as a water taxi pulled up to a hotel, offloading a man and woman. The man got out first, then helped the woman. She smiled up at him, then gave him a kiss when she stood next to him.

Pocketing his cell, Gerard turned away from the canal, barely registering the flock of tourists who wandered by him, chatting anxiously in Spanish about making their dinner reservation, as he made his way through them. He blended in with a group of businessmen, his well-coiffed blond hair and sharp cheekbones drawing more than one admiring glance from women and men alike.

Gerard ignored them all. He kept his eyes scanning ahead, an old habit. But his mind was an ocean away. Laney McPhearson, Henry Chandler, and Jake Rogan had met with Northgram about missing children. He frowned. *Missing potentials. What was going on?*

He'd heard no rumblings about moving on the children. And as one of Samyaza's top lieutenants, he would be in a position to know.

Gerard stopped. He realized he had walked all the way to the Doges Palace at St. Mark's Square—the seat of Venice's power for a thousand years. But all power came to an end eventually. Even the thousand-year run of the doges.

But our rule never ends, Gerard thought fiercely. *We are always the top of the food chain.*

But now someone was trying to chop away at that food chain —interfering with the power structure by taking out potential allies down the road. Of course, it didn't currently affect him, and it seemed to be causing problems for the other triad.

He should call Elisabeta, though. But just the thought of coming to her with little to no information was too frightening a possibility. He'd seen her rake people over the coals for less.

Resolved, Gerard pulled out his cell phone. He had some work to do.

CHAPTER 22

BALTIMORE, MARYLAND

Danny stared out the window. Henry had returned last night from his trip to Chicago, but Danny had made a point of not talking to him any more than necessary. Today, he'd given him the same treatment.

And he'd actually felt good about it. It made him feel like he had a little control in their relationship. But right now it was making the drive to the Chandler School from the estate feel like it was taking at least twice the amount of time it normally took.

"Um, so do Lou and Rolly know you're coming?" Henry asked.

"Yes," Danny said, not looking at him. Silence descended on the car again. Up ahead, Danny saw the school and felt relief. This car ride couldn't be over soon enough.

Henry sighed as they passed through the gates of the school. "Listen, I know tomorrow is bookstore day. But I have a conference call in the morning that might go long. How about if we go to the bookstore in the afternoon instead? Grab an early dinner?"

Danny looked over and shook his head. "No. I already made plans to go with Maddox and Max."

"I'll talk to Maddox, see if they mind going later."

"No. I already made plans. We'll go without you."

A look of hurt flashed across Henry's face. Ever since Danny had first arrived at the Chandler Group, he and Henry had gone every single Tuesday to the bookstore. Together.

Danny felt a momentary stab of guilt but shooed it away. Henry had to realize he wasn't a kid anymore.

Henry pulled into his parking spot behind the school. "Okay. I'll tell security."

Danny whirled back. "We don't—"

"*That* is not negotiable, Danny, and you know it. I know you're not a kid. But you're also not ready to face every threat out there. If you leave the grounds, you bring security."

"Fine," Danny said through clenched teeth as he opened the door. Grabbing the file from between the seats, he stepped out of the car. "Come, Moxy," he ordered.

"Danny, I—"

Danny slammed the door on Henry's words and stomped into the school. He didn't look back, didn't wait to see if Henry got out of the car. A part of him boiled at the way he was being treated, and another part of him couldn't figure out why he was acting this way. He made a conscious effort to shove the fight with Henry from his mind. Right now, there was something more important he needed to focus on.

As he and Moxy walked down the hall, their footsteps echoed around them. A couple of kids walked past and gave Danny a smile. It was a struggle to smile back. The file felt heavy in his hand.

Up ahead was the door that led to the courtyard where Cleo's cage sat. Through the glass in the door, Danny saw Lou and Rolly. Laney had introduced both new kids to the giant cat before she left, and they seemed fascinated by her.

Now Lou was sitting on the bench outside Cleo's cage, and Rolly was leaning against the cage, feeding something to Cleo.

Danny thought it was probably bacon, because that seemed to be Cleo's snack of choice.

Ever since the new kids arrived, the three of them—Danny, Lou, and Rolly—had hung out in the same spot. Well, the five of them, if you included Moxy and Cleo. When they could, they would let Cleo out to run around.

Now Danny pushed open the door and stepped out. Lou waved and Danny gave her a half-hearted wave back. Moxy ran across the field to the cage, running up and down the length of the cage as Cleo did the same from inside.

Rolly jumped out of the way so as not to get knocked down by Moxy. He shook his head. "I still don't get their friendship."

Lou smiled. "They just accept each other—the basis of any good friendship. Right, Danny?"

Danny stopped next to the bench. "Uh, yeah. And I think maybe they just understand each other. Maybe kind of like Laney understands them."

Rolly plopped onto the bench next to Lou. "Friendship—the unifying force of the universe."

Lou rolled her eyes at Rolly's dramatic proclamation, but all Danny could manage was a weak smile.

"All right, Danny," Rolly said. "What's up? You've got a look on your face like you've been called to the principal's office."

Danny fingered the file behind his back. How did you say something like this? "Um, I... uh... I found some information on your sister."

"Really?" Rolly paused. And then looked away from him. "Where is she?"

Lou met Danny's gaze, and Danny saw the realization dawn in her eyes. She put a hand out and touched Rolly's sleeve. "Rolly."

Rolly let out a breath. When he spoke, his voice was quiet. "She's dead, isn't she?"

Danny nodded. "Yeah. About two weeks after she disappeared."

Rolly took a shuddering breath and stared off into the distance. Finally, he turned back to Danny. "How?"

Danny swallowed. "She was at one of the camps. She stopped a Fallen who was going to kill another kid at the camp. She got in between them."

A little smile crossed Rolly's face. "She was always doing that. She stepped between me and my dad I don't know how many times." He put a trembling hand to his mouth.

Lou reached out to him. "Rolly, what can—"

Rolly shook his head. "Nothing." He started to walk away, stopping to rest his hand on Danny's shoulder. "Thank you for finding out."

Danny nodded at him.

Rolly took a few steps away from him before turning around. "Who was it? Who was it that killed her?"

Danny paused. "It was Pascha."

Shock crossed Rolly's face before his jaw tightened. Pascha had been the Fallen who had recruited both Lou and Rolly—and who had almost killed them.

Lou stood. "Rolly—"

He put up a trembling hand. "I just need a little time. Okay?"

He didn't wait for a response, just turned and walked across the field before he disappeared around the side of the building.

Lou came to stand next to Danny.

"Is he going to be all right?" Danny asked, not taking his eyes from where Rolly had disappeared.

Lou wrapped her arm around Danny and leaned her head on his shoulder. "Eventually."

CHAPTER 23

ATLANTA, GEORGIA

Laney stepped out of the house and into the hot Atlanta sunshine. After they'd wrapped things up in Chicago, Laney and Jake had flown down here to see the Watson family. Tomorrow they would head to see the Seeleys—a full twenty-four hours of seeing heartbreak up close and personal.

Now, as they left the Watsons' house, even the heat couldn't touch the ball of cold that had lodged in Laney's chest. She glanced back at the house. *That poor family.* The pain they were going through was palpable.

They were a nice family. The mom and dad had been high school sweethearts. Sophia had been their youngest, their surprise child. Their other kids were already grown and out of the house. And now they were alone.

Laney twirled the ring around her finger. Mr. and Mrs. Watson had had no clue about any special abilities their daughter might have, and Laney had gotten no inkling of any abilities from them, either. They described Sophia as smart, fun, happy—the same way all caring parents described their children.

Jake took her arm as they headed down the porch steps. "You okay?"

Laney shook her head. "That family is devastated. And I feel helpless."

The Watsons had readily agreed to meet with them this morning, obviously desperate for any help in finding their daughter. But Laney and Jake hadn't been able to offer them anything. And the Watsons hadn't been able to shed any more light on their daughter's disappearance.

"I don't know how a family gets through that," Laney said, trying to imagine how she or Kati would cope if someone took Max.

She couldn't imagine it—and she didn't *want* to imagine it.

A picture of Victoria flashed through Laney's mind. Had she been as devastated when she gave away Laney? Laney shook her head. No. Victoria had known where her daughter was.

She glanced back at the house. It was the not knowing that was eating these families up.

Jake leaned down to her. "I think we have an audience."

Laney glanced across the driveway. A little boy in a cowboy hat peered at them from the fence that separated the two yards. He had watched them when they had arrived as well.

Laney nodded to Jake. "Why don't you go check in with Henry? I'll be just a minute."

"Okay." Jake kissed her on the cheek before heading to the car. He leaned against it and pulled out his phone.

Laney turned toward the boy, trying to figure out how to speak with him without terrifying the poor kid.

"Are you a cop?"

Laney glanced down, surprised that the kid was now only a few feet away. He sure moved quietly. And he didn't just have the cowboy hat; he had the complete sheriff ensemble, including shield, gun holster, and boots. The kid was a little younger than Sophia, maybe five or six.

Laney shook her head. "Not exactly. But I am trying to find Sophia."

"She was my friend."

Laney wasn't sure what to say to that. "You miss her, huh?"

He nodded, his eyes focused on the ground. "She played basketball with me."

Laney didn't know what to say. How do you comfort a little kid when something so horrible has happened? Do you say everything will be all right? Because that wasn't the truth. Do you say it will get better? Because in Laney's experience, the pain of loss never got better, you just got used to it.

"Did you see anyone watching her?" Laney asked.

The boy shrugged and kicked at some loose gravel on the sidewalk. "I don't know. Maybe."

Laney felt the tingle of possibility take root. She tried to keep the urgency out of her voice. "Who did you see?"

"Couple of guys. They hung around for a few days."

"Hung around?"

The boy nodded and pointed down the street. "They had different cars, but always the same guys."

Laney's pulse began to beat faster. "You're sure?"

He nodded. "Yup."

Laney looked over at Jake, who must have read the surprise on her face. He started over. Sophia hadn't been a chance kidnapping. They'd been watching her.

Laney turned back to the boy. "Do you remember what they looked like?"

"I don't know. They were white, like you. And big like him," he said, pointing at Jake.

Jake came and stood next to Laney, catching the end of the boy's comment. "Did they have red hair like her or brown hair like me?" he asked.

The boy shrugged again. "I don't know. They had on baseball caps. Really dirty ones."

"Is there anything about the guys you do remember?"

The boy nodded. "One had some ink like my friend Darrell's uncle."

"Ink like a tattoo?"

The boy nodded.

"What was it of?" Laney asked.

"It had angel wings. It means he's a park ranger."

Laney pictured a feathered wing. *A park ranger?* Why would he think that meant—

Next to her Jake went still, his eyes intent. "Were there words above the wings?"

"Yeah."

Jake knelt down, keeping his voice even. "Was your friend Darrell's uncle an airborne ranger?"

"I don't know. He died in Iraq."

"Did you tell the cops this?" Laney asked.

The boy shook his head. "They never asked."

Laney looked over at Jake, and he nodded. They had something. It might be small, but it was something.

Jake reached into his pocket and pulled out a twenty. "Thanks, kid."

The boy looked at the money and smiled. He started to run off, but then turned back. "You'll help find Sophia, won't you?"

Laney swallowed. "We'll do our best."

The boy's shoulders drooped. "Adults always say that. It usually means no."

Laney watched him disappear into the house next door.

"So it's possible the guys who grabbed Sophia are former military," Jake said.

"So we have a lead."

Jake's smile was grim. "A small one. But maybe we can make it a little bigger."

CHAPTER 24

BALTIMORE, MARYLAND

Early the next morning, Henry wound his way down Sharecroppers Lane. Before a meeting, he liked to take a little time to focus on the topic under discussion. Usually a walk helped him fine-tune his points.

But today it wasn't working. Today all he could see was Danny's face. Last night, Danny had only responded to him in monosyllabic grunts. This morning was no better. When did this get so hard? It felt like his and Danny's conversations were loaded with landmines. And he seemed to be setting one of them off every time he opened his mouth.

"Henry?"

He looked up as Kati stepped onto the sidewalk. Then he glanced back at the path that led to the bomb shelter. "Visiting Dom?"

Kati nodded, looking a little pale. "Yes."

"Are you all right?"

Kati smiled—it looked a little forced, Henry thought. "Yes, fine. Just, um, a little headache. How about you?"

"Just trying to clear my head. Are you heading back to your cottage?"

She nodded.

"Mind if I walk with you?"

"I'd like the company," she said, taking his arm. "I thought you'd be at the bookstore."

Henry shook his head. "I have a meeting in a little bit."

They walked along in silence for a few minutes before Kati spoke. "So, where's Jen?"

"What makes you think I'd know?"

Kati laughed. "I don't know who you two think you're fooling —besides each other."

"She's at the school, helping the kids get settled."

"She's good with them. And Danny. He really seems to like her."

"Better than he likes me," Henry mumbled.

Kati stopped. "What does that mean?"

Henry shook his head. "Nothing. It's just been a long day."

Kati laughed. "Henry, it's not even noon."

He groaned. "I know."

She pulled him toward her porch swing. Henry thought about resisting—the meeting time was getting close—but to be honest, he really wanted to talk to another parent. He took a seat, and Kati turned toward him, waiting.

Henry sighed. "I don't know what I'm doing. Every time I speak to Danny lately, I seem to be saying the wrong thing. And he hates the security I've placed around him. But until I know it's safe, I just can't remove it. He acts like I'm ruining his life."

"He's a teenager."

Henry leaned his head back. "I know, I know. I guess I hoped that with his intelligence, we could skip this stage."

"Not happening?"

Henry let out a rueful laugh. "No. And I can't help but wonder if I did the right thing bringing him into my life. Would he have been better off somewhere else? I thought I was making it easier for him, but lately… I don't know. I think I've made it harder for him."

Kati was quiet for a moment. "Danny's road was always going to be rough. He's different. There was never a chance for him to go to a regular school and just hang with friends on the weekend. The way his brain works, he's caught between two worlds: the world of kids his age and the world of geniuses."

Henry sighed. "I know. I just wish I could make it easier for him."

"You have. You took him out of a home where he was abused and unwanted and gave him your love and protection. You gave him a safe place. More than that, you gave him a family."

"But I wish I could be a better friend to him."

Kati shook her head. "That's not your job. Your job is to say no —to be the bad guy. Because what you're doing is for his benefit down the road. So no, you don't get to be his friend. Your job is to be his parent."

Henry looked down at her. "How'd you get so good at this?"

Kati smiled. "Nobody is *good* at parenting. We all just muddle through, doing the best we can."

Henry stood up. "All right then." He glanced at his watch. "If we hurry, we can probably catch them for lunch."

"What about your meeting?"

"I'm going to cancel it. Some things are more important."

CHAPTER 25

Danny wandered down the book aisle, his eyes scanning the sci-fi titles. Nothing was catching his interest. He tried to ignore the Chandler security agent at the end of the aisle, who was pretending to leaf through a copy of *Men's Health*.

Turning down the next aisle, Danny picked up the library edition of *Buffy the Vampire Slayer*. He had hoped they'd have it. He knew he could order it online, but there was something about finding books at the bookstore that was, well, just fun.

Except today. Today, the bookstore wasn't fun.

He kept replaying his conversations with Henry in his head. Every time he'd seen Henry since their fight at the school, he'd wanted to apologize. But instead, he just kept on being a jerk to him. It was like someone else had taken over his body.

He sighed. Henry was the one person in his life he could always count on. And now, he felt like there was this giant wall between them. A wall he himself had created.

Danny put the book back on the shelf, promising himself he'd grab it on the way out. He headed back to the kids' section to see if Max had found anything.

A few rows away from the kids' section he could hear Max

talking excitedly. "But Maddox, there's no way Black Widow could win in a fight against Captain America. He's—he's *Captain America*."

"I don't know, kid. She's a pretty good fighter. I think if she really wanted to, she could take him."

"Well, who would win in a race, the Flash or Superman?"

"Can Superman fly?"

"No. He has to run."

"Then I think the Flash. He's had more practice."

"Yeah. I think so too."

Danny smiled as he rounded the corner. Maddox who was sitting on a purple cube, obviously not meant for someone his size, and Max was sitting cross-legged on the floor, a serious expression on his face.

Max's face lit up when he saw Danny. "Danny! I found a book on dinosaurs." Max turned the book around for Danny to see. It was upside down.

Danny felt his mood lift. "That looks awesome."

Maddox struggled to his feet with a grimace. "Hey. Find anything?"

Danny shrugged. "Not really. Any chance we could go get something to eat and then come back?"

"Yeah." Max scrambled to his feet. He ran over to Maddox and took his hand, looking up at him. "Can we get milkshakes? Please?"

Maddox shook his head. "Yes. But only if I can get one too."

Max smiled. "Of course, silly."

Max skipped ahead of Maddox and grabbed Danny's hand, half pulling him out of the kids' section.

Danny smiled in spite of the chaos in his mind. It was hard to stay in a bad mood around Max's energy.

They made their way to the front door. Danny pretended not to notice Maddox subtly signal to the other two security members that they were heading out.

R.D. BRADY

Outside the store, they headed left. There was a diner only a few blocks away. Max chattered on, oblivious to Danny's mood and their entourage. Danny saw one member of security twenty feet ahead and knew the other one was about ten feet behind them.

He tried to swallow his anger and be logical, but failed. How much more of a freak could he be? It was already bad enough that he had nothing in common with kids his age, but now he had his own security force. Henry might as well hang a giant sign on him in neon colors: *Come one, come all, and stare at the freak.*

Max reached up and took his hand. "It's okay, Danny."

Danny looked down at him. "What okay?"

"The guards. They're here to protect us. It's a good thing."

"How did you—"

The screech of brakes cut off his reply. Danny jerked his head up, feeling his eyes go wide.

A white panel van leaped up onto the curb. Maddox immediately grabbed Danny and Max, shoving them out of harm's way. Danny slammed into the sidewalk, scraping his palms and knees, and Max crashed to the ground next to him. But the van plowed right into Maddox, pinning him into the brick wall next to them.

Danny scrambled to his feet, pulling Max to his. All the while he kept his eyes on the van. The side door flew open and two men jumped out, firing at Maddox, who was still pinned to the wall.

"Maddox!" Max screamed.

Danny clamped a hand over Max's mouth and pulled him away. The two Chandler guards were racing toward them, but the two shooters from the van dropped to their knees and aimed for the guards, forcing them to take shelter behind parked cars.

Danny yanked Max into a nearby alley, his heart pounding. *Oh God. Oh God. Oh God.* Danny's hand was clasped tightly around Max's. And for the first time in his life, he couldn't seem to think.

Next to him, Max stumbled. Danny grabbed the collar of Max's shirt, all but carrying him down the alley.

110

His breaths coming out in panicked gasps, Danny pictured the city grid. He knew the alley led to another street that ran parallel to this one. "Come on, Max," he said as he broke into a run.

Max's little legs churned next to him. But a short way down the alley, a chain link fence blocked further progress. *No.* This wasn't in the schematic. Panicked, he looked around, spotted a door. He pulled Max over to it, yanked on the handle—locked. He glanced back at the street. Gunfire still blazed.

Max's terrified face stared up at him.

It was either back the way they came, or over the fence. The fence was at least twenty feet high. But there was a dumpster pushed up against it.

He pulled Max over to it. "Come on, Max. We're going over."

"Where do you think you're going?"

Danny whirled around. Two men had slipped into the alley behind them. They weren't the same gunmen from the van.

The taller of the two barked at his companion. "Grab the abomination."

Abomination? Danny's heart galloped in his chest.

The other man pulled out a gun. He was shorter but beefier than the first one, and his face had a ruddy glow. Danny flashed back on another violent man who could have been his brother.

"No guns," the tall one yelled, his eyes focused back toward the street.

The short man grunted and replaced the gun with a knife as he stalked toward Danny and Max.

Danny pulled Max behind him. "Max, you stay behind me, okay?"

"Danny?" Max's voice trembled.

"It'll be okay."

Danny moved his right leg forward, establishing his stance like Laney had taught him. He tried to ignore the shaking in his hands. Laney's words drifted through his mind as if she were right next to him. *Remember, if you're ever in a fight, you'll be scared. Ignore it. You can be scared* after *you do what needs to be done.*

The man laughed when he saw Danny adopt a fighting stance. "What are you going to do, kid? You think you can fight me?" He lunged, aimed right for Danny's chest.

Danny didn't think. He just reacted.

He stepped aside, latching his left hand on to the man's knife hand. With his right he slammed the heel of his hand into the man's nose. Then he switched his right hand to the man's wrist, bringing the side of his left hand down at the crook of the man's elbow.

The man's arm automatically bent. Danny pushed it farther with his right. The knife plunged into the man's chest. Danny wasn't sure whose face was more shocked—his or the attacker's. But he didn't let up. He kicked the man at the knee, then, wrapping his hand around the man's throat, shoved him to the ground.

Danny stumbled back, his eyes locked on the man on the ground and the blood pooling around him. He couldn't believe what he had just done. He hadn't even thought; he just did it. Just like Laney told him.

His head jerked up as a shot took out the second man. Maddox ran down the alley toward them. He stopped by each of the men and gathered their weapons. Then he walked toward Danny slowly. "Danny, you okay?"

Danny felt like he was moving in slow motion. He glanced up at Maddox, whose clothes were ripped and singed. A cut above his eye was already healing.

Max ran around Danny and threw himself at Maddox. Without breaking his stride, Maddox swooped Max up. "It's okay, Max. I've got you."

Danny watched it all, but he felt distant, disconnected.

Maddox knelt down in front of him. "Danny, look at me. Look at me."

Danny tore his gaze away from the men on the ground and

forced himself to look into Maddox's eyes. He struggled to think through the thick syrup in his thoughts. "Those men... they wanted to kill us. Or take us."

Maddox nodded. "And you didn't let that happen."

Danny stared up at Maddox. "The security team?"

"Both of them were shot, but they'll be okay."

Danny nodded. His eyes went back to the man he'd stabbed. *I did that.* He felt sick. *Oh my God, I did that.*

Again Maddox's voice cut through the fog in Danny's brain. "Danny, listen to me: You did what needed to be done. You saved yourself. You saved Max."

Danny started to shake, but he nodded, turning to look at Max. "Max, are you okay?"

Max flung himself at Danny, his body trembling as he wrapped his arms around Danny's shoulders. "I want my mom."

Danny pulled the boy close, tears choking his throat. *And I want Henry.*

CHAPTER 26

Henry slammed the car to a stop at the edge of the police barricade. Kati was already out the door and running toward Maddox. He stood a head taller than everyone else and was easy to find.

Henry scanned the area, looking for Danny. A white van had crashed into the side of a bank on the left. Cars parked on the street were riddled with bullet holes, their windows smashed. Blood stained the bank wall as well as the sidewalk.

Maddox had called and told them what had happened. He'd said that Danny and Max were unhurt. But Henry couldn't get himself to calm down. He needed to *see* that Danny was all right. He needed to know he was safe.

When Kati reached Maddox, she nearly collapsed in his arms. He helped her toward a waiting ambulance. And sitting at the back of the ambulance were two small figures huddled together under a blanket.

Henry grabbed onto the doorframe for support. *He's okay. He's fine*, he told himself, but his trembling limbs didn't seem to hear him.

It took him a few seconds to get his emotions under control.

He let out a breath and started walking over to them, his legs still feeling a little unsteady. Yesterday's disagreement with Danny crowded into his mind. What if Danny didn't want to see him? He couldn't still be mad—not after this. Could he?

As he made his way through the crowd, a police officer tried to intercept him, but another whispered in his ear, and the officer waved him on. Henry kept his eyes on Danny. Kati had pulled Max into her arms and was sitting in the back of the ambulance, rocking him back and forth.

Danny's eyes caught Henry's. For a moment, Danny went still, and Henry's heart broke. *He's still mad.* Then Danny jumped off the back of the ambulance and ran toward him.

Henry caught him and wrapped his arms around him.

"I'm sorry, Henry," Danny said.

It took Henry a moment to speak past the tears in his throat. "It's okay. All that matters is that you're okay. You *are* okay, aren't you?"

Danny just nodded into Henry's chest.

As Henry held him, he looked around. Six men had attacked them. The security force had killed three; another two had escaped. And then there was the one on the way to the hospital. The one Danny had somehow fought off. Henry's arms tightened as he imagined how easily he could have lost Danny.

Above Kati's head, Henry caught Maddox's gaze. Maddox looked like he wanted to kill someone. And Henry felt the same way. But that anger had been pushed to the back by the fear and terror that had taken root. *Why did someone come after the boys?*

He glanced at the destruction around them and pulled Danny a little closer.

And had they been scared away? Or were they just beginning?

CHAPTER 27

Laney ran up the steps to Henry and Danny's home. Henry had called her and Jake on their flight back and told them about the attempted abduction. He'd assured them that the boys were fine, but Laney was still shaken. Who would go after the boys? Why? Was it related to the other missing kids, or was this a whole new danger?

When they landed, she had headed straight here, while Jake had headed to the hospital to see if he could talk to the remaining assailant.

The one Danny stabbed. Laney shivered at the thought.

When she'd started teaching Danny self-defense, she'd mainly thought of it as a way for him to build his confidence. She never thought he'd have to actually use it—especially this soon.

At the front door, Laney didn't even knock. She just let herself in, calling out. "Henry? Danny?"

Henry appeared in the hallway ahead. Laney rushed over and gave him a hug. "You okay?"

He nodded, but Laney could see the fear in his eyes. This attack had really shaken him.

"Where's Danny?" Laney asked.

Henry nodded toward the kitchen. "In there."

Laney headed down the hall quickly. She stopped in the doorway, soaking up the picture of Danny. He sat at the kitchen table, pushing macaroni and cheese around on his plate, looking like he always did. Jen sat across from him. She caught Laney's eye and gave her a quick nod.

Laney sagged against the doorway in relief. *He's fine.* "Danny."

Danny looked up and then stood.

Laney made her way quickly toward him, wrapping him in a hug. "Thank God you're okay."

He just hugged her tighter. Laney rested her head on his, her heart rate calming. *He's not hurt,* she reassured herself.

Finally, Danny released her.

She took his face in her hands. "Are you okay?"

Danny nodded. "Yeah, I'm okay."

Laney sat on the chair next to him as Danny reclaimed his seat. She took his hand. "I am so proud of the way you defended Max. The way you defended yourself."

Danny ducked his head down, his voice small. "I nearly killed that man."

"You didn't have a choice," Jen said softly.

Laney nodded, feeling his pain. "Jen's right. You didn't start that fight. And the only other option was to let him grab you or Max. Or worse. You did the right thing."

"Then why do I feel so bad?" he asked.

Jen and Laney exchanged a look. They both knew what he meant. They'd both taken lives. And even though they'd saved others or themselves by doing so, it never sat easy with either of them.

"Because violence isn't easy," Jen said.

"And it shouldn't be," Laney said.

Henry entered the kitchen and took a spot across from Danny, his hands resting on the back of a chair. "Patrick is down at Dom's with Kati, Max, and Maddox. They're going to stay there tonight."

Laney nodded, knowing Kati would find the bomb shelter much safer than the cottage. God, what must this be doing to her? She was already scared. This attack might just have pushed her over the edge.

Laney looked between Henry and Jen. "Have either of you talked to Kati? I couldn't reach her."

"She's dealing," Henry said.

Jen shook her head. "No. She's terrified."

Laney nodded, not having a clue how to fix that. "I'm going to head to the shelter. Stay there for the night. Unless you guys want me to stay here?"

"Actually, I think I'll stay at Dom's too," Danny said.

Henry looked over at him. "What? Why?"

Danny looked back at Henry, his face serious. "You want to find the guys that did this. You should be able to focus on that without worrying about me."

"Danny, it's not like that," Henry said. "I—"

Danny shook his head. "I'm not mad. I'm not hurt. I *want* you to find these guys. And I think you'll be able to focus better without me, that's all." He paused. "But when you're done, can you come to Dom's too?"

Henry nodded. "Absolutely."

Jen tapped Danny on the shoulder. "Why don't we go grab some of your stuff?"

Danny nodded. "Okay." He stood and then paused, looking at Henry. "You will come to Dom's later, right?"

"Yes. As soon as I can," Henry assured him.

Laney watched Danny leave with Jen, Moxy trailing behind them. She ran her hand through her hair as soon as they were out of view. "I can't believe somebody went after the boys. Do we have any idea who?"

Henry pulled out the chair across from her and sank into it. He glanced back the way Danny had disappeared before turning back to Laney. "Not yet."

"Do you think this was some sort of retaliation for the Fallen in Chicago?"

"I don't see how. *We* didn't kill that guy."

"So then what? The missing kids?"

"I don't see that either. I mean, there's no indication that either Danny or Max are anything other than normal boys. There's no angelic background there. And I haven't gotten a sense off of either of them. Have you?"

Laney shook her head. "No. Nothing."

"What about Kati's husband, David?" Henry asked. "Is there anything there?"

Laney pictured David Simmons as he was the one and only time she'd ever seen him. "The car crash that killed him was really bad. But if he were a Fallen or a nephilim, he would have survived it."

"I thought he was impaled?"

Laney nodded. "Yeah, but not through the heart. David was just a normal man."

"And Danny's family has no indications of abilities?"

"No. So is this even connected?"

"Maddox said none of the attackers had abilities. But they were organized," Henry replied.

"Humans," Laney said, disgust rolling through her. "The Council."

Henry shrugged. "Maybe. I just don't know."

"Did Northgram ever get back to you?"

"He did. He gave me some names, but I've already had operatives go through their lives. They seem clean so far, at least with regard to the missing kids." He shook his head. "I don't think it's any of them."

"Do you think Northgram's holding out?"

"I think he knows something. I'm just not sure if we're even on the right track. I think... I think maybe we're asking the wrong questions."

Images of the missing kids swirled through Laney's mind, along with images of Max and Danny. Were these different events connected? Or was this threat something altogether new?

"Well, Jake's at the hospital," Laney said. "He'll see what he can find out."

Henry nodded. "And Jen's going to head to the police department and see what she can learn."

"In that case, I'll take Danny down to Dom's and let Jen get going."

Laney studied Henry. His shoulders were taut and he was gripping a napkin like he wanted to strangle the life out of it. She spoke slowly. "Henry, are you going to be okay?"

Henry's eyes cut to her, and the anger in them startled her. "Someone came after Danny. And they're going to pay for that."

CHAPTER 28

Laney walked through the shelter. She'd just read Max a book and tucked him in, and Dom was sitting with him now, waiting until he fell asleep.

She wasn't sure where Kati and Maddox had gone, but she knew Danny had gone upstairs for some fresh air. She glanced over at the entrance. She should probably go check on him.

"I'll go," Patrick said, standing up from the couch.

"No, it's okay. I can—"

Patrick put up his hand. "Laney, I need to do something."

And Laney saw the fear and anger in his eyes. Patrick loved both Max and Danny. And this attack was hitting him as hard as everyone else. *Maybe that's the point,* a voice whispered at the back of Laney's mind. *To put all of you off your game.*

Well, if that was the plan, it was working. She hadn't been able to focus on the missing kids since she'd heard. "Okay. You go. I'll see if there's anything new on the missing kids."

Patrick kissed her on the cheek and headed out.

Laney watched him go and kept watching long after he had disappeared from view. Then, giving herself a mental shake, she headed for Dom's office. *Why go after the boys?* she wondered for the thousandth time. *And why were the attackers humans? Was it the Council?*

"He saw you get impaled, Maddox! Do you really think he's just going to bounce back from that?"

Laney's head jerked up and she stopped just outside Dom's office. It was Kati's voice she heard, and she was obviously crying.

"He's okay. He's fine."

"He's not fine," Kati said, her voice breaking. "He sees ghosts. And now someone tried to kill him."

Ghosts? Laney inched forward, aware she was eavesdropping but unable to stop herself. She remembered what Max had told her about Drew and Rocky, but that was just his imagination —wasn't it?

"Kati, you're working yourself up."

"Shouldn't I be?"

"Kati…"

"Could you just leave me alone?"

The room went silent for a moment. "Okay. I'll be with Max."

Maddox walked out of the room. He paused for a moment when he saw Laney. Then he nodded and kept going.

Laney leaned against the wall. She hated that Kati was going through all of this. But she didn't know how to make it better.

Pushing off the wall, she walked up to the door of Dom's office and knocked softly on the frame. "Kati?"

Kati looked up. Tears were running down her cheeks. Laney immediately crossed the room and pulled her friend into a hug.

Kati sobbed against her. "They came after my little boy."

Laney led Kati over to the couch. "I know, honey. I know."

Laney stayed with Kati, letting her cry, and doing a little crying herself, for the better part of an hour. Finally they were cried out. Laney got up to grab some tissues from the box on Dom's desk, then brought them back to the couch, handing some of them to Kati.

Kati wiped at her red-rimmed eyes. "What am I going to do?"

"We'll keep him here. Keep him protected."

"Until when?"

"Until we catch the guys responsible," Laney said with a confidence she didn't feel.

Kati just nodded numbly.

Laney watched her friend, worried about how she was handling all of this, but also worried about what she had overheard. "Kati, what did you mean when you said that Max could see ghosts?"

Kati's head popped up in surprise

Laney cringed. "Sorry. I kind of overheard."

Kati sighed, curling her legs under her. "I don't know why I didn't tell you. I guess I just figured you had enough going on without more drama."

Laney took Kati's hand. "You guys are my family. I know these last two years have been crazy, but that hasn't changed."

Kati squeezed her hand back. "I know. I know. I think I've just wanted to keep it to myself. If I did, then maybe it wasn't real."

Laney nodded. "I get that. But any chance you could tell me now?"

Kati spoke slowly. "It started a few months ago. Max kept talking about these imaginary friends. I never really thought much about it. Not until Sally."

"Sally? His friend from the park?"

Kati nodded. "Her full name is Sally Richards."

Laney paused. "Why do I know that name?"

"Because she was the little girl who went missing about two years ago."

Laney flashed on a little girl with red hair and bright blue eyes. "Right. Her body was just found yesterday."

Kati nodded.

"What does she have to do with Max seeing ghosts?"

Kati sighed. "Max is the reason they found her."

CHAPTER 29

TWO DAYS AGO

"Mom, can we go to the park today?" Max asked as he ran into the living room in his new Spider-Man shirt and jeans.

Kati looked up from her paperwork. She hadn't slept much the last two nights; ever since Max had mentioned David, she'd just tossed and turned. So early this morning she'd gotten out of bed and driven to the school. She'd picked up a bunch of paperwork from Laney's desk, and was planning on a day working from home. She just needed a change of scenery, she assured herself on the way back to the estate. And it wasn't because Max said he spoke with his dead father.

Kati looked into Max's hopeful face. "Um, I don't know, honey. I have a lot of work to get done."

"Can Maddox take me?"

Maddox was just coming up from the basement, a basket of laundry in his hands. "What? The park? When I have an incredible morning of laundry folding planned?"

Max laughed, ran over to Maddox, and grabbed his leg. "Please, Maddox. *Please.*"

Maddox caught Kati's eye. She nodded. "If it's okay with Maddox, it's okay with me."

"Maddox?" Big blue eyes stared up at him.

"Agh, he's using his powers of cuteness on me. I cannot resist. Okay, Max. Go grab your jacket."

"Yes!" Max sprinted out of the room.

Maddox placed the laundry basket on the counter. "Okay if I leave this here?"

"Sure, no problem. And thanks for taking him. I'm a little distracted this morning."

Maddox leaned against the counter. "I noticed. Everything okay?"

Kati struggled to keep her voice even under Maddox's intent stare. "Yeah. Just didn't sleep much."

Maddox glanced over his shoulder toward the stairs, then sat down next to Kati. "Last night, Max kept saying that he promised Sally he'd play with her today. Have you met Sally?"

Kati shook her head. "No. Sally's one of the imaginaries."

Max walked into the kitchen just then, his jacket on upside down, the collar near his waist. "She's not imaginary."

Kati laughed at the sight. "Come here, you." She pulled it off him and put it on correctly, zipping it up. "So what does Sally look like?"

"She has red hair like Laney."

"Oh, I see. And where does Sally live?"

"At the park. That's where her dad left her."

His words left Kati with a chill. She opened her mouth to ask him more questions but he ran over to Maddox. "Up."

Maddox twirled him up. "All right. We're out of here."

Max waved at his mom over Maddox's shoulder. She gave him a half-hearted wave in return. She could hear them laughing on their way to the car, and she smiled. Maddox was good for her son—almost like a father.

Then Max's words from the night before came back to her: *He said he should have taken the other road that night.* She shook her head and said aloud, "It's nothing. He's imagining things."

She turned her attention back to the paperwork in front of her. She tried to focus, but Max's words seemed to be on an unending loop in the back of her mind: "That's where her dad left her."

Imaginary. Sally is imaginary, she thought. *And he just guessed about David. Or maybe I mentioned it once and don't remember.*

She forced her mind back to her work. But after another twenty minutes of getting nowhere, she finally pushed it aside and pulled over her laptop.

I'll just do a quick search, ease my mind, and get back to work, she thought as she entered "Sally, missing, Baltimore" into a search engine. Then she got up and made herself a cup of coffee and tried not to notice the tremor in her hands.

She placed the coffee next to her computer as she took a seat, then scanned the search results. Almost immediately, Kati's heart slammed to a stop. There, at the bottom of the first page, was a picture of a little girl with red hair. Kati quickly clicked the news story next to the picture.

Sally Richards, age seven, had gone missing two years ago. The last person to see her had been her father, who had visitation rights. He claimed she had said she was tired, so he'd put her down for a nap, and when he'd gone back to check on her later, she was gone.

Kati sat back from the laptop, feeling numb. She only hesitated for a second before grabbing her jacket and rushing out the door.

She told herself to calm down as she approached the playground a short time later. She could see Max; he was the only kid there. But he was holding an animated conversation with himself.

Or with Sally, she thought.

Maddox caught sight of her and walked over. "Kati? Is everything all right?"

Kati made herself nod. "Yeah. Good. Has anyone else been here?"

Maddox shook his head. "No. It's just been us."

Kati nodded and walked over to Max. He caught sight of her and his face broke into a grin. "Mom!" He ran over, throwing his arms around her. "I thought you couldn't come."

She tried to smile. "I thought I'd take a little break. Have you seen your friend Sally today?"

Max nodded. "She's in the sandbox."

Kati glanced over to the empty sandbox, the hairs on her arms rising. Then she knelt down to face Max. "Max, you said Sally's dad left her here. Do you know where?"

Max nodded. "Yeah. " He pointed to a large oak tree twenty feet away from the playground. "Right there, under the tree. Can I go back and play?"

Kati could only nod; the lump in her throat was too large for her to talk around. She stood on shaky legs. Pulling out her cell phone, she dialed.

A deep male voice answered. "Detective Mike Chapman."

Mike had been Rocky's old partner back in Syracuse.

Kati cleared her throat. "Hey, Mike. It's Kati."

"Kati!" She could feel the smile through the phone. "How are you guys doing? How's Baltimore?"

"Um, it's good. How's Syracuse?"

"Not bad. Little cold, but hey, par for the course, right?"

"Right," Kati agreed. "Listen, Mike, I was wondering, do you know anybody on the Baltimore PD?"

Mike paused. "Everything okay, Kati?"

"I'm not sure. I, um... I need a favor, and I'm hoping you can help me out."

CHAPTER 30

Kati stood at the edge of the playground, her gaze darting between Max and the parking lot. She had explained to Maddox about finding the information on Sally online. She knew he wasn't convinced, but that was okay.

"You know it's probably just his imagination," Maddox said.

Kati nodded. "I know." But she didn't believe that. The more she watched Max, the more convinced she became that he wasn't playing alone.

Maddox nudged her. "They're here."

Kati glanced over at the police car that had pulled into the lot. A tall African-American officer stepped out of the car and a black lab hopped out after him. The dog sat still as the officer snapped a leash on him. Then the two made their way over to the playground.

Kati nodded at Maddox. "I'll be right back."

She headed toward the officer, who waited at the edge of the playground for her to join him. The lab sat patiently next to him, wagging his tail. "Ms. Simmons? I'm Officer James."

Kati nodded. "Call me Kati. Thanks for doing this."

The officer nodded. "Mike said you might have something. Where are we looking?"

Kati pointed over to the big oak. "Can you check under that tree there?"

"No problem. Be back in a bit."

Maddox walked over to join Kati. Neither of them said anything as they watched the officer and dog do their job. Kati realized she was holding her breath and forced herself to breathe.

The dog sniffed the ground dutifully, but seemed unconcerned. But when it got within about ten feet of the oak, it went still. Then it started going in circles, sniffing the ground in frantic motions. Finally it reached a spot two feet from the tree, sat, and howled.

The sound went right through Kati. She grabbed onto Maddox's arm. "Oh my God."

CHAPTER 31

PRESENT DAY

Laney wasn't sure what to say—or think for that matter.

"They found Sally Richards's body at that exact spot," Kati said, her face pale, her hands clutching a couch pillow.

"Are they sure it's her?" Laney asked.

Kati nodded. "It was a little girl, and she was wearing the same dress that Sally was reportedly last seen in. It was her."

A sense of unease rolled over Laney. What did this mean? Did it mean anything?

"Are you sure he didn't..." Laney's voice trailed off. She couldn't think of any way Max could possibly know where Sally Richards's body was. Max had been only three when the girl disappeared.

"His friends aren't imaginary," Laney said.

Kati shook her head. "No."

Laney felt stunned. Max had said that Drew and Rocky had stopped by to visit him. She felt a little warmth at the idea. But that warmth cooled a little when she remembered what he'd said next. *Something's coming. Something bad.*

"Why didn't you tell me any of this?" she asked.

"I don't know. I wanted to. I guess I was hoping it wasn't true. I mean, look at everything that's happened. You're the ring bearer. Saving me and Max was part of your destiny coming true. And your mother is—well, she's someone important. And Jake and Henry and the others... But me and Max, we've always been, you know, not really part of it. But now..." She paused, as if she was afraid to say the words aloud. "Now I can't help but think that Max has a role, too. And I really, *really* don't want him to."

Laney nodded. "I understand that. Really, I do. But we can protect him. We can keep him safe."

"How?" Kati's eyes looked wild. "By keeping him under guard for the rest of his life? He's only five. Even if it's true, even if he really does play a role in all this craziness, it can't be until years from now. Doesn't he deserve a chance to be a kid?"

"He does. Of course he does. And we'll make sure he has it." Laney paused. "Does Maddox know?"

"Yes. I asked him not to say anything." She looked Laney in the eyes. "And I'm asking you not to say anything either."

"But after today—"

Kati shook her head. "No. It's not related. No one knows about Max. And all the kids that are going missing are angelic, right? That's not Max."

"Does anyone else know?"

"Just Dom."

Laney sat back. "Dom?"

"I talked to him earlier today. I thought he might have some insight."

"Did he?"

Kati shrugged. "He spoke about the root race. And he said Max was psychic. That he could see ghosts, and that ghosts could reach out and touch him, even if he didn't want them to."

Laney shivered at the thought. "Anything helpful?"

"Well, he offered to run a couple of assessments, including blood and DNA testing. But I declined."

Laney smiled in spite of the circumstances. She could picture Dom being excited about figuring out the origins of Max's ability. "That sounds like Dom."

Kati gave her a half smile that quickly evaporated. She shook her head. "But it can't be related to the attack today."

"Maybe ..." Laney tried to figure out how any of this fit. If Max was actually psychic—which Laney still wasn't sure she believed—how would anyone else even know?

Kati shook her head. "We still don't know which one of the boys those men were after. It can't be Max. I mean, what's more likely: that they were trying to grab the five-year-old son of a normal, single mom, or that they were trying to grab the teenager of a billionaire nephilim?"

"Well, when you put it like that," Laney said, trying to smile. "But Kati, you will let us keep Max under protection until we find the people responsible for the kidnappings, right?"

Kati looked at Laney for a long moment before finally nodding. "Yes, of course. I would never do anything that would risk Max's safety."

CHAPTER 32

Danny closed his eyes and took a deep breath, inhaling the cool night air. Sitting with his back against Dom's shelter, his arm around Moxy, he tried to wrap his head around everything that had happened.

Those men had wanted to hurt him and Max. Or maybe just him. Or just Max. He still couldn't be sure which of them they'd been going for. He pictured Max. *Was I the target, or was I just in the way?*

A wind blew and the trees rustled, making Danny shiver a little, but he didn't want to go back inside for a jacket. For the first time he could recall, Dom's place made him feel a little claustrophobic.

He heard the blast door inside open and mentally laid bets as to who was coming after him. When Patrick stepped out, Danny said, "I lost."

"What do you mean?" Patrick sat down next to him, Moxy in between them.

"I bet myself it would be Laney who'd come to take me back."

Patrick ran his hand through Moxy's fur. "Actually, I asked her to let me check on you. And I'm not here to bring you back—just here to see how you're doing. You shouldn't be alone right now."

Danny gave a mirthless laugh and gestured to the trees. "There are at least two guards in those trees. And Laney had Cleo brought back from the school. She's prowling around here somewhere."

Patrick nodded. "They just want to make sure you're safe."

Danny opened his mouth to argue, then shut it. Why did he want to argue every time someone said something like that? He knew Patrick was right.

Instead he leaned his head back and stared up at the stars. They were out in full effect tonight. The image of the man lying in the alley came back to him. But that image then shifted to his father, Keith Wartowski.

He shoved the thought aside. "Have you heard anything from the hospital?"

Patrick shook his head. "No. Nothing."

Danny nodded, not knowing what to say.

"Do you want to talk about it?"

Danny shook his head. "Not really."

Patrick didn't say anything. He just sat next to him, waiting.

Danny knew what he was doing. He was letting the silence play out until Danny spoke. And after a few moments, Danny realized he wanted to do just that. "You were a Marine, right? In Vietnam?"

Patrick nodded. "Yes. I was one of the last out of the country."

"And after that you became a priest."

"Yes."

"Why?"

Patrick was quiet for a moment. "I saw and did a lot of horrible things when I was a soldier. And when I got out, I needed some peace. I needed to feel like I was giving back. Like I was doing good work. The priesthood offered me that."

Danny looked over at Patrick. He loved Patrick, but he didn't understand him. Danny's life revolved around facts and certainties. Patrick's revolved around faith and God—things Danny's logic couldn't work his head around.

Patrick reached over and squeezed Danny's hand. "What happened today wasn't your fault. You did what you needed to do."

Danny looked away, feeling a catch in his throat. "Wasn't it? I nearly killed that man. I'm not any better than he is. Not any better than—" He cut off, an image of his father again floating into his mind.

"Not any better than who?"

Danny was silent for a moment. "My father," he said at last, hating how tiny his voice sounded.

Patrick leaned back and nodded. "You don't talk about him. But from what I gather, he was at times a violent man."

Danny scoffed. "At times." He went silent again, not wanting to talk about his former life, but at the same time the words felt like they were going to burst out of his chest.

He pictured his father: his big beefy face, his big beefy hands. Danny winced. Finally he spoke, needing the words to come out.

"He never liked me. I was never tough enough, never strong enough. My brothers, they're like him. Rough, violent. He never knew what to do with me. Kept telling me I needed to be a man."

"How old were you when you left home?"

Danny sniffed. "Eight."

Patrick sighed. "Parents can leave lasting effects, even if their behavior is completely wrong. Probably *especially* if it's wrong."

"The guy in the alley. He kind of looked like my dad."

"And it brought up lots of memories?"

Danny nodded, picturing the belt his dad liked to use.

"Danny, we're not our parents. Laney can probably explain to you better the genetic argument, but I'll tell you what I think, okay?"

Danny nodded.

"I think we each choose our families and the struggles we're going to go through before we're born."

Danny opened his mouth to speak. "What—"

Patrick put up a hand. "Just bear with me. I think we learn from every horrible situation we're in. I think we can *grow* from every situation, although not everybody does. Look at you. You've found a new family with Henry, with all of us. One in which we love you and would do anything in our power to protect you."

"Yeah, but I didn't—"

Patrick took his hand. "I've met too many kids that have been abused, Danny. And I've seen them close themselves off. You didn't do that. You kept reaching out for something to hold onto —something to believe in. And you and Henry found each other. You found someone to trust, even when your earlier experiences taught you that trusting was dangerous."

Danny was taken aback. He had always been a person of logic, not belief. Yet he recognized that Patrick was right: his faith in Henry was absolute. He might not like the barriers Henry had surrounded him with, but he never doubted, not even for a moment, that Henry was doing it out of anything but love.

"But I didn't do anything." Danny said.

"You need to give yourself more credit, Danny. You found a better situation. You found your true family. You're not like your father. His life made him who he is. Your life made you who you are."

Danny tried to imagine his father as a kid. "Do you think…" He paused. "Do you think if my father had someone in his life when he was younger, like I have Henry, do you think he would be different?"

"I do," Patrick said. "I know that as people get older, it's harder to change behavior. But if you provide them with that kindness early enough, you can change someone—for the better."

Danny's mind drifted to the missing kids. What about them? If they were still alive, would this situation change them? Was there anyway it couldn't?

He glanced at Patrick out of the corner of his eye. Patrick was absentmindedly petting Moxy, but his face looked troubled, the creases around his eyes more pronounced.

"Do you think they'll be able to find those kids in time?" Danny asked softly.

Patrick didn't ask whom he meant by "they." When he turned to Danny, his face was confident, with no sign of doubt. "I think that Laney, Henry, and Jake have done some amazing things. And I think finding those kids will be one more amazing thing."

More than anything, Danny wanted to believe him. But logic ruled his mind. "But statistically, the likelihood of those kids still being alive is really slim. And it's getting slimmer each day."

Patrick put his arm around Danny and gave him a squeeze. "You're right. But sometimes you just need to have a little faith."

CHAPTER 33

Henry hung up the phone and stared out the window in his office. Not that he could see anything with the dark. But he knew his men were out there, patrolling the estate. He'd put extra men on duty. In fact, he'd called in every single member of his security force that wasn't already on active assignment.

The memory of Danny shaking when Henry wrapped his arms around him after the attack slashed through him. He curled his fist. He wasn't an angry man. He prided himself on his ability to keep calm under almost all circumstances. *But they went after the boys.*

He let out a breath, trying to find his calm. He tried to picture the men responsible, but that was the problem: there was no one to picture. They were in the dark. Jen and Jake had gone to get what information they could, but Henry hadn't heard back from either of them.

Henry stood up and stretched, his mind roaming over the operatives he had in the field, calculating how long it would take to get his people in place. He had put his operatives on notice that they might be needed. When they had a target, he wanted to be ready. He glanced back at his desk. But right now they had nothing.

He felt a slight tingle along his skin, then glanced up as his doors burst open and Jen strode in. She had left an hour ago to see if she could encourage the medical examiner to speed up the autopsies. Anger punctuated her steps.

Dread washed over Henry. "What happened?"

Jen walked up to his desk. "The cops lost the bodies."

"*What?*"

"The bodies of the attackers. They've disappeared from the morgue."

"What about the guy in the hospital?"

"Died about an hour ago—and he's gone too. Video was compromised and the guys were in and out." Jen shook her head. "Damn it. I should have gotten there sooner. But I wanted to see that the boys were all right. I should have—"

Henry walked around the desk. He reached out to take her by the arms but then thought better of it. Instead he shoved his hands in his pockets and sat on the edge of the desk. "What about the bodies? Did they get anything?"

Jen shook her head. "Not even a fingerprint. How could they not have at least fingerprinted them?"

Henry clenched his teeth. "So we have nothing?"

"Not a damn thing."

Jake walked in. He took one look at Henry's face and paused mid-step. "What happened?"

"The bodies are gone," Jen said. "*All* of them. And we have nothing on them. Not even fingerprints."

At Jen's last remark, Jake smiled and walked forward, placing a piece of paper on Henry's desk.

"What's this?" Henry picked up the paper and scanned it.

"Whose fingerprints are those?" Jen asked, leaning over Henry's shoulder.

Jake took a seat in one of the leather chairs in front of the desk. "That's our guy in the hospital."

Jen looked over at him. "How'd you get these?"

Jake shrugged. "I rolled the guy's hand on a soda can when I went to the hospital. Then I spoke with some of my friends down at the lab, had them expedite their scan."

Henry closed his eyes. "Thank you, Jake."

"Who is he?" Jen asked.

"Lawrence Kelly, former military," Jake said.

"Rangers?" Jen asked.

Jake shook his head. "No. Marines."

"One of the guys at the Watson abduction was a Ranger though, right?" Jen asked.

Jake nodded. "That's what we think. We've got guys from two separate branches involved in this."

"What's Kelly's story?" Henry asked.

"Served two tours in Afghanistan, one in Iraq. Honorably discharged after being wounded by an IED on his last tour."

Henry raised an eyebrow. "Wounded? Did he need follow-up medical care?"

Jake smiled. "Yup. First thing in the morning, I'll head to the VA, see if they have a record of him."

"You can't contact them now?" Jen asked.

Jake let out a bitter laugh. "You ever dealt with the VA?"

She shook her head.

"Well, let's just say they aren't very helpful after hours."

They're not overly helpful during hours either, Henry thought, but kept it to himself. "Okay. Which VA?"

"Kelly's from Stamford, Connecticut. There's a VA there, so I'll start with them. But don't get your hopes up. The VA records are a mess. Then I'll go meet with his family, see what I can come up with."

Henry pictured the rooms he'd seen on the news, stacked high with VA medical folders. Veterans sometimes had to wait more than a year to be seen by a doctor.

"See what you can do," Henry said. "Because right now, Kelly is our only shot."

CHAPTER 34

SACRAMENTO, CALIFORNIA

Nathaniel lay the phone down slowly, a tremble in his hand.
They had failed. He sat staring at the wall, not really seeing
anything.

How could they have failed? The Shepherd had specifically
requested this target. Nathaniel didn't know why this child was
important, but he knew that he was.

He stared wildly around the room, as if some answer was
going to materialize in front of him. *What am I going to do? I can't
tell him.*

His eyes fell on the crucifix on the far wall. The eyes of Jesus
seemed to stare right into him. *He died for our sins. Perhaps now I
will die for my mistake.*

He shook the thought off as soon as he had it. The Shepherd
had never harmed him, nor anyone he knew of. But there was
something about the man that terrified him nonetheless.

The Shepherd was the reason he had everything he had.
Nathaniel liked to think he had achieved all of his success on his
own. But down deep, he knew the truth. For years he had toiled

away, trying to gather followers, but had met with little success. It was the Shepherd who had shown him the way, who had provided him with the tools he needed to gather his flock. It was only with the Shepherd's help and guidance that Nathaniel had succeeded.

And now Nathaniel had failed him.

He sat in his chair for a while, dreading the phone call he knew he had to make. Finally, the clock on his desk warned him that he couldn't put it off any longer. He picked up the receiver and punched in the numbers. It took him three tries to get the number correct, his hands were shaking so hard.

The Shepherd picked up quickly. "Nathaniel." There was a pause. "What a pleasant surprise."

Nathaniel swallowed, trying to get some moisture into his now dry mouth. "Uh, yes, Shepherd. Um... I have an update." He went silent.

"I'm waiting."

"Uh, yes, um. It seems the latest acquisition did not go as well as planned."

"Exactly how 'unwell' did it go?"

Nathaniel took a breath and then blurted out the details. "They failed to grab the boy. Three members of the team were killed. A fourth was hospitalized."

The Shepherd spoke slowly. "Will they be able to trace it back to you?"

"No. The team was disposed of before they could get any identities on them. The police have nothing."

"How did this happen?"

"I'm sorry, sir. We thought we had enough men. We didn't realize they had an abomination on the security detail."

The Shepherd paused, then sighed, his voice resigned. "Of course they did. I should have warned you of that possibility."

The Shepherd went silent again and Nathaniel racked his brain for something to say, but for the first time in his life, his golden tongue failed him.

Finally, the Shepherd spoke. "No matter. We can still get him."

"But sir, they'll put rings of protection around him now. We'll never get to him."

"Oh, they'll gather the wagons and not let the boy out of his sight, I'm sure. But we'll get him."

Nathaniel waited for the verbal blow to come. "I'm sorry, sir," he said again. "I should have—"

"Don't worry about it. It is not insurmountable, just a slight delay. We can go ahead without the boy and grab him at another time, if necessary."

Nathaniel felt a weight leave his shoulders. He sagged in his chair. "Thank you, sir. We won't let you down again."

"Humans are fallible, my son. Mistakes are made. The point is not to make the same mistakes again. If an opportunity arises to take the boy, you will be better prepared, won't you?"

Nathaniel swallowed, wondering if the threat he heard was real or imagined. "Yes, sir. Of course."

"Good night, Nathaniel." The Shepherd hung up the phone without waiting for Nathaniel's response. But Nathaniel didn't mind; he was still too relieved that the Shepherd wasn't disappointed in him.

Straightening his spine, he dialed Tyrell. "We need to take the boy. If there is any opportunity, you take it."

"Yes, sir."

"Make sure you have enough to take out the abomination. We cannot fail the Shepherd again."

"Yes, sir. I'll need more men."

Nathaniel gripped the phone tightly. "Take all that you need."

CHAPTER 35

Laney ran her hands through her hair. *Crap.*

She was sitting in one of the offices off Dom's living area, staring at all the data on the abductions—again. And nothing new was popping out. Adding in the information on Danny and Max only seemed to make it worse.

She thought back to her conversation with Kati. Were Max's abilities, if they were even real, related?

And if Laney hadn't known about them, how on earth could anyone else? Frustration welled up in her. She wanted to hit something.

Jake had left early this morning to go speak with the VA in Stamford. She had thought about going with him, but she wasn't quite ready to leave Max and Danny. She glanced at the clock; she had expected Jake to call by now.

She looked back out into the living area. Danny and Max were playing *Skylanders*. Max's face was lit up and Danny smiled whenever Max looked at him. But every time Max looked away, Danny's smile disappeared.

Maddox caught her gaze. He eased off the couch behind them and headed toward her. Laney swirled her chair toward him. "Hey," she said as he stepped in.

"Hey, back. How's it going?"

Laney shook her head. "It's not. I can't find a link between Danny or Max and these other kidnappings. I think we're going down the wrong road. Can you think of anything about the attack that might give us another angle?"

Maddox shook his head, taking a seat. "Not really. I mean, I was pinned to a wall by a van for most of it."

Laney cringed. "Ouch."

Maddox just shrugged. "Been through worse."

"Did they know you were a nephilim? Is that why they took you out first?"

"I don't think so. Honestly, I think they aimed the van for me because I was the biggest guard. They looked shocked when it didn't kill me."

Laney thought back to all the other abductions, and her frustration built again. "But see, even that doesn't fit. All the other abductions were, for lack of a better word, subtle: in and out, no witnesses. This was a gun battle in the middle of the street."

"But Danny and Max are different from those other kids. They always have security."

"True, but why target them at all? Neither is a Fallen or nephilim. Apart from Danny's intelligence, they're just normal kids."

Maddox glanced back into the other room, his eyes falling on Kati. She was in the kitchen mixing up a batch of cookies.

Laney leaned forward. "She told me."

Maddox's eyes grew large. "She did?"

Laney nodded. "Yeah."

Maddox's shoulders sagged. "Good. I didn't feel right telling you, but I'm glad you know."

Laney's gaze drifted to Kati, who was now scooping cookie batter onto a baking tray. Her normally upbeat expression was gone, her face was drawn, and there were bags under her eyes. Laney realized she'd even lost some weight. Damn.

"Do you think that Max was the target? That it has to do with his abilities?" Maddox asked.

Laney shook her head. "I don't see how. No one knew about his abilities."

Maddox stood. "I know. But it seems like an awfully big coincidence."

Laney sighed. "I hate coincidences."

"Me too," Maddox muttered as he left.

Max's laugh pulled Laney's gaze back out the door. Max stood in his monkey pajamas, a giant grin on his face as he maniacally pushed the buttons on the video controller. With a yell he threw up his hands and did a little victory dance.

Was it even possible? He looked so young, so innocent, so happy. *Wouldn't psychic ability make him more, I don't know, serious? Mature?* He looked just like any other five-year-old.

Laney flipped through the notes she'd made on the missing kids. None had reported psychic abilities. But didn't Dom mention something about including psychic abilities in their search?

Of course, the science on psychic ability didn't really hold up. *So says the reincarnation of Helen of Troy*, Laney thought wryly.

Three hours later and one phone call from Jake and she was no closer to any answers.

Jen stepped in. "Did Jake find anything?" she asked without preamble.

Laney turned her chair toward Jen, who'd already taken a seat. "Um, not really. Just that Kelly's family said he came home a changed man. He became really religious."

"How religious?"

"He was convinced the end of days was near."

Jen raised an eyebrow. "Does the family know where he is now?"

"No. Jake showing up was the first they'd heard of him in months. And Jake got the feeling that frankly, they'd rather *not* hear from him until he lets go of his new religious conversion."

"So we have nothing."

"Not necessarily," Laney said. "I'm trying the religion angle. A lot of soldiers seem to find religion in the service, especially if they've seen combat."

"No atheists in a foxhole?"

"Exactly. So I've been trying to find religious groups that focus on former military."

"Maybe those that have an end of days theme."

Laney nodded. "I'm working on it."

Laney caught sight of Kati and gave her a smile. Kati smiled back before heading to Dom's kitchen area and pulling some snacks out of the closet. But every few seconds she would glance over to where Max was, her gaze worried.

"Have you talked to her?" Laney asked, nudging her chin toward Kati.

"A little," Jen said. "She's scared. She doesn't know what to do."

"She thinks Max is in danger here. That she'd be safer elsewhere."

"Do you think she's right?"

Laney's eyes traveled to Max, who was trying to tackle Maddox to the ground. Maddox picked him up and tossed him onto the couch.

Laney smiled as Max's giggles rang out. How could anyone want to hurt that little boy? "I don't know. I can't see why they'd be after Max. I mean, he's five."

"And Danny's older than any of the other missing kids. But he makes more sense. I mean, he's Henry's son. He's brilliant."

"But grabbing either of them would throw all of us in a panic." Laney gave a mirthless laugh. "I mean, look at us. We're all hunkered down here, guarding them, as if the two blast doors wouldn't keep someone out."

"So you think someone tried to grab them just to throw us off our game?"

Laney ran her hands through her hair. "I don't know. I mean, does anyone even know we're looking for these kids?"

"Well, the person who was watching Northgram sure knows."

Laney nodded. "True, but we think that was in the works well before any of this started happening. Still, I guess someone might have picked up on our involvement. We haven't exactly been covering our tracks."

Jen glanced over her shoulder at Max before looking back at Laney. "It can't be Max. I mean, his most unusual trait is his imaginary friends."

Laney paused. She knew she didn't have the right to reveal Max's abilities yet. Not until she spoke with Kati. So she shrugged, trying to keep her voice nonchalant. "Don't all kids have imaginary friends at his age?"

Jen smiled. "I have no idea. The last time I was around kids Max's age I *was* Max's age."

Laney smiled. "So what about Danny?"

Jen traced an imaginary shape on the table. "I've been thinking about that. Do you think maybe someone thought Danny was Henry's biological son?"

Laney glanced over at the teenager. He'd grown in the time she'd know him, but he was nowhere near Henry's height. Henry's hair was darker than Danny's, his cheekbones more pronounced.

"I don't see how," she said. "They don't really look alike. Besides, Danny's IQ made him well known even before Henry. Unless these guys did zero background, they'd have to know they aren't related."

"So we don't know who they were after. It could have been either of them."

Laney's eyes traveled back to the boys. "Which means they're both still in danger."

CHAPTER 36

The New Age music drifted toward Gerard as he stepped out of the house onto the patio. On the other side of the pool, candles burned within the white-draped pergola. A muscular shirtless man stood next to the massage table, working the kinks out of Elisabeta Roccorio's back. White marble glinted back at Gerard from all surfaces, including the towering Aphrodite at the end of the pool, water pouring from the pitcher in her arms.

Gerard walked around the pool. He kept his eyes down as he approached, noting that Elisabeta hadn't worn anything for the massage. A flare of jealousy sparked through him, but he tamped it down.

The masseur caught sight of him and whispered into Elisabeta's ear, then helped her up and into a white robe. With a flick of her hand, she dismissed the masseur, who headed back toward the house with a quick nod to Gerard as he passed.

Elisabeta took a seat in one of the lounge chairs next to the pool. Her dark hair contrasted with the white surroundings, as did her olive complexion. A fact he knew Elisabeta was well aware of.

Her small dark eyes flicked toward Gerard. "I trust you have a good reason for interrupting me?"

Gerard bowed his head. "Yes. We've discovered a problem."

She arched a perfectly sculpted eyebrow. "Problem?"

"Some of our children are going missing."

She frowned. "Has another group of our brethren popped up?"

"I don't think so. The children. They are young. Very young."

"How young?"

"All are under ten."

Elisabeta's gaze cut to him, her voice low. "They are potentials?"

Gerard nodded, noting the anger cross Elisabeta's face.

She sat back. "We cannot allow the potentials to be harmed. Not until we know which one is the key. Is there any trace of them?"

"The children have disappeared. No bodies have been recovered. I believe a human group is responsible for their abduction."

"To what end?"

"I do not know."

Elisabeta fell silent. Gerard stared across the water, knowing his silence was all she wanted from him at this moment. A few minutes passed before she spoke.

"The children need to be found. They need to be protected."

"I can take a group—"

"No. We can't trust our brethren with this knowledge. They would want to know why."

"What about the Council? Can we use them?"

Elisabeta shook her head. "No. I am not ready to reveal anything to them either. And they would dig until they learned why the children are important."

"We could always just kill whoever the Council sends."

Elisabeta smiled. "If only it were that easy. But no—the

Council is paperwork and trails. Someone would know. Someone would investigate. And they need to stay in the dark until the last."

She was right, of course. The Council was like a dog with a bone when they caught the scent of something. "How then would you like me to proceed?"

"We need the enemy of my enemy."

"I don't understand."

Elisabeta smiled again and stood, letting her robe gape open. She walked to Gerard and ran her hand up his chest. "So handsome. But not very bright, are you?"

As she walked past him toward the house, she called over her shoulder. "I need you to take a meeting."

CHAPTER 37

BALTIMORE, MARYLAND

Laney sat in Henry's office, going through information on cults and religious groups in the United States. She'd needed to get out of the bomb shelter. She just couldn't focus with everyone around.

Not that they were interrupting her. But she kept getting up to make sure Max and Danny were all right. Finally she told herself it would be quicker if she just worked elsewhere. So she and Henry had traded places so she could get some work done.

Of course, that thought had proven to be ridiculously optimistic. Laney shook her head for the umpteenth time as she stared at the information on the latest group she'd brought up: Heaven's Gate. The two founders, Bonnie Nettles and Marshall Applewhite, believed they were the two witnesses spoken of in the Book of Revelations. They somehow mixed their belief in an upcoming apocalypse with a belief in resurrection through suicide.

Oh, and then a spacecraft was going to take their essence to the next level of development. Applewhite convinced thirty-eight members of his group that he was right, and they all committed suicide on March 19, 2007.

Laney couldn't help but think of the similarities to other groups who argued that humanity was broken up into different time periods of development: the Mayans, theosophists, Christianity, even Cayce mentioned different root races dominating at different times. But was any of this related to the missing kids? Was she going off on wild tangents?

"Hey, beautiful."

Laney looked up with a smile as Jake walked across the room. She got up and walked over to him. "I didn't hear you."

"Ah, good. My ninja skills are still operating at peak efficiency." He gave her a long kiss.

Laney leaned into him. "I've missed you."

He leaned his chin on her head, holding her close, and spoke softly. "How about after all this winds down, we go take another little trip, just the two of us? Maybe the Greek isles this time?"

Laney smiled as she imagined lounging on a white sandy beach with Jake, not a care in the world. She leaned back to look into his face. "That sounds perfect."

He leaned down and kissed her again.

Laney sighed when he pulled away. "Things *will* wind down, won't they?"

"God, I hope so."

Laney held Jake's hand and led him over to the couch. He took a seat next to her, angling his body to face hers. "So, how many crazy religious groups are there?"

When they spoke earlier, Laney had said she was going to research any religious groups that might attract someone like Kelly.

She sighed. "Hundreds."

Jake's eyes grew wide. "You're kidding."

Laney shook her head. "I really wish I was. And that's not even counting the more established religions that warn of the end of days."

"Any of them more likely than the others to attract military types?"

Laney nodded. "Some. But we're still numbering in the hundreds. And there's still no guarantee those are the groups we're looking for."

"So where are we?"

Laney shook her head. "No closer than we were before."

"Well, I might have something. Kelly went over to Afghanistan with a few guys from his high school."

"They were friends?"

Jake hedged. "Apparently, they *used* to be friends. But Kelly's conversion seems to have put a strain on those friendships."

"Do they know anything?"

"He came home with them but only stayed in town for a few weeks."

"They know where he went?"

"Somewhere out west. That help any?"

Laney groaned. "Oh, sure. That knocks about three hundred churches off the list, not including, of course, the internet sites."

Jake leaned over and took Laney's hand, his eyebrows knitting together. "What's going on, Laney? This isn't you. You see a challenge and run for it. So what's different this time?"

Laney sighed. "I don't know. I guess it's the kids. I can't get their pictures out of my head. And now all I can think about is how lucky we are that Max or Danny or both of them aren't part of that group. And the end result of it all is, I can't seem to focus."

"But Max and Danny *aren't* part of that group. And we *will* find those kids. We'll get them back."

Laney nodded, her mind going to places she didn't like. In graduate school, she'd taken a class on child predators. At the time, she'd been able to look at the topic clinically. But now, with real children in danger, it was proving incredibly difficult to maintain that professional distance. And everything she learned about predators was playing in her mind on a nauseating reel.

She closed her eyes, trying to banish the images. When she opened her eyes again to look at Jake, her voice was whisper quiet. "But even if those kids are alive, what shape are they going to be in when we get to them?"

CHAPTER 38

SACRAMENTO, CALIFORNIA

Nathaniel walked down the hall. They would shift their base of operations in a few days. He took a deep breath, sensing the fulfillment that was less than a week away.

The tune from a children's show wafted down the hallway toward him. Steeling himself, he opened the door. Over a dozen children ranging in age from one to ten were scattered around the room. The oldest, a boy with black hair, caught sight of him first and turned his back. Nathaniel ignored the slight. The boy was an abomination. He didn't matter.

On the far side of the room, Zachariah was playing with the one-year-old twins. The little boys were laughing as Zachariah made a teddy bear dance for them.

"Zachariah," Nathaniel said sharply.

The smile immediately dropped from Zachariah's face. The twins caught sight of Nathaniel and clung to Zachariah, who whispered something to them.

A girl of around eight came over to take care of the boys as

Zachariah made his way to Nathaniel. He stopped directly in front of him. "Yes, Father?"

"There have been complaints that the children are making too much noise at night. It is your responsibility to keep them quiet. If you cannot handle it, I will replace you with someone that can."

Fear flashed across Zachariah's face and he opened his mouth to say something before thinking better of it. Shutting his mouth, he composed himself, then spoke. "I'm sorry, Father. Some of the children were scared. Are there any more coming?"

Distracted by a five-year-old painting a rainbow, Nathaniel didn't answer right away. The child looked downright angelic with her long blond hair, porcelain white skin, and bright blue eyes. As he gazed at her, Nathaniel found it almost impossible to believe that she was an agent of evil.

"Just one," he said, his eyes still on the child. Then he turned back to Zachariah. "Can you handle that?"

Zachariah nodded. "Yes, of course. It's just that, whenever a new one arrives it upsets them a little." His words came out in a rush. "But it will be all right tonight. I'll keep them quiet."

Nathaniel sensed doubt in the boy. His anger, always just below the surface when he saw his son, surged to the forefront, and his voice lashed out. "Are you questioning God's plan?"

Zachariah took a step back. "No, Father."

"We do not get to question God. If God acts, then His act is justified. If God instructs us to act, then the act is justified. Who are we to question God? To judge God? Who are you? Do you think to know more than God himself?"

Zachariah shook his head quickly, taking a step back. "No, sir. Of course not, sir."

"There is no confusion. We may not understand God's plan, but we *do* need to follow it. We are His followers. We submit entirely to Him."

Zachariah nodded. "Yes, sir."

Nathaniel glanced around the room again. "They are not chil-

R.D. BRADY

dren, Zachariah. Do not get attached to them. You know what they are."

"Yes, Father. They're abominations. Just like me."

Nathaniel narrowed his eyes, trying to determine if Zachariah was being sarcastic. He shook his head. *No.* Zachariah knew what he was. He knew his place.

Nathaniel nodded. "See that you remember that."

Then he left the room, shutting the door behind him. Even if Zachariah was getting attached to them, it wouldn't matter. His fate was sealed, just as was theirs.

CHAPTER 39

BALTIMORE, MARYLAND

Henry stood with his arms crossed, watching Danny and Max run across the field just behind Dom's. The wind blew furiously, pushing and pulling the multicolored dragon kite across the sky.

Danny looked over at him and smiled. Henry returned the smile. But as soon as Danny looked away, the smile dropped from Henry's face. He resumed his inspection of the land surrounding them.

Jen, Laney, Kati, Maddox, Patrick, and Jake were also scattered around the boys, making a circle of protection. More guards were positioned farther away, and Henry had even ordered two snipers in the trees. He wasn't taking any chance with the boys' safety.

The adults were trying to act like they were having a good time, but their faces were strained, worried. The boys had been desperate to get out of the bunker and run around. It was a good idea, but even with all the precautions, Henry still worried. They were all still worried.

Henry's phone beeped, and he pulled it out of his pocket. The text was from Jen:

Quit worrying. They're fine.

A second text came in:

That means smile.

He looked over at her and she raised an eyebrow.

He smiled.

The wind died down and the boys' kite dropped. Maddox walked over to help them get it back in the air again. Henry's phone rang.

He shook his head with a smile when he answered. "I *am* smiling. See?"

He looked over but Jen wasn't on her phone.

"Actually, I can't see you right now, but I'm hoping we can change that."

There was something familiar about the voice, but Henry couldn't place it. He glanced at the number. He was unfamiliar with that as well. "Who is this?"

"You know me as Gerard Thompson."

Henry went still. Gerard Thompson had been an assistant to Sebastian Flourent. Turning his back to the group, Henry anxiously scanned the trees. "What do you want?"

"I heard about your little problem with the missing kids."

"And you've called to tell me where you've taken them?"

Gerard laughed. "Ah, what a great sense of humor. No, I do not have them. And neither do any of my brothers."

"Why should I believe you?"

"Because I'm telling the truth. I don't have them. And you don't think I do either. But I believe I may know where they are."

Henry stared over at Jen, who looked back at him with concern. He turned his back so that she couldn't read his expression. "Okay. So tell me."

"I'm afraid I need to do that in person. Which means you'll have to meet me."

"Why can't you just send me your information?"

"And have that super-genius of yours track me down? No, I don't think so. Face to face or nothing."

Henry scoffed. "Well I guess I'll have to choose nothing."

Gerard's tone was serious. "Henry, I'm not joking. I know where those kids may be. And I will offer you that information."

"In exchange for what?"

"The promise that you will see that no harm comes to the children."

"Why do you care?"

"Let's just say that in this situation we have similar goals."

"How did you even know they were missing, if you're not responsible?" Henry asked.

"Why, because you told us, of course. You, Ms. McPhearson, and Mr. Rogan."

"The Fallen across the street from Northgram. He was yours."

"I neither confirm nor deny that."

"Did you kill him?"

Gerard paused. "Hypothetically speaking, I could see how someone would want to make sure that their own spy didn't fall into enemy hands."

Henry shook his head in disgust. "And why me? Why am I the one who gets the pleasure of your call?"

Gerard chuckled. "Well, you're the only one I can trust, now aren't you? Delaney McPhearson could control me with that stupid little ring of hers. From what I know of Jennifer Witt and Maddox, they'd just try to take my head off. And none of you will allow a human to meet with me alone."

"So you want *me* to meet with you alone."

"Of course. And if I see or sense any of the others nearby, you'll never find those kids."

Henry watched Danny and Max play in the field. Jen narrowed her eyes and started heading toward him.

He sighed. "Fine. When and where?"

"I'll text you a location in two hours."

CHAPTER 40

"You can't be serious," Jen said, her arms crossed as she sat at the granite island in Dom's kitchen.

Henry sighed. He'd waited until they'd returned to the bunker to tell them about Gerard's offer. "Look, I know. But if there's a chance, I have to take it."

"Henry, the last time you were near Gerard, it didn't go that well," Laney said.

"They tortured you," Jake declared bluntly.

"Gee, I'd forgotten. Thanks for the reminder." Henry shook his head. "Look, I know it's a risk. But we're at a dead end. We don't know where the kids are and we don't have any leads. And if Gerard knows something, we need to know it too."

"We're whittling down the religious groups," Jen said. "With a little time—"

"Some of those kids have been missing for a month," Henry replied. "They don't have time."

"He can't be trusted," Jake said.

"No, he can't," Henry said. "But there was something in his voice. I think this is on the up and up."

"We don't even know if those kids are still alive," Laney said quietly.

Henry knew how much that thought consumed her. He took her hand. "But we need to act like they are until we know for sure that they aren't. And that means doing everything we can to find them—including meeting with Gerard."

"Fine. But if you're going, I'm going," Jen said.

"No," Henry replied. "Gerard was clear on that point. I'm the only one he trusts to not try and kill him or control him in a meeting."

"Apparently he's not stupid," Laney mumbled.

Jake grunted. "Then we're putting a tracker on you. I'll stay back but be close enough—"

"No," Henry said, more forcefully this time. "Look, I know it's dangerous, but it's a chance we have to take. It's a chance *I* have to take. And I'm not risking those kids lives by breaking Gerard's terms."

Jen glared at him. "You're not going in there alone."

Henry sighed. He knew that tone; she wasn't going to back down. He shouldn't have told them. He should have just met with Gerard and then told them about it afterward. But it was too late for that now. If Gerard had information, they needed it.

He sighed. "Okay. You can come. But you guys have to stay back."

"Deal," Jake said. "When's the meet?"

"He's going to text me with a location in three hours."

CHAPTER 41

Henry stared at the building in disbelief. *You have got to be kidding me.*

He looked down at his phone again—the phone in which he'd disabled the GPS so the others couldn't follow him. *Yup. This is it.*

After Henry had snuck off his estate, Gerard had sent him to three separate locations. At the first one, Henry had been required to get out of the car while two humans searched it. At the second two, he'd sat and waited in the car until a new message came in, sending him somewhere else. And now he sat in the parking lot of the fourth location, his disbelief growing. A giant mouse towered over the front of the building.

He was at Chuck E. Cheese's. *Where a kid can be a kid.*

A family of six headed to the front door. The kids excitedly ran ahead of the parents, who dragged their feet, looking resigned to their fate. A mom and two kids were walking out as the family of six walked in. Both kids were crying, and one was being held over the shoulder of the very tired-looking mother.

Henry typed into his phone: I'm here. Even as he sent the message, he hoped Gerard would send him to another location.

The response was short in coming. Back right hand corner of the dining area.

Blowing out a breath, Henry stepped out of the car. The air had gotten a little cooler, but he took off his fleece anyway. He didn't want Gerard to think he was concealing a weapon and cause a scene.

Henry crossed the parking lot and opened the front door. Noise accosted him immediately: games, yelling kids, and music. *How can anyone think with all this?*

He got into line behind the family of six. Another family was ahead of them. Henry glanced around and realized that he was the only adult not attached to a child. *Crap.*

He looked past the family ahead of him at the pimply teenager letting people in. "Are you here for a birthday party?" the teenager asked the father in front.

"Yes. Eddie's."

The kid nodded, grabbed a stamp, and dutifully stamped the hand of each person in the group. He did the same for the next family, although apparently they were just here for the fun of it.

When Henry reached the front of the line, the kid gawked up at him. "Um, are you here for a party?"

"Yes. My nephew. Eddie."

The kid grabbed a stamp and placed it on the back of Henry's hand. Then he waved him in, having already lost interest in him.

Henry headed toward the back corner. Kids ran past him. He spotted Gerard sitting at a booth in the back, near the birthday area. As Henry wound his way around excited children and stressed parents, he thanked God that Danny had never asked to be taken here.

Gerard stood as Henry approached. "Henry. Good to see you."

Henry nodded and took the chair across from him. "Why on earth are we meeting here?"

Gerard looked around with a shrug, resuming his seat. "Why

not? Lots of kids. Lots of innocents. Lots of noise. No one will notice us, and all these kids will make sure you don't make a scene."

"I don't think *my* making a scene is the issue."

Gerard smiled. "Well, *I'm* certainly not going to do anything. Each of these parents has a cell phone ready to record their little darling. Or us. We're both protected."

Henry nodded. "Fine. So tell me, where are the kids?"

Gerard sighed. "Straight to business." He pulled a file from the chair next to him. "We don't have an exact location, but I have background on one of the key players in this little adventure."

Henry took the file and flipped through it. It was a deep background check on Phillip Northgram. "We've already spoken with him. How does this help us find the kids?"

Gerard took a sip from his cup and then stood. "Read it. You'll see."

"That's it? You're leaving?"

"I've done what I planned. And you and I both know that Jake Rogan is undeniably scouring the city looking for you."

Henry had to admit that that was probably true. It was why he had disconnected the GPS on his car and phone and told everyone the meet was set for an hour from now. "I still don't get why you're doing this."

"And you don't need to. For once, we are not at cross purposes. Let's just leave it at that." And with that, Gerard headed for the exit.

Henry watched him leave, his eyes narrowed. Whatever the reason, Gerard helping them couldn't be good. Obviously he wanted the children protected, or at least not in the hands of whoever had them. But why? What was Gerard's plan for them?

Henry shook his head as he stood. It didn't matter. At least not right now. Right now, finding the kids was all that mattered. And if a little confab with the devil's envoy was what was required to secure their safety, then so be it.

They'd worry about what the devil wanted after they got the kids back.

CHAPTER 42

K ati walked around the island in Dom's kitchen. Dom offered her a bag of cookies. "Chocolate chip?"

She smiled. "No, thanks."

He smiled and tottered off. Kati watched him go, a reluctant grin on her face. He'd been a happy distraction and, strange as it sounds, a comfort these last few months. But the smile soon slid from her face. In the last year, Max's life had been in danger twice —and so had hers. And each time it was because they were close to Chandler Group activities or personnel.

She hated thinking that. It felt traitorous. But the Fallen kept coming for Laney and Henry. And people were getting caught in the crossfire. And the last time, she'd nearly lost Max.

Kati wrapped her arms around herself. She wasn't cut out for this type of life. Laney, Jen, Jake, Henry—they all seemed to be able to take the violence in stride. But not Kati. She hadn't had a good night's sleep in about a year.

Actually, you've slept better since Maddox moved in. Well, that was true; she had to admit her subconscious was right. But she still wasn't sleeping as well as she had before all this began.

Max's laugh grabbed her attention. He was playing *Skylanders* with Danny. He looked so young. Her heart caught. *And he is going to have a chance to get older. I promise.*

Everyone else was up at Henry's office. Everyone except one. She glanced at where Maddox was sitting.

Kati stood up, giving herself a shake. *Okay. Let's do this.* She walked over to Maddox.

He looked up. "Everything okay?"

"Yes. Um, I was just thinking, maybe we should spend the night at the cottage."

Maddox's eyebrows raised. "Why?"

Kati swallowed. "I just think it would be good for Max to sleep in his own bed—above ground. Do you think it's safe?"

Maddox nodded, speaking slowly. "Yes, *I* do. But why do *you* think it's safe?"

"You're good at your job. And Henry has the whole estate locked down. I just think it would be good for Max."

Maddox stood up and looked down at Kati. His voice was low. "You and Max are not a *job*."

Kati's head jerked up. "I know. I know that."

Maddox looked down at her, his eyes searching for something. She wasn't sure what.

Finally, he nodded. "Okay. Let's go."

CHAPTER 43

As soon as Henry climbed into his car, he opened the file on his lap and scanned the first page quickly. It was just background on Northgram.

We already know all this, he thought as he read. *Why would Gerard think this matters?*

He scanned the second page. They had all this information as well. What the hell? He flipped to the next page. *This is a huge waste of time. Damn it. I never should have—*

He stopped in mid-rant as his eyes locked on a line halfway down the third page. He immediately fumbled for his phone, dialing quickly.

Jake answered almost immediately. "Henry, where the hell—"

Henry cut him off. "Northgram had a first wife."

"What?" Jake said.

"Phillip Northgram. He's on his second marriage, not his first. He paid to have all traces of the first marriage wiped. Apparently they got married early, right out of college."

"Who's the first wife?"

"Her name's Linda."

"Hold on," Jake said. Henry could hear Jake yelling at someone in the background to run a check on Linda Northgram.

Henry drummed his fingers on the dash.

Jake came back on the line. "There's nothing on that name. What's her maiden name?"

Henry scanned the sheet. "Grayston."

"I'll call you back." Jake hung up.

Henry stared at the phone, then dropped it in the passenger seat. He started the car and slowly pulled out. As he headed back to the estate, his mind was a million miles away. He kept glancing over at the phone, willing it to ring. A few minutes later, it did.

Henry pulled over. "What have you got?"

"Linda Grayston, age fifty-two. Currently residing in Happy Meadows Sanitarium."

"*Sanitarium?* How long has she been there?"

"Ten years."

Henry felt his new hope begin to ebb. She'd been locked up for a decade. How could she be related to any of this? "What's she there for?"

"She's a paranoid schizophrenic."

Henry stared at the folder on the passenger seat. "What the hell?"

CHAPTER 44

Kati watched from the doorway as Maddox tucked the blankets around Max. It had taken them a while to leave Dom's. Max had wanted to stay and finish his game that never seemed to end. Kati had finally just turned the machine off. Max had then been angry and refused to leave, so Maddox had just scooped him up and headed out.

Maddox had carried Max the whole way back to Kati's cottage, and he'd fallen asleep en route. Now Kati's heart skipped as Maddox pushed Max's hair out of his face and placed a kiss on his forehead.

When Maddox stood up and joined Kati in the hall, he said, "I couldn't find Lamby. Did you bring him?"

Kati's hand flew to her mouth. "Oh, no. I must have left him at Dom's. Max will be so upset if he wakes up and realizes Lamby's not here. Can you go get him?"

"Do you think you'll be okay here for a few minutes?"

Kati nodded. "Yeah. I even saw Cleo prowling around out back. We'll be fine."

Maddox studied her for a moment. "Okay. I'll be back." He headed down the stairs.

Kati waited until she heard the front door close, then she sprinted for Max's room. She ran to the bed and carefully bundled her son into her arms. He mumbled but didn't wake.

Moving as fast as she could, she made it down the stairs. It was a struggle to open the front door while holding Max, but she managed it. And she nearly let out a screech when she did: Cleo sat directly on the opposite side of the door.

"Oh, Cleo, please move," Kati begged.

Cleo stared at her for a moment before stepping aside. Kati breathed a sigh of relief as she stepped past the cat. *I'll have to put Max in the car and then come back to close the door,* she thought.

But behind her she heard the door creak. She glanced back. Cleo had the door handle in her mouth and was pulling it shut.

"Thank you," Kati whispered.

Her heart pounding, she struggled to move quickly under Max's weight. When had he gotten so heavy? She hugged him to her. He was growing up so fast. *And I mean to see that he continues to.*

She leaned him against the car, again struggling to hold him while opening the back door. Then she maneuvered him into his booster seat and quietly buckled him in.

"Mom?" Max's sleepy eyes watched her. "What are you doing?"

"It's okay. We're taking a little ride. Go back to sleep."

He nodded, and Kati could tell he was already drifting off. She looked around for Cleo, but the big cat had already disappeared somewhere. So she eased the car door shut and ran around to the driver's seat.

Buckling herself in, she glanced back at Max. Sound asleep. She let out a breath. *Stage one complete.*

As she pulled the car away from the curb and headed for the main gate, she rehearsed the words in her mind. A guard stepped out of the booth as she pulled up to the gate.

"Hi, Ms. Simmons." He glanced in the back seat and saw Max asleep. He lowered his voice. "Where are you two off to?"

She put a finger to her lips and waved him closer, whispering. "Just running some errands."

"Are you sure that's all right?" He looked uncertain.

Kati nodded. "Oh, yes. They found the men who were responsible. And they weren't after Max. It was Danny."

The man still looked uncertain, so Kati pushed a little harder. "I really need to get going."

He nodded and hit the button that operated the gate. "Well, have a good time."

"Thanks." Kati let out a breath as she drove off the property, but she was careful to keep her speed low until the guard was out of view.

Then she hit the gas.

CHAPTER 45

Maddox headed back to Kati and Max, the beloved stuffed lamb clutched in his hand. He shook his head. A year ago he was fighting for his life; now he was on stuffed animal retrieval.

But Kati was right. If Max woke up and Lamby wasn't there, there would be waterworks.

He smiled as he saw the cottage up ahead. All the lights were off, except for the front hall. It was funny. With Kati and Max, he felt like he had found a home—a family—for the first time in a long time.

He pictured Max asleep in his bed and imagined Lamby curled up in his arms. A feeling of contentment drifted through him. How crazy that such a small act—a little boy sleeping with a toy—could bring such peace. But Maddox knew it was more than that. Max was a sign of the goodness in this world. The innocence in it.

He climbed the steps and quietly let himself in the door. There was no sound from upstairs. *Maybe Kati feel asleep, too.* He hoped she did. She needed to get much more sleep than she had been lately.

Maddox took the stairs two at a time and headed to Max's room, expecting to see Kati asleep in the chair next to the bed. Slowly, he pushed the door open.

The chair was empty. And so was the bed.

Maddox went still. He turned and strode toward Kati's room, his heart beginning to pound. *She just brought Max to sleep with her,* he rationalized.

But the house was quiet. Too quiet.

He pushed open Kati's door. Her bed was empty too.

"Damn it," Maddox cursed. He turned and ran down the steps. He was out the door and on the sidewalk in seconds. He scanned the cars parked there. Kati's was gone.

He yanked his cell phone out and dialed her number. Kati's familiar ring tone rang from back in the house.

He ran to the front gate at top speed, not even bothering to hide his ability. The guard was startled, and clumsily got to his feet when Maddox appeared in the doorway.

"Kati," Maddox barked. "Did she leave the estate?"

The man nodded. "Uh, yeah. About ten minutes ago."

Maddox stepped into the small booth, crowding the man. "You *let* her out?"

"Sh-she said she had some errands to run. No one said she couldn't leave the estate."

Maddox's heart was now at a fevered pitch. He knew she was scared. He should have seen this coming. And the guard was right: no one had said Kati couldn't leave the estate. All their focus had been on keeping people *out* of the estate, not in it.

He took a step back, his eyes going past the man to the Chandler Jeep outside. "I need the keys to that Jeep. And contact Jake. Tell him Kati left with Max and that I'm going after them. Which direction did they go?"

The man fished the keys out of his pocket and handed them over. "Right. Toward the highway."

Without a word, Maddox turned on his heel and sprinted for the car. The engine roared to life and Maddox peeled out of the parking lot. He turned right and slammed on the gas, praying that he was the only one who'd noticed that Kati and Max had left.

CHAPTER 46

L aney walked out the back door of the Chandler main house.
Henry had taken off to Happy Meadows with Jen about a
half hour ago. Hopefully Northgram's first wife could offer them
something.

Laney had wanted to go with him, but she thought it would be
better if she stayed with Kati and Max. She was worried about
how Kati was handling all this. And she was hoping she could talk
Max and Kati into sleeping in the cottage tonight.

Laney pulled out her cell phone and called Kati, but her call
was sent right to voicemail. *That's odd*, she thought. She hung up
without leaving a message.

She called Dom, who picked up on the first ring. "Hey, Laney."

Laney smiled. "Hey, Dom. I'm trying to reach Kati."

"Oh, Kati decided to sleep at the cottage tonight."

"She did?"

"Yeah. She thought Max might want to be in his own bed."

"Oh. Well, that's good."

"Yeah, um, but maybe you guys could come by for breakfast?"

Laney smiled, knowing Dom had liked having everybody

around these last few weeks. "I think we can arrange that. I'll call you tonight." They said goodbye and Laney hung up.

So, Kati's at the cottage. Laney smiled. *That's a good sign.*

With a little more energy in her step, Laney turned onto the path that led to Sharecroppers Lane. A few minutes later, she stepped out onto the sidewalk and headed for Kati's cottage.

The door to the cottage was wide open.

Laney stopped in shock. She turned, her eyes scanning the street. Kati's car was gone.

Her cell phone rang. She yanked it open. "Hello?"

Maddox's voice was urgent. "Kati took Max. I'm leaving the estate now. She was heading for the highway. I'm going to head east."

Laney had started running the moment Maddox began speaking. Now she yanked the door to her car open and hopped into the driver's seat. Quickly turning it on, she threw it into gear, pulled a tight turn, and gunned it for the main gate. "Then I'll take west."

CHAPTER 47

K ati glanced in her rearview mirror: still no one behind her. She eased off the accelerator, but her heart still raced. She felt like she was doing something wrong even though she knew she was doing the right thing for Max.

The only way to keep him safe is to get him away from all of that.

She glanced back at her son, who was still sleeping peacefully. Her heart felt like it was going to burst. She loved this little boy more than anything in the whole world. The idea of him being in the line of fire was just too difficult to contemplate.

The rest of them didn't understand. They didn't have kids. She pictured Henry. Well, he probably understood. And Kati was willing to bet that if there was a way to keep Danny out of all this, Henry would grab it with both hands.

Headlights flashed on her car as another car entered the highway behind her. Kati's heart rate tripled. She moved into the right lane to let them pass. The man in the white Toyota didn't even glance at her as he picked up speed and raced off.

Kati let out a shaky breath. *I am not cut out for this cloak-and-dagger stuff*, she thought. Every nerve ending she had was taut.

She shook out her right arm, then her left, and rolled her

182

shoulders, trying to ease some of the tension out of them. Lights appeared behind her, farther back down the highway this time.

Kati focused on the road, but her gaze kept straying to the lights behind her. The car was getting closer.

She picked up just a little bit of speed.

Still the car closed the gap, and as it got closer, she could see that it was an SUV. Her heart sank when she recognized it: one of the security Jeeps from the estate.

Kati gripped the steering wheel. *Doesn't matter. They have no right to stop me.*

Her decision made, she ignored the headlights and kept her eyes on the road ahead. The Jeep came up behind her and then changed lanes and came up abreast of her. And even though she told herself not to look, she couldn't help herself. She glanced over.

Maddox glared back at her.

Oh, no. She knew there was no way he was going to let her go. She pictured the two of them driving neck and neck for miles until one of them ran out of gas. Because that was exactly what Maddox would do. And in fact, if he ran out of gas first, he'd probably flag down some poor schmuck, throw the guy out of his own car, and continue the chase.

She gritted her teeth, her hopes of escape dimming. *Damn.*

She put on her blinker and took the ramp leading to the rest area.

CHAPTER 48

As Maddox followed Kati's car into the rest area, he tried to tamp down his anger. There were two other cars in the parking lot, but no one in them. He didn't sense any nephilim nearby.

He pulled into a parking spot a few down from Kati and took a moment to breathe deep and try to keep the anger and fear he felt from spilling over. Then he opened the door and stalked over to her car.

Kati got out and waited for him on the sidewalk. Seeing her there in the dim light, her shoulders hunched, looking terrified, brought all his fear right back to the surface.

"What the hell were you thinking?" he demanded, towering over her.

She flinched. "Max isn't safe there. I need to get him away. And you would never agree to taking him away."

He stared at her, dumbfounded. "How the hell do you know that? You never even asked me."

Kati's mouth fell open for a moment before she shut it. "You would consider that?"

Maddox ran a hand through his hair to keep from shaking her. "Kati, there's not a lot I wouldn't do to keep you two safe."

Kati looked up at him for a long moment. Then she looked away. "I'm sorry, Maddox. It's just—all I could think about was keeping Max safe. And I thought getting away would do that."

Maddox let out a breath as a tear rolled down Kati's cheek. Such a simple little thing, but that tear managed to wipe away all his anger, leaving only his fear and frustration. "You need to trust someone sometime. Laney, Henry. Or me. You can trust me, Kati."

She took a stuttering breath. "I know. It's just—I can't have Max in the middle of all that. I just can't. I love Laney, I do, and I know she's the reason we're alive, but right now, I don't think it's safe for us to be around her, or anyone from Chandler."

"Including me?"

Kati's gaze flew to his face and she grabbed his hand. "No, Maddox. But you've had so many years of your life taken away already, it doesn't seem right to ask you to give up more of your life. "

"Kati, you and Max have *given* me a life."

She stared up into his eyes, and then her gaze shifted toward the car. "He's awake."

Maddox glanced back. Max was now sitting in the driver's seat of Kati's car. "I'll get him."

Maddox walked over and opened the door. Max stood on the seat and Maddox pulled him out, careful not to hit his head on the doorframe.

Max smiled. "Hi, Maddox."

"Hi, Max."

"What are you doing here?"

"Looking for you two."

Max squirmed down. "I'm glad you found us. Mom's going to need you."

Maddox looked down. "Why's that?"

Max tugged his hand, pulling him closer.

Maddox knelt down. "What is it, little man?"

Max's face was strangely serious. "It's not your fault. And it's not her fault either. You have to make sure she understands that."

"What's not my fault?"

"What's about to happen. It was supposed to be this way."

Maddox felt cold shoot through him. He straightened quickly and cast his eyes around, looking for any hint of a threat. The parked cars were still empty. A few other cars drove past the rest area, but none pulled in.

"Maddox?" Kati called.

He didn't respond, his senses on high alert. It was as if the very air had changed, like right before a storm. Somewhere nearby, he heard a footfall.

"Get down!" Maddox yelled at Kati, pulling Max to the ground as gunshots rang out. Kati dove to the ground with a scream. She army-crawled toward Max, tears streaming down her face.

Maddox pulled out his weapon, but he was caught out in the open. He yanked Max behind him. "Get under the car!"

But before he could do anything else, two bullets slammed into his chest and another two entered his thigh. He crashed to the ground. More bullets peppered his torso.

"Maddox!" Max screamed. A man in black appeared out of nowhere and grabbed Max by the feet, pulling him to the other side of the car.

Kati got to her feet to run to Max, heedless of her own safety. Maddox tried to yell for her to stop.

Bullets slammed into her, throwing her back.

Maddox struggled to get to her, to get to Max—to do something, anything—but a constant barrage of bullets wouldn't let him. Pain echoed through his system with each wound, only to be replaced immediately by a new pain in a new spot.

The agony seemed to go on forever, but through it all, he saw a van pull up. The man in black loaded Max inside, and then the remaining shooters got in as well, but not before all but emptying their weapons into Maddox. The tires squealed as the van pulled out of the rest stop, onto the highway, and then they were gone.

Finally all was silent. Maddox sucked breath in through his teeth, his whole body on fire. He looked over at Kati's limp form. Her body lay unnaturally on the pavement, blood pooling around her. Too much blood. *No. No!*

Then her hand moved, just slightly. Immediately Maddox forgot his pain and climbed to his knees. He looked down the highway, but the van was long gone. He looked at his car and Kati's: neither was going anywhere any time soon.

He pulled out his phone—miraculously it was undamaged—and dialed Laney as he struggled to his feet.

"Maddox, do you have them?" Laney asked.

"No. I'm at the rest area just west"—he winced, the pain washing through him again—"just west of the estate. A van, black, at least six men. They've got Max."

"License plate?"

"No. It was an old Ford E250."

"You and Kati okay?"

Maddox looked over at Kati and his heart clenched. "Kati needs an ambulance. She's been shot."

"I'll be right there," Laney said.

"No!" Maddox barked out. "Find Max. Do whatever you need to do. But find him." He disconnected the call.

Maddox staggered over to Kati, his pain fading. "Kati?"

He reached down and unzipped his sweatshirt, then yanked it off. There was only one bullet wound, in her shoulder. He pressed the sweatshirt against the wound, but the blood only seemed to seep around it. Fear coursed through him. *No.*

Kati's eyes fluttered open and she gasped.

"Breathe, Kati. Breathe."

She clung to him, trying to get her breath, pain etched in her face. "Where's... Max?" she whispered.

Maddox looked down at her and saw his own fear reflected back at him. "They took him."

CHAPTER 49

L aney pressed down on the accelerator. She flew past the rest area where Kati lay bleeding, forcing herself to not look. She gripped the steering wheel tighter. *I have to get Max.*

She glanced at the dashboard. There was a new shiny button there, next to the air vents. She had let Yoni play around with her car one day, a few weeks ago, and he'd installed nitro—enough for one burst of speed. Laney took a deep breath and pushed the button.

The car burst forward.

Laney focused on keeping her arms tight on the wheel, knowing that if she lost concentration for even a moment she'd be a flaming wreck on the side of the road. The world flew by. If she hadn't been so scared for Kati and Max, it might have been exhilarating.

Finally the speed burst began to wear off, and as she looked up ahead, she saw the taillights of a van.

Laney struggled to think of how she might get the van to stop. She wasn't a good enough shot to blow out the tire while she was driving. She could possibly use wind to take them down, but that was also dicey while both of them were in motion.

Besides, both of those options would result in the van crashing. And she was pretty sure the kidnappers hadn't bothered to strap Max into a car seat.

"Damn it!" she yelled as she closed the distance.

Her cell phone rang. Laney called out for the car to answer it.

"Laney?" Jake yelled.

"I'm behind them." Laney had called Jake after hearing from Maddox. He'd promised to be right behind her.

"I know, I see you. We'll take them from the front."

How can he see me? But before she could ask the question, it was answered: she heard the chopper flying overhead. It flew well ahead of her and the van, then came down right in the middle of the highway, blocking both lanes.

The van screeched to a halt. Laney swung her car sideways to block any retreat, then jumped out. The van immediately went into reverse.

Laney called on the wind.

A giant gust blew down the highway, its force directed entirely at the reversing van, keeping it where it was. The wheels spun in place, and smoke rolled from under the tires. Then the back wheels lifted off the ground.

Jake ran for the van, flanked by two others. He put two rounds through the engine. The other men took out the tires.

Laney released her focus. The back wheels of the van slammed down to the ground just as a burst of gunfire burst from the passenger side window.

Laney dropped to the ground, her heart in her throat as Jake's partners laid down suppression fire. Jake launched a canister of tear gas through the front window.

White smoke billowed out. Three men stumbled from the van. Jake and his partners threw them to the ground and collected their weapons.

Laney leapt to her feet and ran toward them. As she hit the smoke, her eyes began to sting, and she started to cough violently.

Panic surged through her as she looked at the van. *Oh, God, he's still in there.*

Jake waved her back. "Stay there!" He slipped on a gas mask, ran to the van, and entered.

Laney took a few steps back, trying to get clear of the smoke, but her eyes still stung. She held her breath. *Please, please let Max be okay.*

When Jake stepped out the sliding van door, his arms were empty. He walked over to Laney, and when he pulled off the mask, the look of failure on his face made her heart catch in her throat.

Laney started to shake. "No, Jake, no."

"I'm sorry, Laney. He's not there."

CHAPTER 50

Laney sat in the waiting room, thinking about how many hospitals she had been to since this all began. It was too many.

Maddox sat down next to her and handed her a coffee. "Anything?"

She looked up at him and saw the worry etched into the hard lines of his face. "A nurse came out. They removed the bullet and are sewing her up. She'll be brought into recovery soon, but she probably won't wake for a while."

Maddox looked away. "I want to kill somebody," he said softly.

When most people said that, Laney blew it off as a figure of speech. But as she looked at Maddox, she knew it wasn't. "As soon as we find the bastards that did this, you get the first shot."

Maddox nodded abruptly.

A doctor stepped out from the double doors at the end of the hall. Laney stood. "That's the doc."

The tall African-American woman walked over. "Ms. McPhearson?"

Laney nodded, trying to gauge what the doctor was going to say from her face. But the woman was giving nothing away.

The doctor stopped in front of them and gave a tired smile. "Your friend did well. They're moving her to recovery now. I can bring one of you in."

Laney let out a breath. "Thank God."

Next to her she felt Maddox jolt slightly. She looked up and saw the relief on his face as well. She squeezed his forearm. "You go. Be there when she wakes up."

"You sure?"

Laney nodded. "Yes. Take care of her."

"I will." Maddox followed the doctor back through the double doors.

Laney sank back into her seat, trying to figure out what to do. She knew she should track down the bastards who did this, but honestly, all she wanted to do was curl up in a ball and cry. She couldn't get the image of Max hurt and alone out of her brain. And now, mixed with it, was the image of Kati, blood pouring from the bullet wound in her shoulder.

She felt the tears burning the back of her eyes. *I failed them both.*

As she was taking a few slow, shaky breaths, trying to get herself under control, her uncle stepped into the waiting room. He walked over to her and quickly pulled her into a hug. "We'll find him," he whispered.

Laney let the tears fall. They stayed together like that for a few moments before Laney pulled back. She wiped at the tears on her cheeks and Patrick did the same.

"How is she?" Patrick asked.

Laney gestured toward the doors that led to the operating suite. "Maddox is in with her. She came through the surgery fine."

Patrick took her hand. "That's good news. Any leads on Max?"

Laney shook her head. "No. Not yet. Jake's at the police station. He says all the men in the van were former military, but they won't answer any questions, except their name, rank, and serial number. We think they had another car waiting and transferred Max over, then used the van to lead us down the highway."

"Have you told Henry?"

She shook her head. "I didn't want to call until I could tell him something about Kati."

"Go ahead. I'll stay here."

Laney nodded and headed down the hall. As soon as she turned a corner, she leaned against the wall and closed her eyes. Someone was grabbing children, had gone after the boys, had taken Max and shot Kati. And right now their only lead was that one of the guys might have been in the military.

Goddamn it. She opened her eyes, torn between anger and fear. They had no good leads, and now Max was in the middle of all of this. She pulled out her phone and punched in Henry's number, realizing that now *everything* hinged on the Happy Meadows Sanitarium.

Great. Our best chance of finding all those kids is in the hands of a paranoid schizophrenic. What could possibly go wrong with that?

CHAPTER 51

CLEVELAND, OHIO

Henry pulled into one of the visitors' parking spots at Happy Meadows Sanitarium. He and Jen got out of the car and stopped to take a long look at the place.

The building was composed of grey brick, with a black, wrought iron gate enclosing the grounds. No shrubbery or flowers dotted the edges to break up the monotony. In fact, the only colors to be seen anywhere were black and grey.

Jen looked at him out of the corner of her eyes. "You know, I can't say I see anything 'happy' about this place."

Henry nodded. "Yeah. So much for truth in advertising."

He glanced up at the windows. A few patients stared out at them. One banged his fists repeatedly before he was dragged away.

Henry swallowed a curse. Gerard had sent him on wild goose chase. "Goddamn it. We don't have time to chase down false leads."

Jen took his hand. "Well, right now we don't have any other leads. So let's at least check it out, okay?"

Henry looked over at her and felt his heart stutter a little bit. "Okay."

They headed up the broken concrete steps. The front foyer had a deep green tile on the floor and a smell of antiseptic. There were no chairs to wait in, although indentations in the floor demonstrated where some chairs had once been bolted down. No pictures broke up the dull color of the grey walls, only signs:

No Smoking.

You Must Sign In.

All Visitors Must Be Announced.

All valuables should be left in your car. The Happy Meadows Sanitarium is not responsible for any lost or broken items.

Jen glanced at Henry, her eyebrows raised. "Welcoming."

"Yeah. Not where I'd like to spend my golden years."

A fortysomething woman behind a Plexiglas window stared at them. She did not smile. Henry did as he leaned down to the counter. "Hello. My name is Henry Chandler. I spoke with Dr. Marsden about visiting with Linda Grayston."

"ID," the woman said. She hit a button under her desk, and a drawer slid out from underneath the counter. Jen and Henry fished out their driver's licenses and dropped them in. The drawer pulled back.

Squinting at the cards, the woman inspected Jen and Henry; Henry struggled not to squirm under her attention. Finally she nodded, dropped the licenses back in the drawer, and slid them back out. A door buzzed open to their left and the woman went back to her paperwork.

Jen looked at Henry with a shrug before heading for the open door, where an orderly in his late thirties appeared, dressed all in white.

"Mr. Chandler? Dr. Witt? I'm Casey. Dr. Marsden asked me to take you to see Linda." The man barely spared Henry a glance, saving his attention for Jen.

She ignored him.

As Casey led them down the hall, he turned to her. "So, are you a psychiatrist?"

"No," she replied. She didn't elaborate.

Henry tried to hide his amusement. "Um, what can you tell us about Ms. Grayston's condition?"

Casey stopped walking and looked up and down the hall. "Um, I know Dr. Marsden said I was supposed to help you, but I don't think I should provide patient information." He paused, looking expectantly at Henry.

Henry pulled a fifty out of his pocket and slipped it silently into Casey's hand. The man smiled, pocketed the money, and continued to lead them down the hall. "Well, Linda is a paranoid schizophrenic with an extra dose of persecution complex."

"Persecution? By who?" Jen asked.

Casey perked up under her attention. He leaned toward her as he whispered. "Fallen angels. Says they're all around us."

Jen and Henry exchanged a glance but said nothing.

Casey didn't seem to notice. "Anyway, don't get within her reach. She'll grab you. She's not violent, just kind of clingy."

Henry's phone buzzed just as Casey unlocked a door toward the end of the hall. Henry glanced down and gestured for Jen and Casey to go ahead, then he stepped to the other side of the hall and answered. "Laney? I haven't met with her yet. I'm about to go in."

Laney's voice was shaky. "Henry, somebody took Max."

"What? What happened?" Henry listened in growing disbelief as Laney explained about Kati taking off with Max.

"How's Kati?" he asked when Laney was done.

"She made it through surgery well. Maddox is with her now. He looks like he wants to rip someone apart."

"I can't blame him. Do you have any leads?"

"No. Nothing. We have the three guys in the van, but they're not talking."

"I'm so sorry, Laney." The silence felt heavy between them

before the realization hit. "That means they were after Max, not Danny, at the bookstore." Part of him felt relief, and another part of him felt horrible for feeling it. "Do you know why?"

"No."

Henry heard something behind her denial. "Laney, you can read potentials." It was a skill she had realized after working with the kids at the Chandler School. She knew which kids would develop abilities and which wouldn't. "And there's nothing there with Max," he said slowly. "Right?

"Right. He's not a potential." Laney paused. "Do you think maybe they grabbed him to get to me?"

"Do *you* think they grabbed him to get to you?"

She sighed. "I don't know. But I think that's why Kati ran. To get Max away from all of this."

Henry closed his eyes, knowing how guilty Laney must feel. "Even if that's true, it's not your fault."

She gave a bitter laugh. "If it's true, then yes it *is* my fault. If I had stayed away from them, Max would be safe right now."

Henry wasn't sure what to say, because she was right. It was the same worry he had about everything Danny was being introduced to.

Before he could speak though, Laney did. "But listen, meet with Linda, get whatever you can, and get back here as fast as you can. Okay?"

"Yeah. Will do."

Henry slipped the phone back in his pocket and leaned against the wall, suddenly feeling exhausted. Someone had Max. He pictured Max and Danny holding hands.

Oh, no. Danny. Henry pulled his phone out to call him, then stopped. No, right now he needed to meet with Linda and cross this stupid errand off his list. Then he could speak to Danny. But first he called Laney back.

She picked up almost immediately. "Henry?"

"Have you told Danny that Max is missing yet?"

"No. Not yet."

"Good. Can you do me and favor and not tell him?"

"What? Why not?"

"I just..." Henry sighed. "I just don't want Danny to worry. Let's just keep this from him until we have something to work with, okay?"

"Henry, Danny could help us search—"

"I know. But I don't want him involved in this. Max is like a little brother to him. Just don't tell him until I get back at least, okay?"

There was a long silence on Laney's end of the phone. "Okay. But we tell him as soon as you get back."

"Thanks, Laney." Henry disconnected the call and bowed his head. *Max.*

A middle-aged nurse headed down the hall toward him, pushing a cart. She gave Henry a strange look. He shook himself into movement, pushing away from the wall. They needed to wrap up this meeting and get home. They were needed there—not on this ridiculous errand.

He knocked on Linda's door.

Casey opened it up with a smile. "They're having a nice little chat."

Henry ducked under the doorway and got his first look at Linda Grayston. She was skinny, too skinny, with stringy brown hair that hung past her waist. Her fingers were gnarled, probably from arthritis. Her eyes had sunken into her wrinkled face. If he didn't know she was sixty-one, he probably would have guessed she was in her late eighties.

Linda sat at a table, leaning forward toward Jen, her voice intense. "They're here. We have to be careful. The end of days is coming. You need to—"

Her words cut off abruptly as she caught sight of Henry. She went still, then leapt from her chair. With one finger pointed at Henry, she screeched, "Abomination! Abomination!"

"Oh, shit." Casey pushed off of the wall. He walked toward Linda, his hands raised in a calming gesture. "It's okay, Linda. There are no abominations here. It's okay." His voice was as soothing as it could be, considering he had to shout to be heard over Linda's screams.

Linda's shrieking continued; if anything, it got louder. "Abomination! Abomination! They're here!"

"Well, I'd say that's our cue," Jen murmured and stood, pulling Henry toward the door. They stepped outside and closed the door behind them.

Another orderly hustled down the hall, followed by a nurse with a dark complexion and hair streaked with grey. They both bustled into the room. Henry watched as Casey and the other orderly held Linda down while the nurse injected her with a syringe.

"Abomination! Abomination! They're..." Linda's voice suddenly changed to a slow whisper. "... here." She sagged into the arms of the two orderlies. They carried her toward the door.

Casey caught Henry's eye as he walked past. "Sometimes they just lose it. Sorry." He and the other orderly carried Linda down the hall.

"Abomination," Jen whispered. "The same word the men who tried to grab Danny and Max used."

Henry nodded. There *was* something here. He watched the orderlies disappear around a corner with Linda. *And that something is disappearing into the bliss of anti-psychotic medication.*

The nurse came out of the room and sighed. Her nametag read Agnes. "Sorry about that." She looked up at Henry and then shook her head. "Well no wonder she lost it."

"Sorry?" Jen said.

Agnes shook her head. "Casey shouldn't have let you guys in there."

"Dr. Marsden cleared us to visit her," Henry said.

The nurse nodded wearily. "I'm sure he did. But I'm guessing he didn't know how tall you are."

"What does my height have to do with it?" Henry asked.

The woman stripped off her gloves and dropped them in a hazardous waste disposal bin before leaning against the wall. "Linda has this idea that fallen angels are giants. So one look at you, and I've no doubt she thought they had finally come for her."

"Ah," Henry said.

The nurse shook her head. "You know, when she's lucid, she actually makes a pretty decent case. She's told me all sorts of stories about 'giants in America' that fought with Native Americans before Columbus ever stepped foot here. If she weren't schizophrenic, she probably would have been a great history teacher or maybe a writer."

The woman shrugged, pushing away from the wall. "Well, I'm afraid that's all you're going to get from Linda tonight. That drug will have her knocked out for hours. Sorry you wasted your trip." She turned to head back down the hall.

Henry stepped forward. "Ma'am?"

Agnes looked back over her shoulder.

"Has Linda had any other visitors?"

"Not for years."

"So she did have visitors at one time?"

"Just her son."

"Her son?" Jen asked.

The nurse nodded. Henry and Jen exchanged a look.

Henry looked back at the nurse. "Any chance we could buy you a cup of coffee and you could tell us a little about him?"

CHAPTER 52

Thirty minutes later, Henry and Jen hurried from the hospital to the car. "You take the wheel," Henry said, tossing Jen the keys and heading for the passenger door.

Jen caught the keys one-handed and ran to the driver's side. She took off as Henry pulled out his phone and dialed.

Laney answered almost immediately. "Anything?"

"Yes," Henry said. "Linda and Phillip Northgram have a son named Nathaniel."

Laney's voice exploded through the cars speakers. "What? How the hell did we miss that?"

"His mother took him away when she left," Jen said. "Apparently she didn't think Phillip was 'father material.'"

"Well, that's the first thing about her that shows some good sense. Goddamn it. Hold on," Laney said.

Henry could hear her telling someone to run a check on Nathaniel Northgram.

"Try the mother's maiden name too. Grayston," Henry said.

Laney relayed the information before getting back on the line. "What can you tell us about him?"

"He's a minister somewhere out west. And according to

the very chatty nurse we spoke with, he's one step away from being institutionalized himself. Has the same preoccupation with fallen angels, or abominations as they call them, as his mother. I think this is the break we've been waiting for."

"Let's hope. When will you be back?"

Henry looked at the clock on the dashboard. "A couple of hours."

"Then hopefully by the time you get here, we'll have something to move on."

"Good." Henry was about to disconnect when Laney cut in. "Henry, what is her persecution complex about? Who does she think she's being persecuted by?"

"Believe it or not, fallen angels."

Laney paused. "Did you guys get any sense off her?"

"No," Henry said slowly. "We didn't sense anything."

"But there was something," Laney pressed.

"Well, she didn't react to Jen at all. In fact, the two of them were chatting pretty amicably until I stepped into the room. And then she completely lost it."

"Any idea why?" Laney asked.

"The nurse said she's obsessed with giants. She thinks my height may have somehow indicated to her that I was a nephilim. But Laney, she's psychologically disturbed. Full-blown schizophrenic, with the papers to prove it."

"She told me about how giants once ruled the United States," Jen cut in.

Henry looked over at her. "What?"

"Before you came in," she said. "She was talking about how the Smithsonian had covered up evidence of the giants in America. That the government was conspiring with the Fallen and that none of us were safe."

"Huh," Laney said.

"Huh?" Jen asked. "What does that mean?"

"It means," Laney said, "that Linda may not be as crazy as she sounds."

"Care to elaborate?" Henry asked.

"It's not important right now. Look, don't head back here. I need you guys to head to Chicago."

"Chicago?" Jen asked.

"That's where Phillip Northgram lives," Henry said.

"Exactly," Laney said. "We'll run down what information we can from here, but I'm hoping maybe you can get something from the source."

"Will do," Jen said. "What are you looking for?"

"Anything he can tell us about his son." Laney paused, and when she spoke again her voice had a hard edge. "And guys? Don't be nice."

CHAPTER 53

SACRAMENTO, CALIFORNIA

Nathaniel sat at his desk. Tyrell had called. The mission had been a success. Three men had been captured, but no big loss. They could all be trusted not to speak.

Nathaniel opened his book, dipped his pen in the ink bottle, and crossed out the name *Max Simmons*. He scanned the list. All fourteen names were crossed off now.

But he knew this was only the beginning. The Shepherd never failed to find the abominations. When this first duty was success-fully accomplished, there would be more. The Shepherd, Nathaniel, and his followers: they were the last vanguard against the unholy.

A knock sounded at the door. Beatrice peeked her head in, her voice nervous, her eyes wide. "Nathaniel? He's here."

"Who's here?"

"The Shepherd."

Nathaniel stood up, nearly knocking over the inkwell. "You left him waiting? Send him in!"

Beatrice scurried out of the room, and Nathaniel quickly wiped up the ink with tissues. *Why is he here?*

He threw out the stained tissues, trying to calm his heart. *Is he displeased?*

He watched the door, his anticipation and fear growing. *We've done everything he's asked. He should happy, right?*

Beatrice opened the door again. "Nathaniel, the Shepherd is here."

The Shepherd walked in, his dark hair brushing against his shoulders, his trademark sunglasses in place. His grey coat reached to his knees. But as he walked, Nathaniel caught a glimpse of the black suit underneath.

Nathaniel felt his knees go weak. He was in the presence of greatness. He enacted a deep bow. "You honor us with your presence."

The Shepherd stood over him, his voice deep. "Rise, my friend. You have been a loyal servant to his Lord. He is most pleased."

Nathaniel stood, pride bursting within him. *The Lord is pleased.* He sighed, contentment welling up in him. "Thank you. I am His most humble servant."

The Shepherd waved Nathaniel back to his seat.

Nathaniel obediently sat, then started as he realized he had abandoned his manners. "Sir, would you care for something to eat or drink?"

"No, I'm quite all right. And your lovely wife has already asked."

Nathaniel nodded. His Beatrice could always be counted on to be a good hostess. "How may I be of service to the Lord today?"

"You have proven yourself a loyal subject, Nathaniel. But now, God asks for a greater service. A greater sacrifice."

Nathaniel leaned forward. *A greater sacrifice.* He had always wanted the opportunity to prove how strong his faith was. "Anything, Shepherd, anything."

"Are you familiar with the story of Abraham and his son Isaac?"

Nathaniel nodded. "Abraham was ordered by God to take his son to the top of Mount Moriah and sacrifice him in God's honor. God spared Isaac at the last moment. But Abraham, through his willingness to sacrifice his son, demonstrated his true faith in God."

The Shepherd nodded. "Yes. Although according to the Quran, it was Ismail who was to be sacrificed."

Nathaniel looked up sharply. The Quran? Why would the Shepherd mention that text?

The Shepherd waved his hands. "No matter. The importance is the willingness to sacrifice—even that which is most important to you."

Nathaniel felt some of his joy ebb a bit. His son, Zachariah, was not the most important thing to him. If the boy was what he was being asked to sacrifice, it would be only a small sacrifice after all. "What is it He would have me do?"

The Shepherd smiled, and a long line of white teeth glinted back at Nathaniel. "The Lord has found a way to strike a blow to our enemies by placing a lion in their midst. A Trojan horse, if you will."

"I don't understand."

"We have been unable to target the abominations once they have come into their powers. But I have found a way to do just that. And I need your son to do it. Are you willing to make this sacrifice?"

Nathaniel nodded, trying to keep his face a mask. "Yes. But why my son?"

Even through the dark glasses Nathaniel could feel the Shepherd's gaze holding him in place. "I know Zachariah is an abomination. I know you and your wife have prayed for a way to remove this blight. But He does not make mistakes. You were given your son for a special purpose. He is to be our weapon. And with him, we will strike a blow to the very heart of the enemy."

Nathaniel felt the truth in the Shepherd's words and felt some of the burden of his son lift from his shoulders. Since the day he had learned of his son's nature, he had been disgusted by him. Disgusted and ashamed. But deep down, he had known that God had not cursed him with an abomination without reason. God had provided him with a way to serve His cause.

Nathaniel smiled. "Whatever needs to be done, we will do."

The Shepherd sat back in his chair, his hands across his chest. "The Lord will be most pleased."

CHAPTER 54

BALTIMORE, MARYLAND

L aney sat at the conference table in Henry's office, staring at the first page of search results on Nathaniel Grayston. Patrick was at Henry's desk, on the phone with some of the higher-ups in the Roman Catholic Church, trying to see if they knew anything about Nathaniel and his church.

Maddox was still at the hospital with Kati. Laney had ducked in to see her before she and her uncle left. But the meds were keeping Kati pretty out of it—which was probably a blessing.

Now Laney gripped the table edge as she pictured Kati, looking pale and small in the hospital bed. Laney had tried to stay at the hospital, had wanted to, but she felt like she was going to start climbing the walls. There was just too much pain and death in the building, and the truth was, there was nothing she could do to help there.

But here, she could help the missing kids. Her heart clenched. Here she could help Max.

Patrick had driven them back from the hospital and she'd checked her messages on the drive over. Victoria had called, but just to express her concern for Kati; she didn't have any new information. Laney planned on calling her later.

Laney glanced at her watch. Henry and Jen should be taking off for Chicago right about now. It would take them another twenty minutes or so to reach Northgram's home once they landed. She imagined Jen literally squeezing the information out of Northgram. It wasn't an unpleasant thought.

Her anger began to boil. He must have known something earlier. *And Max would be safe if the bastard had been up front with them in the first place.*

The office was quiet. No Cleo, no Danny, no Moxy. She'd sent Danny to the school so that Yoni and Cleo could watch over him. They still hadn't told him about Max. As far as he knew, Kati had decided to take Max to his grandparents.

Laney felt guilty about the lie, though she couldn't fault Henry for wanting to spare Danny some anguish. Yet at the same time, Laney knew that if they were going to find Max and those kids, Danny would be a huge asset.

Enough, she thought, realizing that all this agonizing over what had happened wasn't getting her anywhere. *Back to work.*

With a conscious effort, Laney turned her attention back to the computer. She clicked on the first search page: Nathaniel Grayston's church's webpage. Once they'd had a name, he had been easy enough to find, at least online. They were still having difficulty pinning down his actual physical location.

A picture of the reverend sat on the top right corner of the site. He wasn't an attractive man. In fact, he was edging toward ugly. His chin seemed to almost disappear into his neck and his eyes seemed awfully small for his face—a lot like his father. In many ways, he was completely unremarkable. The kind of guy you'd see on the street and not think twice about.

And this was the man who was gathering all these children for God knew what purpose. A chill cut through her. *If they're still alive.*

She banished the thought almost as soon as she had it. She had to believe the kids were still alive. Otherwise all this was for nothing, and Laney couldn't accept that. She *wouldn't* accept that.

Besides, they could have killed Max at the rest stop. They hadn't. They'd gone out of their way to abduct him. They must have a reason for that. Which meant there was still time. There had to be.

She looked back at Nathaniel's picture. Why was it that the monsters of the world never truly looked like monsters? They always seemed to look like the nice woman at the post office or the nice coach of the soccer team. Life would be easier if the evil were as obvious on the outside as it was on the inside.

Nathaniel's ministry was called the Feast of the Lamb. The website was a mix of patriotic themes, including the American flag, a bald eagle, and a dominance of the colors red, white, and blue. But also a mix of Christian symbols: the cross, lambs, the Ten Commandments on stone tablets.

He was a minister who seemed to be based somewhere in California, traveling all along the coast to share his version of the Good News. He also seemed to go out of his way to cater to veterans, which fit with the people they'd connected to the abductions so far. But the actual official address for the church was only a PO box. Jake had handed off the van search and was now trying to track down Nathaniel's physical address.

On the right hand side of the screen was a collection of clips from his most popular sermons. Laney clicked on the first link and was redirected to YouTube. She hit play.

Nathaniel pounded his fist on a wooden pulpit, a giant statue of Jesus looming over him. "The abominations will destroy our way of life. Only the righteous deserve a place on this wonderful planet that God has given us."

His voice was full of authority and determination. His face was strong, his gaze unblinking. A true believer.

"The abominations are the snake in the garden," he thundered. "The devil in the desert."

Laney froze the frame. Nathaniel's eyes were larger now and filled with anger. A chill began to crawl over Laney. *And this is the man who has Max.*

She bowed her head. *Oh God, please help us.*

She looked over as Patrick hung up the phone and headed toward her. "Anything?" she asked.

He shook his head and took a seat across from her. "Not yet. They're going to make some calls. See if they can learn anything."

"We need to find them, Uncle Patrick."

He reached over and squeezed her hand. "I know, honey."

Jake walked in. And Laney's heart began to pound: he was smiling.

He walked over to her and nodded. "I found Grayston. His ministry takes him all over, but he owns a couple of buildings outside Sacramento, California. They're listed under his ministry, the Feast of the Lamb, although they're hidden under a few dummy corporations. Wheels up in thirty minutes."

"Oh, thank God. Something tangible," Laney said, getting to her feet.

Patrick looked up. "Wait. What's the ministry's name?"

"The Feast of the Lamb," Jake said.

"Why?" Laney asked, watching her uncle. Something was brewing in that head of his.

"The Feast of the Lamb," Patrick said slowly. "It's referenced in the Book of Exodus."

"What's the Book of Exodus?" Jake asked.

Laney answered Jake, but kept her eyes on her uncle, not liking the look on his face. "It's the tale of the Israelites escape from slavery in Egypt."

"You mean the whole manna in the desert story?" Jake asked.

Laney nodded. "Among other tales."

Jake turned to Patrick. "So why does that matter?"

Patrick's eyes were troubled. "I'm not sure."

"Well, I'll leave you two to figure that out," Jake said. "I'm going to arrange for us to head out there. We leave in fifteen minutes for the airfield."

Laney watched Jake leave the room. She turned when Patrick sat down next to her.

"I'll stay here with Kati," he said. "She'll need someone there when she wakes."

Laney nodded. She knew there was no way Maddox would be able to stay behind. And she also knew Kati was going to need someone to help her through the next couple of hours, or worse, days—especially if things went sideways.

"Okay." A shudder ran through her as an image of Max cold and pale flitted through her mind.

"What's wrong?" Patrick asked.

"What's wrong?" Laney nearly choked out the words, all the fear, anger, guilt, and doubt boiling over. "Are you kidding? All these kids... Max." Her voice broke on Max's name. She looked at her uncle, sitting there calmly although she knew he loved Max as much as she did. "How are you keeping it together? I can barely think straight."

He shrugged. "Faith."

"But how? All these horrible things are happening. I mean, *children* are in danger this time. Children. Don't you think if ever there was a time for us to get a little help from the guy upstairs, this was it? And He seems to be awfully quiet right now." Her heart pounded. She felt so frustrated, so angry. It was all just wrong, on every conceivable level.

Patrick was silent for a moment. Then he took Laney's hand. She looked over at him and he gave her a small smile.

"How can you smile?" she asked.

"Because I see this situation a little differently than you do. You think God has abandoned these children, left them without help. But think about all the people that are scrambling to help them. Everyone here is doing everything in their power to help those children. And you, Jake, Henry, Maddox, Jen, and countless others won't stop until those kids come home."

"But shouldn't He be helping too?"

Patrick squeezed Laney's hand. Then he leaned over and kissed her on the forehead. "He did. He sent them you."

CHAPTER 55

Danny watched as Moxy chased Cleo around the yard, the two of them playfully pouncing and dodging in turns. Normally watching the two of them play made him smile. But today, nothing did. Henry had shipped him back to the school without even an explanation. Just said that he needed Danny here. Danny kicked a rock across the lawn.

Cleo must have heard something, because her head turned quickly and she went still. But then she was a blur of motion, running across the lawn.

Lou and Rolly froze in place as Cleo stopped and sniffed each of them. In spite of his mood, Danny felt a smile bubbling up. They both liked Cleo, but they were still a little intimidated by her. "It's okay," he said. "She just wants you to rub her ears."

Rolly reached out a tentative hand, patting Cleo on the head. The big cat purred a little.

Lou reached over as well. "Hey, Cleo."

Cleo rubbed against Lou and then sauntered back to Moxy. Lou and Rolly exchanged grins as they jogged toward Danny.

"Hey, Danny. We didn't know you were coming back," Lou said.

"Yeah, well, Henry ordered me back." He could hear the bitterness in his own voice.

"Ordered?" Rolly's eyebrows inched upward.

"Yeah, you know." He gestured to Moxy and Cleo. "Like a pet."

Lou frowned at him. "You know Henry probably did it to protect you."

"Yeah." Danny turned his back. "Danny, who always needs to be protected."

Lou and Rolly were silent for a moment before Lou spoke. "Well boo hoo for you."

"What?" Danny whirled around.

"Poor Danny: too many people trying to keep him safe. Too many people who love him and don't want him harmed. Poor baby."

Rolly took her arm, his voice filled with censure. "Lou..."

She shook him off. "What? You and I, we have no one left. *No one.* I mean, you just found out your sister is dead, and I don't see *you* walking around feeling sorry for yourself."

Rolly winced and took a step back.

Lou's mouth dropped open. "Sorry. I didn't—"

Rolly put a hand up. "It's okay."

Lou turned back to Danny. "You have this whole group of people who are trying to protect you, and all you feel is annoyed at them. Even though there's every reason for them to be worried."

Danny stared at Lou, his mouth open. "But I—"

"But you what? " Lou lashed out, and there were tears in her voice. "Do you know how long it's been since people cared about what happened to *me*? I mean, really cared? Jen is the first one in a long time. And here you have all these people caring about you and all you get is angry at them for it."

Danny stared at Lou. She stared back, almost daring him to look away. Finally he turned and looked at Rolly. "Is this what you think, too?"

Rolly shrugged. "I get that it sucks to have so much security. I *do* get that. But I think Lou's right. You have all these people who care about you. I don't think you appreciate it."

"I appreciate it. I just—" Danny shook his head. "I don't know. I just get really angry when they tell me what to do."

"Yeah... but they kind of have a reason," Rolly said. "I mean, I don't know Henry well, but he doesn't seem unreasonable."

"And you did almost get grabbed the other day," Lou said.

"Yeah, yeah," Danny mumbled.

"Did you ever wonder why?" Rolly asked.

"Why what?" Danny asked.

"Why they sent you here now? I mean, Laney, Henry, Jake, Jen. They're all out of town," Rolly said.

Danny's head jerked up. "What? How do you know that?"

"Jen called me. Told me she'd be gone for a little while. Told me to—" Lou broke off abruptly.

"Told you to keep an eye on me?" Danny asked.

Lou nodded. "Look, Jen's not the overly warm and fuzzy type. If she wants me and Rolly to keep an eye on you, there's a reason."

Danny looked between the two of them, wanting to be angry at Jen's high-handedness, but somehow, he wasn't able to. All he felt was confused. "But why? I mean, if I was really in danger, why send me here? Why not back to Dom's?"

"Maybe something's happening on the estate they don't want you to see."

Danny nodded, realizing he'd been so angry about being sent here he hadn't wondered *why* he'd been sent here. "You're right."

Lou started to smile. "Well, maybe we should try to find out what that is."

CHAPTER 56

The plane engine droned on like a very loud white noise machine. It should have put Laney to sleep, but sleep was the last thing on her mind. She had called Henry before they left; he had been about to land in Chicago.

Laney clenched her fist. They had to cross the damn country to find these guys. Hours wasted just sitting in a plane. And they still didn't know if they were even on the right track. This could all be for nothing.

She craned her neck around the side of her chair. Maddox was a few seats back, eyes closed, looking peaceful. But she knew he was anything but. When he'd arrived at the airfield he'd barely spoken, but his eyes had said volumes about his pain, anger, and fear.

Laney turned away, knowing her eyes looked the same as Maddox's. And that that wasn't going to change until they found the kids.

She glanced down at her phone. But staring at it didn't make it ring. Patrick had said he'd listen to Nathaniel's sermons and call back if he had any ideas. She knew she should have offered to help him, but she couldn't stand to hear the vitriol that leaked from the reverend's mouth. Every time he said the word "abomination," her stomach clenched painfully with images of Max.

"Anything?" Jake asked from next to her.

Laney looked over at him. "No. And I don't know how Uncle Patrick can still be listening to that man. He's got a stronger stomach than I do."

"He seemed to think there was something special about the name of Nathaniel's church."

Laney nodded. "Yeah, but if you're asking me what it is, I don't know. Lambs are important in Christianity—as sacrifices, as analogies. Even Jesus was called 'lamb' because of his sacrifice. But as to what exactly that has to do with all of this…" Laney shrugged.

"What was all that with Northgram's wife?" Jake asked, interrupting her thoughts. "How did Nathaniel's mom know Henry was a nephilim? Jen said she mentioned giants ruling America in ancient times."

"Oh, there were definitely giants thousands of years ago," Laney said distractedly. *Why would Nathaniel take the kids? What was his angle? Did his father and the Council have something to do with this?*

And why Max? It couldn't be because of his abilities. There was no way they could know about that.

"Earth to Laney."

Laney looked over at Jake. "Sorry, what?"

"You said giants existed thousands of years ago."

"Right," she said. "Do you think—"

Jake put up his hand. "I'm afraid you're going to have to explain that little comment."

Laney looked at Jake. "Oh. I thought we talked about this once."

He shook his head.

"Okay." Laney paused to gather her thoughts, glad that she was able to think about something other than the current situation. "Well, you remember when I was shot?"

Jake looked at her for a long minute. "It rings a bell."

She smiled. "Right. Well, seeing as I was on bed rest, I did a lot of reading."

"I remember."

She thought of Jake lugging cartons of books back to her house for her over the weeks she'd been recuperating, and she wound her fingers through his. "Well, part of what I was researching was Henry. We knew he was different, but we didn't know why. I thought there might be something in the historical record about tall people with extreme abilities."

"And you found something."

Laney nodded. "I found the Mound Builders of North America."

"And these alleged Mound Builders were giants?"

"Well..." Laney drew out the word.

Jake let out a sigh. "Go ahead."

Laney smiled. "First, you have to understand the geological history of the United States—or North America, really. Until the 1920s, scientists believed that Native Americans had only been in the United Sates for a few thousand years."

"Why? I mean the land has been here forever."

Laney nodded. "True, but there were geographic barriers that were believed to isolate it."

Laney saw the awareness spread across Jake's face. "Ah, right. The Clovis First Theory."

Laney nodded. "Yes."

The Clovis First Theory referred to the belief that humans migrated to North America from Siberia around 9500 BCE. Allegedly, these first peoples followed big game across the Bering land bridge created by the lower sea levels. Those first immigrants were then believed to have largely died out within five hundred years, although no one is really sure as to why. And the land bridge disappeared as the sea levels rose at the end of the Ice Age, isolating the continent once again.

"If I remember correctly, " Jake said, "the belief was that humans entered prior to 9500 BCE and then not again until the 1500s with European settlers."

"Yes. In fact, a big part of the problem with the Clovis First argument was that the archaeological evidence suggests that the Native Americans migrated from the south, meaning South America, not the north as in Siberia.

"But the bigger problem was that everyone accepted the 9500 date. So archaeologists would dig down to the 9500 strata, the Clovis barrier, and then stop. Why dig further when there was no chance humans had been there?"

"And I'm guessing somebody finally dug deeper?"

Laney nodded. "Yes. Some, like geologist George Carter, said humans had been in North America as early as 100,000 BCE. Louis Leakey even found evidence that California had been inhabited as early as 200,000 years ago."

"Wait—Leakey? As in Lucy?"

In 1972, Louis Leakey had become famous for finding traces of ancient hominids. His project eventually led to the discovery of "Lucy," the first hominid skeleton, three million years old.

Laney nodded. "Yes. And when he advanced his hypothesis that there had been a much earlier appearance of humans in North America, he was all but drummed out of archaeology. It wasn't until the 1980s when an archaeological team began digging at the Mount Verde site in Chile that the Clovis Barrier began to crumble. At that site, they were able to carbon date their finds and all their results consistently came back to 10,500 BCE, with evidence suggesting earlier sites at an astounding 35,000 BCE. And then, once people started digging below the Clovis barrier, the finds started to spring up."

Jake nodded thoughtfully. "But if there *was* an ancient advanced civilization, the Bering Strait must not have been the only way to get to the continent. They must have sailed." He grimaced. "Or I guess flew."

Laney took his hand with a squeeze. "You said it, not me. But Cayce did mention that descendants of Atlantis and Mu escaped to North and South America after the destructions, around 50,000 BCE."

"Mu?"

"Formally known as LeMuria—consider it Atlantis's sister country. Atlantis was rumored to be off the east coast of North America. Mu was off the west coast."

Jake stared at her for a moment and then shook his head. "Don't think I'm ready to jump into a whole new mysterious ancient civilization. How about you just explain what any of this has to do with 'giants' in America?"

"Actually, I read a book with pretty much that very title. Anyway, we had these ancient sites cropping up all over the US once archaeologists started digging below the Clovis barrier. And along with those finds, people began to pay more attention to the legends of Native American people who spoke of an ancient race that lived here long before them."

"Long before?" Jake asked.

Laney nodded. "There have been legends around for hundreds of years, if not longer, about tribes of giants who once lived in North America. Often they were described as having red hair."

Jake raised an eyebrow. "Ancient relatives of yours?"

"Unlikely," she said with a laugh, but then stopped and looked thoughtful. "Actually, I have no idea. I can add that to my ever-growing list of questions for Victoria."

She shook her head to clear it of Victoria thoughts. There was no time for that right now. "Anyway, one of the best-known legends involved a cave in Lovelock, Nevada. According to the story, a race of giants once lived in the area, raining destruction on the indigenous people who also lived there. Finally pushed to their breaking point, the indigenous tribes joined together and tracked down the giants."

In her mind, Laney saw the Native Americans chasing down the people who were alleged to have been eight to nine feet tall. "The indigenous tribes managed to all but eliminate the giants. The final few that remained were chased and trapped in a cave. The native people set a fire at the cave's entrance. A few giants ran out and were killed. The rest were asphyxiated."

Jake scoffed. "And there's proof of this?"

"Well, sort of. After the giants, bats took over the cave. And they left bat guano six feet deep. In 1911 a company began mining the guano."

"For gunpowder," Jake said.

Laney looked over at him in surprise.

"Guano turns into saltpeter. The main ingredient in gunpowder. Navy SEAL, remember?"

She smiled. "Right. Anyway, when the company started mining, they came across skeletons and fossils. Of course, the company didn't care. And for years they mined, literally tossing out all the ancient finds."

Jake cringed.

"I know. Finally, archaeologists were notified, and they managed to salvage ten thousand artifacts and two giant red-headed skeletons."

"How long until the archaeologists showed up?"

Laney shook her head, thinking about all that could have been learned from the site if it had been studied properly from the beginning. "Ten years. And even then, they didn't realize how significant the find was. The skeletons they documented were over eight feet tall. They also found a ton of arrows, suggesting that the tale of how the giants ended in the cave was true."

"So what happened to the remains? How come they're not front and center in some museum somewhere?"

"The skeletons were sent to the Smithsonian, and then they seemed to have disappeared."

"Disappeared? They're probably just in a box somewhere in some dusty storeroom."

"Probably. But there are those who say that the Smithsonian seems to have developed a 'habit' of losing evidence of paleo-Indians of large size."

"Wait. A habit? How many finds were there?"

"Dozens. From the mid-nineteenth century until the early twentieth, there are literally dozens of reports of giant skeletons being found across the country. All the skeletons ranged in size from six feet to nine feet. Some news reports even suggested taller finds. In fact, early settlers accepted the fact that there must have been an ancient race that had settled North America prior to the Native Americans."

"Why?"

"Because the skeletons were associated with these phenomenal mounds."

"And let me guess: because they didn't believe the Native Americans could construct such a monument?"

Laney nodded.

Jake was quiet for a moment. "Guess that makes sense. That was the time period when the roads were being dug and farms were being established."

Laney's mouth fell open. Wow. He'd really come a long way from when they'd started this whole crazy adventure.

Jake grinned. "Hey, I *have* learned it's useless to fight the strange. After you've died and been brought back, learned you're part of destined triad, and spent time fighting with angels, your views of history become a little less rigid. Now I'm just trying to roll with it. You said something about the mound builders. You mean like the serpent mound in Ohio?"

"That's one of them. But actually, there were a lot of mounds, all across the United States, that settlers came across when they started expanding west. And when they dug into the mounds, people found these huge skeletons."

"All of them were giant sized?" Jake asked.

Laney shook her head. "No. I remember one. It was a cabin that had been built for a twelve-year-old boy. It had toys, and a bed, and the remains of a young boy, buried in a mound."

She stopped talking, feeling the grief she always did when she thought of that burial, compounded by the fact that more children were in danger of dying now. Or already dead.

She blew out a breath. "Whoever these mound builders were, they loved. That was obvious."

"So who do you think they were? Fallen? Early Native Americans?"

"To be honest, I think they might not be either. I'm not entirely convinced they were even homo sapiens."

Jake's eyes went wide. "What?"

"There have been over twenty different types of hominids discovered, and more seem to crop up each year. Most have a combination of characteristics that can be found in homo sapiens, but they are definitely not homo sapiens—which complicates the whole 'where do we come from' question."

"And you think the giants are one of these alternative hominid groups?"

Laney nodded and rubbed the bridge of her nose, where a headache had started to develop. "I'm guessing *Homo denisova*. Very little has been found of them except for some toe bones and a very large tooth. If the scale is correct, they were much bigger than homo sapiens, maybe even eight or nine feet tall."

Jake let out a low whistle. "Wow."

"And it just gets more unusual. DNA tests reveal that the denisovans bred with another unknown species that was neither Neanderthal nor human. And then the problem was, they were supposed to have become extinct over 250,000 years ago, but remains were found indicating they were still around as recently as 10,000 years ago."

"Which means they could be the origin of the ancient tales of giants."

Laney nodded. "Legends of an ancient race of giants can be found across the globe. Take for example the tales of Viracocha, down in Bolivia. He was the Incan god who was supposed to have spawned a race of giants. And Viracocha himself was supposed to have been incredibly intelligent, with great powers."

"A Fallen?"

Laney shrugged. "Maybe. The archaeological site of Puma Punka was said to have been created by Viracocha and his giants. And it is incredible."

Laney pictured the ancient ruins that looked more like the remnants of a construction site than an ancient temple. "The site has these incredible H-shaped blocks that fit together perfectly. Each of them is close to, if not over, one hundred tons. And now the blocks are scattered about, like a child's building blocks. But it's not just the size of the blocks that's impressive, it's the precision with which they were carved and the niches that were carved into them. If you didn't know any better, you'd swear they were done with a machine."

"What happened to them?"

"The best guess is that a giant flood came and destroyed the site. The site is ten miles inshore though, so it had to be a pretty big flood. But it dates to at least 12,000 BCE, and others put it closer to 24,000 BCE."

Laney shook her head. "Anyway, stories like that have been dismissed by academics. There was no proof. But when I started looking into heights and abilities, I don't know, there were these similarities."

"Such as?"

"Well, just like the flood myth, which is found over and over in cultures around the world, the myth of giants also litters the globe. And then the old newspaper articles in the States—they were years apart and came from different parts of the country. That's odd. Because remember, this is the late nineteenth century. Communicating across great distances wasn't exactly easy. Plus, some pieces of those skeletons do remain, and they *are* massive."

Jake was quiet for a moment. "So you don't think Linda's preoccupation with giants is related to the missing kids?"

Laney's enjoyment of the discussion crashed to the ground as reality roared back and slapped her in the face. She shook her head. "I don't see how. I mean, these ancient skeletons were huge, and some nephilim like Henry or Maddox are tall, but besides that, I don't see any connection."

Jake was quiet for a moment. "So. Are we even sure Nathaniel Grayston has the kids? Are we sure we're heading in the right direction?"

As Laney looked at him, all the doubts she had crowded into her mind. "I don't know, Jake. But right now, he's our only lead. And if he doesn't have them..." Laney couldn't finish the sentence.

So Jake finished it for her. "Then we have no idea where they are."

CHAPTER 57

SACRAMENTO, CALIFORNIA

Nathaniel sat behind his desk, staring at the family picture he kept to the right of his blotter. Zachariah was only ten in the shot and smiled brightly. He and Beatrice had thought they were so blessed with him. But that was before they knew who he was. *What* he was.

Now Nathaniel knew God had a higher purpose for him. God had not forsaken them. They had passed the trial of their son and were now to be given the keys to an everlasting reward.

A knock sounded at the door.

"Come in," Nathaniel called.

Beatrice stepped in. "Zachariah is here." There was no trace of warmth in her voice, no motherly concern. She had turned all of that off the day they had discovered what the boy was. To her, Zachariah was now a distasteful stranger.

"Send him in."

Beatrice nodded, stepping back out of the room.

Zachariah appeared in the doorway. "You needed to see me, Father?"

Nathaniel nodded, waving him in. He stood up and walked over to his son, placing his hand briefly on the boy's shoulder. "My son. You will never know God's grace. You are cursed. There is no changing that. But there is hope for you. The Shepherd has shown us a way for you to honor this family."

Zach looked up, his eyes identical to his mother's. The similarity only made Nathaniel cringe more. He shook off his disgust at the abomination cloaked in familiar dressing.

"You have been given a duty—a higher calling. By this act, you open the door to everlasting salvation. That must count for something."

"Yes, Father."

"I have always thought you were our curse: a punishment for our sins. But now I see that you are our reward for following His ways. Through you, we open the door to eternal rewards. The Shepherd has a plan for you."

"Me?"

Nathaniel smiled, imagining his name being linked with glory for generations to come. All would know of Nathaniel Grayston. He placed his hand on his son's shoulder with a squeeze. "Yes, son. I am proud it is our family who has been called to this mission."

Zachariah's eyes filled with tears. "Yes, Father. Thank you, Father. What must I do?"

The boy's tears confused Nathaniel, until he realized that Zachariah must think that Nathaniel was proud of him. *Oh well, if it helps the mission, so be it.*

He took Zachariah's shoulders and peered into his eyes. "You must go into the belly of the beast. Are you strong enough for that?"

Zach nodded. "Yes, Father. I am."

"Good, good. You may go." Nathaniel walked back to his desk. His thoughts of his son were already gone. He was too wrapped up in thoughts of the glorious future that awaited him.

CHAPTER 58

L aney rested her head on her hand and stared out the window at the clouds. Jake had just left to go to the cockpit and speak with Clark.

The SIA was supposed to meet them on the ground and offer some backup, although Jake wasn't sure if they'd get there in time. And Laney and he knew there was no chance they were going to wait. If the kids were at the reverend's church, there wasn't a minute to lose.

Laney tried to keep her mind focused on concrete details and not on the missing kids. Images of Max, though, kept trying to crowd into her mind. And each time they did, she shoved them away.

She mentally pulled up the layout of the church's property. It wasn't large—only about two acres. But it was surrounded by undeveloped land, isolated. There were three buildings: the church itself, and two other buildings that had been built by Nathaniel. *I wonder if—*

Her phone beeped and she looked at it, realizing she'd missed a text from Jen. They had landed in Chicago. She was about to call her back when her iPad beeped. She shook her head, remembering a time when going on a plane meant not communicating with anyone at all, and pulled the iPad into her lap. She clicked on the Skype icon and her uncle's face popped up on the screen. "Laney?"

"Hey, Uncle Patrick. How's Kati?"

"She's," he hesitated, "okay."

Dread washed over her. "What happened?"

"She woke up and asked for Max. When she remembered what happened, she had to be sedated."

Laney leaned back heavily against the chair and closed her eyes. She wanted so much to be with Kati right now. Logically, she knew she was helping Kati more in the long run by being here, but it didn't make being away any easier. *Get him back for her. That's how you can help her.*

She opened her eyes, noticing the background behind her uncle. He was sitting on a grey couch, and behind him was a table with four chairs. "Where are you now?"

"The doctor's lounge down the hall from Kati. They let me borrow it."

"Okay. I'm guessing you found something?"

He nodded. "I finished watching Grayston's sermons. He's very much a fire-and-brimstone type of preacher. I don't think the New Testament holds much appeal for him. Nathaniel's version of religion is a hodgepodge of different scriptures strung together to justify his worldview."

Laney nodded. That had been her guess as well. "So what is his worldview?"

Patrick sighed. "That we are on the precipice of a new world order, something similar to the Rapture, where only the holy survive. The new age arrives with certain signs and certain actions."

"What signs?" Laney asked, but was distracted when Jake walked down the aisle and took the seat next to her. He squeezed Laney's hand and nodded at the screen. "Hey, Patrick."

Patrick nodded back. "Jake."

"I just spoke with the pilot. We'll be landing in about forty-five minutes. It'll be another fifteen minutes to the church from there." He glanced between Laney and Patrick. "What's wrong?"

"Nothing more than before. We were just talking about Nathaniel's sermons."

"And actually, there *may* be more wrong than before," Patrick said.

"What do you mean?" Laney asked, her dread growing.

"I've been listening to the webcasts. For the last year, they've taken on a theme." Patrick went quiet, his face troubled.

"Okay..." Jake drew out the word. "Care to share what that theme is?"

"Sorry," Patrick said with a shake of his head. "He's been talking about the state of the world."

"And I'm guessing he's not saying the state is good?" Laney asked.

Patrick nodded. "He speaks of different events in the world, like the red tide breakouts across the globe. Of course, instead of explaining about the algae blooms causing the coloration, he speaks about the seas running red with blood." He hit some buttons on his phone. "I just sent you a clip of one of his sermons. Take a look at it."

"Hold on." Laney pulled out her phone. A second later Patrick's email arrived. Laney brought up the image. Frozen on the screen was Nathaniel.

"I queued it to the part I thought you should see," Patrick said. "Just hit play."

Jake reached over and ran the video. On screen, Nathaniel jumped to life. "We are in a dangerous time—a time of action. Apathy is not an option."

Off screen, there were murmurs of agreement.

"What will it take to wake people up?" Nathaniel thundered. "They are blind to the truth. The rivers run red with blood. Just a few weeks ago, Sydney, Australia's waters were bathed in blood."

The camera cut away to the congregation, shaking their heads in horror.

"Each week another meat recall is announced. Storms are becoming more severe. Manhattan has been flooded. Hurricanes, tornadoes of increasing intensity are scattered across this great nation. And the darkness of spirit... it pervades every corner of our society. It snuffs out the light of the Word."

The camera panned back to the crowd. People were on their feet now, shouting their agreement.

Nathaniel moved around the podium to stand in front of it. The camera operator zoomed in on his face. Nathaniel's eyes were filled with fire. "Now is the time of decision. What will you do? Will you do what needs to be done? Will you?"

The audience was ecstatic in their support.

Nathaniel smiled—a smile that made Laney's skin crawl. "Good. Because the time is here."

The clip stopped with a close-up of Nathaniel. Laney stared at the image frozen on her screen. He looked smug, self-righteous. Happy.

Her stomach rolled. "Okay, all horrible. But so what? Isn't horrible his thing?"

"Yes, but it's the passages he's been using to bring home his points. They all come from Exodus."

"Not much Sunday school for me, I'm afraid," Jake said wryly. "We're still talking about the escape from Egypt, right?"

"A little more than that."

Laney felt the shock root her in place. She glanced up at Patrick, horror crawling across her skin. "He's aligning modern misfortunes with the ten plagues."

Patrick nodded. "Yes."

The ten plagues. In the Bible, the land of Egypt was besieged by ten horrific plagues: water turning into blood, infestations of frogs, flies, locusts, and gnats, darkness, diseased livestock, thunder and hail, and finally the death of all the first-born. Off the top of her head, Laney could think at least seven events in the last few years that fit those plagues. And she was pretty sure that, with a little research, she could make a case for the other three.

"Grayston's ministry—it's not just a church," Laney said. "It's a doomsday cult."

Patrick nodded. "Yes. I think that's right."

Laney looked back at Patrick. "When was that posted?"

"One week ago."

Jake looked between them. "Doomsdays cults tend to count down to a big event, right?"

Laney nodded, staring at the screen again. "If those kids are alive, I think they're running out of time."

CHAPTER 59

CHICAGO, ILLINOIS

Henry and Jen drove past the Northgram home. The house sat on about two acres with a six-foot wrought iron fence surrounding it. Like every other house on the street, the yard was immaculately maintained.

Henry had had an operative watching the house since their first meeting with Northgram. The operative reported that Northgram's wife and two children had left ten minutes ago for a movie with some friends and that he hadn't seen any other signs of surveillance. But remembering the Fallen across from Northgram's office building, Henry wasn't ruling that out.

They pulled into the driveway of the people who lived two houses down from Northgram. They were out of town for an extended holiday, so Henry and his group were borrowing their driveway. In neighborhoods like this, people simply didn't park on the street.

Henry looked around. "You sense anything?"

Jen shook her head. "Nope."

"Me either. All right, let's go—but keep an eye out."

"I always do." Jen opened her door and Henry stepped out as well.

Henry nodded to the men in the SUV as they crossed the drive. One got out, and Henry handed him his keys. The man hopped into the driver's seat of the SUV Henry had driven.

Jen started to walk down the drive. "Let's go."

Henry jogged a little to catch up to her. He took her hand and she glanced up in surprise. He grinned. "Just a young couple out for a walk."

She rolled her eyes. "You really think that's necessary?"

Henry smiled back. "No."

Jen laughed.

They made their way leisurely down the street. Each lot was at least one and a half acres, and every home looked like it was ready for its own magazine spread. But no one was out. No cars in the drive. No kids' toys on the lawns.

"Kind of has a Stepford quality to it, doesn't it?" Jen asked with a shiver.

Henry nodded. "Yeah."

The Northgram home was no different than the others on the block in that regard. Two turrets dominated the three-story rock face home, giving it the appearance of a small castle. But it was one of only two on the street that had a full fence encircling the yard.

As they approached, Henry asked, "See anybody?"

"Just a lawn crew down the street."

Henry nodded. He hadn't seen anyone either. He spoke into his cell. "Now."

A second later a reply came back. "You're good. All their cameras and power are down. Be careful."

"We will," Henry said softly before disconnecting the call. He glanced over at Jen. "Shall we?"

She smiled—a smile that looked a little predatory. "Let's."

Northgram had four guards at his estate at all times: two

outside, two inside. Henry held his tranquilizer gun in front of him. "I'll go round the back. You get the guy at the front gate."

Jen nodded with a grimace, holding up her own tranquilizer gun. "I still can't believe you talked me into this."

"Well, we're the ones breaking in today."

"Yes. But tomorrow they'll undeniably be right back to being the bad guys."

Henry sighed. "I know. But the good guys have to play by rules the bad guys don't."

"Fine." Jen drew out the word. "I'll give you ten seconds to get in place before I take out the guy in the front. Meet you in the living room?"

Henry smiled. He loved how Jen just assumed this wouldn't be a problem. Who was he kidding? He loved a lot of things about Jen. "See you there."

He sprinted for the back of the estate. They knew one guy patrolled the front and one stayed at the back. The other two seemed to roam the entire house, crossing paths, but Henry wasn't worried. From what they could tell, they were only human. Apparently Northgram didn't trust any Fallen.

Through the fence, he caught sight of the guard coming around the side of the pool. Henry put on a burst of speed and jumped the fence, landing ten feet behind the guard. The guard turned quickly, but Henry had already fired. The tranquilizer dart caught the man in the thigh.

Henry sprinted forward, grabbing the man's hand before he could raise his weapon. "Good night." The man's eyelids drooped, then closed. Henry gently lowered him to the ground.

Henry's head whipped up as he heard the sound of a crash from inside.

Jen.

He vaulted over the pool. In two steps, he was at one of the sets of French doors that lined the back of the house. He ripped one of the doors off it hinges, tossed it aside, and rushed in.

Jen stood at the other end of the room. Northgram was on the floor at her feet, a broken vase next to him.

She raised an eyebrow. "You all right?"

"Um—yeah," Henry said. "I heard a crash."

Jen shrugged. "Phil here was trying to make for his panic room. I didn't want to have to break down that door, so I threw a vase at him."

Henry chuckled. "A vase?"

She shrugged again. "It was handy."

"The other three guards?" Henry asked.

"Sleeping it off." Her eyes twinkled. "Did you get your one little guard?"

"Yes, thank you very much. And he was not little."

Jen grinned. "Sure—whatever makes you feel better."

Northgram groaned from the floor. "If you two are finished."

Jen crouched down next to him. "Careful, Phil. You're probably going to have a nasty headache. Let me help." She pulled him up by the back of the shirt and then half dragged, half carried him to the sunken living room.

Henry tried not to smile as Jen unceremoniously dumped Northgram into a chair and made a big show of wiping her hands on her jeans. Then she glanced at Henry. "The floor is yours."

Henry nodded and came around to stand in front of Northgram. "Phil, you have not been entirely forthcoming."

Northgram shrank back in the chair. "Yes I have. I've told you everything I know. I sent you that list of members."

Henry sat on the ottoman directly in front of Northgram, allowing the man to look him right in the eyes. "You never told us about your son."

Northgram paused, his eyebrows knit together. "Michael? He's only ten. He has nothing to do with this."

"Not Michael. Your other son," Jen said.

Northgram stared between them for a moment, completely confused.

"Nathaniel?" Jen prompted.

Northgram blanched. "Oh."

"Yes, 'oh,'" Henry said. "He's the one behind the abductions of the children."

Northgram shook his head with a sigh and stretched his legs out. "Really? Well, I can't say I'm too surprised. His mother was never really *there*, if you know what I mean."

Henry held back his anger. "Great. Well, now that you remember your own child, how about you tell us about him?"

Northgram sighed. "I haven't seen him in years."

"Then why don't you tell us about the first wife you've kept hidden?" Jen suggested.

Northgram looked up, his eyes narrowed. "Why?"

Henry inched forward. "Because she asked nicely."

Northgram leaned farther back. "Okay, okay. But I don't see what it has to do with anything."

"We'll decide that," Jen said. "Talk."

Northgram straightened his pants. "It was a mistake. Linda and I were both young. And she was fun and wild. And maybe a little off."

"A little off?" Jen asked.

Northgram shrugged. "She heard voices sometimes. But she had other... virtues."

Jen made a sound of disgust.

Henry waved his hand. "What else?"

"I don't know what you want. We were twenty when we got married. Linda got pregnant a year later. We were thrilled. And then everything fell apart."

"Why did everything fall apart?" Henry asked, his patience thinning.

"There was a problem with the birth: a placental eruption. Linda nearly died, Nathaniel nearly died. And Linda came out of it a changed person."

"Changed how?" Jen asked, stepping forward.

"Religious. *Extremely* religious. Although she didn't align herself with any particular group. She read the Bible over and over. Found old esoteric texts and believed every word in them." Northgram shook his head. "She became this crazy person."

"So how did she end up with Nathaniel, and why did you hide them?" Jen asked.

"I wasn't *hiding* them. I was distancing myself from them. Look, I loved Nathaniel. I had every intention of bringing him into the family business."

"You mean the Council?" Henry asked.

Northgram hesitated before nodding.

"So what happened?" Jen asked, not even trying to hide her disgust. "Child rearing proved too much for you?"

"No. I even began instructing Nathaniel on my business. We spent every weekend talking about history and the importance of our place in it."

Henry looked at Northgram, trying to figure the man out. He had spent time with his son, grooming him in the family business, and then let him go? "So how did he end up with Linda?"

Northgram ran his hand through his thinning hair. "Linda and Nathaniel have always been close. And one day, he told her about the Council. About what we did, how we made our money. It convinced her that I was the devil. But she didn't tell me right away. First she gathered documentation on Council activities. And then she gave me an ultimatum: I let her and Nathaniel go— providing them with whatever they need, but never seeing them— or she would reveal everything she knew."

Henry stared at him, his disgust growing. "So you let your son go off with an unstable woman to save yourself?"

Northgram stared back at Henry, arrogance in his tone. "You don't understand. I have responsibilities, *duties*. And Linda was smart. She made it clear that if anything happened to her, the documents would be released."

"Well, aren't you just father of the year," Jen muttered.

Northgram glared over at her. "She *was* unstable, and apparently so is he. So I think *I* made the right choice."

"You made your son a monster by leaving him with her," Jen growled.

"He was already well on the way to being a monster. There was nothing I could do to change that."

"Yeah, you're right. Your DNA damned him from the start," Jen retorted.

Northgram glared at her, his jaw clenched.

"Did you give your son the list of children?" Jen demanded.

"What?" Surprise flashed across Northgram's face. "No, of course not."

"You're sure?" Henry asked.

"Yes. Look, I realize we're not on the same side. But targeting children? No. That's a line I won't cross."

"And no one in your organization would either?" Jen asked.

"No, of course—" Northgram paused.

"What? Who are you thinking of?" Henry demanded.

Northgram shook his head. "No one. I mean, I don't know."

"Don't know what?" Henry asked.

Northgram shook his head again. "I can't."

Jen reached over and grabbed the front of his shirt. "Oh, yes, you can."

Northgram tried to push Jen's hand away. It was a useless effort. "You don't understand. He's dangerous."

"What do you think I am?" Jen countered.

Northgram blanched.

"Now," Jen ordered.

"Okay, okay." Northgram swatted at Jen's hand again. She shoved him away.

Henry towered over him, his arms crossed. "Who?"

"I'm not really sure."

Jen stormed forward. "Oh, for the love of—"

Northgram put up his hands. "No, no. I'm talking. It's just that

I don't know his name. No one does. I'm not even sure if it's a man or a woman."

Henry looked at him, remembering what Laney had told him about her conversation with Clark. "The real head of the Council."

Northgram nodded. "But I don't know who he or she is. And it doesn't pay to look. Some have tried in the past, and, well… at least their funerals were well attended."

"God, you're cold." Jen said.

"No, I'm a businessman. And messing with the Council is bad for business."

Jen glared at Northgram, and Henry had the distinct impression she was trying to keep herself from pummeling the guy. He gave Jen's arm a gentle squeeze. "Jen."

She stared up at him and Henry was surprised by the fear that flashed in her eyes. And it hit him: why she was taking this so personally. She identified with the kids. Twenty years ago, *she* would have been one of the kids rounded up. He spoke gently. "Why don't you get some fresh air? Maybe call Laney."

She nodded. "Yeah. The air in here *is* getting a little rank." She turned around and walked through the doorway Henry had destroyed earlier. Henry watched her go.

"Good job," Northgram said. "She really doesn't—"

Henry's head whipped around. "Understand this. If you don't tell me something I can use to find your son and these children, I will happily let her unleash some of the disgust she has for you. And I'll unleash a little of my own."

Northgram paled. "I—but—"

Henry stared him down, and Northgram shut his mouth with a nod.

Henry took his seat again in front of Northgram. "Now. Let's start back at the beginning. Tell me everything you know about your son."

CHAPTER 60

After speaking with Jen, Laney turned off her phone and stared out the window. So, Linda had blackmailed Northgram into giving her custody of their son. But more frightening, Northgram suspected that the unknown head of the Council was really behind the abductions.

Was this just a red herring to throw them off the trail of his son? Laney shook her head. She didn't think so. From what Jen said, father and son didn't seem to have much of a bond.

But why would the head of the Council target the kids?

Crap. More puzzle pieces that don't fit. Nathaniel was leading a doomsday cult. What did he want the children for? Were they some sort of new generation? Indoctrinate them early? Or were they some sort of sacrifice?

Are we even on the right track? Laney thought as she glanced back to where Jake and Maddox were deep in discussion. No doubt debating what weapons to take on the raid.

Laney turned back around. Clark had said the head of the Council had been shrouded in mystery since its inception. And that anyone who tried to find out who it was met a quick and decisive end. Was it possible that the same person was somehow behind any of this? Was it just a wild goose chase?

Perhaps it didn't matter. She needed all her people tracking down information on Nathaniel right now; she couldn't afford to pull any of them to start looking into the mystery leader. And even if she did, whoever she assigned to the new investigation would have to watch their back.

Laney rubbed her hands over her face. God, this sucked. She needed the information, but she didn't want to risk anyone's lives.

Victoria flashed through her mind. Mysterious, enigmatic, and infuriating as hell with her secrets, but she was also really good at ferreting out details people wanted to keep hidden. If anyone could uncover the Council head's identity, it was probably her. But would she be able to do it without getting killed?

Laney pulled out her phone and dialed. Victoria's voicemail picked up immediately, as Laney had known it would. She waited for the beep. "Victoria, it's Laney. I need your help. Call me."

There was one other thing she could do that she knew would increase their odds—but it meant going back on her word. *I guess that's what being a leader is all about. Doing what's best for the group at the expense of the individual.*

She dialed and waited.

"Hello?"

"Hi, Danny. There's something I need to tell you."

CHAPTER 61

BALTIMORE, MARYLAND

Danny hung up the phone and stared out the window. *Max.* His heart ached and he felt the tears threatening to break. *How could someone take Max?*

He'd known that something was up. He'd gotten into the system and saw that Henry was calling everyone up. He thought they were just going after the kids without him, which he understood. But it was far more than that.

His heart lurched again. *Max.*

There was a knock on the doorframe behind him. "Hey, we're going to—" Lou cut off as Danny turned around.

Rolly stepped forward. "Danny, what's wrong?"

Danny wiped at his eyes. "Somebody grabbed Max."

Lou's mouth opened, but no words came out. Rolly rolled a chair over to sit next to Danny. "Do they think it's the same guys who grabbed the other kids?"

Danny nodded.

"When did it happen?"

"Yesterday," Danny said, feeling hollow.

"Yesterday?" Lou asked, coming to lean against the table. "Did you just find out?"

Danny nodded. "Henry didn't want me to worry."

"So that's why they sent you here. And that's where the rest of them disappeared to," Lou said.

Danny nodded numbly.

"Do they have any clues?" she asked.

Danny cleared his throat. "They, um, they know who the reverend is."

"The reverend?" Rolly asked.

Danny looked over at him. "He's the one they think grabbed them. They're heading to his place right now."

"So it's a religious thing?" Rolly asked.

Danny shook his head. "No, not really. From what Laney said, it's more of a 'pick and choose your favorite parts of the Bible to justify your cause' thing."

"But they know where he is," Lou said. "Which means they'll get the kids back. They'll get Max back."

Danny shook his head. "They don't even know if the kids will be there. Laney didn't say that, but I could read between the lines."

"Do they think…" Lou paused, her eyes meeting Danny's. "Do they think the kids are still alive?"

"Laney didn't say. But I…" He broke off. The thought of Max being dead was too painful to bear. "And it gets worse. When they grabbed Max, they shot Kati. She's in the hospital."

Lou sank down heavily in a chair. "That's horrible."

"Actually, it's not," Rolly said.

Both Lou and Danny stared at him in disbelief.

Rolly put up his hands. "No, I don't mean it that way. I mean, yes, it's horrible that Kati was shot. But they didn't shoot Max. They took him. That must mean they want him for something. Which means there's a good chance he's still alive."

"He's right." Lou gave Rolly a smile before turning to Danny.

"Can you help? I mean, you're like a super-genius, right? Is there something you can do to find him?"

Danny looked at the two of them. His thoughts were slow, his horror getting in the way of ability to think—just like in the alleyway. And then he stopped. *Stupid.* The alleyway. When he'd gotten back home, he'd promised himself he'd keep Max safe. And he did —the only way he could.

Hope began to build inside him. "Actually, there is. In fact, I'm pretty sure I can find him. But I need to get out there."

"Out there? Out where?" Lou asked.

Danny shook his head. "Not sure yet. Somewhere west."

Rolly and Lou exchanged a look before Lou spoke. "Great. I've never seen the west coast. We'll come with you."

"What?" Danny asked.

"Look, Danny, we've all been talking," Lou said. "We all know what it feels like to be ripped away from your life. We want to help."

"We?" Danny asked. "Who's we?"

Rolly gestured toward the door. "Me, Lou, some of the other guys."

Danny shook his head. "I don't know…"

Lou stood up, her hands on her waist. "Look, when they find the kids, they're going to need help. Rolly and I can be that help. Maybe a few of the other students with abilities, too."

Danny shook his head. "No way. Henry would kill me. *Jen* would kill you."

"Maybe. But they don't need to know until after the kids are back. They're just *kids*, Danny. We want to help. What's the point of being super-powered if you can't use your powers for good? You know what they say, with great power comes…" She let her words dwindle off.

Danny bit his lip, his gaze shifting from Rolly to Lou. He thought of Max. He was such a good kid. He didn't deserve this. None of those kids did.

Then he realized something else. He knew Henry was behind the attempt to keep Max's abduction from him. Yet for the first time, he wasn't mad. He understood what Henry was trying to do. But what Henry had to realize was that he wasn't just a kid. He was someone who could help.

And he hadn't yet done all he could. He felt a little guilty. Because he had kept something from Henry, too—something that could help them find Max and maybe all the other kids.

Lou and Rolly were watching him expectantly. At last Danny nodded. "Okay, but you need to do exactly as I say."

He waited until Lou and Rolly both nodded back at him, then he looked at his watch. "And we need to go now. There's not much time. And first things first: do either of you know where Yoni is?"

CHAPTER 62

SACRAMENTO, CALIFORNIA

Laney's phone rang just as the plane was preparing to land. She glanced at the unfamiliar number before she answered. "Hello?"

"Laney? It's Victoria."

Laney breathed deeply. *Thank God.* "Hi."

"Hi. How are you?"

"I've been better."

"I can imagine. I'm sorry about Max. What can I do to help?"

"I was hoping you'd offer. And there is something I need you to do." She chewed her lip. Could she even ask Victoria this?

"Laney, talk."

"It could be dangerous."

"Is it important?"

Laney thought about the missing kids, the resources needed to identify them, and the stakes. And the fact that this one unknown player kept being mentioned. "Yes. It is."

"Then tell me what you need."

Laney blew out a breath. "Okay." She explained to Victoria

about the High Council, the mysterious leader, and the fate of those who had gone digging. "No one knows who he or she is. It might not be related, but it just feels like it's important."

"It's a hole, and you want it filled."

Laney nodded. "Exactly."

"I'll see what I can find out."

"Victoria, it could be dangerous. Apparently tracking down this person is not good for one's health."

"I'll take precautions."

Laney wanted to say more but didn't. She'd warned Victoria; now it was up to her. Laney tried to lighten the mood. "I'm surprised you don't already know who it is."

Victoria remained silent.

Laney gasped. "You *do* know? I was just joking."

"I don't know for sure. Let's just say I suspect."

"Who? Who is it?"

Laney could picture Victoria shaking her head. "Let me verify it first. And if it's who I think it is, we'll talk."

"Well, this person you suspect, would they target the potentials?"

Victoria was silent for a moment. "Yes, if it's him. Yes, he would."

"But why?"

"For fun. He gets bored easily."

Laney gaped at the phone. For fun? Over a dozen children's lives hung in the balance because someone was having *fun*? "You're kidding."

"Sadly, I'm not."

"But—" Laney's mind whirled. "So do you think it's possible this guy could have given the list to Grayston?"

"Oh, that would definitely amuse him. He likes being a puppet master."

Laney stared around the cabin, knowing her mouth was gaping but unable to close it just yet. She realized there was actually a sick sort of continuity in the Council leader's behavior. He had used emissaries to attend meetings, had treated them like puppets—just like Nathaniel. He got them to do his bidding and then disposed of them. But now his bidding included the lives of children. "That's sick."

"Yes, it is. But we don't yet know it's him. So let me see what I can find out and I'll get back to you. Is there anything else?"

Laney stared at the phone as she tried to collect her thoughts. Anything else? There was so much. She tried to pull her mind back to the immediate issues. "Um, yeah. We're trying to get a handle on Grayston's finances."

"Following the money to all his followers and hidey holes."

"Exactly. And you tend to be pretty good at finding the unfindable. Can you run down that angle?"

"Of course." Victoria paused. "You sound like you think there's something to find."

"I'm not sure. We know someone donated the land that Nathaniel built his church on. But it was done anonymously, and we haven't been able to find anything on them."

"And you think it's important."

"I don't know." Frustration rolled through Laney. "But kids' lives are at stake. I don't want to overlook anything. It could just be some rich donor who supports the church but for public image reasons doesn't want his association known."

"But right now it's an unknown, and you'd rather not have any of those."

Victoria's words hit her like a slap. "You don't think—I mean, it's not possible that the land donor and the Council head are one and the same?"

"I'll find out."

And Laney had no doubt that she would. Victoria went silent but Laney was okay with that. It was a comfort just having the connection. Finally, Victoria spoke again. "How are *you* doing with all of this?"

Laney slumped down in her seat a little more. "I'm okay."

"Really?" Victoria asked.

"Well, maybe 'okay' is stretching it. I'm getting by."

"You'll get to them in time, Laney. You're the ring bearer. And there's a reason you are—you'll do whatever needs to be done to protect the innocent. It's your blessing and your curse."

"Uncle Patrick said pretty much the same thing. But sometimes I worry…" She broke off.

"Sometimes you worry what?" Victoria prodded gently.

"Sometimes I worry I'm not up to the task. Everyone keeps looking to me with all these expectations. And I worry I'm going to let everyone down, which means…" Laney couldn't finish the sentence. She didn't want to voice the fears aloud.

"Which means people die. And in this case, children."

Laney nodded and her voice shook. "Yeah."

"Laney, you didn't create this evil. Evil was around in this world long before you. But you can fight it. And you will. You need to stop putting all this pressure on yourself. You will do everything in your power to save these kids. But if you can't, that blame is not yours to shoulder. It's Grayston's."

Laney nodded, knowing Victoria was right, but also knowing she would blame herself regardless.

"And Laney, people's faith in you isn't misplaced. You can do this. You *will* do this."

Laney looked around the cabin. Most people were sleeping. She sighed, feeling the mantle of responsibility settle on her shoulders. "Yes, Mother."

CHAPTER 63

Laney looked at the three building complex. The church was hidden behind the two newer buildings, which looked more like warehouses than places of religious worship. As for the church, all she could see was a white steeple in need of a paint job.

There were no adornments and no religious iconography identifying the location. Just a handmade sign planted in the ground in front of the main building: *The Feast of the Lamb. Members Only.* In fact, unless you knew what you were looking for, you'd drive right by and never guess there was a church here.

From what they'd found out online and through a conversation with the local police department, they knew that about three dozen church members lived here, including the minister, his wife, and son. But there were no people in sight at the moment, although there were a few cars in the parking lot.

Jake gestured toward the warehouse-like buildings. "I'm guessing one of those is the residences and the other the administrative office."

Laney nodded, a thought striking her. She quickly dialed her uncle and put him on speakerphone. "Has Grayston ever posted a sermon from his church?"

There was a note of surprise in Patrick's voice. "Actually, no. They're always from the tent, when he's on the road."

"But he does have sermons here, right?" Maddox asked from over Laney's shoulder.

"Yes," Patrick replied. "But they're reserved for his official church members."

"That seems a little odd," Jake said.

"Now that you've brought it up, it does," Patrick said.

"Thanks, Uncle Patrick." Laney started to disconnect the call.

"Wait."

Laney paused. "What?"

"When you go to the church, put me on video so I can see it."

"What? Why?" Laney asked.

Patrick's voice sounded strained. "I just have a feeling."

"Care to expand?" Laney asked.

"No," Patrick said. "But it might help if I can see it."

Laney nodded. "Okay." She disconnected the call and slipped the phone back in her pocket.

"What do you think it means that he never posted sermons from here?" Jake asked.

Laney shrugged, looking back at the buildings. "I don't know. Maybe nothing."

Jake looked at Maddox and Laney. "You guys have a copy of the warrant?"

Laney nodded, but Maddox jerked his thumb toward the tall blond Chandler operative behind him. "I gave my copy to Jordan. He's more likely to talk first."

"Don't bet on it," Jordan Witt, Jen's brother, muttered.

"Are you getting anything?" Jake asked, his voice low.

Laney shook her head. "No. Whoever is in there is fully human. At least I think they're human. Maddox?"

He shook his head. "I'm not sensing anyone either."

Laney looked at Maddox's determined face and said a silent thank you that she had brought him into Max's life.

"Well, hopefully that's a good thing," Jake said.

Laney glanced at the six police officers behind them and the handful of Chandler operatives. The SIA agents hadn't been able to reach them in time, so they'd had to make do with local cops. The police had been decidedly unhappy when Clark had called them to let them know what was happening in their own back yard.

Laney was worried they might be a little *too* unhappy, but it was too late to do anything about that now. She leaned over to Jake. "Do you realize this is the first time we're doing one of these with legal backing?"

Jake nodded. "Feels weird, doesn't it?"

It was Clark who'd managed to finagle the warrants to search the church's property. While it was nice to have the legal authority, Laney knew they'd be going in with or without legal backing.

Jake surveyed the group of twelve men and women. He met Maddox's eyes. "Maddox, your group takes building one. Laney, your group takes two. I'll take the church."

Laney nodded.

Jake leaned down. "Be careful."

She looked up into his eyes. "Same goes."

Jake nodded and turned back to the group. "Okay. Let's go."

They separated, each group heading to their own building. As Laney's group approached building two, a woman stepped out of it. Her eyes widened when she caught sight of Laney and the men charging toward her, and she dashed back in.

Shit. "Let's go!" Laney yelled. She ran faster.

One of her men reached the door first and moved in. Laney went in after him. The desk at the front was deserted, but they could hear voices coming from the hall to the right.

Laney gestured for two of the men to head to the left while the other two followed her. There was only one door down this hall, and it was open.

She inched forward. The voices got louder and now she could

hear a whirring noise. She peeked her head in. Two women were frantically trying to shred documents.

Laney stepped into the room. "Hands up."

One woman shrieked, dropping the papers she was holding as her hands flew into the air. The other woman didn't even pause to look up.

"Stop!" Laney ran across the room, pushing the woman away from the shredder and shoving her up against the wall. "Who are you?"

The woman didn't wear any makeup and her dress was extremely modest. She glared back at Laney.

"Laney," one of the Chandler operatives called, pointing to a picture on the desk.

Laney glanced at the picture of the preacher and his family. Then she turned back to the woman. "Beatrice Grayston, where is your husband?"

Beatrice sneered, turning her once beautiful face into an ugly mask. "You're an agent of evil. You can't stop the righteous."

"Where are the kids?" Laney asked.

The woman's eyes narrowed. "They're not children. They're abominations."

Laney pushed the woman harder against the wall and spoke through gritted teeth. "Where. Are. They?"

Beatrice smiled. "You're too late."

CHAPTER 64

nger soared through Laney. It was taking every ounce of her self-control not to wipe the smug look off Beatrice Grayston's face. She shoved her toward one of the police officers. "Take her before I kill her."

"Laney," Maddox's voice called through her radio.

Laney pulled it free. "What is it?"

His voice was somber. "I need you to see something."

No. Laney felt her heart miss a beat. She turned to the Chandler operative at the desk. "Go through the papers. See if it tells us anything about the kids."

He nodded. "You got it. Go."

Her legs felt like lead as she walked out of the office, and her heart was trying to pound its way out of her chest. *Please let them be all right. Please let Max be all right.*

Even with the leaden legs, though, she found herself running for building one.

When she got there, a group of women was being herded out. Laney barely glanced at them as she made her way past. She stopped in the doorway and caught sight of Maddox at the end of the hall. He waved her down.

Swallowing, she took some calming breaths, keeping her eyes focused on Maddox. He looked okay—angry, but okay. Not devastated. She let out a breath. It was bad news, but not what she feared most.

She reached Maddox's side. He glanced down at her before nodding toward the doorway. "They were here."

Laney stepped in and felt the world tilt. Children's toys were scattered around the room, along with some articles of clothing. She turned to Maddox. "Bodies?"

Maddox shook his head. "No."

Laney grabbed on to the back of a chair and took several deep breaths. The oxygen flooded her system.

Maddox gestured around the room. "But we know they were here."

He led her across the room to a poster of two kittens in a basket. He lifted it up. Underneath, the words "please help us" were scrawled in crayon. And beneath that were fourteen names.

Laney's heart nearly stopped when she reached the last name on the list: Max. She looked up at Maddox. His face was expressionless, but Laney could read the anger in his eyes.

She looked around, trying to shove her emotions away so she could concentrate. "Any blood? Drugs? Signs of violence?"

Maddox shook his head. "No, nothing like that. But I have men searching the yard."

Laney nodded, swallowing hard. She closed her eyes. *Looking for graves.* She opened her eyes again. "But if Max was here, that means we missed them by less than twenty-four hours."

Maddox nodded.

A day. They'd missed them by a *day*. "Goddamn it."

"Laney?" Jake called through the radio.

Laney yanked the radio off her belt. "Yeah."

"I need you and Maddox to join me in the church."

Maddox's eyes stared intently. Jake sounded frazzled, and she'd never heard him frazzled.

"What's wrong?" Laney asked.

"I—" Jake went silent. "I think you need to see this."

Laney's mouth was suddenly dry. "Is it the kids?"

Jake's words rushed out. "No. No. It's not that. Sorry. No."

Laney closed her eyes. She was going to have a heart attack before the day was done.

"So what is it?' Laney asked.

"You have to see it for yourself. It's something…" Jake paused. "Unexpected."

CHAPTER 65

As Maddox and Laney headed toward the church together, neither of them said a word. What could they say? They had just shared a moment where they thought all of the children were dead. They both needed a little time to come down—or, more accurately, up—from that moment.

Some of the members of Jake's group stood outside the church, looking shaky.

What's in there that could be so bad? Laney looked at Maddox, but he just shook his head.

A sign out front said the church had first been erected in 1832. While it could use a paint job, it looked like a thousand other churches strewn across the nation: white, a tall steeple, a set of brick stairs leading up to the front door.

Jake stepped out the front door and waved them in, his face grim. Laney steeled herself as she headed up the stairs. When she stepped into the church, her jaw dropped.

Maddox's reaction was a little more vocal. "Fuck me."

Two chandeliers made entirely of bones and skulls dangled from the church rafters. More bones were used as decorations on the walls, and the entire back wall of the church was covered in skulls.

Laney moved forward on automatic pilot, taking in the macabre scene. Skulls capped the end of each pew, lining the main aisle.

"What the hell is this?" Maddox whispered.

"It's a church of bones," Laney answered.

Jake stepped up. "I don't have your archaeological background, but I'd say these bones are old."

Laney nodded as she walked over to the wall decoration nearest her. Four skulls were arranged together in the center. Like the spokes on a wheel, six arm bones were arranged around them, with a smaller bone positioned at the end of each. *A kneecap, maybe?* Then femurs were used to create an outer circle. Almost all of the bones had turned brown in color, and a few looked extremely fragile.

Laney looked back at Jake. "I think you're right."

"Who does something like this?" Maddox asked.

"Believe it or not, this is not the first church of bones I've seen." Laney said. "There's a very famous church of bones in the Czech Republic: the Sedlec Ossuary."

"It's a church?" Jake asked.

Laney nodded. "Yes. Back in the thirteenth century one of the priests went to the Holy Land and allegedly brought back dirt from Jesus's burial place. He spread the dirt across the cemetery, which turned the cemetery into a very popular place to be buried. But by the sixteenth century, they were out of room. So the priests began digging up the oldest graves. Then, in the nineteenth century, an artist decided to use the bones to decorate the church."

"But... why?" Maddox asked.

Laney shook her head. "I don't know. But the Czech church is considered to be the most beautiful ossuary in the world."

"And they still use it as a church?" Jake asked.

Laney nodded. "Yes, a Christian one."

"And there are others?" Jake asked.

"Yes," Laney said. "They're not cults or associated with Satanism, despite how macabre they appear. Usually it's just a matter of doing something creative with an overabundance of bones."

Jake paused. "Do you think that's what's happening here?"

Laney shook her head. "I doubt it. But we should check local cemeteries just to make sure they're not missing anybody."

"Lovely," Maddox muttered.

Jake pulled on one of the skulls from a nearby church pew; it came up easily. He glanced inside. "Laney, you want to look at this?"

Laney made her way over to him and glanced inside the skull. On the inside of the cranium was a sticker, with numbers printed on it in faded ink. She looked back at him, feeling her eyes grow wide. "Someone catalogued this skull."

"What does that mean?" Maddox asked.

She glanced around the church. There were easily thousands of bones. "It means that some of these were part of a collection—probably a museum's, although we can't rule out a private collection."

She focused on one of the chandeliers. The work was exquisite, in an incredibly creepy kind of way. Her eyes once again roamed the room. It would have taken a long time to arrange all these bones, not to mention collect them in the first place. A museum would be the most likely source. But why wouldn't they notice them missing?

Although, she mused, if they were taken from a large enough museum, their disappearance might go unnoticed. She thought of the bowels of the American Museum of Natural History. She'd gone there with her uncle once to visit a colleague. There were storerooms upon storerooms in the basement, rooms that no one had visited for years.

In fact, all large museums had far, far more relics and artifacts stored away compared to what they had on exhibit. Were all of these bones from a large museum? One that wouldn't even notice the theft for years, if ever?

Laney's attention was drawn to a giant candleholder up where, in a traditional church, the altar would be. She squinted at it. *That's not right.*

She walked over and looked at it. The base was constructed of a few small bones, but the pedestal was made up of two large bones placed back to back.

The longer bones had to be femurs. But as Laney stood next to them, she saw that they rose as high as her chest. Even minus the height of the base, that meant they were almost four feet long, more than double the size of most femurs. And that, in turn, meant that whoever these bones came from was over nine feet tall.

Laney glanced across the raised area at the front of the church. There was an identical candleholder on the opposite side.

"Laney? What's wrong?" Jake asked.

She gestured to the candleholders. "These bones. I think they're human femurs, but they're the wrong size. They're way too big. To have a femur this size, a person would have to be about nine feet tall."

Maddox walked up to her. "Laney, there's no one that tall. The tallest man on record was, what? Eight feet?"

Laney nodded. "Eight foot eleven. Robert Wadlow, and he only survived to age twenty-three."

"Okay. But still, there's only been one of him."

Laney looked at Jake, and she knew he was also thinking about their discussion of ancient giants, and the bones that had gone missing from many of the finds.

"I'm not sure about that," he mumbled. He pointed to a skull in the middle of the back wall. It was noticeably larger than the others.

Laney walked over and inspected it. From its size, you would guess maybe it belonged to a gigantopithecus. But it was obviously human. She walked back down the aisle. Now that she was looking for it, she realized that most of the bones were at least a little larger, if not a lot larger, than normal human bones. Where had they all come from?

Remembering her uncle Patrick, she pulled her iPad out of her backpack.

"What are you doing?" Maddox came to stand next to her.

"I promised Uncle Patrick I'd show him the church."

She quickly connected with her uncle. "Hey, Uncle Patrick. We're at the church." She paused. "It's an ossuary. Is that what you were expecting?"

Patrick jolted before shaking his head, his expression grim. "No. I thought it might clue us into Nathaniel's goals, his view. But a church of bones? That, I wasn't expecting."

"Well, prepare yourself." Laney began to pan around the room.

"Laney, come look at this," Jake called.

Maddox held out his hand. "Give it here. I'll show Patrick around."

Laney nodded and handed over the iPad before hurrying over to Jake. He was standing in between the two candleholders. "What is it?"

Jake pointed down. "Look. There was something here before."

Laney crouched down and ran her hand along the floor. Sure enough, there were holes in the floor where something had been bolted in. Her gaze roamed the floor, finding three other spots where nails had been.

She looked out at the pews and then back. "There was an altar here, and someone removed it."

Maddox stepped over to them, with Patrick's face leading the way.

"It was taken recently," Jake said.

"But why?" Laney asked, looking around.

"I think I may know," Patrick said quietly.

CHAPTER 66

U nfortunately, the signal cut out on the iPad before Patrick could explain what he meant. Laney, Maddox, and Jake headed outside to get a stronger connection. Laney was perfectly fine with that. She didn't want to spend any more time than necessary in that creepy church.

As they walked, Laney mentally created a list of experts they would need to call in to examine the church. It was a long list, and it was going to be time consuming. Time the kids didn't have.

Jake flipped open the iPad cover, but before he could reestablish the connection, Jordan jogged across the grass to join them. "We've rounded up eighteen members of the ministry. All women."

"All?" Jake asked.

Jordan nodded. "And they won't say where the rest of the church members are or where the minister is."

"What about the kids?" Maddox asked. "Have they said anything about them?"

Jordan nodded. "One of them let it slip that the kids were alive a few hours ago."

"*All* of the kids?" Laney asked, prepared for the worst answer.

"Yeah. But then one of the other members yelled at her and she clammed up. We've pulled her to the side and are trying to get more information, but to be honest, I don't think she knows much more than that."

"What about the paperwork in the office?" Laney asked.

"Still going through it, but so far nothing helpful. Most of it has to do with administrative duties. Some sermons."

"Sermons?" Laney asked.

Jordan nodded. "They look like drafts, mixed in with some drafts for his website."

"Could you have someone grab those? I think we should take a look at them."

"Will do," Jordan said before heading back.

By now, Jake had Patrick back on the screen. "You said you might know why the altar is missing," Jake was saying.

Laney, Jake, and Maddox crowded around the tablet. Patrick nodded. "I read through the church's sermons online. The pastor focuses on righteousness. His people of course being the righteous, doing God's will. Lately, though, all of his sermons are coming from Exodus."

"Right. The ten plagues, we know that," Laney said.

"Yes. But when I put together his sermons on the plagues, the name of his church, and the missing kids…" Patrick swallowed. "I hope I'm wrong."

Laney's heart began to beat faster. He was never wrong on these things.

"Go ahead, Patrick," Jake said.

Laney could feel Maddox tense next to her.

"I think this is his warped interpretation of Passover."

"Passover? The Jewish holiday? That's related to the ten plagues?" Maddox asked.

"Passover is a commemoration of the Jews' liberation from slavery in ancient Egypt. But that liberation was accomplished thanks to God, who inflicted the ten plagues on the Egyptians.

The term 'Passover' comes from the final plague, when God slaughtered the firstborns of the Egyptians, but 'passed over' the homes of the Jews."

"And how does this relate to this church?" Jake asked.

"In the first Passover, Jews killed the fatted calf and put its blood upon their doors, to signify that God should pass over that home. When God came to smite the firstborns of the wicked, he left untouched the children of those with the mark of the fatted calf. And thus the Jews were spared," Patrick said, his eyes boring into Laney.

Laney felt the shock roll over her when she realized where her uncle was going. "You don't think...?" She couldn't bring herself to say it.

Patrick nodded. "When the ten plagues besieged Egypt, the righteous were able to save themselves from God's wrath by the sacrifice of a lamb. The murder of an innocent."

Laney pictured the faces of all the children who were missing, bile rising in her throat.

"The children. You think they're the sacrifice," Jake said quietly.

Patrick nodded. "Yes. He's focused on sacrificing. In rituals, blood is often used to sanctify. And by using the children, there's the added bonus of ridding the world of abominations."

The logic was twisted. It was sick and perverse. And Laney had the horrible feeling that it was right.

Another thought came to her then, one which shook her to her core. Her head jolted up and she stared at her uncle, hoping she was remembering it wrong. "Uncle Patrick, what day does Passover occur on?"

He nodded at her, his face filled with concern. "It begins on the fifteenth. That's the day the Israelites were supposed to kill the fatted calf."

Laney felt the world tilt. *And today is the fourteenth.* "We have only one day left to save them."

CHAPTER 67

Laney strode toward the police van in the parking lot. She nodded at the officers standing next to it. "I need to speak with Beatrice Grayston."

They nodded and pulled Beatrice out of the back.

Beatrice glowered at Laney, her lips clamped shut.

"Where's your husband?" Laney asked.

No response.

"Where'd they take the kids?" Laney asked.

Beatrice's eyes were bright, her face red. She spat out each word at Laney. "'The way of the wicked is an abomination to the Lord, but he loves him who pursues righteousness.'"

The venom in the woman's voice was so strong that Laney was tempted to take a step back. How was she going to break through this woman's shield of righteousness? *All right, what do I know? She's a committed follower, a wife.* She thought about the picture on the desk. Maybe...

"You're a mother. What if it were *your* son who was in danger?"

Beatrice snorted, all but rolling her eyes at Laney. "I will execute judgment on him with plague and bloodshed; I will pour down torrents of rain, hailstones and burning sulfur on him and on his troops and on the many nations with him."

Laney narrowed her eyes. *What the hell?* She ignored the woman's ranting. "You must be proud of your son. I hear he's a big part of the ministry."

Beatrice's jaw tightened.

Laney pushed on. "He looks just like you. It would be a shame if you never saw him again."

Beatrice laughed.

Laney looked at Jake, who had walked up next to her. She didn't understand what was going on here. There'd been plenty of pictures in the office, but only that one of the son. And it was obviously years old. And Beatrice's desk itself had absolutely no pictures of the son, although she did have pictures of herself and the reverend. Was she just not the motherly type?

Jake tugged on her arm. Laney stood for a moment, looking at the woman and thinking of Henry's description of Linda. Apparently, men really do marry someone just like their mother.

Laney nodded back at one of the officers. "Put her back."

The officer grabbed Beatrice by the arm, but Beatrice resisted; there was one last verse she needed to spit out. "'But the fearful, and unbelieving, and the abominable, and murderers, and whoremongers, and sorcerers, and idolaters, and all liars, shall have their part in the lake which burneth with fire and brimstone.'"

Laney just shook her head.

"'Let every oppressor perish from the face of the earth; Let every evil work be destroyed'!" Beatrice yelled as the officers manhandled her back into the car.

Laney walked away with Jake. *What the hell was all that?*

She and Jake stopped over by the Jeep. Jake looked at Laney. "Did you recognize the quotes?"

Laney nodded. "The first was Proverbs. The third was Revelations, and I think the second was Ezekiel, which is kind of ironic."

"Ironic? How?" Jake asked.

"Ezekiel had visions of the future, like Cayce. In fact, some people even argue that Cayce *was* Ezekiel in a past life."

Jake shook his head. "All right, well, let's table that tangent for a moment. That last quote, though, where was it from?"

"I think it was the Book of Enoch."

"The book about the angels falling."

"Yes." Laney looked over to the SUV Beatrice had been loaded into. Was she just ranting, or was there something in those passages?

"I'm not the biblical scholar you are, but is there anyway she actually just told us where the kids are?"

Laney's hope began to build. "What do you mean?"

"Well, maybe she's suggesting that the kids are in the spot where the angels fell," Jake said.

Laney shook her head, the hope ebbing. "That can't be right."

"Why? Does anybody know where the angels first fell?"

"Mount Hermon," Laney said absentmindedly. "It's also called the Gates of Hell."

Jake gave a low whistle. "Hermon's caught between Israel, Syria, and Lebanon. It's a magnet for violence."

"I know." Laney wondered again if perhaps that was more than a coincidence. There must be a reason why the Fallen chose that particular spot.

She pictured the tall mountain peak. It had always been shrouded in difficulties. Millennia ago, a pagan city had sat at its base at a time when all the communities around had turned to one god.

In fact, it was as if the place itself was always luring people to their baser, most narcissistic selves. Jesus himself had been to the foot of the mount at Caesarea Philippi, and had called upon Peter to build his church on this rock—and to defy evil.

There was also something else about Hermon, something on the edges of her mind. She pulled out her phone and called her uncle, wishing he were here in person. He'd probably have a better angle on this than anyone.

Patrick picked up quickly. "Is everything all right?"

"Maybe," Laney said, putting the phone on speaker. "Mount Hermon was mentioned." She quickly recapped what she had told Jake and what Beatrice had said. "But there's something else about Mount Hermon, isn't there?"

"Hermon—it means 'Forbidden Place.' And for all of history that's what it's been. People have given the mount itself a wide berth, building only around its base. There's supposed to be a cave within it that leads to the underworld. At the foot of the mountain was a town named Panias, where pagans worshipped the god Pan, in contrast to all the surrounding religious towns at the time."

Laney nodded. "And Jesus gave his famous speech about Peter building his church at its base."

"Yes," Patrick said. "There's debate about whether Jesus was directing Peter to build it right there, or if it was a more general command."

"Why would Jesus tell him to build it right there?" Jake asked.

"Well, it was an interesting speech," Patrick said. "You see, Jesus seemed to be calling his followers to arms. Telling them they needed to battle evil."

"You mean physically battle?" Laney asked.

"If Mount Hermon was, or I suppose *is*, a gateway to Hell," Patrick said, "then Jesus's speech takes on a different meaning, doesn't it? He seems to be calling on the church to be a vanguard against a physical evil."

Laney swallowed. *Well, that's slightly terrifying.* "Okay. Anything else?"

Patrick was silent for a moment. "There is one more thing." He paused. "Mount Hermon is rumored to be the location where the anti-Christ will be born."

Laney turned to Jake, her eyes going wide. She'd forgotten about that part.

Jake shook his head. "But Hermon can't be part of all this. I can't imagine Nathaniel would be able to sneak over a dozen kids into that area. It's a perpetual war zone."

Laney nodded wearily. "Plus, he's never been out of the country, at least that we know of. I can't see his first trip being this one. It doesn't feel right."

"And there's no indication that he has any connections over there," Jake said. "And he'd need connections in order to do what he plans. Plus, if this is all supposed to go down tomorrow, he couldn't make it in time."

"I agree," Patrick said. "One of the other themes inherent in all of Nathaniel's sermons is patriotism. I think wherever this is going to happen, it's in the States."

"So what did Beatrice mean?" Laney asked, frustration rolling over her. "Was it nothing? Because it seemed like she was gloating."

"I don't know, Laney," Patrick said. "Because if she was referring to where the angels fell, it wasn't in the United States. Not even close."

"Not even close," Laney echoed. Which is exactly how she felt about the likelihood of them finding the kids in time.

Not even close.

CHAPTER 68

CHICAGO, ILLINOIS

Henry closed the phone. *Damn it.* They'd come up empty at the church.

He'd stepped outside to take Laney's call, leaving Jen with Northgram. The man hadn't shared any more relevant details, just babbled on about the hardships of having to deal with a difficult first wife.

He shook his head. The man was a jerk, but Henry didn't think he was holding back. They just had to find the right questions. He could hear Jen's voice as he approached the back door. Maybe Jen had found the right ones.

As Henry stepped back into the room, his thoughts were still on Laney's ideas of the children as the sacrifice. The logic felt right; now all they needed was a location.

Jen's eyes were narrowed and she stood a few feet from Northgram. "You grimaced."

Northgram squirmed farther back in his chair, looking away from Jen. "No, I didn't."

Jen stalked across the room. "Yes, you did. Why?"

"It's nothing, nothing." He turned to Henry, his eyes pleading.

"I'd suggest you tell her," Henry said dryly.

Jen reached for the front of Northgram's shirt.

Northgram tried to bat her hand away, unsuccessfully. "Okay, okay. I mean—I didn't lie. Linda never belonged to a church. She used to take him camping at the Grand Canyon. She called it 'their church.'"

Henry waved him on. "And?"

"And I thought that, being he seemed to like the Grand Canyon, it could be something we could do to get closer."

"Go camping?" Henry asked. Northgram was wearing a Cartier watch, creased khakis, a new pink Polo shirt, and loafers minus the socks. The man definitely did not look like the roughing it type.

"Oh, God, of course not." Northgram curled his upper lip in distaste. He looked like he'd eaten a lemon. "But there were these finds from the Grand Canyon at the Smithsonian."

The Smithsonian. Laney had mentioned something about the Smithsonian. "One of the exhibits?" Henry asked, straightening.

"No. I, um, arranged for a tour behind the scenes."

"What find?" Jen asked.

"Well, there was this cave in the Grand Canyon. It was found some time around 1900. Had these mummies, and other artifacts. " Northgram shrugged, looking away. "I thought he'd like it." He went silent, not making eye contact with either of them.

"He didn't?" Henry prodded.

Jen was less diplomatic. "For God's sake, get to the point!"

Northgram threw up his hands. "I don't know! Nathaniel freaked out. And when we came home, Linda freaked out. That's when she left."

"But why?" Henry asked.

"There was a room in the cave. And each shelf had the mummified remains of giants."

Abominations, Henry thought, remembering Linda's cries.

"Were the finds dated?" Jen asked.

Northgram nodded. "Yes. But the dates had to be wrong."

"Why?" Henry asked.

"They dated to before the last Ice Age."

Jen glanced quickly at Henry and then back at Northgram. "But why did that freak out your wife?"

"She said it was the ultimate defilement of God's church."

"So if Nathaniel was looking to sanctify ground…" Jen said slowly.

Henry nodded slowly. "He might start there."

CHAPTER 69

SACRAMENTO, CALIFORNIA

There has to be something we can do. Laney paced in the hangar of the private airport outside Sacramento, California. They didn't know where Nathaniel had gone, but with that many children to transport, it had to be somewhere closer to here than Baltimore.

Laney ran her hands through her hair, her nerves on a razor's edge. Fear was clawing its way up her throat and she was having trouble thinking around it. What if Nathaniel was heading out of the country? Or to the other side of it? They only had twenty-four hours. What if she was pushing everyone in the wrong direction?

And every time she tried to calm and focus her mind, she pictured Max being sacrificed on a bone altar.

Laney reached the end of the hangar and turned to head back to the other side. The door opened and Jake stepped in. He had been helping with the interrogation of the women from the ministry.

Laney hurried over to him. "Anything?"

Jake shook his head. "No. The women say they don't know where the rest of the group has taken the kids."

"They have to know," Laney said.

"Actually, I don't think they do. Apparently, the group was very patriarchal. Women weren't part of the decision-making. They were just expected to follow the men's dictates. I don't think they know where the kids were taken."

"But Beatrice Grayston. *She* knows."

Jake nodded. "I agree. But she's not talking. In fact, the only things she's said so far are what I'm guessing are more passages from the Bible."

"Like what?"

"'He who justifies the wicked and he who condemns the righteous are both alike an abomination to the Lord,' or something like that."

Laney ran her hands through her hair. More abomination quotes. But what did it mean? Was it just her equivalent of name and serial number? "It's Old Testament, I think Proverbs again. But I don't know how it relates. Maybe she's just spewing out her greatest hits of Bible verses."

"Her version of a soldier's name and serial number."

Laney gave a little laugh. "Yeah, that's just what I was just thinking."

She turned, needing to walk more, but Jake caught her before she could and pulled her into his arms. She stiffened, unable to enjoy the embrace, too stressed to think straight.

"Laney, look at me."

She looked up into the face she knew so well.

"It's going to be okay," he said.

"How can you say that? We have less than a day to find those kids, and we have no clue. Nothing. They've disappeared."

"Okay. So let's go over what we *do* know."

Laney looked at Jake, thinking he was crazy. He couldn't expect her to focus right now, not with... She took a breath. No.

She needed to focus. She didn't have the luxury of letting fear take over. She owed the kids and Max her best. And right now, they weren't getting it.

Laney swallowed it all down. All the fear, the frustration, the anger. She shoved it into a corner of her mind, promising herself she'd deal with all those emotions later. Right now, she needed to help the kids. She couldn't let any emotions get in the way of that.

She headed back to the table they'd set up in a corner of the hangar, with all the papers and information they had. She blew out a breath, trying to exhale all her fear and anxiety. "Okay. Nathaniel thinks the kids are abominations who need to be sacrificed. We know they were alive a few hours ago when he moved them. And the kids are most likely safe until tomorrow."

"Good. And we know Nathaniel's mom is a paranoid schizophrenic."

"Which means there's an eight percent chance that *he* is, too." Laney felt herself calm, the logic making her feel more in control.

Jake nodded. "And the mother is obsessed with the Fallen. It's safe to say that that's where Nathaniel got his ideas."

Laney nodded. "But what about his dad? Henry said the mother's symptoms started to show around the same time she realized his involvement with the Council."

"So what does that mean?"

Laney paused, rolling the thoughts over in her mind. "The mom thinks the Fallen are abominations. The father makes his money from the abominations. The son is caught in between, but I think we could say he's more influenced by the mother who raised him."

"So what does that tell us?"

Laney shook her head. "I don't know. But I feel like that's important."

The phone rang and Laney picked it up. "Henry. What did you find out?"

"Well, there might be something."

Across the hangar, a group of men in black special ops uniforms appeared. *Must be more SIA.* Jake indicated he'd deal with them and headed over to them. Laney kept her focus on the conversation with Henry.

"How old was Nathaniel when his mom took him?" she asked.

"Eight."

Laney paused. Long enough for the father to have some influence. "Did Northgram share anything about his Council business with him?"

"Yeah. Actually, he had just started to. That's what seems to have set the mother off."

"How so?"

"Remember how Linda told Jen the Smithsonian had been hiding evidence of the giants?"

"Yeah."

"Well, Northgram said he used to take Nathaniel to the Smithsonian every weekend."

An idea began to form in the far reaches of Laney's mind, but she couldn't quite reach it yet. The Smithsonian... something about the Smithsonian.

Henry continued. "He also said that Linda and Nathaniel used to go camping a lot at the Grand Canyon. They considered it 'their church.'"

Laney pictured the three-hundred-mile-long canyon with its multicolored rock faces. A mile deep and eighteen miles wide, it was believed to have been created by wind, water, and volcanic activity—basically everything Mother Nature had in her toolbox.

"I can see that," Laney admitted grudgingly. "But I don't see how it helps."

"It might," Henry said. And then he explained about Northgram showing Nathaniel the Smithsonian find from the Grand Canyon.

Laney thought for moment, feeling the tingle of understanding crawling around at the edges of her brain. The Grand Canyon had a number of interesting rumors surrounding it. One of them involved ancient sites hidden within its caves. In fact, a number of the landscapes in the Grand Canyon retained Egyptian names: Isis Temple, Tower of Set, Tower of Ra, Horus Temple, Osiris Temple.

Suddenly she went still. "What exactly did Northgram show him?"

"Some large mummies and a giant Buddha with a lotus flower."

"It's the Grand Canyon City," Laney exclaimed.

"Are you sure?" Henry asked, but Laney could hear the excitement in his voice.

"It has to be. I'll explain it all later. Just get here." Laney disconnected the call and sprinted for the lounge where everyone was gathered. She threw open the door.

"Everyone gear up. We're heading to the Grand Canyon."

Jake was the first to move. "You heard her. Move."

There was a scramble of motion as each man and woman grabbed their gear and ran for the planes. Maddox grabbed Laney's arm before she could do the same. She looked up at him.

"You're sure?" he asked.

Laney nodded. "I'm sure. I'll explain it on the plane."

Maddox shook his head. "You're sure, that's good enough for me. I'll go in the other plane. Contact me with the plan." And with that Maddox ran for the second plane.

Laney hurried over to the first plane. Jake was already waiting for her at the bottom of the steps. She climbed them quickly and Jake pulled them up, locking the door. The engine was already running and the plane began taxiing for the runway before Laney had even taken her seat.

She buckled herself in as Jake sat down next to her. "Okay, so what did you learn?" he asked.

"Henry said that Northgram used to take Nathaniel to the Smithsonian. He showed him the artifacts that were taken from Grand Canyon City."

"City? What city?" Jake asked.

Laney sat back. "Around 1909, a newspaper reporter named Kincaid was going down the Colorado River. He allegedly saw some interesting stratifications in the rock walls at one point along the river, and intrigued, he pulled ashore and started to climb. Once he got over an overhang, he spotted a cave entrance —a *man-made* cave entrance. He went inside and found a huge space that had been created inside the rock. And a number of artifacts that he couldn't explain."

"Such as?" Maddox asked.

"The walls were alleged to have been carved with writing similar to hieroglyphics. He found seeds, copper hooks, pottery, jewelry. And the place was huge, with multiple rooms off two main passages that were hundreds of feet long. They also found mummified cadavers, some of them giant-sized. Even a large statue that was alleged to have resembled Buddha holding a lotus flower."

"But what does that have to do with the kids?" Jake asked.

There was so much energy running through Laney, she was bouncing in her seat. She was right. She knew she was right.

"There's another legend about the Grand Canyon. It comes from the Hopi tribe. According to them, in the ancient past there was a giant cataclysm. But the Hopi were spared because 'star beings' led them to an underground hiding place where they waited out the tumult. For decades, even centuries, they waited. And then one day, when it was safe, they emerged. According to them, this was the dawn of the modern age. And hence—"

"That was the place where the Fallen first emerged in the modern world," Jake said.

Laney nodded. "Exactly. It's only recently that the Hopi revealed the location of that exit: the Grand Canyon. And some people say that the place that they hid out was Kincaid's cave."

"Great. So we head for the cave."

Laney nodded, but her excitement began to wane.

Jake frowned. "What? This is good news."

"The only problem is that no one knows exactly where in the Grand Canyon the cave is. According to Kincaid's description, it's forty-two miles up the Colorado River from El Tovar Crystal Canyon—a place no one has been able to identify. And the entrance can't be seen from the river."

"So what are you saying?" Jake asked

"I'm saying it's going to be hard to find. So we need to come up with a plan."

"But you're sure this is the place?"

Laney nodded. "If you were a diehard patriot and planned on sanctifying the ground, wouldn't you choose the place where you thought the Fallen had first arrived in America?"

CHAPTER 70

GRAND CANYON NATIONAL PARK, NEVADA

Nathaniel stood on the bank of the Colorado River, gazing up at the rock face next to him. Then he looked down the long canyon, imagining what it must have been like to stand here a hundred years ago, not a soul around for maybe a hundred miles.

He breathed deeply. The Grand Canyon. The greatest expression of God's love and power.

He'd been to the Grand Canyon many, many times. He and his mother had camped here at least once a year up until the time she had been institutionalized. He felt guilt tug at him. She had shown him the way. Put him on this path. He hadn't wanted to put her in that place.

But she had gotten erratic. The hallucinations had become a daily occurrence. Then he hadn't been able to find her for a week. He had been beside himself.

When finally he did find her, she'd been walking in the woods. She'd lost her shoes, her feet were scratched up, and some of the cuts had become infected. At that point he felt he had no choice but to call his father, who had made the subsequent arrangements.

But even his mother's hospitalization had been for a reason. It had forced him to rely on himself, to fine-tune his understandings. And it had given him an in with his father. He'd plucked his father's strings of guilt like a virtuoso. It had clarified his mission, his role in God's plan. It had led him to the Shepherd.

And it had led him here.

"Sir, we're ready for you," Tyrell said.

Nathaniel nodded and walked over to the base of the rock. The ladder had been bolted in place. There was a chance someone might discover it, but this part of the Canyon wasn't traversed very often. They should be safe, at least long enough to finish their business.

Tyrell held up a climbing rope. "Sir, let me wrap this rope, just as a precaution."

Nathaniel wanted to wave the rope away, but just the thought of being on that ladder gave him a sense of vertigo. So he stood still while Tyrell wrapped the rope around him, tying it so it would rest under his armpits while he climbed, the knot in front of him.

Tyrell took a step back. "All set, sir."

Nathaniel nodded, took a deep breath, and began to climb. The first few feet were fine. But the higher he got, the more the wind pulled at him. Halfway up the climb, he had to stop. He rested his head on the rungs, sweat pooling on his brow.

He tried to swallow but his mouth was dry. The ladder shook, and Nathaniel clung even tighter.

"Reverend?" Tyrell called.

Nathaniel glanced down to see Tyrell just a few feet below him on the ladder. But one glance down was enough. He felt himself sway.

"It's all right, Reverend. Just look straight in front of you. I'm right here. I won't let you fall."

The Reverend nodded and took a shaky step, then another. Tyrell coaxed him on, even at times helping to brace him as he reached for the next rung. It seemed to take an eternity, but finally Nathaniel reached the top. Four strong arms reached down and helped him over the edge.

He collapsed on his back, enjoying the feel of solid ground beneath him. He stared up at the bright blue sky, trying to get his shaking limbs to stop.

Slowly, he became aware of the low voices of his men, of their averted gazes. His cheeks flamed. *Always the weakling.*

He quickly pushed himself up to his knees.

Tyrell unhooked himself and dropped down to Nathaniel's side. "Take it easy, sir. That's right."

Nathaniel wanted to shoo Tyrell away, but he couldn't; he needed his help to stand.

Tyrell kept a strong grip on Nathaniel's arms until the reverend could stand on his own, then stepped away. "Sir, the lights have been strung up. It's all ready for you."

Nathaniel tried to straighten his shoulders, recapture some dignity, even though he still burned at how weak he had been. As he looked ahead, he saw the entrance that had been hewn out of the rock thousands of years ago.

He looked around at all the men. *I brought them here.* These men might be physically powerful, but *he* was the one they looked to. The one they answered to.

He straightened even more. "Yes. Let's see."

Tyrell stepped aside and let the reverend lead the way. Nathaniel walked toward the cave entrance. The metal gate, placed there by the Smithsonian in 1909, lay open.

Excitement bubbled in Nathaniel's stomach, along with a little fear. He thought of the hands that had carved it out and curled his lip. They had been here. They had *defiled* this place. And he, Nathaniel Grayston, would make it a holy place once again. And save himself and his followers while he was at it.

With a renewed sense of purpose, he stepped through the gates, whispering, "Let God's will be done."

CHAPTER 71

They arrived outside Las Vegas late that night. Dark had already fallen.

There was no way they were going to be able to investigate the Grand Canyon at night. The area within the canyon where they thought the cave was located had thousand-foot-tall cliff walls that were practically sheer. And there were no lights there at night. They would be seen from miles away if they initiated a search.

So Henry had arranged for everyone to bunk down for the night at a private airport. It wasn't the Ritz, but no one cared. Everyone wanted to be ready to go at first light.

Laney pulled on a sweater as she walked outside the hangar. They might be in the desert, but the temperatures dropped precipitously at night. She wrapped her arms around herself, trying to get a little added warmth, and hoped the kids were warm too. The door cracked open behind her and Jake stepped out.

Laney smiled as Jake stepped behind her and wrapped his arms around her. For a few moments she just closed her eyes and enjoyed the embrace, letting herself forget all the craziness surrounding them. When at last she opened her eyes again, she felt more centered, more confident. Jake always had a way of making her feel more capable, just by being around.

"Everything good inside?" Laney asked.

Jake nodded against the top of her head. "Yes. We'll be ready to go by four a.m."

"Good. We should probably get some sleep, although I don't think—"

Headlights were coming their way, still distant but visible. Laney frowned. "We have any more people coming in?"

Jake stiffened and stepped back. "No. The only ones due are Jen and Henry, but they won't be here for another hour." He opened the door behind him and yelled. "Might be trouble."

There was a flurry of noise and movement behind her, but Laney didn't turn to see. She kept her eyes glued to the approaching headlights and drew her Beretta. Others poured out of the hangar and took up positions.

Maddox stepped up next to her. "Who the hell is that?"

"I have no idea." Laney raised her weapon. A second later she felt the jolt of awareness, and then for just a moment she saw herself from far away.

"Oh, for the love of God," she growled, lowering her weapon and gesturing for everyone else to do the same.

The van pulled to a stop in front of them and its side door slid open.

"What the hell are you doing here?" Laney said.

Lou hopped out of the van with a sheepish grin. "We thought we'd help."

Cleo slipped out behind Lou and rubbed up against Laney. Laney rubbed behind the cat's ears. "Hey, girl. It's nice to see you too."

Cleo was followed by Rolly, Theresa, and two other teens from the school. Yoni walked around from the driver's seat, his hands up. "Hey, I didn't even know they were on the plane until we landed. Someone helped them board through the cargo hold."

"Who?" Laney asked.

Yoni nodded toward the passenger seat, and Danny stepped out.

Laney shook her head. "Seriously?" She fixed her eyes on Danny. "Et tu, Brute?"

"Sorry, Laney," Danny said, but he met her gaze. "But they can help."

"And you?" Laney asked.

Danny's blush deepened, but he met her eyes. "I'm here to help, too."

"Danny, I know you care about Max," Laney said. "But you can't help. It's too dangerous."

"From what I understand," Danny said, "your problem is that you can't find the cave."

Laney looked at him for a moment, a little kernel of hope beginning to bloom in her chest. "Yes."

Danny smiled. "Then perhaps I can help."

"How?" Laney asked.

Danny's smile turned into a grin. "I placed a tracker on Max."

CHAPTER 72

Laney yawned as she crowded into the hangar office with Jake, Maddox, Henry, Danny, Yoni, Jen and Jordan. Henry and Jen had arrived a few minutes ago and they wasted no time setting up and figuring out their plan.

Laney glanced outside, where the rest of their group had bedded down for the night. She knew she needed to get some sleep as well, but the image of Max alone and scared made it impossible.

Jake unrolled a map of the area onto the desk in the small office, drawing her attention back to the group.

"Getting into the cave is going to be the hard part," he said. "From Kincaid's description, we know you can't see the entrance until you're almost eye level with it. Other than that, all we know is that it's alleged to be forty-two miles down the Colorado River."

"Well, that's about par for the course for us," Yoni mumbled.

Jake nodded. "Once we locate the cave, we'll need to quietly take out any security outside. Laney and Maddox, you'll take the group at the top. Yoni and I will take out any security at the river."

"What about the cave entrance?" Jen asked. "They'll have a guard there."

Jordan nodded. "They'll be my responsibility. Once we locate the cave, I'll find a spot on the rock cliff opposite the cave and take out any sentries."

Laney shook her head. "But if they see you or if you take out the sentries, they'll know we're there."

"Laney," Jordan said. "I won't let them see me. And I won't take any action until we're about to go in, or if they notice what's happening to the other guards."

Laney nodded. Her stomach was still in knots, but she knew there was no other choice. There was only one entrance, and at some point, the people in the cave were going to realize what was happening. They just had to keep that from happening for as long as possible.

"That all sounds fine to me, as long as we can locate the cave in the first place," Jen said.

Jake nodded toward Danny. "Well, thanks to Danny, we have a good chance of that."

Danny ducked his head, a blush spreading across his face. Apparently, after the incident at the bookstore Danny had inserted a tracker into Max's shoe.

Laney shook her head. *Smart.*

Of course, Danny could have just called them and told them that rather than bringing himself and his friends into danger, but Laney was so damn happy they had a way of tracking the kids, she couldn't be upset about that. All she'd been able to do was hug Danny.

Still, one thought kept that optimism from blooming fully: if Max was deep inside the cave, there was a very good chance that the signal from the tracker wouldn't be able to reach them. Laney chased the thought away. *Let's stay positive.*

Jake nodded toward Jordan. "Jordan's already arranged to borrow a Grand Canyon Tours helicopter. They'll sweep over the area where we think the cave is located and look for any sign of Nathaniel's men—or better yet, a signal from Max's tracker."

The stretch of canyon where they believed the cave was located was wide open. There was simply no way they could sneak up on it, except maybe on foot. And it would take forever to cover the area that way. Plus, their opponent could have the higher ground. They'd see and hear them if they came in by boat or by air.

Since a quiet approach wasn't an option, they'd decided to risk a chopper. There was simply no other way to reconnoiter in time. Hopefully they could pass themselves off as just one of the many tourist helicopters that passed over the Grand Canyon daily— even though the area they'd be visiting wasn't a typical tourist destination.

Danny had wanted to go in the chopper, but everyone had voted down that idea. In fact, everyone else wanted to go themselves.

It was finally decided that Yoni and Jordan would go. They weren't sure if there were any Fallen helping the reverend's team, but if there were, they couldn't take the chance that those Fallen might sense Henry or Jen or Laney. That would blow their cover before they even began.

Laney had her doubts about the efficiency of flying around for miles in a helicopter. If Max's tracker didn't come through, the odds were low that they'd happen to pass over the right spot, or recognize it if they did. *It's the ol' needle in the haystack approach.* But she kept those thoughts to herself.

Maddox appeared to share her doubts. "And if that doesn't work?"

Jake looked over at him. "Then we head down the river in boats and fly low over the top of the cliff until we find them."

"But that'll let them know we're coming," Jen said.

"I know." Jake let out a heavy breath. "But if we can't find the cave with the chopper, we won't have any other choice."

"And if we have to go with option two," Laney asked, "how many kids will we lose?"

Jake didn't say anything. He just shook his head.

But Laney heard the unspoken words.

All of them.

CHAPTER 73

J ust after dawn the next morning, Laney, Jake, Henry, and Jen crammed into the small office, the radio keyed up. Laney rubbed her hand over her eyes. They stung. She'd managed to get about two hours of sleep last night and was trying to compensate with lots of coffee. Now as they listened intently to the radio, she felt like her nerves were on a string. *Come on guys. Find something.*

"Just heading over the ridge now." Jordan's voice came through loud and clear.

"No hits," Yoni said. "But that's probably just because of Jordan's flying. My mother flies better than this."

"Shut up, Yoni."

Yoni chuckled, but no one in the room even cracked a smile.

Yoni and Jordan had gone up in the chopper fifteen minutes ago. They'd been searching the area for ten minutes without any sign.

Laney couldn't stand to just sit idly and wait, so in her head, she began to rearrange the plan. Henry and Maddox could be lowered onto the top of the cliff. Jen could go along the bottom. Maybe if they ran fast enough they could find and take out the guards without anyone noticing. *Maybe I can send Cleo with Jen. She would at least distract the guards—*

"Coming up on the eastern ridge."

"No hits," Yoni called.

Laney tried not to scream in frustration. *Come on, just a little help.* A small something that meant that their going in might not seal the fates of all of those kids.

"Hold on a second," Yoni's voice called, a glimmer of hope in it. "Jordan, cut a little more to the other canyon wall."

Laney held her breath. *Please, please.*

"I have a signal!" Yoni yelled.

As if on a string, everyone in the office leaned forward. "See anyone?" Jake asked.

"Hold on," Yoni called. "Yeah—two spotters up top. I don't know about below. Do you want us to circle back around, make another pass over them? It might raise alarms."

"No. That's all right. Get back here. We leave as soon as you get back," Jake ordered. He looked at everyone in the room. "Time to go hunting."

CHAPTER 74

L aney made sure everyone had what they needed and that the teenagers understood their roles in this. They were coming along, but staying in the back—the *far* back. If all went well, they'd never be anywhere near any violence.

Laney zipped up her vest, placed a Beretta in her holster, and slid her knife into the sheath attached to her thigh. She picked up her P90 and checked the cartridge. All good.

Jake walked over and handed her earplugs. She looked at them for a moment and then up at him. "What are these for?"

"We're going to be shooting inside a cave. We'll be lucky if we aren't all deaf by the time we get out."

Right. She hadn't thought of that. The cave walls would trap all the sound in, sending it back at them. "We might not be able to hear the kids with these things on."

"True. But we definitely won't be able to hear them if we go in without the earplugs."

Laney knew he was right. Gunfire out in the open was loud; in the tight cave space, it was going to be deafening. "And Jake, remind everyone that guns are a last resort. We want to take these guys out as quietly as possible."

Jake placed his hand over hers and squeezed. "I told them. But I'll tell them again." He gave her a kiss on the cheek before heading off to hand out more earplugs.

Laney sighed. She knew Jake had it handled. But it was hard not to micromanage on this mission.

Henry stepped next to her. "You ready?"

Laney took a deep breath. "Yes." Then she nodded at something behind Henry. "Incoming."

Danny, Lou, and Rolly walked up to them.

"Hey, guys," Laney said.

Danny handed Laney what she thought was a rock. But when her hand closed around it she realized it was metal, painted a reddish brown. She held it up. "What is this?"

"It's basically a small drone." Danny pointed to the top. "Wings come out of here, allowing it to fly. But it can go back to this form and lie on the ground, unobtrusive."

Laney inspected it and noticed the small hole at the front. "Is that a camera?"

Danny nodded. "I'm not asking you to let me go with you. But if I'm over with Jordan, I'll be close enough that I can control this guy and give you the layout before you go in."

Laney wanted to say no. She didn't know what they'd find in that cave. For all they knew, Nathaniel had already sacrificed the kids. And if he had, she couldn't let Danny see that. Henry would never forgive her if she did. She would never forgive herself.

She looked over at Henry. He had tried so hard to keep Danny out of all of this. But now Danny was here, and Laney thought Danny's idea was a good one. Still, as much as it killed her, she had to leave the decision to Henry. She cocked an eyebrow at him.

Henry gave her a tiny nod, then turned his gaze to Danny. When he spoke, his voice was confident, maybe even proud. "He can do it. He's the best one for the job."

Danny's jaw dropped for a moment before a smile broke out across his face.

R.D. BRADY

Laney tried to hold back her own smile. "Okay, tell Jordan. And Danny, you're wearing a vest."

Danny nodded quickly.

"We'll get him suited up." Lou wrapped her hand around Danny's arm with a grin and dragged him off. Rolly slung an arm around Danny from the other side.

Laney smiled at the camaraderie of the moment, happy that Danny finally seemed to be finding his place with kids his own age.

But the smile soon slid from her face. She looked up at Henry. "We're doing the right thing letting them help, aren't we?"

Henry looked down at her. "I hope so, Laney. I really hope so."

CHAPTER 75

Laney headed for the locker room, looking for a little peace before everything went to hell. As she approached, she heard a noise from inside. She stepped in and saw Jen sitting on a bench, pulling on her wetsuit. She was going to be part of the team that crashed the beach.

Laney took a seat on the bench across from her. "You up for this?"

Jen zipped up the front of her suit. "You know I am."

"Good, good."

Jen straddled the bench in front of her. "Are *you* up for this?"

Laney rubbed the ring on her finger. "Yeah."

"Lanes?"

Laney thought for a moment about lying, but she just didn't want to. And Jen would see through it anyway. "I'm just so scared this time. It's one thing risking *my* life, but all those kids. And now we've got the teen titans with us as well."

"Well, those guys will hang back in the boats until we get the kids out. And then, and *only* then, will they move in."

Laney bit her lip. "I know this is the best plan in this situation.

299

But there are just so many things that could go wrong. And the price of those mistakes…" Laney shook her head.

"Hey. We've done this before. And we're still here, aren't we? We've fought ridiculous odds before and won. This is just one more challenge. And we'll defeat this one, too."

Jen was right. They had done the impossible before. But somehow with children caught in the middle, especially Max, the cost of this confrontation felt so much higher than any of the others.

"Besides, this time we're only fighting humans. How hard can it be?" Jen's words were glib, but they were belied by the concern in her eyes.

"Yeah," Laney said softly, "but they're humans with children as shields."

CHAPTER 76

Laney stood with the assault force in a field a mile from the Colorado River. They were splitting up the group here. Most would go in by the river, but a few of them would descend from the top of the cliff. They'd already alerted local law enforcement.

Laney was leaving two of the teenagers and Cleo at the top to watch their backs. Cleo had already been dropped off. She was making her way toward the cave and was under strict instructions to not engage with any humans.

Laney and Henry would be part of the cliff top team. Two helicopters were sitting quietly a hundred yards behind them. But right now, they were waiting to hear from Jordan and Danny to find out what they were walking into.

Jake put his arm around Laney. "It'll be okay. We have at least twelve hours until the sun goes down. We have time."

"If Nathaniel keeps to the schedule," she mumbled. "Who knows what his plan really is? He's mixed a bunch of Bible verses together into his own personal scripture. Who's to say the timing of the sacrifice isn't something else he decided to revise?"

"Don't go borrowing trouble," Jake warned. "Let's focus on what we can affect, not things that are out of our control."

Jordan's voice called over the radio. "Danny and I are in position."

Laney waved to everyone for quiet, then turned on the monitor on the hood of the Jeep.

Jake grabbed the radio. "Guards?"

"One at the cave entrance. And it looks like another two at the base of the cliff," Jordan responded. "But I can't see into the cave."

Laney's gaze caught Jake's. They'd have to adjust. Which meant Jake, Yoni, and Jen were going to swim in first, ahead of the boats. Laney's gut clenched at the thought.

They're trained for this, Laney thought. Both Yoni and Jake were Navy SEALs. They'd done this a million times. And Jen swam like she was born in the ocean.

Jake looked over at Laney.

She nodded back at him. "Send Danny's little friend in."

Jake relayed the message over the radio.

The monitor came to life as Danny's robot activated. First, all they could see was the rock on the far side of the river. Then a buffet of wind tossed the little thing, and they were staring at the water below before Danny righted it again.

"Okay, anybody else feeling a little sick?" Yoni asked as he came to stand next to them.

Laney put an arm around him. "I thought you SEALs were made of tougher stuff."

Yoni swallowed. "Just not a fan of heights."

"There's the entrance," Jake said.

Laney turned her attention back to the monitor. She realized that she was holding her breath, and let it out. As the drone's camera zoomed in, she saw the guard in the doorway. He was about thirty, with a scruffy beard, an old camouflage jacket, and some scuffed-up boots. He was leaning against the cave entrance, smoking a cigarette.

The guard glanced over in the direction of the bot. Danny quickly downed it. Unconcerned, the man looked away. But Laney got enough of a look at him to recognize him: Larry Kelly, the man Jake had fingerprinted at the hospital. *The man who took Max.*

"How's Danny going to get the drone past him?" Laney whispered, even as she realized the ridiculousness of whispering.

"Just wait," Jake said.

All of a sudden the guard straightened and walked to the edge of the cliff. Danny wasted no time bringing the bot back to life and zipping it into the cave.

"What happened?" Laney asked.

Jake grinned. "Jordan set up a small rockslide."

Laney didn't respond; her attention was drawn to the sight on the screen. Danny had moved the bot to the ceiling. Laney's mouth hung open.

The cave was massive. Nathaniel's men had strung lights along the path, providing a good view. In front of the drone was a passage that Laney couldn't even see the end of. But she could tell that different rooms cut off of the main artery.

"Laney?" Jake asked.

"There's no question it's man-made—at least parts of it. Someone carved this out of the rock." *Who could have done this? What tools would they have needed? This was obviously not...* Laney shook her head to refocus. Academic curiosity could come later. "Tell Danny to check each of the rooms."

"No guards yet," Maddox said.

Laney realized he was right. The only guard was the one at the entrance. "Where is everybody?"

"They're probably not expecting anyone. They've managed to grab all of those kids without anyone even getting close," Jen said quietly. "They're getting cocky."

Danny took the bot down the passage and peeked into the first few rooms. They were empty, and Nathaniel's people hadn't bothered to light them. It wasn't until they approached the twelfth room that light shown through the doorway.

"This place could hold thousands of people," Jen said.

Jake nodded, his face concerned. "Yeah. And these guys are tucked way in the back. Can't be sure, but I'd say that the main passage is at least a hundred and fifty yards."

"That's a lot of distance to cover silently," Yoni said.

On screen, a room appeared that did have lights strung up. Sleeping bags were scattered across the floor. Boxes were stacked in the back—food and water, Laney figured.

"Danny, hold there," Jake ordered, staring at the screen. "I count eighteen sleeping bags."

"Figure another two or three guys on guard duty," Yoni said.

"So we're talking over twenty guys," Maddox said. "Tell Danny to keep going. We need to see the kids."

Jake relayed the command. The bot was on the move again. Up ahead, there was a lot of light. Laney leaned forward as if she could somehow see more. The bot moved into a large room.

The ceiling was much higher in here, and giant stalactites hung from the ceiling. Surrounding the room were dozens of individual alcoves, each tall enough to hold a man standing upright—a very *tall* man. The large room was shaped like a dome and reminded Laney of the Pantheon in Rome.

Danny positioned the bot near one of the stalactites, giving them a bird's-eye view of the room. Around twenty men lounged below them, obviously not impressed by their surroundings. Some played cards. Some read books.

Laney stared at the screen. "Where's Grayston?"

"There." Jen pointed to the bottom right of the screen.

And sure enough, there he was, sitting at a makeshift table, eating. Not a care in the world.

Yoni leaned forward. "What's that?" He pointed to something sticking out behind the reverend.

"Danny, move the bot behind Grayston," Jake ordered.

The scene changed, and Nathaniel came more into focus. But Laney lost interest in him as soon as she saw what had caught Yoni's attention.

Laney thought she had prepared herself for what she was going to see in the cave. She was wrong. She grabbed Jake's hand. He squeezed hers back.

Yoni's voice was full of revulsion. "Is that...?"

Jen answered his unfinished question. "Yes. It's the altar of bones."

CHAPTER 77

L aney felt her mouth go dry. The structure on the screen was a macabre creation, even worse somehow than the whole church. Skulls, femurs, knee sockets, all types of bones had been used to create an altar.

But it wasn't just its appearance that was making her sick. It was the knowledge of what Nathaniel planned on using it for. This was where Nathaniel planned on sacrificing the children.

"Who the hell creates something like that?" Yoni demanded. "What kind of fucking asshole comes up with that?"

Jake put his hand on Yoni's shoulder. "Yoni."

Yoni looked up at him, tears in his eyes. "They're kids, Jake. Just kids." For the first time, Laney realized how hard this mission was going to be for Yoni. Now that he had Dov, this mission was hitting too close to home.

"I know," Jake said.

Yoni looked at him for a long moment. "Just tell me when I can shoot somebody." Then he walked away, heading toward the other Jeep.

The silence was heavy after Yoni left. Everyone stared at the screen. Jake was the first to recover. "Danny, check the opening behind the altar."

Laney blinked, noticing the bloom of light just on the edge of the screen. "What is that?"

Danny brought the bot closer. About ten feet behind the altar was another room. Light shone dimly through the opening.

The bot moved closer.

Laney held her breath.

Jen stepped closer to her, her shoulder brushing Laney's, and took Laney's hand. Laney squeezed her friend's hand but didn't take her eyes from the screen. Then the bot flew into the room, once again along the ceiling.

And there, crouched along the floor, their faces dirty, were the fourteen missing children.

Laney gasped, her heart breaking at the sight. The smaller kids were cradled in the bigger kids' laps. Some slept, but most just stared, not saying a word.

Laney scanned the group frantically, her eyes finally coming to rest on a little boy on the left, his little arms holding on to a two-year-old girl who seemed to be crying quietly. "Max," she said, reaching for the screen.

"Everyone, grab your sheets. Find your kids," Jake ordered.

Laney swallowed, shoving aside her heartbreak at the sight of Max. She grabbed the stack of photos in front of her. They had divided up the kids prior to the bot search. Each of them was responsible for identifying each kid in their stack.

Laney scanned the group on the screen. Her heart broke a little more each time she ticked off a name on her list.

"All of mine are there," Jake said.

"Mine too," said Maddox.

"All of mine," Henry said.

Jen nodded.

Laney let out a breath. "Mine as well."

Then she noticed an older boy in the back, a boy she didn't

recognize from the pictures. He had a small girl in his arms and was pacing along the far wall. He stopped and ran his hand through a smaller boy's hair, saying something to him.

Laney pointed. "Does anyone have that tall boy on their list?"

They all shook their heads.

"He looks older than the rest," Jen said.

Laney looked at Jake. "Can you ask Danny to get closer to him?" There was something about the boy that was familiar.

Jake relayed the request. The bot moved closer, and Laney caught her breath. "That's Nathaniel's son."

"Are you sure?" Jake asked.

Laney nodded, watching the boy lean down to another child and give him a hug. "Zachariah Grayston. He's fourteen."

Laney watched the teenager as he moved among the kids, speaking to a few of them. Everything in his movements was compassionate, caring. But he was the son of Nathaniel and Beatrice Grayston.

Jen looked over at her, her confusion plain. "So is he a good guy or a bad guy?"

Laney shook her head. "I have no idea."

CHAPTER 78

Laney leaned her head back against the chopper seat. They would be dropped a quarter of a mile from the cave, would make their way over to it, set up their ropes, and rappel down—after the river team took out the spotters on the bank and Jordan took out the guard at the entrance. They'd lucked out with regard to the spotters on the top of the cliff: according to Jordan's report, they had climbed down.

Laney ran over the plan in her mind. They were going to use the rocks they'd seen at the top of the cliff to secure their ropes. Someone had suggested bolting them in, but the bolt guns would be way too loud and they couldn't take that chance.

She pictured the rappel down, the fast disengagement, and making her way through the cave. Everything had to be silent or they risked warning Nathaniel's men. And that couldn't happen.

Henry's voice came through her headphones. "We're descending."

Laney opened her eyes and looked at Lou and Rolly, who were seated next to her. The other teenagers were part of the river patrol and would hold back until the kids were secured. But Lou and Rolly had begged to be allowed to do more.

Laney nodded at them. "You guys ready?"

Lou nodded and Rolly gave her a big thumbs-up. Laney hoped they were taking this seriously.

The chopper landed with a short bump a few seconds later, and they quickly hopped out. The chopper took off immediately and the other chopper took its place. Another six members of their team disembarked. They were ready to go.

Laney tapped her mike. "We're on the cliff. Heading for the rappelling spot."

Maddox's voice answered. "Our swimmers are in the water. Five minutes."

Cleo appeared from behind some rocks and Laney received no sense of danger from her. She was calm. Laney suddenly realized that the group was looking at her expectantly. "We have five minutes. Let's go."

They took off at a fast clip.

Laney kept an eye on her GPS, and after a few minutes she put a hand up for everyone to stop. The cave entrance was precisely 1,462 feet straight down from where they were.

"Set up the anchors," Laney said quietly, even though it would be impossible for the guard down at the entrance to hear her even had she spoken more loudly. The distance alone would make it difficult, plus a wind blew hard against them, pulling away any sound.

Four anchors were quickly established, and Laney locked herself on to one of the ropes, as did Henry and two other members of the team. They were the first wave. As soon as they unclipped, the second wave would follow.

"We can help, Laney," Lou said, stepping up to her.

"You *are* helping. You're watching our backs. " Laney nodded to the radio attached to Rolly's belt. "Remember, if you see or hear anything, you contact Jordan *immediately*."

Rolly nodded. "We will."

Cleo padded up and touched her head to Laney's. Laney rubbed the big cat's ears. "I'll be okay. You look after these two, all right?"

Cleo gazed at Rolly and Lou for a moment, as if memorizing their faces, before walking away.

"We're being babysat by a cat?" Lou grumbled.

"Yup," Laney replied.

Rolly crossed his arms over his chest. "We can handle ourselves."

"I don't doubt it," Laney replied. "But if something does go wrong, wouldn't you *like* Cleo's help?"

Lou glanced over at Cleo. The cat's shadow stretched out behind her, making her look even larger than usual. "Okay. Good point."

Laney waved them back. "Now scoot."

Lou and Rolly backed up to give the team room. Laney gathered the rope and held it to her side. She spoke into her microphone. "We're ready."

"Thirty seconds."

"Earplugs in, everybody." Laney handed her radio to another member of the team and inserted her own earplugs. Then she watched the woman with the radio. The woman raised her hand, then dropped it.

The first wave flung their ropes over the edge and all but flew down the side of the cliff. Laney had never rappelled so far in one leap. She forced herself to not think about just how far it was. Instead she pulled up a mental picture of Max. *I'm coming, Max. I'm coming.*

Henry landed a few seconds before she did and had already disengaged himself by the time Laney landed. She quickly followed suit, then pulled her P90 from her hip. Normally she liked the Beretta, but she wanted the laser sight for this particular mission.

She looked toward the entrance, where the guard they'd seen through the bot already lay sprawled on the ground. From the corner of her eye, Laney saw Jen crest the cliff and roll into a smooth crouch, her weapon in hand.

Laney moved in behind Henry. So far, so good: no one seemed the wiser. Then a familiar electric tingle ran over her. She grabbed Henry's arm and mouthed, *Fallen.*

How many? he mouthed back.

Laney put up one finger.

Henry nodded, his jaw taut. There was nothing they could do about it now. They were committed. But Laney worried that the Fallen had sensed them as well, and was already warning Nathaniel. *Damn it.*

Laney followed Henry into the cave. Laney stayed to the right of the passage; Henry took the left. Henry peered into the first opening and shook his head. Then he glanced over at Laney and went still, pointing at the opening in front of her. Silently, Laney swung her gun onto her back and withdrew her knife from the sheath on her thigh. She held her breath and waited.

Henry held out his hand and counted down with his fingers: *three, two, one.*

A man rounded the corner. Laney wrapped her arm around his neck and covered his mouth with her hand as she plunged her knife into his back. She left it there while she wrapped her other hand around his neck and twisted. The man's eyes bulged wide for a second and then he went still.

Laney lowered him quietly to the ground, reminding herself that his death was necessary. This man was willing to sacrifice kids. But the horror of what she'd done remained. It didn't really matter if it was for the greater good: each life she took also took away a piece of her.

A little shaken, Laney pulled her weapon back in front of her. Henry moved forward and Laney followed as the rest of the team filed into the cave behind them. They were silent as they continued down the passage, checking each room as they came to it, but no one else emerged.

Laney began to feel a thin ray of hope. Whoever the Fallen was, he hadn't sounded the alarm. No one yet knew they were here. *We can do this. The kids are going to be—*

Twenty feet ahead, a man stepped out of the cavern where the sleeping bags had been. He rubbed his eyes and looked down the passage at all of them.

Everyone went still.

And then all hell broke loose. The man let out a yell and turned to run back into the cavernous room. Henry's bullet cut him down.

"Move!" Jake yelled, sprinting forward.

Laney ran with him, praying for the kids. Two gunmen leapt out of an opening farther down the passageway. Gunfire blasted down the passage toward them, and they all immediately dove into the nearest room, unable to move forward.

Panic twisted in Laney's gut. They needed to get to the kids. They couldn't just sit here.

Maddox must have had the same thought. He pushed away from the others, stepping right out into the barrage of bullets, and charged down the passage with a yell.

He ran right past the large cavern and toward the two gunmen. Bullets blasted into him, but he didn't slow, even though Laney knew each wound was incredibly painful. Jen and Henry sprinted after him. Each of them was shot multiple times as well, but they didn't drop. Instead they offered themselves up as a shield for the rest of the team to get in place.

The gunmen's focus on the trio allowed the rest of them to make it down the hall as far as the opening of the cavern where the first man had appeared. There were more gunmen inside, but working together, and led by Jake, the team made quick work of them. Maddox took out the two men farther down the hall.

Laney saw Jake pulling his earplugs out, so she did the same.

"Where are the rest of them?" she yelled as she ran forward and flattened herself against the wall beside the room at the back where they'd seen the children. She steeled herself for what she might see, then she glanced inside.

The room was empty.

The kids were gone.

CHAPTER 79

"Where are they?" Maddox limped up next to Laney. Blood still seeped from some of his wounds. His shirt was dotted with bullet holes and his face was pale. But his healing was already well on its way.

"I don't know." Laney looked around the large room.

The room towered above them, rows of giant alcoves hewn into the rock walls, one atop the other. It was like a giant theater, with luxury box seating all up and down the walls. Along the bottom were seven separate openings. Discounting the one they'd entered through, that meant six possible escapes for Nathaniel and the kids.

Jake jogged over. "We need to split up. But I don't like spreading us out so thin."

Laney rubbed the ring on her finger. "Let me see if I can help with that." She closed her eyes and tried to sense the kids. She knew they didn't have their powers yet, but maybe there was some small nugget in them she could pick up.

Maddox blew out a breath. "Laney, we need to—"

"Maddox, quiet." Jake ordered.

Laney struggled trying to sense something—anything. *Come on, where are you?*

Suddenly a small tingle began somewhere to her right. There was another to her left, and one somewhere behind her. The one behind her was the strongest—that must be the full-blown Fallen she had sensed when they first rappelled down. But the other two? Had some of the kids come into their powers?

She opened her eyes and pointed at the three openings. "They split them up. I sensed something through there, there, and there."

Laney looked at Maddox, who nodded. "We'll take this one," she said, nodding to the one where she'd gotten the strongest reading. If there *was* a Fallen, she was the one best equipped to handle him.

"Good luck," Jake said, running to one of the other openings while barking orders at the rest of the group.

As soon as Laney ducked into the entryway with Maddox, a surge of electricity rolled over her. She grabbed Maddox. "Did you feel that?"

"No. What?"

"It's got to be the kids. I can feel them."

"One's at full force?" Maddox asked.

Laney nodded. "Yeah. Let's go."

She ran forward, need overriding caution. The passage was dark. Laney pulled out her flashlight and placed it along the top of her weapon to guide the way.

One minute in, Maddox grabbed her hand. "Hold on. I hear them."

Laney quickly doused her light. They moved forward cautiously. After a few more feet, a light shone from farther ahead. Laney could hear voices as well.

"—betrayal! Someone has betrayed us! A Judas in our midst! Was it you?"

"No, no, of course not," a second voice screeched.

A child cried out.

"Shut them up!"

Laney and Maddox inched forward and peered in. Nathaniel was pacing in front of a group of children, and two other men were with them. Laney did a quick count of the kids: five, including Nathaniel's son. But no Max. She shoved the heartbreak away. *Save these kids, then find Max.*

One of the men waved his gun toward the children. "We should sacrifice them now, even if it's early." The children shrank back.

The tingling struck Laney again, and her eyes flew back to Nathaniel's son. *He's the Fallen.* Her mouth fell open. *Holy crap.*

Maddox nudged Laney. He pointed to the man on the right. Laney indicated the man on the left. Each man cradled an assault rifle comfortably in his arms. *More military training,* Laney thought.

Nathaniel, unarmed, continued to pace in front of them, sweat pouring down his face, mumbling to himself—a man unhinged. They'd leave Nathaniel for last.

Maddox counted down.

The man on the left reached down and grabbed one of the kids. "Well, I'm not waiting."

Neither did Laney. She sprang from her covering and drilled him right through the forehead. The children screamed as Maddox took out the other one.

Nathaniel didn't pause. He grabbed the child nearest him and yanked her up, placing a knife to the girl's neck.

Laney stepped into the cave, her weapon pulled to her shoulder. She hadn't seen the knife. *Damn it. I should have shot him when I had the chance.*

"Take another step and I kill her," Nathaniel screeched, his eyes bulging.

Maddox stepped forward. "No."

Nathaniel pressed the knife tighter to the girl's neck. A tear rolled down her cheek. Her eyes begged Maddox for help.

Laney tensed. She didn't have a shot. *Shit.*

With a blur of motion, Zachariah Grayston appeared in front of his father, grabbed the hand that held the knife, and pulled it from the girl's neck with a twist of his father's hand.

Nathaniel screamed.

Zachariah pulled the girl away from him and gently pushed her toward the other children. "Go."

The reverend squirmed, tried to get out of his son's grasp. But Zachariah just twisted his arm harder.

Nathaniel dropped to his knees, his face contorted in rage. "What are you doing? Let me go."

Zachariah's face was contorted as well, but by sadness, not anger. "No, Father. No more. It's over."

Nathaniel at last yanked his hand from his son's grip. He scrambled to his feet, his knife aimed at his son. "How can you defend them? They're abominations!"

The boy shook his head slowly. "They're not abominations. They're just children."

Nathaniel glared at his son, spit curling at the sides of his mouth. "You disgust me."

"I know, Father. I'm sorry."

The reverend lunged toward his son, but Zachariah stepped out of the way, latched on to his father's arm at the wrist and shoulder, and twisted it. With a quick move, his father's arm snapped at the elbow.

Nathaniel screamed and the knife dropped from his hand. He cowered on the ground, clutching his arm and moaning.

Maddox and Laney stepped forward.

Zachariah snatched the knife from the ground and whirled around. He waved it between Maddox and Laney. "I won't let you hurt them. They're not abominations. They're just children."

Maddox raised his hands, his voice calm. "I know. We came to help them, not hurt them."

Tears streamed down the boy's face. "They're just kids. They deserve to be just kids."

Laney kept her voice calm as well, but her heart broke for the kid. "They do. And my friends and I will make sure that they're safe and cared for. You've helped them. Now let us help too. My name's Laney."

Zachariah started, his eyes growing wide. "Laney? Max said you'd come. I didn't believe him." His gaze turned to Maddox. "You must be Maddox."

Maddox nodded.

The boy lowered the knife and looked back and forth between Maddox and Laney. His eyes were filled with so much pain that Laney sucked in a breath. He gestured to the children behind him. "They're not abominations."

"No. They're not," Maddox agreed, inching forward.

Zachariah dropped the knife to the ground, then turned, holding his arms out. The children flocked to him.

Maddox quickly retrieved the knife from the ground and tucked it in his belt. Laney, though, kept her eyes locked on Zachariah. The sadness in his face was almost unbearable. She saw his lips move but she couldn't hear what he was saying above the sounds of the children.

Until, that is, he looked up at her. "They're not abominations. But I am."

CHAPTER 80

Laney helped usher the children back along the passageway. She had sent Maddox ahead, knowing he wanted to find Max. She wanted to as well, but Maddox would move more quickly.

A number of the children were being carried by officers and agents. One agent stayed back with Nathaniel; he'd be leaving the cave last. They didn't need his histrionics upsetting the kids any further.

Laney walked next to Zachariah; she was worried about the boy. He seemed to have sunk into himself. He didn't say a word, except to one of the twins he held in his arms.

A Chandler operative jogged back toward them from the main cavern. Laney looked up. "Report?"

The man smiled. "We've got them. We've got them all."

"They're okay?"

The man nodded with a smile.

Laney felt her knees weaken and she closed her eyes for a moment. *Thank you.* "Where are they?"

"They're being led back to the main cavern now."

Laney smiled. "Then let's go greet them."

She picked up the pace. Soon she was stepping out into the large cavern, and there was Maddox, a little boy wrapped in his arms. The boy caught sight of her at the same time that she saw him. His brown eyes grew large and he squirmed out of Maddox's grip. "Laney!"

Max sprinted across the space toward her.

Laney ran toward him, then dropped to her knees, threw her arms wide, and pulled him close. "Max," she whispered, tears clogging her throat and preventing her from saying anything more.

Max hugged her just as tightly, and Laney was content to stay there for a few moments, letting relief wash over her.

Finally Max pulled back. "I knew you'd come."

Laney smiled. "I will always come for you."

"I know. I told the other kids they didn't have to worry. That you guys would get here in time."

"Are you okay?"

He nodded. "Yeah. But some of the kids need some help."

Laney looked around for the first time and realized that some of the kids were lying on the ground, with adults tending to them. She stood up but didn't let Max out of her arms as Jake walked over. "What's wrong?"

Jake put up his hands. "Nothing serious. A little dehydration, a few scrapes and bruises. One seems to be going into shock. We'll patch up those who need it and get those who are okay out of here."

She nodded. "What about Nathaniel's men?"

"A few were killed. The rest gave up without much of a fight. I have some SIA agents babysitting them until we can get the kids out of here."

"Good." Laney caught Maddox's eye and waved him over. She handed Max to the big man, and Maddox looked delighted to have the boy in his arms again. "Maddox, can you arrange for the first group of kids to be taken out?"

They'd already arranged for the kids to be taken out by boat, figuring it would be easier to lower the kids down than have them climb or be hauled up.

"I'm on it," Maddox said, Max tucked into his side. And Laney realized how right that sight was. Even though Maddox had only been in Max's life for a short time, he'd become the father figure. Even now, Maddox looked happier than she had ever seen him.

"What?" Maddox asked.

Laney shrugged. "Nothing. Just thinking you two look good together."

Max leaned his head on Maddox's shoulder. "And we're going to be together for a long, long time."

"Is that right?" Laney asked.

When Max looked at her, his face was serious. "Yes."

Maddox leaned his head into Max's. "Absolutely." He nodded at Laney. "I'll get the first round moving."

CHAPTER 81

L ou and Rolly paced along the top of the cliff, occasionally peering over—although after she'd done that twice, Lou decided it would be best for the contents of her stomach if she let Rolly do the checking from now on. They hadn't heard anything since the gunfire ten minutes ago.

"You think they're okay?" Rolly asked again.

Lou nodded with a confidence she didn't feel. "From what I hear, that's the dream team down there. They'll get the kids."

He nodded. "I'm sure you're right." Then he paused. "Don't you think they should have a name?"

"A name?

"Yeah, you know: a superhero name. Like winged avengers."

Lou smiled as she pictured Jen in a superhero costume. She'd hate it. "How about the Good Guys?"

Rolly shook his head. "Nah, too on the nose. How about Heavenly Warriors?"

The two of them spent the next few minutes debating names until Lou found herself holding her stomach and laughing. "Fluffy Knights? Can you see Jake walking around with that name?"

"What? Fluffy like angel wings and Knights like, you know, the round table."

"Yeah, keep working on that."

They were silent for a bit, just looking around.

"You know, it's been a while since anyone contacted us," Rolly said slowly.

Lou nodded, doubts beginning to creep their way into her mind. "What if they're in trouble and we're just hanging around up here? We should go check."

A voice sounded over the radio. "Jen to cliff top."

Rolly struggled to get the radio off his belt. He fumbled it a few times, almost dropping it before he got it stabilized. Lou had to restrain herself from yanking it out of his hand.

"Cliff top here," Rolly said.

"We've got the kids—all of them. We're sending the first group out with Maddox. Hold tight until we send someone for you guys."

"Um, gotcha. Over and, uh, out." Rolly replied before grinning at Lou. "The dream team racks up another win."

Lou grinned back, bursting with happiness. "Okay, maybe we didn't help, but yes!" She put up her hand and Rolly high-fived her. Then they hugged and did a quick victory dance.

As Rolly looked around, his smile dimmed. "Hey, did you see where Cleo went?"

Lou shook her head. "No. Where the hell could she go?" There were a few rocks she could hide behind, but the giant cat would have to lay practically flat.

Suddenly a tingle of electricity rolled over Lou, and her head whipped toward two figures who'd just appeared on the horizon. She grabbed Rolly. "Down!" Seconds later, gunfire raked the ground in front of them.

The two teenagers rolled out of the way. Lou started to get to her feet, but two Fallen sprinted toward them and arrived before she could manage it.

Lou looked up into a smirking face—a face she knew and wished she didn't. "You."

Pascha Bukin had been the Fallen who'd recruited her and the rest of the teens for the hideous training camp. He'd escaped in the confusion when Jen and Henry had led the assault.

He smiled. "Yes, me. And I found some new friends."

Lou glanced over at Rolly. His face was furious. *Please don't do anything stupid*, she thought.

Rolly's voice was cold. "What the hell are you doing here? Are you here for us?"

Pascha laughed. "Such an ego. We're not here for you."

Lou's jaw dropped. "You're here for the kids."

Pascha shrugged. "At least one of them, anyway. You two we have no use for." He raised his gun.

From behind him, Cleo let out a shriek and leapt at both men, raking their backs with her claws. They screamed in horror. Cleo landed on the second nephilim and swiped him across the neck.

Lou took advantage of the distraction and threw herself forward, tackling Pascha at the waist. As she slammed him onto his back, she pictured the girl he had brutally killed the first night in the camp. She wanted to snap his neck.

Rolly wrenched the weapon from Pascha's hand and held it to his heart. "You want the honors, Lou?"

"Get off me!" Pascha ordered, bucking to try and throw them off.

Lou stared at Rolly and then at Pascha. Pascha had killed Rolly's sister as well as hers—but they couldn't both kill him. At the same time, she wasn't sure she could bring herself to pull the trigger. "Rolly, are you sure—"

Rolly pulled the trigger, not stopping until the magazine was empty.

Lou jumped back, her eyes wide. She felt a little sick but shoved it away. She stared at Rolly, stunned. "You did it. You killed him."

Rolly got to his feet. "If we didn't stop him he would have just killed someone else's family. He killed Charlotte. He killed Alicia."

Lou knew he was right. If they didn't stop him, he would have killed those kids without a thought. She glanced over at Cleo, who was licking her paws after her snack. One glance at the body of Pascha's friend made it clear he wouldn't be healing.

Rolly leaned over and whispered in Lou's ear, "Remind me to never make Cleo mad."

Lou nodded as Rolly pulled her up, but then went still as electric tingles ran over her. "What's wrong?" Rolly asked.

"Five. There are at least five more."

She ran to the edge of the cliff. Below, she could see the kids being lowered to the beach. Downriver, she could just make out a boat heading toward them.

"That's not our guys, is it?" Rolly asked.

"No."

"Are you sure? I don't feel anything."

"That's because they're Fallen, not nephilim. You can't feel them—" Her eyes flew to Rolly's as the realization hit her. "Which means Maddox won't feel them either. He'll think it's the good guys."

She ran back to grab the radio from where it had fallen during the attack. Two bullet holes had removed any chance of it working. "Shit. We need to warn them."

"How?" Rolly asked. "With this wind, we can yell as loud as we want and they won't hear us. And we can't jump down three thousand feet."

Lou spotted the ropes Laney and the rest of the group had used to reach the cave. She glanced over at Cleo and then Rolly. "I think it's time we tested just how strong we are."

CHAPTER 82

Maddox held Max close in his arms as he headed toward the cave entrance. Four other members of their force followed behind him, and each one carried a child. The plan was to keep the kids strapped tightly against the adults, and then for the adults to rappel down the side of the cliff.

Maddox hugged Max a little closer to him. He hadn't let him go since he found him, except to let him hug Laney. Maddox's heart still pounded at the thought of how close the boy had come to dying.

Max draped an arm around the big man's neck and snuggled into his shoulder. Maddox reached up and patted the boy's back. This little boy had made him vulnerable.

Maddox had survived all that time with Amar by locking down his emotions, not letting himself care. Even when he helped the teenagers escape from the camp, he'd viewed it as just a job. It was the only way for him to do what he needed to do.

But Max had crawled under his defenses and right into his heart. And Maddox knew he would tear the world down if that's what it would take to keep the boy safe.

Max tilted his head back to face him. "Is Mommy okay?"

Maddox nodded. "She's going to be so happy to see you."

Max gave a big yawn. "Yeah."

Maddox smiled as he stepped out of the cave, then nodded to the man behind him. "Go ahead."

The man walked to edge of the cliff with a child no older than two strapped to his chest. Without hesitation, he latched into one of the ropes and started to rappel down. The other three quickly followed, leaving only Maddox and Max.

Maddox whispered down to Max as he approached the ledge. "Close your eyes, Max, so you don't get scared."

"I won't get scared. I'm with you."

Maddox kissed him gently on the forehead. "That's right. And I won't let anything happen to you."

They made it to the bottom of the cliff without incident. The boat was only about twenty yards out. Maddox placed Max on the ground. "Okay, little man. We're going to go for a boat ride."

Max grasped Maddox's hand, then took a step back and stared behind Maddox. "I don't want to go with him, Maddox."

"Don't worry, Max. I'll be with you."

"Well, hello, Maddox," came a familiar voice.

Maddox sprang to his feet just as Gerard walked up, flanked by three men. Maddox's men drew their weapons.

"You should warn them, Maddox. I've been told to try to not kill too many of you. But if you resist..." Gerard shrugged.

Maddox put up a hand, signaling the men to hold while his mind raced for a way to keep the children from getting caught in any crossfire.

Gerard's eyes widened at something over Maddox's shoulder, and Maddox had to keep himself from looking back to see why. Then with a low roar, Cleo slid past him and planted herself between Max and Gerard. Lou and Rolly stepped up next to Maddox.

"Where the hell did you three come from?" Maddox whispered.

"Um, the top of the cliff?" Rolly said.

Gerard glared at the three newcomers. "Children fighting to protect children? How cute."

"Maddox?" Lou asked, not taking her eyes off Gerard.

"The kids are your priority," Maddox said. "You guys keep them safe. Cleo and I will deal with these guys. And our reinforcements are right there."

"Um, about that," Rolly began. "The boat that's heading toward us isn't the good guys."

Maddox cursed, and he felt Max tremble behind him. Anger ripped through him. He wanted to tear these assholes limb from limb.

"How about some of the Chandler operatives get the kids out of here?" Lou asked as the boat beached and four men dropped out. There was a tremor in her voice. "I think you might need the help."

"I think we all might need some help," Rolly muttered.

Maddox felt Max tremble in his arms, and he let the rage flow through him. *Bastards.* Not taking his eyes off Gerard, he swung Max down to the ground. An operative took Max's hand and pulled him back to where the other men stood.

"No! Maddox!" Max tried to grab for him.

"Go with him, Max. I'll be there in a minute."

Gerard laughed. "You always have been cocky. How about I help knock your ego down to size?"

Maddox glared back, but his next words were for Rolly and Lou. "Whatever you do, protect those kids."

CHAPTER 83

L aney reached down and gently picked the crying two-year-old girl up from the floor. "It's okay, honey," she cooed.

Zachariah walked over, a bottle in his hand. "She usually quiets down when she's had her milk."

Laney took the bottle with a nod. "Thanks."

Zachariah ran a hand over the little girl's brown hair and then walked away. Laney watched him with narrowed eyes. What was going through his head? So far he'd been nothing but helpful; his focus had been entirely on taking care of the kids. But Laney knew there was a wellspring of emotion under the boy's surface.

She walked over to Jen, who glanced behind her, no doubt trying to see if Laney was heading for someone else.

Jen placed her hands up in front of her. "Oh, no."

Laney ignored her refusal and handed the little girl over. "Oh, yes. You got her?"

Jen held the girl awkwardly, looking completely out of her depth. "Um, yeah. Sure."

Laney tried not to laugh. "Just jiggle her a little bit if she starts to get antsy. And here's her bottle."

"Jiggle her? What does that even mean?"

This time Laney did laugh. She patted Jen on the shoulder. "You're a smart woman. You'll figure it out."

She turned away from Jen and let her eyes scan the cavern. All of the kids had someone attending them. The plan was to wait until Maddox came back before sending down the next wave. She glanced at her watch. The second boat should by arriving in another fifteen minutes.

Jake came to stand next to her. "Well, I think this went better than we ever thought possible."

Laney nodded. She was still watching Zachariah, who was walking slowly toward the altar of bones. All of a sudden, he reared back and kicked the altar, then punched it. The hits rebounded through the cavern. Some of the kids cried out.

"Shit." Laney sprinted across the space, Jake at her side.

"Stop!" Laney yelled.

And Zachariah stopped in mid-kick.

What the—? Oh, crap. She'd forgotten about the ring. She walked quickly over to Zach. "Put your leg down and quietly come with me."

Zach followed Laney into the cavern the men had been using to sleep. He stared at her, his eyes wide, shrinking back from her. "How did you do that?"

Laney put up her hands. "Sorry about that. I sometimes forget I *can* do that. But I needed you to calm down. We don't need the kids getting any more scared than they already are."

Zach's shoulder slumped. "Oh, man. I didn't—I mean, I wouldn't—"

Laney stepped forward. "I know. I know you wouldn't do anything to hurt them."

"It's just…" He stopped and looked past her.

"It's just that you're angry. And you needed to lash out. Trust me, I understand that feeling very well."

He looked at her for long moment. "What are you going to do with me?"

Laney crossed her arms over her chest. "Well, that's up to you to a certain extent. You're still a minor, so you can't go out on your own."

Zach nodded, staring at his feet.

"But we have this school we've set up for people like you."

"Abominations?"

Laney shook her head. "No," she said softly. "You are not an abomination. You're different. You're special."

"I don't feel special."

Laney gave a laugh, feeling a sense of déjà vu. Zach took a step back. Laney put up a hand.

"Sorry. But I can't tell you how many times I've had people tell me I'm special and I've thought exactly the same thing."

"You're like me?"

Laney nodded. "Yes. But also a little different. It's how I was able to get you to stop. And I *am* sorry about that. I try not to use that particular ability unless absolutely necessary."

"But how are you—"

If Zach said anything more, Laney didn't hear it, because a picture of Max trembling and clutching Maddox suddenly pierced her mind, and her head jerked up as if it were pulled by a string. Fear shot through her. *Max.* And then the awareness of the Fallen seeped through the cave walls and into her.

Turning from Zach, she sprinted out of the room and into the passage, yelling back into the cavern room, "We have trouble!"

She didn't have time to explain any more than that. She needed to get to Max. *Now.*

She raced toward the entrance of the cave. As she approached, her radio sprang to life. "—on the beach—Jordan—need—"

Laney yanked it off her belt. "Say again, Danny."

"Laney, thank God," Danny's panic was obvious in his voice. "Something's happening on the beach. Jordan found a lower position to offer them cover. Gerard is there."

Laney burst out onto the cliff and ran to the ledge. She

scanned the area below. She could barely see the group on the beach. Zach appeared at her side, followed by the rest of the group, Jake in front.

"What is it?" Jake said.

Laney caught his eyes. "Bad guys. *Fallen* bad guys."

Jake cursed before grabbing his radio and striding back to his men, issuing orders to get ready to go down.

Laney turned to Zach. "You should stay here."

"Are the kids in trouble?"

"Yes."

"Then I'm going."

A gunshot sounded from the beach and Laney's heart all but stopped. She knew it would take her minutes to climb down the ladder. Minutes the people on the beach didn't have. She put her hand on Zach's shoulder. "If you're going down, do it as fast as you can. You don't want to be an easy target."

"How are you getting down?" Zach asked.

Laney didn't answer. She ran as far from the edge as she could, then, taking a deep breath, she sprinted for the edge and leapt.

CHAPTER 84

L ou slammed her fist into the Fallen's stomach, pulled his head down, and kneed him in the face. She flipped him to the ground and then, grabbing the little girl next to him around the waist, she sprinted for the fallback position.

A Chandler operative ran toward her. She all but threw the girl at him. "Take her!"

The Fallen she had just dropped got to his knees and lined the operative and girl up in his sights.

Lou ran forward just as he pulled the trigger. She jumped in the air, the bullet catching her in the chest. Pain surged through her and tears sprang to her eyes as she crashed to the beach, sand filling her mouth. *Jen's right. Getting shot hurts.*

The Fallen stepped toward her, smirking. "That was stupid."

Cleo screeched behind him and jumped, tackling him. Lou rolled away as Cleo's claws raked the man's chest.

"Thanks, Cleo," Lou mumbled as the pain began to lessen. She lay on her back for a moment and caught sight of something being thrown off the cliff above. It took her a moment to realize that it wasn't a some*thing* but a some*one*.

Her stomach bottomed out as she scrambled to her feet. "Laney!"

Laney's body was tight, pointing like an arrow at the beach. As she neared the ground, a gust of wind came out of nowhere, grabbed her, and turned her onto her feet. She slowed and then touched down in a plume of sand.

One of the Fallen immediately ran toward her, but Laney waved him away with a flick of her wrist. A blast of wind grabbed a second Fallen and threw him against the rocks. Still another Fallen tried to run away, but Laney stopped him with a single word. "Stay."

Then a human ran at her. He threw a hook at her head. Laney ducked easily, while landing her own punch to his ribs. She followed it up with a roundhouse to his knee, a punch to his armpit, and a knife hand at his throat.

And Lou knew that without her own abilities, she wouldn't have been able to see any of it. It had all happened that fast.

Gerard took one look at Laney and hightailed it for the boat with two others.

Laney ran for them, but they sped away before she could reach them. "Cowards!" she yelled. The two remaining Fallen were quickly finished off by Maddox and Jordan.

Lou ran back to the kids and did a quick head count. She let out a breath: everyone was present and accounted for. She turned to the SIA agents. "I think we're clear."

"Everyone all right?" Laney asked as she walked up.

Max sprang at her. "Laney!"

She picked the boy up in her arms. "Gotcha."

"Is it over?" Max asked.

Rolly walked over with a limp. "Yeah. I'd kind of like to know that, too."

Laney looked down the river at Gerard's boat, which was now disappearing from view. "It's over. At least for now."

CHAPTER 85

Laney called Clark and requested more help. The other boat had been disabled, but no one, thank God, had been killed. Clark told her he'd arrange for search and rescue to get to them ASAP. Laney disconnected the call and sat back against the rock face.

Maddox walked up. "So, you jumped off a thousand-foot cliff?"

"So it seems."

"How'd you know we were in trouble?"

She glanced over at where Cleo was licking her paws. "Cleo told me."

"Uh, okay." Maddox looked behind him and then back at Laney. "Well, good luck." He walked off.

Good luck? What did he—

"What the hell were you thinking?" Jake yelled as he stormed up to her.

Oh. Laney got to her feet with a sigh. "I wasn't really thinking. It just seemed like the fastest way to get to the beach."

"How did you even know it was going to work?"

"I didn't. I just—"

"You *didn't?*" Jake threw his hands in the air. "Never, ever, *ever* do that again."

Laney reached out to him. "Jake, I—"

He ran a hand through his hair and glared. "You scared the hell out of me."

"I—"

"I need to calm down." He stormed off. He only got three feet away before he spun around, grabbed her by the shoulders, and planted a huge kiss on her lips.

Laney felt her knees buckle.

When Jake pulled away, his face was still furious. "Never, ever again." He stormed off again, and this time he didn't turn back.

Yoni looked at Jake's retreating back before turning to Laney. "Personally, I think that was completely badass. You looked like Captain America. You know, if Captain America was a redheaded woman."

Laney sighed. "Thanks, Yoni. I think. The kids okay up top?"

Yoni nodded. "Well, seeing as you wrapped everything up so quickly down here, Jen, Henry, and a few others stayed with the kids. We should have them all down in a little bit."

"Okay. Good."

Yoni turned to go but then stopped and looked back at Laney. "And don't be too hard on Jake. You didn't see his face when you did your swan dive. He really was terrified."

Laney nodded, feeling a lump in her throat. She remembered how she felt when she'd seen Jake shot in Egypt. She knew exactly how terrifying it could be.

Cleo came over and rubbed against her. Laney tried to ignore the blood around her muzzle. "Hey, girl."

Then she stepped back as she realized that Cleo shouldn't be here. Last time she'd seen her, she had been on the cliff top with Lou and Rolly. "How'd you get down here?" she murmured.

She caught sight of Lou and Rolly sitting on a rock. Both looked a little dazed by events.

R.D. BRADY

"Lou, Rolly." Laney waved them over.

As they approached, Laney blanched at the sight of the bullet holes in their shirts. "You two okay?"

"We're good," Rolly said, although some of his usual exuberance was missing.

"How did you guys get down here? And how'd Cleo get down here?" Laney asked.

Lou and Rolly exchanged a grin. "We kind of lowered her over the cliff with the ropes," Rolly said.

Laney's eyes grew wide. "What?"

"Well, there wasn't a choice," Lou explained in a rush. "The radio was toast, and the bad guys were heading in. And the kids were already on the beach. So we—"

The rest of her explanation was lost as Laney pulled her in for a hug. "Thank you." She turned to Rolly and hugged him too. "Thank you both."

"Hey, does this mean we're official members of the Angel League?" Rolly asked.

Laney pulled back. "The what?"

"We figure you guys needs a name. That's the one we like so far. You know, like the Justice League."

Laney laughed. "Fine with me."

Rolly whacked Lou in the arm. "Told you she'd like it."

Lou smiled but then turned back to Laney. "Um, by the way, there were a couple of Fallen up on the cliff top. One of them was Pascha."

"What? How did you guys—"

"Cleo helped us take care of them."

The two teenagers stared at their feet, looking a little shaken. Compassion washed over Laney. *They're so young.* "I'm so sorry."

Lou shrugged. "Had to be done. At least the kids are safe."

"Yeah." Laney's eyes traveled back down the river in the direction Gerard and his friends had disappeared. But what had that all

338

been about? They'd only brought a few fighters. Not enough to overpower the group. So what was the point?

"They didn't want all of the kids," Lou said, as if reading her mind.

Laney's head swung back to Lou. "What?"

Rolly gestured toward the top of the cliff. "When Pascha found us, he told us they weren't after *all* the kids. They just wanted one."

Laney felt her jaw fall open. Just one. Her gaze raked the beach until she spotted Max, once again safely snuggled in Maddox's arms. Max was the only child who didn't fit the pattern: no angelic abilities and no chance of developing them. She remembered the old game from childhood: which of these things is not like the others? She felt lightheaded and leaned back against the rock face.

Oh God, Max.

CHAPTER 86

Laney let out a breath as she was buzzed into the corrections wing. Last night, they'd managed to get all of the kids down from the cave without further incident, and had taken them all to a regional hospital. No major injuries, thank goodness. But now they had to figure out what to do with them.

Most would go back to their homes. But then what? Laney knew a few of them would one day come into their powers. Should they tell their parents? Wait until the kids were older?

And what were they going to do with the handful of kids who couldn't, or shouldn't, go back to their families? At least three of the families were neglectful, if not downright abusive. Combine a lousy upbringing and superpowers and you had a real recipe for disaster.

But what could they do? Legally they couldn't intervene unless they could prove abuse, and even then they'd have a hard time convincing the courts to let a corporation have custody of a child.

Laney shook her head as she made her way down the empty stalls. Those were questions for later. Right now, she just had one thing to truly focus on.

She nodded at the guard, who opened to door to the interrogation room. Inside sat Nathaniel Grayston, in an orange jump-suit, his hands and feet shackled, even though his left arm was in a cast.

He looked up as Laney stepped in. For a brief moment, he looked confused; then recognition dawned and his look turned to hate.

Laney pulled out the chair across from him. "Oh, good. You remember me."

"You are the devil's spawn."

Laney thought of Victoria and shrugged. "Well, that's still up for debate. Your horribleness, however, has been well documented."

Nathaniel shook his head. "And on her forehead was written a name of mystery: Babylon the great, mother of prostitutes and of earth's abominations."

Laney raised an eyebrow. "Are you calling me the mother of whores?"

The reverend narrowed his eyes. "You are an abomination."

"You seem quite obsessed with that word. But you see, me, those children, your son: we're not the abominations. *You* are. And you've lost."

"I haven't lost."

Laney made a show of looking around the room. "Do you see where you're sitting? This would be the loser's room."

Nathaniel just glared back at her.

"But believe it or not, I'm not here to gloat. I have some questions for you."

He stared at the wall behind her.

"How'd you find the children?" Laney asked.

"It's the computer age. Everyone can be found."

"Yes, but how did you know who they were? *What* they were?"

The smugness was once again back on his face. "Why would I tell you?"

Laney looked at him for a long moment, her arms crossed over her chest. "You'll tell me because you *want* to tell me. I can see it on your face. You want me to know why you think I've lost. You want me to understand."

Nathaniel smiled. "You have lost. I am but a soldier in this war."

Laney tried to keep her face expressionless. A soldier? Was he working for Samyaza? Was that who'd given him the list? Was that why Gerard was there? But if so, why had Gerard led them to him?

Out loud, she said, "If you're but a soldier, who's the general? Who's calling the shots?"

Nathaniel looked back at her and Laney forced herself to stay quiet. He wanted to tell her—she could feel it. He was desperate to let her know how much smarter than her he was. Finally he spoke. "We are but humble servants of the Shepherd. He shows us the way."

"The Shepherd? Who's the Shepherd?"

"He is the one with the knowledge. He is the one God smiles upon. And through him, God smiles upon us."

"Okay. But does your Shepherd have an actual name?"

"Names are not important."

"So he never told you." The Shepherd. Was he the mysterious donor who'd given them the land? Laney paused and studied Nathaniel. "Who gave you the bones?"

"What bones?"

"Your church."

Nathaniel smiled. "Phillip Northgram. He had the bones of the abominations hidden away in the Smithsonian. I brought them out into the light. To remind us, each time we pray, how critical our mission is. How victorious we will be."

He didn't give any indication that Northgram was his father. He could have been talking about his accountant for all the warmth he demonstrated.

"And he gave them to you as a gift?"

Nathaniel smirked. "I didn't give him a choice."

Ah, Laney nodded. "Blackmail."

The reverend shrugged. "Northgram has resources and money. I needed them. And the Shepherd helped show me what to ask for. He helped me fulfill my dream."

Laney tamped down her anger at the idea that this man's dream involved a church full of bones and the death of over a dozen children. "What does this Shepherd look like?"

"The hand of God."

Oh, great. I'll just have Clark put out an APB for the hand of God. Should have him in custody by lunch. "Yes, well, I was thinking of something more helpful: hair color, eye color, height, gender."

Nathaniel glared at her, his expression smug. "I will never betray the Shepherd. Remember: the war is still going. I am one small casualty. The Shepherd will continue the fight."

"What do you mean?"

"Oh, you'll find out. You'll find out in glorious fashion."

Laney stared at him and he smiled back. Finally, deciding she'd get no more useful information from the man, and frankly eager to be away from his evil, she turned and left.

She was surprised to find Jake just outside of the door. "Where'd you come from?"

He took her hand as they stared in the window at Nathaniel. "Thought you might like a little company after meeting with Sir Creepy."

Laney squeezed his hand. "You're not wrong."

Jake gestured back toward the room. "What did he mean by all that?"

"I don't know. He's not exactly acting like a man defeated, is he?" She looked up at Jake. "We got all of his followers, right?"

"The ones in the cave, yes. But we're still going through his computer. There are undeniably more still out there."

Laney's gaze was drawn back to Nathaniel. "What do you think about all this 'Shepherd' talk?"

"Maybe he's the benefactor."

"Yeah, I was thinking that too." She paused. "Do you think there's any chance the Shepherd and Samyaza are one and the same?"

"I don't know. But Victoria might."

Laney suddenly felt very tired. "I'll call her once we get the kids settled."

Jake placed his hand on her shoulder. "You know, Grayston could have just made up 'the Shepherd.' If he inherited his mother's schizophrenia, this Shepherd could be nothing more than a hallucination."

"Wouldn't that be nice." She looked through the window at Reverend Nathaniel Grayston. He just sat there smiling, nodding to himself. *He's delusional, just like his mother,* she assured herself.

But another part of her brain wondered: *But what if he isn't?*

CHAPTER 87

TWO WEEKS LATER

VENICE, ITALY

Gerard walked down the hall, trying to figure out what he was going to say. He had failed to get her the child. And since then, she had sent him on one meaningless errand after the next. He'd had to prove himself all over again to her. He glowered. It was humiliating.

But he pulled back the anger as he remembered the state of the last person who had disappointed Samyaza. All things considered, she had been kind to give him this time to redeem himself. With a steadying breath, he rapped on her study door.

"Come in," Elisabeta called.

He opened the door. Elisabeta stood by the open terrace. A gondolier rode by, his voice wafting in on the evening air.

"Samyaza, I—"

She put up a hand. "Sh."

Gerard went silent. Elisabeta swayed silently to the man's

song, turning to Gerard only once the song could no longer be heard. Her eyes pinned him in place. "You have not had a good year, Gerard."

He wanted to defend himself. Explain that it was the ring bearer who had disrupted all his well-laid plans. But he knew better than to offer excuses. He bowed his head. "Yes, Samyaza."

She walked over and patted him twice on the cheek. "You're lucky you are so handsome. But if you do not improve, even your good looks won't save you."

Gerard swallowed. "Yes, Samyaza."

She walked away and took a seat on the chaise lounge near the terrace. Her gaze drifted back toward the canals. Gerard watched her, confused. What was going on? He appreciated that she wasn't angry, but it was... not like her.

"I have a way for you to make it up to me," she said at last.

Gerard stepped forward. "Yes, Samyaza. Anything."

"I need you to find out who is the head of the High Council."

"You mean Northgram?" Gerard pictured the man. They had a full dossier on him, and a team that kept track of his whereabouts. But Samyaza already knew that.

"No. Northgram is not the head. There is someone behind the throne, pulling the strings."

"You don't know who?" The words slipped out of his mouth before he could stop them.

Elisabeta turned to him and narrowed her eyes. "No. It never mattered before. They've been an occasional nuisance, but easily squashed. But that's changed now. They went after potentials."

Gerard opened his mouth to contradict her but then shut it. The Council may not have directly threatened the potentials, but it was true that without their influence, the situation never would have arisen. "Would you like me to begin taking them out?"

Elisabeta sighed and shook her head. "You are brave, Gerard, but you need to be smart. You never rush in against an enemy blind. We need to know more about the Council head first. Don't forget about Delaney McPhearson."

Confused, Gerard asked. "Delaney McPhearson? You don't think it's her, do you?

"No." Elisabeta's voice took on an odd, almost wistful tone. "But she exists, and she can hurt us. And there are others who can hurt us as well."

"What? Who?"

Elisabeta shook her head. "Just find out who the true head of the Council is. Spare no expense. You're dismissed."

Gerard nodded and let himself out. But his mind whirled. Someone *else* could hurt them? Who? He'd never heard of such a person; no one had ever even intimated that there were other threats. As far as he knew, they had only the ring bearer to worry about.

And it wasn't just Elisabeta's words that convinced Gerard that whoever this other person was, they were even more dangerous than McPhearson. It was the look on her face.

He'd never seen that expression on Elisabeta's face before, although he had seen it on the faces of countless others.

It was fear.

CHAPTER 88

ONE MONTH LATER

BALTIMORE, MARYLAND

Danny headed down the hall to the computer lab. Laney was having his office painted, which meant he'd have to make do with the computer lab for the next two days.

A few months ago, the idea of having to spend time with the other members of the school would have driven him back to the Chandler estates. But something had changed. He now realized that he had an essential role to play, just like those with abilities. They might be the ones who leapt tall buildings in a single bound, but none of them could navigate the computer world like he could.

He'd also realized that that had been part of the reason why he'd been so angry: he had felt cowed by their abilities. He smiled. *Well, part of it anyway.* He was self-aware enough to realize another part of the reason was that he didn't like being told what to do.

As he rounded the corner, he nearly ran straight into Zach. He stumbled back, and his new friend reached out to catch him. "Sorry."

Danny smiled. "No problem. I was just lost in my thoughts, as usual. What are you up to?"

Zach shifted from foot to foot. "Um, just surfing the net, you know. I never really got to do that."

Danny nodded. Over the last month, he'd gotten to know Zach probably better than anyone at the school. He sensed a kindred spirit. With Lou and Rolly's help, they'd been slowly getting Zach to join in some activities and just hang out. Zach had even been known to laugh now and then. But this Zach in front of him looked stressed.

"Everything okay?" Danny asked.

"Yeah, no, everything's fine. I should let you get to work." He started to walk past Danny.

Danny turned. "Hey, Lou, Rolly, and I are going to watch *Star Wars* later in Lou's room. You want to join us? We're ordering pizza."

Zach shook his head. "Um, I don't know. Maybe."

"Okay, well if you want, we'll be there in around two hours."

Zach nodded. Danny waited, having learned that sometimes it took Zach a little while to decide if he was going to say something. Finally, Zach spoke. "I, um, just wanted to say thanks. You've been a good friend since I got here. My first friend."

"Well, you, Lou, and Rolly—you're kind of *my* first friends, too. At least my first friends my age. So why don't you come meet your friends for pizza later?"

"We'll see." Zach disappeared down the hall.

As Danny stepped into the computer lab, he made a mental note to track Zach down later and drag him to Lou's room, forcibly if necessary. He went to the back corner and flipped on the monitor. He'd spent the last month finishing up the projects he'd been working on, and he really didn't have a lot left to do—just one thing, in fact.

Danny had taken down the church's webpage while he was still in Nevada, but he hadn't had a chance to go through the page itself. Not that he thought he would find anything actionable.

He pictured Zach. Who was he kidding? He was hoping he'd find a way to help Zach. Every once in a while the boy would smile, but for the most part, Zach seemed to constantly be surrounded by his own personal cloud of misery.

Danny read through the postings, cringing at the apocalyptic tone. He knew that most people wouldn't understand what Zach had gone through. But Danny did. He, too, had been raised by a family who despised what he was. Out of everyone at the Chandler Home, he probably came the closest to having a shared experience.

But as he read the posts on the page and viewed some of the clips, he began to get the feeling that he might have gotten off easy in comparison to Zach. And when he considered that he had also escaped that life when he was nine, he *knew* he had gotten the better deal.

Danny spent an hour going through the site, not seeing anything important, but learning a great deal about Zach. He leaned his head on his hand as he stared out the window, trying to figure out a way to help his new friend. Should he share what he'd learned with Patrick? Patrick always seemed to have a way of speaking with people.

As he glanced back at the screen, he noted the crucifix positioned to the right of the title banner. No, perhaps Patrick wasn't the best choice after all; Zach would probably not want to talk with someone religious.

He pictured Laney. She would know what to say, would know how to help make Zach feel like part of his new world. After all, if anyone was good at accepting change and getting past difficult times, it was her.

He was preparing to stand and go talk to her, when he noticed the contact button on the website. *Hm. If there's an email address attached to it, then someone could have access to it.*

He pulled his chair back to the screen and dug around until he accessed the email account. It turned out it was only a Gmail account, with little to no security.

"Amateurs," he muttered with a smile.

He quickly scanned the email list, starting with the latest entry. It had been sent two days ago, with no subject. In fact, the same person had sent ten emails over the past month. *That's odd. Who would send something after the raid?*

Danny had taken the website down even before they'd breached the cave. Although he supposed someone could have tracked down the email address if they really wanted to; nothing truly disappears on the internet. Was it just some member who was unaware that everyone else had been arrested?

He glanced down at the other emails. They all seemed innocuous enough. *Well, as innocuous as email to a crazy cult can get, anyway.* His gaze flipped back to the first ten. More troubling than the fact that they had been sent after the raid was the fact that they had already been opened by someone. *Who's reading these emails?*

Danny opened the most recent email.

THE PACKAGE IS READY. *Northeast fence.*

AND THE SIGNATURE was only a quote and a moniker:

YOU WILL BE BLESSED *in the light of the Lord. The Shepherd.*

. . .

351

HE QUICKLY SCANNED through the other nine emails:

YOU ARE *an abomination and this is your only chance at Salvation.*

YOU WILL NEVER KNOW *God's grace without action.*

YOU WILL NEVER BE *part of that world. They are all abominations in need of deliverance.*

THEY WENT on and on like that, and all with the same signature: *The Shepherd.*

Danny stared at the screen, feeling cold. He quickly ran a search for the origin of the emails. They had been sent from a TOR account. There was no way to find the sender. But maybe whoever opened them hadn't been as smart as the sender.

Sure enough, Danny was quickly able to identify the IP address of the computer where the emails had been opened. He gasped when he recognized the number, but double-checked to be sure he was right. He was.

The IP address was from the school.

Danny checked the time stamp when the last email had been opened. An hour ago. *When Zach was in the lab.*

He quickly pulled up the security footage from that time. *Please let me not be right,* he prayed silently, not sure who he was talking to. As he ran the footage, he saw what he didn't want to see: Zach, sitting at a computer in the back of the lounge, alone. *No, Zach.*

Zach sat back in his chair, staring at the screen in front of him. Finally he got up and headed out, his shoulders low. Danny struggled to find the camera angles to follow him, and finally just jumped ahead to the northeast fence.

A backpack lay just inside the fence.

Danny fast-forwarded a few minutes.

And watched Zach step into the frame.

Zach walked up slowly, picked up the bag and pulled it onto his shoulders, then walked out of view.

Danny sat back. *What do I do?*

He didn't know for sure that Zach had done anything wrong. And if he told Security, Zach would never be able to fit in here.

I need to find out more, Danny thought as he stood, his heart beginning to pound as he thought of all the possibilities.

He scrolled through the live camera views, trying to find out where Zach was now. Finally he found him heading for the gym. Danny immediately headed for the door, Moxy on his heels. He ran out into the hall and nearly knocked over Lou.

She stumbled out of Danny's way. "Hey, what's the rush?"

"Sorry," Danny said, not stopping.

Lou ran up behind him. "Danny, what's going on?"

All the fear he'd been trying to shove down came boiling up. "I think there might be a bomb in the school."

CHAPTER 89

Laney fought exhaustion as she walked down the stairs of the school. Jake walked up behind her and swept her into his arms.

"Put me down," she said with a laugh.

"Nope, I need to get in the practice."

"The practice?" Laney asked lightly.

He looked down at her and Laney felt her heartbeat triple in speed.

"You two coming?" Henry called from the driveway. He stood next to his Range Rover. Jen watched from the other side, one eyebrow raised.

They had been working non-stop ever since Nevada. Today, they had finally decided to take a little time for themselves. They were going to go have lunch, somewhere with linen napkins, and there was even talk of a movie. For the first time since they'd learned about the kids, Laney felt like they could all breathe a little easier.

She felt the blush bloom across her cheeks as Jake lowered her to the ground. But before letting her go, he dipped her and gave her a kiss worthy of a sailor who'd been at sea for months.

Laney felt a little wobbly when he let her back up. The clap from the teenagers across the drive only made her cheeks bloom hotter. But she couldn't help but smile. She wrapped her hand around Jake's arm as they made their way to Henry and Jen.

It was going to be a good day.

CHAPTER 90

Danny turned the corner outside the gym so fast that he bounced off the opposite wall. Lou grabbed his arm and pulled him along. "We should tell someone."

Danny shook his head, breathing hard. "No. Not until we know for sure."

The gymnasium doors were just up ahead. Construction equipment lined the hallways leading there. Months ago, Laney had arranged for the gym renovation; it had begun while they were out in Nevada.

They came to a halt at the door and Danny peered in. Zach sat on one of the bleachers, the bag next to him.

Danny leaned back. "He's there."

Lou glanced around him. "Okay, let's go—"

Danny grabbed her arm, stopping her from entering. "No. You need to stay back here and listen. And if you need to, evacuate everyone from the school."

"What? Why?"

He glanced over at Zach. "Because you can get everyone out of the school faster than I can. We've done the fire drills. It takes five minutes to clear this place."

Lou spluttered, "I can't let you—"

"Lou, we have to empty the school quietly. We can't set off the fire alarms. You can do that faster than me."

"Yeah, but I can also knock him out faster than you."

Danny looked her in the eye. "Faster than he can push a button?"

She opened her mouth, then shut it. "Okay, so what's the plan?"

Danny took a deep breath. "I'll go talk to him and find out if he even has a bomb. When you hear the code word, you go get everybody out."

"What's the code word?"

Danny gave her a small smile. "Bomb."

Lou let out a nervous laugh. "Right."

He stepped toward the door. She grabbed his arm. "Be careful, okay?"

Danny swallowed hard. "No problem."

CHAPTER 91

The creak of the doors echoed through the cavernous space. As Danny stepped inside, he was convinced that Zach could hear his heart pounding from all the way across the gym.

Zach's head popped up in alarm, but then his shoulders relaxed when he saw it was only Danny. "You shouldn't be here, Danny."

"What, in the gym? I'm here to work on my basketball game." He crossed the room and stopped just a few feet away from Zach.

Zach shook his head. "I knew when I bumped into you in the hall. I knew you'd figure it out."

He turned to face Danny, revealing the bomb strapped to his chest.

Fear coursed through Danny. He forced himself to not take a step back. "Aw, Zach. A bomb? Why?"

Zach had tears in his eyes. "Why? Because I'm a weapon and I'm damned. Do you realize that when my dad told me about this mission, it was the first time he ever said he was proud of me? The first time."

"But you're going to kill all these people."

Zach shook his head. "No, I'm not. Who did you warn? Lou or Rolly?"

Danny hesitated, unsure if he should cop to it or not. Finally, he decided on honesty. "Lou."

Zach nodded slowly. "She'll get everybody out. I'll wait."

"But why do this at all?"

"You won't understand, Danny. You're normal."

"Me? Normal?" he laughed. "You are without a doubt the first person who has ever called me that."

"But your family, they—"

"Henry's not my biological father. Laney, Jake, Patrick, Jen— I'm not related to any of them. They just became my family. My real family thought I was a freak." And as he said the words out loud, for the first time he realized that what his family thought of him didn't hurt. It didn't even matter.

"You're not a freak. You're just smart."

"And you're not an abomination. You're just..." Danny paused, struggling for the right word. "Fast."

Zachariah shook his head. "You don't understand. I'm evil. I was born evil."

"No. You were born *gifted*. Just like Henry, like Jen, like Laney. And those are three of the best people I know. And like Lou! If you're evil, then so is she."

Danny's eyes flicked to the bomb strapped to his friend's chest. He spoke quietly. "You could have let your father kill all those kids. But you didn't. You fought him. You fought *for them. He's* the evil one here, not you."

Zach looked down at the vest and then back at Danny.

"Take it off," Danny said softly. "You don't want to die. You don't want to kill anyone. You just don't want to live this way anymore."

"But there's no out for me. I'm not you. I don't have anyplace to go."

Danny spread his arms wide. "You have this place. They won't

359

turn their back on you. If there's anybody who understands screwed-up families, it's us. And I won't let them turn their back on you." Swallowing, he stepped forward. "Let me help you."

Time seemed to stretch between them.

Finally, Zach nodded.

Danny exhaled, feeling almost lightheaded with relief. "Okay, so how do we get this thing off?"

"Right here." Zach reached down to hit a button next to the timer. But before he could do anything, the timer suddenly came to life. The glowing digits read: 1:00.

Panic crashed over Danny. "Zach?"

"I didn't do it, I swear! It just came to life!" Zach frantically pushed the button again and again. "It's not working."

"Turn around." His hands trembling, Danny tried to undo the knots at the sides of the vest. "They're too tight."

Zach turned to him. "Danny, run. You need to run."

Danny wanted more than anything to turn and flee. But the pragmatic part of his brain knew that he couldn't escape the blast radius. And his heart wouldn't let him leave this boy who'd already had every other person in his life turn their back on him.

"No. I'm staying."

CHAPTER 92

Lou sprinted back to the gymnasium. She'd warned everyone she could find, including Jordan, who she was sure would get everyone out. She needed to get back to Danny.

As she sprinted around the corner, someone else ran up next to her. She glanced over. "I told you to get out."

"When did you become the boss in this little friendship?" Rolly asked, keeping pace beside her. She just grunted at him.

They both came to a standstill outside the gym doors.

"I can't get it off!" Danny was saying, a tremor in his voice.

"Just get out of here!" Zach yelled back.

Rolly bolted through the doors and Lou was only a step behind, having paused to pull the fire alarm.

Zach turned to them and yelled, "Get Danny out!"

Rolly skidded to a halt in front of them, his eyes locked on the bomb vest. "Holy shit."

"I can't get it off," Danny said.

Lou grabbed one of the side straps at one end; Rolly grabbed the other. With one good, super-powered yank, they snapped the strap in two.

"Careful," Danny warned.

They ripped a second strap the same way, which provided just enough room for Zach to carefully wriggle out of the vest.

Twenty-five seconds.

Danny put out a trembling hand. "Give it to me. You guys are fast enough to get clear in time."

"No chance," Lou said.

"I agree with her," Rolly said. "But, um, does anyone have a plan that doesn't involve us all getting blown up?"

"I might," Danny said quietly.

CHAPTER 93

"So what should we see?" Jake said. "I heard the new Marvel movie is good."

"They're always good," Jen said.

Henry caught Laney's gaze in the rearview mirror. "What about you, Laney? What do you want to see?"

"I don't care. Anything. As long as there's a big tub of popcorn and lots of chocolate in it for me."

Jake took her hand. "That I can promise."

Laney's phone rang. Jen turned around. "Ignore it."

Laney wanted to do just that. But some of the parents had been calling about their kids with some concerns. "I'll keep it quick," she promised as she fished her phone from her pocket and put it on speaker. "Hey, Yoni. Did you and Sasha change your mind? We're only a few minutes away."

"You guys need to get back here!" Yoni yelled into the phone. Laney could tell he was running. "Get out!" he yelled at someone on his side of the line.

"Yoni, what's going on?"

"There's a bomb at the school."

Everyone in the car went still for a second. Then Henry threw the car into a U-turn that flung Laney into the door. He floored it as soon as the car was facing the right direction. They whipped down the dirt roads.

"I'm getting everyone out!" Yoni yelled before disconnecting the call.

Laney stared at the phone. *A bomb? What the hell?*

Next to her, Jake was already on the phone with the police, arranging for the bomb squad, medical care, and fire trucks. Laney held onto the emergency bar in the back, trying to keep her head from smacking into the roof each time Henry hit a pothole. But she didn't ask Henry to slow down. She wished he'd go faster.

Jake tried to call Patrick next, but didn't get an answer. Laney tried Danny—no luck. Jen tried Jordan, who they knew was at the school today. No answer from him either.

"They're all probably evacuating people," Laney said, but she saw Jen's look of concern.

Henry urged the car to move faster. "Come on. Come on."

Beside him Jen leaned forward, as did Laney and Jake from the back, as if they could all make the car speed up. Henry whipped around a curve and they braced themselves to keep from being flung against the window.

"We'll make it, Henry," Jen said.

Images of the kids at the school crashed through Laney's mind. *How did a bomb get into the school?* She looked over at Jake. "Call again."

Jake was already dialing. After a few seconds he shook his head.

The car came around the trees. There, resting like it always did at the bottom of the mountain, was the school. There were no flames, no smoke. Laney felt a small measure of relief at the sight. But people were pouring out of the doors.

Henry yanked the wheel to the right and onto the grass,

cutting directly toward the school rather than taking the more winding road.

They were five hundred yards away.

"We're almost there," Laney said.

And then the building exploded.

CHAPTER 94

Henry slammed on the brakes as a cloud of debris from the explosion battered the car. He ripped open his door and started to run. Jen matched his pace. People were running toward them.

Henry grabbed one of the kids. "Sean, where's Yoni?"

Sean pointed back toward the school, coughing. "Back there. With Sasha and Dov."

"You need to gather everyone up. Have them meet by my car. There's a first aid kit in the back. Help's on the way."

Sean nodded. "Got it."

Jen ran ahead and grabbed a man who was bleeding heavily from his arm. Jordan.

Henry sprinted over. "What happened?"

"Lou. She warned us about a bomb in the gym," Jordan said.

Jen made Jordan sit on the ground. Ripping off one of his sleeves, she started to bandage his arm. "How many got caught inside?"

Jordan grimaced. "Not many. Thanks to Lou, we had some warning. And Danny kept the bomber talking so the rest could escape."

Henry felt his world tilt. His gaze flew to the burning building. "Did Danny…?"

"I don't know. I think he was still—"

Henry didn't hear the rest of Jordan's sentence. He was already running. He blew past students who were stumbling from the wreckage. None of their injuries looked life-threatening. But Henry wasn't sure if he could have stopped even if they were. The need to get to Danny overrode every other thought.

He charged up the steps, desperation to save Danny fueling him—even while part of his mind whispered that he was already too late.

CHAPTER 95

Laney had heard Jordan's comment and felt her heart break. *Danny.* Blood thundered in her ears as she raced into the building, right on Henry's heels. Smoke filled the front hallway. She closed her eyes. Seconds later, a strong wind blew in and chased the smoke away. Jake and Jen ran in behind her.

Laney looked at Henry. "Let's go get him."

Jake stepped forward. "Yoni said they were in the gym."

Laney pictured the blast. The biggest explosion had come from that area. She swallowed her horror. "Okay. Then that's where we're heading."

Together they ran. On the way, they came across three injured students in the cafeteria. "We've got them," Jake said, nodding at Jen. "You guys go find Danny."

Jen picked up one of the kids. "We'll find you as soon as we get these guys clear."

"Okay," Laney said, running to catch up with Henry, who hadn't even paused. He also hadn't said a word since they'd come inside. Laney wanted to tell him it was okay, but she had no idea if it really was.

They turned down the hall to the gym, only to find that the

floor above had crashed down into it. Carefully, they climbed through the debris. Laney could sense Henry's growing fear. The damage was clearly worse as they got closer to the gymnasium.

Tingles ran over her skin: two Fallen and a nephilim. She grabbed Henry's arm. "There's someone there."

The gym doors had been completely blown away. It was only when Laney stepped through the gaping hole that she saw the full extent of the destruction. Light streamed in from where the roof should be. Fires raged around the perimeter. But there was no sign of life.

Laney felt her own fear crawling up her throat. Who had done this? Jordan had said that Danny had talked to the bomber. *Someone he knew?*

Laney could still sense the Fallen and nephilim. She looked around. But where?

Her eyes fell on the locker room. Or what was left of it. Its door was completely gone and the wall between it and the gym had largely collapsed. She heard a cough. Henry blurred and was gone. Laney ran after him.

The inside of the locker room was a jumble of wreckage and debris. There were no fires in here, but it looked like most of the ceiling had caved in. Henry must have heard something, because he picked his way through the mess and went straight to the laundry chute. "Hello? Anyone down there?"

"Henry?" Danny called back.

Henry grabbed the wall and closed his eyes. He wobbled with overwhelming relief, and it looked like his legs might give out on him.

Laney felt the tears gather in her throat. "Who's down there with you?"

"Lou, Rolly, and Zach."

"Is everyone okay?" Henry asked.

"Yeah. Well, Lou broke her foot but it's getting better. And I think I dislocated my shoulder when I landed," Danny said.

Laney let a laugh of both relief and disbelief. "How the hell did you guys survive the blast?"

"We dove down the laundry chute," Rolly said.

"It was Danny's idea," Lou shouted up.

Laney grasped Henry's hand and held it tightly. "We'll have you out in a few minutes."

They found the stairs to the laundry-room-slash-bomb-shelter, and Henry pried open the door, with Rolly and Zachariah's help. Laney rushed in as soon as the door was open, and Lou gave her a wave from the floor across the room.

Danny lay on the floor, his face pale. Laney dropped down to her knees. "Danny?"

"I'm okay," he said through clenched teeth.

Henry walked over. He took one look at Danny and said, "Danny, I'm going to pop your shoulder back in. It'll hurt when I do it, but then it'll feel better."

Danny nodded, gritting his teeth, and Henry helped him sit up.

"Rolly?" Henry asked.

Rolly nodded and scooted behind Danny to hold him.

Henry knelt down. "This is going to hurt."

"It's okay. Just do it."

Henry's eyes met Rolly's. Rolly placed his arms around Danny to hold him still. Then, with a quick jerk, Henry wrenched the shoulder back in place. Danny screamed.

Rolly released Danny, who collapsed forward. Henry caught him. Rolly then pulled off his sweatshirt and used it to tie up Danny's arm.

Danny leaned heavily against Henry. "Thanks."

Laney sat back and looked around. "I can't believe you guys are all right. Where did the bomb blow?"

The four teenagers exchanged a look. "Um, up by the ceiling," Lou said.

"The ceiling? There was a bomb on the ceiling?" Laney asked, trying to picture it.

"Not exactly," Rolly said. "We sort of threw it up in the air right before it exploded, and then ran and dove into the chute. That's how Lou hurt her leg. She was the one who threw it, so she was the last one through."

Laney looked from one to the other of them before her eyes finally came to rest on Lou. "You *threw* a live bomb up in the air?"

Lou squirmed. "Well, Danny said if I got it through the skylights in the gym, it would do less damage. So I did."

Laney was stunned. "How did you even know there was a bomb?"

All the teenagers went silent. Then Lou, Danny, and Rolly rushed to explain at the same time.

"I saw it when I was—"

"Someone told me—"

"I don't know. I just sort of—"

"Guys!" Zachariah said loudly, and they all shut their mouths and looked at him, their eyes wide.

Lou shook her head. "No, Zach."

"Yes." His voice was shaky. When he turned to Laney and Henry, his eyes were bright with tears. "I brought the bomb into the school. I'm sorry."

Laney stared at him, dumbstruck. "You brought a bomb here? Why? How?"

Danny sat up. "He got a message, actually messages. But you have to understand. He made sure everyone was out. In fact, he wasn't going to set it off at all, but then the timer came to life all by itself. It's not his fault."

Rolly and Lou nodded their heads in agreement.

Laney met Henry's incredulous gaze. Zach brought a bomb into the school?

"Zach?" Laney asked.

He looked at her with tears in his eyes. "I wasn't going to let anyone get hurt, Laney, I promise. Even if the Shepherd told me to."

"The Shepherd?" Laney suddenly remembered her conversation with Nathaniel.

Zach nodded, wiping away a tear. "He knew you'd take me. He wanted me to destroy this place and everyone in it. But I could never do that. No one was supposed to get hurt, except..." He looked away.

Except you, Laney thought with a heavy heart. She looked at the poor boy in front of her. He'd spent years being abused by his father. His emotions and self-esteem were all over the place. And this Shepherd had used that vulnerability to try and get him to do his dirty work.

But it hadn't worked. Zach wasn't like them. He was good. She saw that in him. She felt it.

But they couldn't let him hurt any of the other kids.

"What are you going to do?" Lou asked.

"I don't know." Laney looked at Henry, trying to gauge his reaction.

Henry was still looking at Zach, his expression inscrutable. "We'll figure that out. But for right now, this stays between us, okay?"

They all nodded.

Tears tracked through the dust in Zach's face. "I'm sorry."

Lou and Rolly leaned into him, throwing their arms around him, and Laney nodded. "I know. But I need to know who gave you the bomb. Who sent you the emails?"

"It was the Shepherd," Zach said.

"Do you know his real name?"

Zach shook his head. "No. No one does."

Laney met Henry's eyes. Maybe no one did, yet—but finding out the name of the Shepherd had just become priority number one.

CHAPTER 96

ONE MONTH LATER

Laney stepped out of her Jeep and surveyed the front of the Chandler School. All of the windows had had to be replaced after the bombing, and a full wing had been shut down. But they had been lucky: there were no major injuries. All thanks to a group of teenage heroes.

Jake walked around the Jeep and kissed her on the cheek. "I'm heading to the gymnasium. See how the repairs are coming along. Catch you later?"

She nodded. "Absolutely."

As he disappeared around the side of the building, Laney gave a contented sigh. The last month had been blissfully non-violent. She and Jake had been in the same cottage every single night, except for when they both stayed out here. And even with the many decisions that had to be made and all the work that needed to be done, just being able to wake up and fall asleep next to Jake made every day so much better.

A group of teenagers sprinted out of the front door with Moxy on their heels. Laney jumped quickly out of the way to avoid being trampled.

"Hey, Laney." Lou ran up and hugged her.

Laney returned the hug. She looked over the group: Lou, Rolly, Danny, and Zach. Her gaze lingered for a moment longer on Zach. There was a glow in his cheeks that hadn't been there when she'd first met him. He smiled shyly back at her.

They had managed to keep Zach's involvement in the bombing quiet. Laney, Henry, and Jake had decided to keep Zach at the school. There wasn't really any place else they could think of that could help him the way they could. But Zach had had to agree to daily counseling sessions, and of course everyone was still keeping an extra close eye on him.

Laney had told Zach that he could pick his counselor. When he'd picked Patrick, Laney had been surprised: she'd thought he'd be reticent about talking with another religious authority. But he and Patrick had really gotten along well. And Laney could see that Patrick was helping the boy heal.

"So, where are you guys off to?" Laney asked.

"Soccer practice," Lou said. "We've got a game later."

"Want to play?" Rolly asked.

Laney thought of everything else she had to do. "What time?"

"Eleven at the back field," Danny replied.

Laney smiled. "I'll be there."

"Yes!" Rolly said, slapping Zach on the back. "Now let's stop by Cleo's cage and see if she wants to play goalie."

The kids headed off, loudly debating what position Cleo would best be suited for. Laney laughed. This was what life was supposed to be like: friends, happiness, and soccer games. And lunch with friends—she had plans to meet Max, Maddox, and Kati at noon.

Kati was still on the mend, but getting Max back had done wonders for her progress. Kati was still feeling fearful, but she was slowly accepting the surreal in her life—including the abilities of her son.

Laney's mood dimmed for a moment as she thought about that. She didn't know what Max's abilities meant. And ever since Nevada, those abilities seemed to be growing stronger. And yet, there had been no more attempts on him. Or maybe they hadn't been after him after all. Their actual target that night remained a mystery.

A whoop from across the lawn interrupted her thoughts. Rolly had grabbed Danny's hat and was running across the lawn. The other three gave chase. Laney laughed at their antics. They had the right idea: live in the now, and leave the problems for when they really were problems.

But the thoughts that had haunted her since the bombing were always there in the back of her mind. Who was the Shepherd? How had he been able to get to Zach? Why had Max been targeted?

Zach had given them all the information he could. Unfortunately he didn't know the Shepherd's name, although he did say he had an usual amount of influence over his father. Zach had seen him once, but besides his shoulder-length dark hair, the only distinctive feature Zach could remember was the dark sunglasses he always wore.

Victoria had also been searching for him, but with no success thus far. Laney tried not to worry about her, but she couldn't help it.

And then there was Max. Why had he been grabbed? Did his psychic abilities have something to do with it? And if so, how could anyone have even known about them?

Laney shook herself from her thoughts. She didn't have any answers right now, and she needed to find a way to live while searching for them. She reached back into her car and grabbed her coffee. On the side of the cup were the words: *Life is Good.* Jake had gotten it for her.

Laney smiled. *Life is good. My new mantra.*

Her phone rang and Laney went still, a sense of foreboding coming over her. *No. Life is good. My life is not that predictable.*

But when she saw that the call was from Victoria, her calm shattered. The ring on the chain around her neck felt heavy, and she knew that this was duty calling. A call from Victoria was practically a bat signal.

Maybe she's just calling to say hi, Laney tried to convince herself —unsuccessfully—as she took the call. "Hi, Victoria."

"Laney." Victoria's voice was urgent.

"What's wrong?" Laney said, alarmed.

"Everything. Everything's wrong."

For Victoria, the queen of understatement, to say something like that was the equivalent of the nation going to DEFCON one.

Before Laney could speak, Victoria rushed on. "I've found the Shepherd. I know who he is."

"Okay, who is he?"

"His name is Jorgen Fuld. But that name is meaningless."

"And he's dangerous?"

"Very."

Laney closed her eyes. This was what she had feared: that there was more underneath it all. "Do you know him personally?" Laney asked softly.

Victoria hesitated, and Laney could picture her wrestling with how to answer. Finally, she seemed to decide on the truth. "I've known him for a long time."

"Care to quantify that?" Laney asked. "Because for most people, a long time would be years. For you, I'm thinking it's longer."

"A very long time," Victoria said softly.

"Is he Samyaza?"

"No. She's a problem, but not the biggest problem."

"Wait—*she?*" Laney asked.

"She's not our biggest problem. You need to understand who

Jorgen really is." Victoria paused. "And you need to understand who I am."

Shock rooted Laney in place. She had wanted to know who Victoria was ever since she met her, but now the old phrase wafted through her head: *Careful what you wish for.*

Laney spoke slowly. "Does that include how you saved Jake?"

"Yes. You need to know everything. If you're going to fight him, fight them. Can you come to me? Jake and Henry as well?"

"Uh, sure," Laney said. "When?"

"The sooner the better. Things are happening fast."

"Things?"

Victoria went quiet for a moment. "It's better to do this face to face. It's time. You need to know what you're up against. And every weapon and enemy you are up against. Especially me."

EPILOGUE

As Gerard led the way down the hall, he glanced back past his five men to Elisabeta. She had wanted to come, to make sure her message was received personally.

They'd found the elusive head of the High Council. *A businessman based out of Seattle. Humans and their fears. Ridiculous.* Gerard had managed to convince himself that he must have misread Elisabeta's mood when she had sent him on this quest. After all, what was there to fear from a human?

Gerard himself had done the reconnoitering on the target. The Shepherd, Jorgen Fuld, was working in his home office. They had already taken out his pitiful excuse for security. Now only the man himself remained.

Elisabeta nodded.

Gerard turned back to the door. Grasping the handle, he twisted it open and rushed in. His men followed right behind him.

"Put your hands up," Gerard barked.

Jorgen continued making marks on the paper on his desk. His

dark hair was pulled back in a ponytail, and he wore sunglasses despite the encroaching evening.

Gerard moved forward. "I said, put your hands up."

Jorgen still didn't take his attention from his papers. "I heard. I just choose not to."

Gerard paused. "Why, you—" But Samyaza stopped him with a hand on his shoulder.

Finally, Jorgen placed his pen down and looked up. He scanned the group in front of him with a bored air until his gaze fell upon Elisabeta. He raised an eyebrow. "Why Sam, how nice to see you again."

Shock momentarily taking his voice, Gerard stepped forward. "How dare you speak to—"

"No," Elisabeta ordered. "No one touches him."

Her words were forceful, but Gerard could have sworn he heard a tremor in them.

"But—" a man behind Gerard said.

Elisabeta's voice lashed out. "No. One. Touches. Him."

The Shepherd gave Gerard a grin. "She's always had a soft spot for me."

Gerard looked back and forth between the man and Elisabeta. Who the hell was he? Gerard didn't sense anything from him. He wasn't a Fallen or a nephilim. He seemed like just a normal human.

Elisabeta took a step forward, waving Gerard back. "What are you doing here? You've never involved yourself in these matters before."

"Well, time does march on, doesn't it? And times have changed, haven't they? The triad has arisen. As has she."

"What does *she* have to do with anything?"

The Shepherd's face went cold. "She has to do with everything. As you well know."

Elisabeta stiffened.

The Shepherd leaned back, his hands across his chest, his

posture casual. But Gerard couldn't help but feel they were the mice standing before the lion.

"So, you know," the Shepherd said quietly. "And now I'm guessing that, in a strange twist of fate, we have the same goal."

Elisabeta's voice was incredulous. "You can't be suggesting we team up?"

The Shepherd stood and stretched with a laugh. He walked around to lean against the front of the desk. "Of course not. We might have the same goal, but our motivations are somewhat divergent, aren't they?"

Elisabeta took the smallest step back. "You were the one who tried to orchestrate the deaths of the potentials. Why?"

He shrugged. "I play the long game, as you well know."

"They were children," Gerard burst out.

The Shepherd's voice was like a whip. "They were soldiers waiting in the wings, either for your side or theirs. Neither of which is in *my* best interest. Besides, it kept the ring bearer busy while I took care of a few details."

Elisabeta said nothing in response.

Gerard stared at her disbelievingly. What the hell was going on?

The Shepherd nodded toward the men. "Now, my dear Elisabeta, why don't you and yours head out while I still allow it?"

"*Allow?*" One of Gerard's men sneered as he stepped forward. "Samyaza, let me teach—"

"We're leaving," Elisabeta ordered. Gerard gaped. "*Now.*" And without another word, she turned and strode toward the door.

As they filed out, one of Elisabeta's men walked within arm's reach of the Shepherd. The Shepherd stepped forward slightly, just enough so that their shoulders brushed.

A crack sounded through the room like a thunderclap.

Everyone went still.

Except for the man the Shepherd touched. He dropped to his knees with a scream, his arm now hanging uselessly at his side.

Gerard looked on, his eyes wide, waiting for the man to heal. But he didn't. Gerard tore his gaze from the man and turned it to the Shepherd.

Elisabeta strode back into the room, but Gerard noted that she stayed a good few feet from the Shepherd. "That wasn't necessary."

The Shepherd's voice was cold. "That was *generous*. And a reminder."

The injured man staggered to his feet, his arm hanging uselessly by his side, his face deathly pale. Two of the other men had to help him out of the room.

The Shepherd leaned casually against the desk, his arms across his chest.

"Let's go, Gerard," Elisabeta said, backing out of the room.

Gerard did the same, not taking his eyes off the Shepherd.

"Oh, Gerard," the Shepherd called as Gerard reached the door.

Gerard stiffened.

"Be a dear and close the door on your way out."

In his mind, Gerard beat this man into a bloody paste. In reality, he pulled the door closed behind him with a polite nod.

What the hell was going on?

DELANEY MCPHEARSON's journey continues in The Belial Origin. Now available on Amazon

FACT OR FICTION?

I want to thank my readers who have been nice enough to write and let me know how much you enjoy the "Fact or Fiction" section at the end of the Belial books. I have to admit, I love it too when I find these sections in other books. So enough gabbing: on to the facts! And once again, they are not in any particular order.

People in Ancient America. Until I started doing research for this book, I just assumed North America had been inhabited prior to the Ice Age. Granted, I didn't expect it to be millions of people, but I expected a pretty sizeable group. Imagine my surprise when I found that scholars argued the opposite: that North America was largely uninhabited until after the Ice Age.

But even though academics argued that people weren't here earlier, many Native American tribes spoke of an ancient people who were in the Americas long before them.

Ten Plagues. The examples used to represent the ten plagues were all taken from real life.

The Clovis Barrier. The Clovis Barrier and the Clovis First Theory are real. The belief was that, prior to the ice bridge across the Bering Strait, there were no people in the Americas. As a result, archaeologists didn't dig below the 9500 BCE strata until late in the twentieth century. And when they did, they started to find more and more artifacts. All of the archaeological evidence mentioned in *The Belial Children* is accurate. So the question is, if the Americas were geographically isolated, where did these early people come from?

Giants in Ancient America. I cannot remember where I first heard about ancient giant skeletons. I've been wracking my brain trying to remember, but it is eluding me. I guess it's one of those things you hear along the way that just sticks with you.

So is it true? Again: a matter of debate. In the early twentieth and late nineteenth centuries there were quite a few newspaper articles about giant skeletons that were unearthed, many of them in connection with elaborate mounds.

Another interesting fact mentioned in different newspaper reports was that many of the skeletons had two rows of teeth. I didn't mention it in the book, but I find that coincidence fascinating, especially considering communication between different parts of the country would have been extremely difficult at the time the newspaper articles appeared.

The Hemlock Cave example was also alleged to be true. :) So, were there giants in America? Well, why not? Life seems to be filled with new discoveries every day. And Hobbits apparently existed, so why not the other end of the spectrum?

If you are looking for more information, consider *The Ancient Giants who Ruled America* by Richard J. Dewhurst.

The Mound Builders. The mound builders did exist. As the United States was first being settled, settlers reported these incredible mounds across the country. Some of them still exist, such as the Serpent Mound in Ohio or the effigy mounds in Iowa. However, many of them were destroyed to make for settlements.

And early settlers of the United States did believe that an ancient advanced race once lived here, due to these sophisticated mounds they found as they began to settle across the country.

According to the early settlers, the mounds must have been created by a race other than the Native Americans—due to the intelligence needed to create such monuments. (Yup, no racism there.)

Different Humans Coexisting. In *the Belial Stone*, Yoni mentioned the race of Hobbits, known as *Homo floresiensis*. Well, Yoni was right, but there's more to the story. In fact, over twenty different types of hominids are known to have existed, and in the last decade, more and more types of hominids have been found. Homo denisova, as mentioned in *The Belial Children*, is an actual classification. They were much larger than *Homo sapiens*, going by the larger teeth found and attributed to them.

And yes, there is an unknown species that bred with the denisovans. What this all means is that the human family tree has a lot more branches than originally believed—and that means our history is a lot more complicated than is currently understood.

Haplogroup X. There is a haplogroup X, and geneticists are a little baffled by its existence. The timing of the appearance of haplogroup X in the Americas does actually align with the two of the alleged destructions of Atlantis (10,000 and around 35,000 BCE). Part of the fun of haplogroups is that, through testing, it can be determined when and where peoples migrated to and from. Haplogroup X does constitute three percent of Native American populations, as well as small portions of populations in Europe and Asia.

Edgar Cayce and America. Edgar Cayce does speak about early America. He said that people were in North America much earlier than was understood at his time. Later archaeological evidence seems to have borne out his predictions. He even predicted the early settlement found in California—a settlement which is at least a hundred thousand years old. He also spoke about the mound builders and Iroquois. Edgar Cayce did say that the noble class among the Iroquois were pure Atlanteans.

If you're interested in reading more on Cayce's predictions

about ancient America, the Mound Builders, and haplogroup X, check out *Mound Builders: Edgar Cayce's Forgotten Record of Ancient America* by Greg Little, John Van Auken, and Lora Little.

Grand Canyon City. In 1909, there were two newspaper reports in the Arizona Gazette regarding G.E. Kincaid's discovery of a cave in the Grand Canyon. The description of the cave in *The Belial Children* is taken from those newspaper reports. Some argue that the newspaper articles were a fake. Others argue that the Smithsonian did indeed dispatch a team to document and collect the find.

The Smithsonian Hiding Finds. A number of different sources claim that the Smithsonian began hiding finds of an ancient race of giants. Allegedly the cover-up began with Smithsonian Director Powell after the Civil War, with the adoption of a policy that argued that any evidence of foreign involvement in the United States was to be quashed.

Keep in mind, we are talking about a time when slavery has just been abolished and Native American lands were being taken away. To say this was a time of racial strife would be an understatement. Throw into that the need for a solid American identity, and I can see how finds that only fueled the racial strife could be disregarded, if not actively hidden.

Or perhaps the finds don't exist. But there seems to be enough evidence that has come to light to suggest that we do indeed have very tall individuals in our history. It would be interesting if we could figure out exactly who they were.

Ancient Tales about Advanced People. There is a legend among the Hopi about being led by an advanced race to a safe location during a cataclysm. And yes, one Native American group did reveal that the Grand Canyon was where they had been led and where they did emerge after the cataclysm had passed.

Library edition of *Buffy the Vampire Slayer* Comics. There are library copies, complete collections of seasons 8 and 9 of the comic books of *Buffy the Vampire Slayer,* which take off where the show left off. Why do I mention this? I loved that show. And yes: I have the library editions.

Mu. Ah, the other legendary city. According to numerous sources, including Edgar Cayce, Atlantis was not the only highly advanced ancient civilization. While Atlantis was off the east coast of North America, Mu was alleged to be off the west coast. Allegedly Mu was destroyed around the same time that Atlantis was. But unlike the inhabitants of Atlantis, the citizens of Mu fled to… Oh, wait a minute. I should probably keep that to myself. I think it may show up in a different book. :)

Quotes. The quotes attributed to the Bible found in *The Belial Children* are actual quotes. There are different versions of the Bible, which word things slightly differently. So if you are reading a quote and it seems a bit off from what you recall, that may be why.

The quotes attributed to the book *The Army of the Belial* are of course my creation.

Edgar Cayce and Psychic Abilities. When Edgar Cayce was a child, he was reported to have spoken with ghosts. Some were nice and some were not. In fact, psychic ability seems to have run in the Cayce family.

There are other researchers who argue that when children are young they are more likely to see and hear spirits. Is that true? I don't know. But personally, I've seen a few incidents involving children that suggest it might be.

Church of Bones. There are churches that are decorated in bones. They are called ossuaries. And as mentioned in the book, the macabre creations are usually created due to an overabundance of bones. If you are interested in checking one out, Google the Sedlec Ossuary.

Doomsday Cults and "End of Days" Religions. Alas, these exist too. Most are harmless, more of a preparation for the end of days than any active attempt to bring it around. But every once in a while a group like Heaven's Gate shows up.

Heaven's Gate was a real end of days cult. All of the information in the novel is accurate about the group. The leader Applewhite did indeed convince his followers that by committing suicide they would be in essence beamed aboard a spacecraft waiting for them out in space.

Subduing Someone with Chapstick. Thought I'd just throw this one in for fun. Yes, there are ways to subdue an individual with Chapstick, or a quarter, or any other small little object. Generally it involves a finger or pressure points. It takes little to no force and is highly effective. Go ahead, Google it; you know you want to. :)

Thank you for reading *The Belial Children*. I hope you enjoyed it. If you get a chance, please leave a review.

Until next time,

R.D.

P.S. Oh, and one more thing: keep reading for a sneak peek of the next book, *The Belial Origins*.

ACKNOWLEDGMENTS

There are a lot of great people who helped make *The Belial Children* a reality. First and foremost, I'd like to thank all the special critters who have read and re-read multiple drafts of this work. Every week, you helped me iron out the mistakes and find a better way to explain my ideas. I am forever grateful.

I'd also like to thank my group of beta readers, who helped make this version of *The Belial Children* a much better copy. Thank you for reading. And thank you for all your work.

Thanks to my family and friends who have supported my efforts along the way.

Thank you to the people who helped with the editing and cover design. To the great team at Damonza, thank you for your excellent cover designs. You delight me every time. And a special thank-you to David Gatewood for all the time you put in. I am extremely grateful that I found such an incredible editor.

Thanks to my favorite beta reader, Elizabeth McCartan, for all your work and your support.

To my three little ones who constantly ask me how my books are doing and whether they're done yet—and who have started writing books of your own—thank you for your smiles, your hugs, and your love. You make each day that much better.

Thank you to my husband Tae. When I started this new career, unbeknownst to me my husband began planning for how we would financially survive when the writing thing didn't work out, or at least took a while to take off. But he didn't say a word beyond words of support. Thank you for always being in my corner and supporting my dreams.

Special thanks to Dave Owens. Dave has been a mentor and friend for over a decade. One weekend we were taking a group of students to meet some retired FBI profilers. On the long bus ride, Dave said I should write a book because of all my knowledge about crime. I had never seriously considered it before then. Oh, I had made up stories in my head during my twelve-hour drives home from graduate school, and I had often daydreamed in class about armed gunmen invading my high school and me handily escaping via the air ducts. But until the conversation with Dave, I never seriously considered writing. That, however, was the day when the seed was planted. And it finally took root a few years back. So thank you, Dave, for being my friend and opening up a whole new world to me.

Thank you to the Syracuse Martial Arts Academy—my second family. You offer me support and friendship in my real life and great ideas for fight scenes in my professional life. And a special sorry to Jason Wallace for all those "unintentional" hits.

Thank you to Katy Meyers for answering my bone questions.

Thank you to all you readers. I still pinch myself when I realize that I am a writer and that people are actually enjoying my books. It is mind-blowing to me. I try to write back to everyone who drops me a note and say thank you for taking the time to write. But right now I'd like to take the opportunity to thank *all* of you for taking the time to read. This has been an incredible journey for me, and it's wonderful to know there are other people who are just as concerned about Laney, Henry, Jake, Patrick, and everyone else as much as I am.

And finally, thank you for your patience in learning about Victoria. There was some groundwork that I needed to lay before her identity was revealed. And yes, you will find out who she is in the next book. Flip to the next page to read an excerpt from *The Belial Origins*, coming this spring.

EXCERPT FROM BELIAL ORIGINS

FORTY-EIGHT YEARS AGO

SPRINGFIELD, ILLINOIS

The images swirled through her mind: violence, despair, and death. Twelve-year-old Emma Riley sat straight up in bed, grasping for something in the empty air.

"Em?" her sister Vicki, age fourteen, asked from the other bed. "You okay?"

Emma's eyes flew open, staring in shock at her room. Her favorite puppy picture was on the wall. Her side of the room was painted pink, her sister's in purple.

It's my room, she told herself. *I live here.* But her pounding heart was taking a while to convince, still feeling the effects of the latest nightmare.

"Em?" Vicki asked again.

"I'm okay." Emma sat up, leaning against the headboard as her breaths came out in pants. She glanced over at her sister. They shared the same bright red hair and blue eyes, although Emma's were so dark they were almost purple. And even though they were fourteen months apart, people often mistook them for twins.

Vicki hesitated for only a moment before climbing out of her bed and into Emma's. She put her arms around her sister. "They're only dreams," she said softly.

Emma nodded into her sister's shoulder, but the fear and horror of the dreams wouldn't let go. She was in a city that was burning. And she and a friend, a tall man who couldn't speak, were trapped by a group of men.

Vicki kept her arms wrapped around Emma's shoulders. "Hey. There's no unhappiness today. Today is party day!" She wiggled in bed, her movements forcing Emma to wiggle as well. Then she crossed her eyes and stuck out her tongue.

Emma laughed, her sister's antics pushing away the darkness in her chest. "Please tell me you're not going to do that in front of my friends."

"Oh, I am *so* going to do that." Vicki hopped off the bed. "I'm also going to do my signature moves."

Vicki thrust out a hip and kicked out the opposite leg while throwing her hands in the air. Her ringlet hair flew in every direction as she moved. She looked like she was having a seizure.

A laugh burst from Emma. "Please, please, I beg of you. Not the signature dance moves. They all know we're related. I'll never survive the embarrassment."

Vicki flopped back down on her bed. "Well, as my birthday gift to you, I will refrain from my incredible moves."

Emma grinned, not for the first time grateful that she had Vicki for a sister. All her friends who had sisters complained about them all the time. But not Emma; Vicki was her best friend. They were attached at the hip and had been since Emma was born.

Vicki stood up again, her blue eyes shining. Then she reached down and pulled on Emma's arm. "Come on. Let's get dressed and get this party on the road!"

THAT NIGHT, when Emma fell back into bed again, she was exhausted. Exhausted and happy. Her mom and sister had outdone themselves decorating the yard. Balloons and streamers had been everywhere. Her dad had even hired a band and set up a giant tent.

And Chris Rosen had asked her to dance—twice. She hugged her pillow to her and wiggled with excitement. This was without a doubt the best birthday of her life.

When she closed her eyes, happiness settled warmly in her chest, and she drifted off to sleep.

The sun was barely up when her eyes popped open. She stared at the ceiling. *No. No. It can't be true.*

But deep in her heart, she knew it was.

One bed over, Vicki murmured and rolled over in her sleep. Emma watched her sister, her heart aching. *I can't do this. I can't leave Vicki.*

But she remembered all the times she had avoided the call. And all the deaths that had followed.

Shaking, she climbed out of bed and quietly packed some clothes in her backpack. She pulled her stuffed bunny from the bed. She'd had him since she was two; she couldn't leave him behind. She stuffed him in the bag, but kept his face out as she zipped it up.

After placing her bag quietly in the hall, she walked over to her sister's bed and knelt down. "Thank you for being my sister. I will never forget you," she whispered, then placed a trembling kiss on Vicki's cheek.

She watched her sister sleep, memorizing her face, then fled from the room before the sobs burst from her chest. Grabbing her bag, she crept down the hall, pausing by her parents' door. They were both still sleeping.

She wanted to run in there, hop in between them, and tell them everything. They would tell her that these were just dreams. They would tell her that everything would be all right. They'd tell her she didn't have to do this—that it was their job to be the adults and hers to be the kid.

But she knew the truth. Her childhood was over.

Her legs shook as she made her way down the stairs.

Her golden retriever Rex sat at the bottom of the stairs wagging his tail. As Emma looked into his big brown eyes, she nearly lost it then and there. She sank down next to him and buried her head in his fur, throwing her arms around his neck.

"I'm going to miss you so much," she said, glad she could say the words out loud. Rex couldn't make it up the stairs anymore because of his hips. Emma usually slept downstairs a few nights a week to keep him company.

Finally pulling away, Emma stood, walked to the back door, and opened it.

Rex looked at her and sat instead of running outside.

"Come on, Rex. This is hard enough. Go."

He hesitated before nature overrode his concern.

She watched him make his way slowly down the steps. Then she walked to the counter and pulled over the phone message pad. She pulled off a sheet of paper and wrote:

I LOVE YOU ALL. But it's time for me to leave. Don't look for me. You won't find me. I'm not hurt. No one is making me leave. I made this choice a long time ago.

. . .

SHE PAUSED, knowing they wouldn't understand that last line. Then she added:

I LOVE YOU SO MUCH. Believe that.
  Love, Emma

A WHINE SOUNDED from behind her. Rex stared at her through the screen, his tail wagging. She opened the door and let him in. She wanted more than anything to take him with her, but at age fifteen, he was having trouble walking. He would slow her down, and she needed to move fast.

She sat down, and Rex immediately sat next to her, placing his paw on her thigh. She rubbed behind his ears. "They don't give you enough credit, do they? You know something's up."

Emma glanced at the clock. She was taking too long, and this was just making it harder. With a shuddering breath, she trailed one finger between Rex's eyes, "Sleep, my friend."

Rex's eyes immediately closed and his legs gave out. Emma caught him and gently lowered him to the ground. She rubbed his belly. "I'll miss you, too, Rex."

Then she stood, swiped at the tears that ran down her cheeks, and slung her backpack over her shoulders, pulling the straps tight. Without looking back, she strode to the front door, pulled it open, slipped outside, and quietly pulled it shut behind her.

Not giving herself time to think, she ran to the side of the garage and grabbed her bike. She pedaled furiously out of the drive and didn't slow down until she was eight blocks away, at the pay phone next to the fruit stand. Hopping from the bike, she picked up the receiver and rang the operator. "Collect call," she said when the operator answered.

She rattled off the number and then waited while the phone rang.

A man picked up, his voice gruff. It was two hours earlier in California.

"Collect call from Lazarus. Do you accept the charges?"

"Uh…" The man paused, obviously shocked. But he recovered quickly. "Yes. Yes. Of course."

"Thank you," the operator said before clicking off.

"Mr. Draper," Emma said.

"Um, yes. Miss Smith?"

Emma let out a breath. He remembered. She had chosen him because she had been assured he would, even years later. But still, it was always a gamble. Of course, if he hadn't remembered, she had other numbers and other people who were paid well to remember her when she called. "Yes. I'll need transportation immediately, as well as IDs."

"Where are you?"

"Springfield, Illinois." She rattled off the address.

"Give me the number of the phone you're at."

She did.

"Give me five minutes." He hung up.

Emma paced by the phone. Time seemed to crawl by. She kept expecting her parents to roar into the parking lot and demand to know what was going on.

"Come on," she urged, staring at the phone. Finally it rang. She snatched it up. "Yes?"

"I have a car on the way to you. It'll be there in ten minutes. It'll take you to an airfield. I've chartered a plane, and it will be waiting for you."

Emma nodded. If he was surprised that a young girl was calling, he didn't let it show. He was as good as she had hoped. Of course, for the amount of money he was being paid, he should be.

"Good," she said. "I'll give the pilot directions when I'm on board. I'll also need some spending cash. About five thousand should be good for now, until I get to a bank. And I'll need credit cards."

"Yes, ma'am. And the name for the new IDs?"

Emma hesitated, picturing her sister doing her goofy dance. An ache pierced through her, threatening to drop her to the ground.

"Victoria," she said softly. "My name is Victoria."

ABOUT THE AUTHOR

R.D. Brady is an American writer who grew up on Long Island, NY but has made her home in both the South and Midwest before settling in upstate New York. On her way to becoming a full-time writer, R.D. received a Ph.D. in Criminology and taught for ten years at a small liberal arts college.

R.D. left the glamorous life of grading papers behind in 2013 with the publication of her first novel, the supernatural action adventure, *The Belial Stone*. Over ten novels later and hundreds of thousands of books sold, and she hasn't looked back. Her novels tap into her criminological background, her years spent studying martial arts, and the unexplained aspects of our history. Join her on her next adventure!

To learn about her upcoming publications, sign up for her newsletter here or her website (rdbradybooks.com).

BOOKS BY R.D. BRADY

Hominid

The Belial Series (in order)
The Belial Stone
The Belial Library
The Belial Ring
Recruit: A Belial Series Novella
The Belial Children
The Belial Origins
The Belial Search
The Belial Guard
The Belial Warrior
The Belial Plan
The Belial Witches
The Belial War
The Belial Fall
The Belial Sacrifice

The A.L.I.V.E. Series
B.E.G.I.N.

A.L.I.V.E.
D.E.A.D.
R.I.S.E.
S.A.V.E.

The Steve Kane Series
Runs Deep
Runs Deeper

The Unwelcome Series
Protect
Seek
Proxy

The Nola James Series
Surrender the Fear
Escape the Fear

Published as Riley D. Brady
The Key of Apollo
The Curse of Hecate

Be sure to sign up for R.D.'s mailing list to be the first to hear when she has a new release!

Made in the USA
Las Vegas, NV
28 January 2021

16646144R10239